BOOK OF LEPRECHAUNS
THE LORE GATHERERS

A NOVEL* BY JONATHAN UFFELMAN

---

* As Shaun McClanahan notes in his book, *Details Matter*, the history of the footnote dates back millennia to the ancient leprechaun battle practice of writing short notes on the feet of the slain about the deceased's heroics. As lore gatherers view every living thing as a story in its own right, the transition from battle record to literary notation was seamless.

Copyright © 2022 Jonathan Uffelman
Cover illustration © 2022 Emmeline Forrestal
emmelineforrestal.com
Cover design by Michael Thomas Holmes
mtholmesdesign.com

All rights reserved.

ISBN: 979-8-88525-695-7

DEDICATION

For Karen: You are the soul and center of everything.

For Ethan and Jonah: If I can write a book, you can do anything.
In years to come, these words will reach across time
and space to remind you that I love you forever.

CONTENTS

		Acknowledgments	i
		Prologue	1
PART I			
	1	The Pot of Gold	5
	2	The Thieving	19
	3	Responsibility	40
	4	The Story	48
	5	Crisis	53
	6	The Reminiscence	63
	7	A New Life	77
	8	Cross Countries	96
	9	Italy	107
	10	The Message	121
PART II			
	1	Alice's Shadow	138
	2	Ancient Rome	146
	3	Captive	159
	4	Prison	167
	5	Gladys	178
	6	Hail Caesar!	185
	7	Caesar's Wishes	197
	8	Prison. Again.	227
	9	Lucius's Wishes	247
	10	Caesar's Soothsayer	246
	11	Deep Magic	257
	12	Home	269
	13	A Reckoning	286
		Epilogue	300

ACKNOWLEDGMENTS

Marcia Popp read a very early, very rough draft of this novel and gave me much needed encouragement. Her support and well-timed words over the last ten years have been more helpful than she probably realizes.

Andrew Ordover read a later draft and provided pages of comments that helped sharpen my thinking and propelled me to a better version. His creativity and friendship have helped shape my life since the day we met in 1994.

David Engelhardt's sound advice helped me get unstuck when I was still writing my first draft and wondering if I would ever finish. He later gave me detailed notes on a more completed draft that helped me refine the story immeasurably.

Tom Willner read an even later draft and is the cheerleader/friend every artist should have. His unequivocal enthusiasm embarrasses me almost as much as my need for it. His own success at just about everything he attempts going back to when we first met almost fifty years ago would make him insufferable if he weren't also one of the nicest, best humans I know.

Emmeline Forrestal and Michael Thomas Holmes are a creative joy, and everyone should hire them. They advised on the overall book design and created a cover that captures the spirit of what I've written more perfectly than I could have ever imagined.

David Gautschy gave the novel a helpful final proof as well as much needed enthusiasm to help get me across the finish line.

Finally, my family. My son Ethan outlined a ten-point plot for this story on a walk with me back in 2013 when he was nine years old. Without him, this book would not exist. My son Jonah wrote what is, in my opinion, the funniest, most clever joke in the book (when he was about ten or eleven). My parents and brother have been inspiring me creatively since the day I was born. My wife, Karen, sees more deeply into the characters and relationships I write than I do. Her thoughts on story, plot, character, and everything else reliably unlock doors I didn't even know were closed. Anyone involved in any kind of artistic endeavor should have Karen Wright to advise them.

If magic exists in the world, Karen, Ethan, and Jonah are it.

PROLOGUE

In the beginning, there were lore gatherers.

What are lore gatherers? Basically, they are leprechauns—a sort of specialty subculture. Do not, however, confuse them with the jolly, jigging stereotypical leprechaun popularly displayed on cereal boxes and American television. This is nothing more than a grotesque cartoon that, frankly, has been encouraged by certain leprechauns who, in the eyes of lore gatherers, aren't above debasing themselves for some cheap publicity.

While you might think they are Irish, you would be wrong. They do not consider themselves affiliated with human culture in any way. As Shaun McClanahan details in his book, *A Brief History of Leprechauns: More Than You Wanted To Know*, leprechauns did originate in the part of the world humans currently call Ireland, but they had been around long before Ireland became Ireland, or the Celts became the Celts—eons, in fact, before the Eurasian tectonic plate broke off from the megacontinent Pangea one hundred and seventy-five million years ago.

But longevity is not their most distinguishing characteristic. What defines a lore gatherer, without question, is art. Art is a lore gatherer's soul and center. If something cannot be done beautifully, it is probably not worth doing. And stories, above all, are their chief interest and delight. Lore gatherers are the keepers of stories. They compile them. *All* the stories. The very first story is about the creation of everything. It is recounted in THE BOOK OF LEPRECHAUNS, vol. 1, *The Book of Firsts*, roughly translated here:

Before the universe existed, there was another time. A

time outside of time. Call it a different plane of existence or a different reality, it doesn't really matter. What does matter is that in this pre-time time, the first leprechaun moved across its face with great magic, making beautiful and wondrous things. Her name was Shillelagh.

Shillelagh was wise and powerful, but she was captured by dark forces and imprisoned. In exchange for her freedom, they demanded the secret of Shillelagh's power. They threatened to kill her and destroy all she had made.

"Alas, my power is great, but it does not last," Shillelagh lied. "I must renew myself from time to time by returning to the place I was born."

And then she told them a story—improvised completely on the spot, mind you—about a place of infinite spaces. The sort of place where a being such as she could stretch to her full size and expand with imagination and possibility. A place where all the ideas that spun through her mind like enormous flaming tops took physical shape, and she was free to explore her staggering creativity uninhibited. On and on she wove her tale, embellishing it, elaborating on it, refining it to the most granular detail.

Despite—or perhaps because of—her immortal danger, she was really enjoying herself.

As any child who has played make-believe knows, sometimes you get a little lost in the game. Shillelagh painted such a vivid picture of this imaginary place for these dark forces, even she started to believe it existed.

When she had finished, the dark forces said with ravenous, drooling hunger, "Take us! Take us!" for they were desperate and envisioned a place with infinite things to devour.

But Shillelagh frowned and said, "Alas, I cannot take you. You have caught me at the end of my power, just as I was leaving to rejuvenate. If I remain bound here much longer, I shall die and never see my home again."

The dark forces thought hard. Or as hard as they could think. Strong and terrifying they were; intelligent they weren't.

At last, they came to a decision: "If we let you go, you will promise to take us!"

"Oh yes, of course," promised Shillelagh, though of course she had no intention of doing any such thing. When the dark forces released her, she wasted no time in overcoming them entirely and placing them in a jar, which she now keeps on her fireplace mantle (or wherever it is such beings keep their knick-knacks).

What happened next, however, surprised her more than anything had in an age. When she surveyed herself, she found lurking within a corner of her soul something that had not been there before: the story she told the dark forces had become real. She had, in other words, lied a universe—our universe—into existence. She was so amused, she decided to keep it and see what would happen.

One of the things that happened was this—

Part I

CHAPTER 1

The Pot of Gold

Evil lurked deep in the Irish forest.

Untouched since creation, this forest looked as if a woodland deity had carelessly spilled an armful of seeds at the dawn of time, cursed violently, then passed out for billions of years in a drunken stupor. Ferns carpeted the forest floor; moss and algae freckled rock and stone; tangled ivy, grasping at sunlight, twisted and hooped skyward, shivering up the spines of gnarled and mighty oaks. Walking these woods, you might expect any fantastical creature to pop from every tree and spore. Even at night, the forest felt alive. Sleeping, but alive. Lush, green, otherworldly. Walking in it, even the most incurable skeptic could not deny that magic—the real thing—courses through the veins of the Earth like blood: ancient, wild, and powerful.

The evil here, however, was neither troll, nor ogre, nor fire-breathing dragon. It was far worse: a roughly seven-inch tall man whose shoes were *fabulous*—a leprechaun gone bad. His name was Dorn.

Dorn had wandered the forest alone for more years than he could count, nursing ancient grudges and feeding on bitterness: envious, spiteful, desperate. But he was weak.

Dorn hated weakness.

Once, he had been powerful. He'd had magic.

Oh yes, he had!

All leprechauns have magic, but where most squandered it, Dorn had *mastered* it . . .

. . . and lightning had danced on the tips of his fingers; he could conjure fire with a breath; he could have been—could still be!—the most powerful leprechaun in any story in any volume in any lore gatherer's book.

But now his magic was, alas, a shadow of what it had been. Barely enough. Only enough to survive.

He needed food. He needed shelter.

He *wanted* revenge.

* * * *

The forest was also home to the beautiful lore gatherer village of Finnegan's Wake. If your eyes could penetrate the powerful magic concealing it, you might have thought Finnegan's Wake was a nineteenth century human village reduced to one ninth of its size and transplanted in the present day.

The name "Finnegan's Wake" was a bit of a misnomer, though it was not a coincidence. For longer than anyone could tell, the village had been called Kilcronaghanmallock. Then, in the mid-twentieth century, around 1940, a copy of the book *Finnegans Wake* by the famous human author James Joyce found its way into the village. Few actually read it because not even lore gatherers understand it. After eighty years of close study, all that their experts have been able to conclude has been: "Well, *he* seems to know what he's talking about . . . ." But everyone agreed the title sounded meaningful and looked good on postcards.

It was about four a.m. and a gentle rain fell. A wind chime effect sounded through the village, created by water cascading down the enchanted and intricately thatched rooftops, each of which was engineered with individualized designs that not only enhanced their visual appeal, but also channeled rainwater into an underground reservoir that supplied the entire village—a perfect marriage of aesthetics, magic, and pragmatism, the lore gatherers' hallmark. The sound even had a calming effect on all who heard it. ᶠ Otherwise, all was quiet.

Well, not quite all. From the window of one slightly rundown cottage, a

---

ᶠ   Walking though lore gatherer forests, humans have, on occasion, heard such sounds and attempted to recreate the soothing effect to no avail. Sadly, humans are simply unable to identify or measure the delicate bodily and psychological currents involved, and so are totally unable to calibrate the methods they employ—wind chimes, crystals, new age music, etc.

lone candle shone through the early morning fog. There, Shaun and Molly McClanahan could be heard packing two knapsacks.

"Where are we going, Da'?"

"You'll see. Do you have the shovels?"

"Will this take long? I don't want to be late to The Thieving."

"You won't be late if you pay attention and do what I ask."

"Did Ma' do The Thieving, Da'?"

"Yes, Molly. The shovels?"

"Did she pass it? Her first time, I mean?"

"Yes. Pay attention please, Molly . . ."

Shaun had been dreading this day. It was a Big Day. He hated Big Days. Big events in Molly's life—even birthdays—always made him feel like an actor without a script who didn't know what to do with his hands. But she was twelve now. All twelve-year-olds had to participate in The Thieving. Twelve was the age, ready or not, and there was nothing he could do. The ritual was, after all, thousands of years old.

He had tried to prepare her, but Molly was just . . . difficult. There she sat twiddling a lock of that thick brown mop on top of her head that she *never ever* seemed to brush, peppering him with questions about The Thieving—"What if? What if? What if?" His anxiety was spiking. The Thieving was important, yes, but this task that he was going to show her was even more so. Didn't she understand that??

No, he reminded himself. Of course she didn't understand that. He had never shown her before. Right.

He took a deep breath.

He wished Alice were here. Alice would have known what to say to her.

"Did you pass it your first time, Da'?"

"Yes, of course, Molly. And you will too. *Please*, do you have the shovels??"

"Urgh!"

Molly had been looking forward to this day, but her dad was already ruining it. She was excited—well, excited *and* scared is what she was. And now her dad was . . . well, being her dad. All he could think about were the stupid shovels and this dumb task he did every day. Whatever it was. What on earth could be so important?

Actually, she had wondered about that for a very long time—every morning when he left the house, in fact, as far back as she could remember. He never talked about the task and never took her. But he took it more seriously than . . . just about anything else, really. Happy as she was to finally be clued in on the big secret, she couldn't help but wonder: did they have to do it today? Couldn't they focus on The Thieving? That's what *she* wanted to talk about. She had *a lot* of questions. And besides, talking helped calm her down.

But her father never talked about anything. Nothing important, anyway. Certainly, nothing about her. Only about his books, his research, and his stupid lists (which frankly she wished he would shut up about). There he sat, glaring at her with those big, round eyes (which his thick glasses magnified), worry practically boiling off his bald head like steam, looking like a bearded, perfectly groomed grey owl staring at the end of the world inside his head.

She wished her mother were here. Her mother would have known what to say to him.

"Da'." Molly stopped and looked at her father, incredulously. "You're not going to wear that to The Thieving, are you?"

Sometimes, Molly's innocent brown face made Shaun feel like a butterfly that had just been pinned to a display case. He looked at his clothes self-consciously. He would have been the first to admit that he had absolutely no fashion sense. His idea of color coordination was to wear different shades of the same color.

"What's wrong with this?" he said.

"All green? Seriously, Da'? It looks so . . . leprechauny. No one thinks it looks very good."

Shaun sighed. "Do you. Have. The shovels?" he said, roughly stuffing a few large books into his knapsack.

"Will there be a lot of people there today? What if I get nervous, Da'? What if—"

"The shovels, Molly!"

"Yes, Da', I got them!" Molly produced two shovels with curved handles, and blades so hard and sharp they looked as if they could pierce concrete.

"Tsk—no, *no*, these are—" Shaun took a long, hard look at Molly. Then, as if coming to a difficult decision, he quietly said: "Go get the other shovels. The ones with sycamore handles."

"Wh—You mean . . . ?"

"Yes."

Molly almost swallowed her tongue. "But . . . those are—"

"I know. Go get them, please."

The shovels with sycamore handles were legendary. Molly had only the faintest memories of them. All she really knew, she had learned from others in the village who spoke of them in hushed whispers. The last time Molly had brought them up, her father told her never to speak of them again.

They were her mother's.

Shaun *never* talked about her.

But Alice's garden had been the best in the village, and in addition to having a thumb so green some said she could raise plants from the dead, she made all her own tools. Each was a work of art, coveted by every serious gardener in Finnegan's Wake. Generous as she was in everything else, however, Alice did not share her tools—especially with Shaun. To this day, he kept them locked at the back of her closet, undisturbed.

Still not sure she had heard correctly, Molly solemnly retrieved them and gave them to her father, who received them like fine crystal. The blades glinted in the candlelight. Even after all these years, they still looked brand new. As her father's fingers traced their smooth handles lovingly, feeling their perfect weight and balance, Molly realized this might be the first time he had ever held them. His hands trembled.

"You never let us use—"

"These are for you, Molly."

"Wh—?"

Shaun nodded and cleared his throat. "It's a special day. Isn't it?" he said, trying not to shake.

Molly nodded, took them from her father, and almost immediately began choking back wracking sobs.

Shaun swallowed and looked at his daughter quivering before him. He never knew what to say when Molly got upset, especially if it had anything to do with Alice. A part of him just wished she wouldn't do it. Some things in life had to be endured, and that was that. Nothing more to say. It was awful, but what could you do? Nothing, that's what. Besides, when she got upset, he got upset, and that was . . . well, even more upsetting.

"The research . . . (*ahem*) You know, Molly, the scholarship is pretty clear," he said, trying and failing to keep his voice steady, "that . . . well, it's humans, Molly isn't it? Blame humans. Okay? This whole . . . The Thieving, this task . . . it's all because of humans. All of it. Too hungry for gold, the lot of them. They'll do almost anything to get their hands on it. Greedy, grasping. They'd love nothing more than to catch an unsuspecting leprechaun and wish for her gold.[♭] They're a leprechaun's most dangerous predator."

Molly nodded, still unable to speak.

Shaun started to put a hand on her shoulder but snatched it away as if he had touched a hot flame. If he touched her, he knew he might not be able to hold himself together. His voice became impatient. "We just . . . it's . . . we just have to do it, Molly."

"Why are they so horrible, Da'? Humans, I mean. Why do they have to ruin everything for everyone?"

"You know . . ." he said, shaking his head, "in my book *Human Atrocities: A Compendium of Horror*, I have a chapter on these things called 'zoos' where they keep animals in cages—"

"WHAT?!?"

"I know, I know. Well, there's a kind of monkey that flings its poop at the humans who come to stare at them."

Molly laughed and wiped a tear from her eye.

"Humans are kind of like those monkeys, only with clothes and slightly worse manners. C'mon. I have to show you this."

* * * *

After a long, carefully choreographed series of twists and turns through the forest, past Shrieking Shamus (an oak tree with a cluster of knots and holes in its trunk that made it look like it was screaming in agony), over Fiddler's Brook, and beyond the Green Place, Shaun brought them to a large fallen pine tree that had been dead for decades. It was not the sort of place for a picnic. Damp and

---

[♭] Leprechauns are like many creatures in human mythology who grant humans wishes—genies, sphinxes, fairy godmothers (among many others, the existence of whom is beyond the scope of this book). Lore gatherers have studied this closely for as long as there have been humans. Why, exactly, leprechauns should be *compelled* to grant humans wishes upon being captured is still disputed, though some philosophers argue it's cosmic punishment for Shillalegh's refusal to keep her end of the bargain with the dark forces that had captured her. All agree, however, that it's a nuisance.

a bit nasty, most walked by it with barely a second look. Molly didn't think she'd ever seen it before. There they waited quietly.

At exactly the fifty-fourth second of the fifth minute, Shaun had them spin in place three times and kneel. Then he muttered a few magical phrases under his breath that Molly couldn't hear, and they began to dig.

The dirt almost turned to sand under Molly's blade. Even the clay. It was the best shovel she had ever used. But leprechauns, if you didn't know, are already extraordinary diggers. A trench that might take a human several days to dig, they complete in little under half an hour, even with their bare hands. Undoubtedly, this talent gave rise to the belief among some humans that leprechauns live underground. This is untrue. While there are records of underground leprechaun civilizations, they have lived primarily above ground for millenia.

Thus, Shaun and Molly dug a ten-foot hole in the earth in almost no time, at the bottom of which lay a large chest.

Molly gawped. "What's th—?"

"Shh!"

Shaun peeked above the hole to make sure no one had followed them. Then, carefully selecting a key from his keychain and unlocking the chest, he muttered a few more magical phrases (which, once again, Molly couldn't hear) and opened it.

"Shillelagh's breath!" Molly whispered.

Even in the darkness of early morning, the gold that filled the chest gleamed with its own light. Midas would have wept. It had everything—coins, chunks, lumps, ingots, bars, blocks, jewelry, doubloons, triploons, you name it. Shaun put a hand on Molly's shoulder and spoke quietly.

"Generations upon generations of our family have accumulated this gold, Molly. Found it, stole it, saved it and, most importantly, protected it. What a magnifying glass does for the sun, gold does for our magic. Many consider it the most potent amplifier of a leprechaun's magical powers."

"Really?" Molly whispered.

"Mm-hmm."

"How come you never told me about this before?"

"You're doing The Thieving today. You're old enough to understand why."

Molly nodded.

"Because this gold, Molly, is technically not ours."

"What?"

"This is why The Thieving is important," Shaun said, pulling out their ledger. "We safeguard this gold for the whole village. It belongs to everyone. We have . . . it's like a magical contract. Everyone's gold is part of a larger communal 'pot' from which the village and everyone in it draws power and protection. We divide the pot among all the families so that if one of us gets captured by a human and loses their gold, the majority remains untouched, and the village stays safe. This is our most scared responsibility. Understand?"

Molly nodded.

"Now, The Thieving tests your ability to hide and find gold *without* magic. Anyone can conceal gold with magic. Magic is the easy part. But we need every available protection. The village wants you as cunning and crafty as possible. Because humans are relentless. Dumb and destructive, yes, but relentless. Now, let's get started."

Together, they took a painstaking inventory of the entire chest, counting every coin and weighing every ingot. Molly found it incredibly tedious, and she kept worrying they would be late to The Thieving. But Shaun did not take shortcuts. Only when he was satisfied that every ounce was accounted for, did they close the lid, lock the chest, and rebury it. Shaun then reactivated the magical protections.

"Da'?" Molly said, "what happens if it gets stolen? The gold, I mean?"

"That can never happen!" Shaun snapped.

"Okay, but what would—"

"The world might end."

It is worth mentioning here that over the years, Molly had observed her father displayed little interest in "managing" stress. For him, stress was more of a lifestyle. His capacity for stress was matched only by his capacity for panic, and he had always treated this task like the most panic-inducing thing in the world. In fairness, he treated *a lot* of things like that. Living with Shaun, you could easily believe just about anything could trigger an apocalypse—illness, being late, a broken teacup. So Molly had learned to take her father and his worries with giant sacks of salt. But this felt different.

"No, but . . . wait, really?"

"C'mon," Shaun said briskly, his mood suddenly dark. "We've got to get back and get some food into you."

* * * *

Dorn was sure the human had not been there a moment before. But now, inexplicably, there he was. Somehow.

They were in a remote part of the forest. Not even lore gatherers came here, much less humans. And humans rarely did anything silently. They were about as stealthy as artillery, and only half as subtle. That was intriguing.

The man's clothes were odd though: a long, white toga with a fringe of purple, and leather sandals. His face was tanned, lined, and rugged, yet open and alert, and his short, salt-and-pepper hair was combed straight forward. He was clearly middle-aged, but sinewy, and impressively fit. Not just fit—strong. But he looked confused.

Dorn practically salivated. Confusion was like a "WELCOME" mat to Dorn.

Most likely, this was a nearby townsperson who had gotten drunk the night before and wandered off—a looooooooong way off—into the forest. As explanations went, it wasn't great, but it was the most reasonable one he could think of for this strange human's sudden appearance.

The actual explanation wasn't even close to reasonable.

* * * *

Dorker didn't like working in his father's bakery. They got along well, his dad and he. They didn't just love each other; they genuinely liked each other (which Dorker thought was almost better). But when it came to their interests, they were just different. Nothing in the world was more wonderful to his father than the smell of eggs, flour, oil, and sugar in a hot oven. A friendly, booming sort of man, with a voice as rich as his jelly pastries, you could get hungry just listening to Dorlish. The thin layer of flour that covered him was now so permanent, hardly anyone noticed it anymore.

Dorker didn't like baking. He had no talent for it. What Dorker liked was books. All the books. He read everything he could get his hands on, from scholarly treatises to the labels on discarded human soup cans. He even liked reading things he didn't understand. The sight of letters and words on a page fascinated him and just made him happy. What he liked most were romances. This is because he was thirteen and certain hormones were now flooding his system, awakening his hitherto dormant libido to all sorts of exciting—and sometimes alarming—realizations.

Dorker was also at that age when different parts of his body were growing at different rates, and nothing worked in unison with anything else. Dorlish said watching him walk was like watching an octopus on land: floppy, possibly boneless, with all its limbs seemingly controlled by unknown and independent command centers. That was a bad combination in an environment with searing hot pans and lots of things to spill.

When Molly and Shaun walked into the bakery, Dorker had just tried to open a bag of flour, which had not so much opened as erupted. He looked like the world's scrawniest ghost.

"Morning Shaun!" Dorlish cheerfully coughed from within the cloud of white that now filled the shop.

"Morning, Dorlish," said Shaun, squinting through the haze. "Is that Dorker? Haven't seen you in a while. You've grown, haven't you?"

Shaun remembered Dorker as a gangly little boy, even at age five. Now, at thirteen years and an astonishing ten and a half inches, he towered over his father.

"That's because I'm part human," Dorker announced, accidentally elbowing his father in the ribs and releasing another small cloud of flour into the air.

Shaun blinked. "Excuse me?"

"What happened was, you see, um . . ." Dorker stammered.

". . . years ago, you see, um . . . my Dad here—"

"Dorker is lying," Dorlish said, handing Dorker a broom. "Trying to, anyway. Hasn't quite got the hang of it yet."

"Ah! Excellent!" said Shaun. "Studying the thirty-two crucial lies [‡] are you?"

Dorker nodded proudly. "I'm on number fourteen already!"

"The Lie Confusing?"

[‡]   Young leprechauns are taught the finer points of lying from the textbook classic, *Thyrty-Two Cruciale Lyes: The Multitudinous Mendacities*, written by Flan McGorvish in 1623, and used by leprechauns all over the world. It is the most authoritative catalogue of lying known to leprechauns, complete with woodcut illustrations.

"No, the Lie Spontaneous!"

"Excellent! Good try, Dorker," Shaun said encouragingly. "Nothing in the texts say the Lie Spontaneous can't also be confusing, so you're halfway there."

"I'm also reading your book, Mr. McClanahan," Dorker enthused. "*A Lie for a Lie?* ᶠ But I had a question. In chapter two, page forty-three, when you say 'incredulous'—"

Dorlish elbowed him meaningfully and gestured at Molly. "Dorker, what have we talked about? We greet *all* our customers when they come into our shop."

"Wha—oh! Right. Um . . . hi!"

Their eyes met.

What is love? Is it a feeling? An action? An instinct? What combination of hormone, blood, and fire transmutes through some strange alchemy into compassion, desire, and tenderness? Would it, like a rose, by any other name, *really* smell as sweet?

Maybe it's too early in the story to ask these questions, but it was not too early for Dorker. It was definitely too early for Molly.

"Can we have one of your sheep-scrapple and apricot biscuits?" said Shaun. "You know the ones I mean. Must get something hearty in Molly's stomach before The Thieving."

"Ah, that's right!" Dorlish beamed. "I almost forgot! Coming right up, Molly."

"Um . . ." Dorker's ears went bright red as he sidled up to the counter like a self-conscious crab, "Molly, um. I was down at Holly's Hedge reading earlier and um . . . you know it's really nice down there. You know? And maybe we could sometime, you know, maybe go for a walk or something down there? Together . . . you know . . . or maybe something . . . together?"

"At Holly's Hedge?" Molly was confused. Even Dorlish looked puzzled.

ᶠ   Shaun's literary supplement to Flan McGorvish's seminal work titled, *A Lie for a Lie Leaves the Whole World MINE!*, catalogues over one thousand types of assertions on the spectrum between True and False, including, truths, half-truths, white lies, mendacities, misrepresentations, prevarications, deceits, deceptions, evasions, distortions, as well as the lie intentional, the lie pragmatical, the lie accidental, the lie convenient, the lie comical, the lie tragical, the lie historical, pastoral historical, comical pastoral, etc., among many many others.

Dorker had that effect on people.

"Yes," said Dorker, licking his lips self-consciously. His mouth had suddenly gone very dry. "Anyway, like I say, it's really nice down there . . . for walks 'n stuff . . ."

"O . . . kaaay . . ."

"Um," said Dorker. "So anyway, um, no, what I *wanted* to say was, you know, good luck."

"At what?"

"Oh, sorry! At The Thieving."

"Oh," said Molly. "Er, thanks."

"Exciting stuff!" Dorlish said, handing Molly a steaming hot biscuit. About five distinct scents mingled into an aroma that wafted straight up her nose and made her suddenly ravenous. "Don't worry, Molly, you'll do fine. You might even have fun! After Dorker's Thieving, it was all he could talk about for weeks."

"*Dad!*" said Dorker.

"See you at the stadium," said Dorlish, as Shaun and Molly opened the door to leave. "Best of luck, Molly!"

"I'll be rooting for you especially, Mol—"

"Dorker, leave her alone," said Dorlish. "She's got to hurry, or she'll be late."

* * * *

When Dorn revealed himself, the strange human had barely flinched, which was unexpected. If anything, seeing a seven-inch tall old man with a suggestive, yellow grin and horrid teeth only sharpened this human's focus. Surprise, as a rule, gave Dorn the upper hand. But this man was so imposing, so imperious, Dorn felt himself immediately wrong-footed, which was strange. Dorn had been unable to dominate a stupid human only once in his life. True, this human's language had been unusual—Dorn had never heard anything like it—and that sort of thing could throw a lesser leprechaun off their step. But Dorn had an excellent ear and was conversing fluently within minutes.

No, what really threw him was the man's nose. It was extraordinary. Magnificent. Intimidating, even. Calling it big didn't do it justice. It didn't just dominate his face, but the entire landscape around them. It projected mightily from beneath his eyebrows like a promontory, or Roman arch. Dorn fancied it could support an aqueduct. Here was a nose so classically spectacular, it could bestride the ocean and launch a thousand ships. But rather than making him look freakish, it just made you feel small. The man looked down over it at Dorn as if from a mountain top.

They had conversed haltingly for several minutes, Dorn trying to glean what advantage he might press to manipulate him. Humans were such black holes of need and desire, finding something that pulled their strings like a marionette was never hard. There was always a button to push, always a lever. But this man was impressively guarded and not so easily cracked.

"Where am I?" the man finally demanded.

"This is what you humans call Ireland, friend," Dorn smiled ingratiatingly.

"Ireland? What's that?"

"What's th—?"

An idea flashed through Dorn like a lightning bolt, and for the first time he was glad he had paid attention to his lessons in human history. That face, the clothes, the language, that nose—a possibility dangled itself before Dorn that was so far-fetched, so outrageously delicious, he could scarcely give it credence. Yet in some preposterous way, it was also the only explanation that made any sense. It had to be right. Could he really be so lucky?

"My name is Dorn, friend," he cooed. "What's yours?"

The man arched an eyebrow contemptuously. "You may call me Caesar. Julius Caesar. You are permitted to bow."

"Oh," said Dorn, celebrating to himself. He bowed deeply. "How NICE to meet you!!"

* * * *

The excitement was palpable at the stadium when Molly and Shaun arrived at the participants' entrance. Molly was the last to show up and suddenly, everything was happening so fast. She hadn't even had time to go home and clean up.

She looked at her father.

The moment had come for him to say something. It was a Big Moment. Possibly the biggest moment of her young life. But his head was at war with itself.

Tell her you love her. Tell her you love her. Tell her you love her! He thought. *Why don't you tell her you love her?!? What's wrong with you? Just say the words! Just say them.* But what if it all goes wrong? What if she fails? What if she can't do it? What if I didn't teach her well enough? What if I failed her? I'm a terrible father. I'm a terrible person. What kind of father can't say, "I love you" to his daughter?!? *I wish Alice were here. She would know what to say. She always knew what to say. She could say "We love you" for both of us. Alice should be here, not me. It should have been me. It should have been me. Why couldn't it have been me? It's all my fault! It's all my fault! I'm sorry, Molly. I'm sorry, I'm sorry, I'm sorry! I love you, Molly. Oh Shillelagh, I'm so sorry!*

In the end, he gave Molly a pat on the head. Two pats, to be exact.

Then he turned and walked away.

CHAPTER 2

The Thieving

"WELCOME, one and all, to The Thieving!!!" announced a voice over the roar of the crowd. The voice belonged to Morgus O'Verunderhill, the village wood worker. In addition to making sumptuous furniture from wood gathered from the surrounding forest, he had a mellifluous baritone that made him a natural for events such as this.

The morning was cool and crisp, and the sun bright in a cloudless sky. A perfect day for The Thieving. The air felt carbonated, as if the arena itself were bottled champagne, making everyone in it loud, giddy, and uninhibited.

The Thieving was a solemn ritual to be sure (for a given value of "solemn"), but leprechauns like an excuse to party as much as anyone. Whole families came with food and drink, banners to cheer on friends and family, noise makers, silly hats, painted faces, and basically anything else they could think of, all in the name of village pride.

"Thank you all for coming out to support the village and this young group of hopefuls!" Morgus continued, his voice echoing around the arena. "We want to especially thank the parents, who have put so much time and effort into preparing their children for such an awesome responsibility. And now, please rise as we all sing the village anthem."

Everyone stood, as a drum, a pennywhistle, and two fiddles began to play. Hundreds of voices rose in magnificent harmony:[*]

---

[*] In 1878, W.S. Gilbert (of Gilbert and Sullivan fame) became one of the few humans ever to catch a

We'll swindle, steal, and scam, and snatch, and seize, and misappropriate;
We'll burgle, bilk, bamboozle, dupe, defraud, deceive, and defalcate.
If treasures of the world exist we know we should have got a hold,
We guarantee we'll find a way to add it to our pot o' gold!

We'll pilfer, plunder, purloin, pinch, and pillage, pluck, and burglarize;
We'll hoodwink, heist, and con, connive, and loot, and filch, and vandalize.
In short if it's not fastened down, it's not that we run hot or cold,
It's just that we will find a way to add it to our pot o' gold!

The audience finished with a raucous cheer.

"Thank you all!" Morgus continued. "Before we begin, if you haven't heard, we're doing something a little different this year. It was controversial, but the vote was unanimous. We'll make this quick, since our young contestants are, as we speak, waiting excitedly in the entry hall . . . ."

* * * *

Just within that hot and narrow entry hall, Molly and a group of quivering twelve-year-olds stood before a rumpled, tweedy man who couldn't tuck his shirt in properly or get his glasses to sit quite right on his nose. His generally lopsided look was enhanced by his lack of coordination and terrible nearsightedness. As he glanced back and forth from the children to his clipboard, he grabbed his reading glasses on and off his face so haphazardly, they kept clattering to the floor. His name was Mr. Links.

"Out there," Mr. Links shouted over the arena announcer, "is an almost lifesize model of our forest. There, you must each find five hidden gold pieces. You must each find your specific stash." Mr. Links then gestured to eleven adults standing further back in the corridor: "You will question the test auditor who hid your specific stash and ask them anything you want for as long as you want. Whether you should *believe* anything they tell you," he said, allowing himself a thin grin, "is entirely up to you. You will have two hours. Take my

---

leprechaun. Little is known about their interaction or his wishes, but any human hearing the village's national anthem could not fail to recognize more than a passing similarity between it and "Modern Major General," from *The Pirates of Penzance*. The original anthem went on for thirty-four verses.

BOOK OF LEPRECHAUNS: THE LORE GATHERERS

advice: do NOT waste your time. These auditors are cunning and have years of experience."

A deafening roar of laughter went up in the arena crowd at some pre-event entertainment. It sounded to Molly as if every lore gatherer in the village were there, and by the volume, possibly every lore gatherer in the world.

"They amplify the crowd to make it sound bigger than it is," a boy named Gregory whispered to her. He was fifteen, having failed The Thieving twice before.

"They do? Why?"

Gregory shrugged. "To mess with us, I guess."

"Then," shouted Mr. Links over the cacophony, "*IF* you succeed, we swap. *You* will each be given five gold pieces to hide. You will have forty-five minutes. Your auditor will then try to find your hiding place. Same rules. They question you for as long as they want. Lying is encouraged, but please note that our auditors are experienced liars themselves, which makes them outstanding *lie detectors*. If they find your gold in two hours or less, you lose. If not, you pass. Now, unless there are any questions—?"

No one raised a hand.

"Then I wish you all good luck."

Mr. Links turned away, then turned back again, dropping his glasses once more. "I almost forgot," he said, "I don't know what you've heard, but this game is not a game. Severe penalties will be deducted if the judges feel even for a moment that you are not taking this seriously. Your parents are expected to have prepared you. And a new rule has been implemented this year. It's controversial, but the vote was unanimous."

Mr. Links looked into their wide, worried faces.

"Starting this year, anyone who does not pass The Thieving will be banished from the village."

"WHAT?!?" Molly cried.

* * * *

"You're upset, I can tell," said Dorn.

"The future?" Julius Caesar curled his lip. "You're trying to tell me I'm *two thousand* years in the future?"

"I'm afraid so, friend."

"Really."

"You must have travelled through time."

"Really."

"No other explanation."

"How, exactly?"

"I wish I knew," said Dorn. This was one hundred percent true.

Caesar's very impressive nostrils flared as he inhaled deeply. In the short time he had spent with Dorn, he had already rightly concluded that only about a third of anything Dorn said was reliable. But Caesar had never seen a leprechaun before, much less one as supremely confident as Dorn. That sort of thing can shake your certainty in what you think you know. Besides, Caesar had no idea how, in the blink of an eye, he had arrived in this forest from his quarters in Rome where he had been enjoying a peaceful moment alone with an especially fine goblet of wine. Something was clearly afoot, but he didn't know what. Or why. He had to be careful.

"Alright," he said. "Prove it."

"Prove it?" said Dorn, licking his lips.

"Yes."

"You want proof?"

Caesar stared at him.

"So what you're saying is, you want proof . . . that you travelled through time . . . ?"

Caesar was disconcertingly comfortable with uncomfortable silences.

"Okay! Proof is what you want; proof is what you get. Sure! No problem. Proof! Ha! Easier done than said."

Dorn looked around, his mind racing. This part of the forest was not exactly teeming with evidence of the twenty-first century, which was just as well. He *really* didn't want to take Caesar to a more populated area. The less he knew the truth about the twenty-first century, the better. Caesar was too cunning to be trusted with anything like the truth. He had to be careful.

Then they heard a low, not-so-distant rumble. Both of them looked up as a small, turboprop airplane flew directly over their heads.

****

"One try and that's it?!? Molly thundered. "That's not fair! How is that even fair? Who came up with such a stupid rule?!?"

The anxiety in the corridor, already high, now rose to critical levels. As Mr. Links pushed his way over to Molly, the other children pretended to get very interested in their shoelaces and tried to sweat inconspicuously.

"Fair?" said Mr. Links, peering intently at Molly. "*Fair?* What's your name, girl?"

"Well, it's not '*Girl*,' I'll tell you *that* for nothing! It's Molly!"

"Molly," said Mr. Links, "Do you think this is a game? Do you think this is about making you comfortable? This is a *test!* Do you understand? The safety of our village depends on you. On all of you. Everyone out there is counting on *you* to protect our gold. This is our greatest responsibility as villagers. None more sacred! If you—if any of you—do not feel up to it, please go home now." Mr. Links glared at her. "Molly?"

Molly desperately wanted to smack the glasses off his face, but what cool-headed sense remained in her over-heated brain restrained her. "No," she said, seething quietly. "I'll play."

Mr. Links nodded. "Oh, and lest any of you get any ideas, there is a spell over the playing field that prevents the use of any magic. I do *not* recommend you test it. Wait here until your name is called."

* * * *

". . . And so, without any further ado," Morgus announced, bringing the crowd to its feet, "let's meet this year's CONTESTANTS!"

The crowd went wild as the children were called into the arena, one by one. All the talk this year was of a pair of twins, Celli and Daen McClure, both of whom were already accomplished tricksters, and both of whom were highly competitive, especially with each other. They hadn't stopped pushing and shoving each other since Molly arrived, and tensions were escalating.

"Bet you lose!"

"Bet *you* do!"

"Oh yeah?"

"Yeah!"

"Hey! Watch it!"

"HEY!"

An open scuffle erupted, and by the time their names were announced,

Shaun took a deep breath. This shouldn't be hard, he told himself. How many places were there to hide gold?

If you have ever played hide and seek with a small child, you know that the number of hiding places is limited, and you can readily guess where a child is likely to be. Leprechauns are like that when it comes to finding gold (especially if humans have hidden it—finding gold hidden by humans is as challenging for leprechauns as finding an elephant-sized pin in a mouse-sized haystack).[F] The village therefore replicated a forest to give them a challenge. But even so, the odds were slanted heavily towards the children. For example, when it was the children's turn to hide, as long as they hid the gold someplace a larger adult couldn't physically get to, they were pretty much assured of success.

In many ways, the question/answer portion was the real test of The Thieving. Leprechauns are taught to mask their intentions and feelings, and an artful leprechaun can learn a lot of information from the unwary even in a casual chat. But brilliant as he was, Shaun had always struggled with lying. Among his failings was a straightforward honesty that had been the despair of his parents and grandparents. He knew all sorts of lying techniques and could recite them alphabetically and categorize them by effect. He could tell you in detail the background and evolution of every subterfuge, as well as the roles each had played in historical events through the ages. But in practice, he was about as cunning as a schnauzer. He just didn't get it.

"Oh!" he said. "Oh no. She's overwhelmed. Look at her! The lights, the pressure—!"

Shaun, please relax.

"How can I relax?!? She's going to fail! Shillelagh's breath! Look! Look, look, look! She can't even get started! Did you hear them say 'banishment'? She's banished if she fails, Alice!! She's panicking! She's panicking, she's panicking, she's panicking! What are we going to do?!?"

Shaun watched in horror as Molly suddenly grabbed Mr. Links by the lapels of his vest and yelled, "WHERE'S THE GOLD? *TELL MEEEEEEEEEE!!*"

The crowd, momentarily stunned, roared back to life with laughter. The

---

[F] This explains why there isn't as much gold lying around that humans have buried as you might think. When humans bury gold, leprechauns invariably find it, steal it, and add it to their own stash in almost no time.

announcer loved it.

"Looks like Celli and Daen aren't the only ones with spirit, eh, folks?"

The audience cheered.

"This is a disaster," Shaun groaned.

"*That's* your question?" said Mr. Links, recovering quickly. "Alright. I'll tell you. Look into my eyes: I buried it, fifty yards that way into the woods, turn left twenty paces, then under a small pine tree with no leaves, two-and-a-half feet down."

"Don't believe him, Molly!" Shaun yelled. "She's going to believe him, Alice! She doesn't *think!* She's not calm and rational. WHY ISN'T SHE CALM AND RATIONAL?!? Why does she—"

Shaun . . .

"Now what is she doing?!? She's closing her eyes!?!"

Shaun! Stop it! Look at your daughter! She's seeing it.

"Seeing what? What is she seeing? She can't see anything with her eyes closed!"

The story behind the story . . . .

Alice had always talked about the story behind the story. According to Alice, any story you hear is only part of the story. Listen to the story, yes, but pay attention to the story behind it. That may be the real story. Alice said it was the most important thing to know about stories.

Shaun never knew what she was talking about. But that was true of a lot of things Alice said. Shaun had learned not to question her. If Alice said it, it must be true, whether he understood it or not. He had written all the books, but Alice was the one who knew things.

Shaun, do you see?

"No!" said Shaun desperately.

She's relaxing. Oh Shaun! Her mind—I wish you could see it. It's so beautiful! It's expanding like a balloon! Do you see? All the anger and anxiety are draining through her feet right into the earth! What she's doing—I never taught her this. I never could have, even if I'd had the chance. She's the real pot of gold. Oh Shaun! Isn't she remarkable!

"Why can't I see it?" Shaun said quietly.

When Molly opened her eyes, the edges of the world sharpened. Details leapt out that she hadn't noticed before: the fibers in Mr. Links's vest were as clear as if she were seeing them under a microscope; light danced across the surface of a dewdrop; birdsong sounded like conversation; she felt as if she could have heard the smell of rain.

"Say that again," she said, looking at him steadily.

Mr. Links raised an eyebrow as he felt Molly's eyes pierce him. "I buried it," he said, his face an almost perfect mask of deception.

Almost.

A single twitch fluttered across the corner of his eyelid that, in her heightened state, flooded Molly with information—nothing she could have articulated or explained, but she didn't need to. Everything made sense.

"It looks like Molly McClanahan has a plan!" Morgus swooned as Molly bolted into the forest. "Look at her go!!"

The crowd exulted.

Oh my. Oh Shaun.

"What?" said Shaun. "What now? She's just running. She doesn't know where she's going. How can she know where she's going?!? She hardly asked any questions! Oh, this is terrible. Someone's got to stop her!" Shaun got up, then sat back down, then got up again.

You can't stop her, Shaun. Your place is here. Just look at her! She looks like a fish swimming in water. There are no boundaries between her and the world. She could navigate by thought alone!

"But—"

Shhhhhhhhhh. Hush, Shaun.

"Celli and Daen are showing speed and determination," Morgus raved, "fulfilling all the hopes and expectations placed on them. Now Celli's in the lead! Now Daen! They're trading the lead, back and forth, elbowing each other, grappling with each other, neither willing to yield an inch of ground, and it's *thrilling* to watch! It's not clear *why* they're racing with each other instead of looking for their gold, but they must have a . . . oh, dear. Now they're fighting again . . . ."

"Alice look!" said Shaun, pointing at Molly. "She doesn't know where she is! She's lost! She's lost, she's lost, she's lost! She just standing at the base of those poplars. She doesn't know where *she* is, much less the gold! She'll be banished, for sure! Oh! Oh! Oh!"

"*Wait.*"

BOOK OF LEPRECHAUNS: THE LORE GATHERERS

"And Gregory is *still* talking to his auditor," cried Morgus. "He must be getting some *great* information to risk spending this much time ... WAIT!! He's pulled out a small table and two chairs and started pouring tea?!?"

The crowd groaned.

"Oh, Gregory. Bad move!"

There!

Shaun watched Molly scurry up the side of a tree, reach into a large knot about thirty feet up, and pull out five gold coins.

"OH NO!" cried Shaun. "IT'S NOT IN THE—Oh. She did it."

Molly held the gold coins aloft, gleaming in the sun. As a final flourish, she grabbed a piece of the tree's paper-like bark, pushed off from the trunk, and descended to the ground, slowly cork-screwing around the tree, bark peeling off behind her like a streamer.

"Ladies and gentlemen, a big round of applause for Molly, the first to strike gold, and a Thieving record, to boot!" The crowd stood and cheered.

Shaun sat down, bewildered.

"How did she ... ? I didn't even see ... ?"

Shaun. My love. Your daughter is extraordinary. You must know that? Truly. What she just did hasn't been done in an AGE of lore gatherers.

"What did she do?"

Shaun—

"But it doesn't matter, right? There's still the second round. It doesn't matter how amazing that was if she loses the second round, does it? I mean it doesn't, does it? She'll still be banished, and then what? Then what?!?"

Shaun, I love you. But you're impossible.

Shaun took a deep, shuddering breath. "I know, my love." He shook his head. "I know."

* * * *

"What do you *mean*, you don't want to go home?!?" Dorn snapped. This was not how it was supposed to go.

"Veni, vidi, and I'm going to get to the bottom of it!"[F] Caesar said. "When

---

[F] Julius Caesar famously wrote, "veni, vidi, vici" (I came, I saw, I conquered) in a letter to the Roman Senate following his victory at the Battle of Zela. He liked it so much that, ever the savvy public relations man, he had decided to adopt it as a pithy catch phrase. He was still tinkering with it.

Alexander the Great was told there were infinite worlds, did he not weep for that he was not lord of any?"

"Did he?"

"I had planned to rule an empire. With the power of flight, I could rule the world!"

"Uh-huh."

"Who knows what other wonders the future holds!"

"Uh-huh."

Dorn's head was throbbing. This wasn't fair. This was too perfect an opportunity. He had been on his own for too long. Some stupid two-thousand-year-old emperor with an over-developed god complex was not going to stop him. Not now. It was time to get creative.

"It's just . . . you know . . . Like I say, O Caesar, I'm happy to help you. With anything and everything you ask. But this future you're so excited about? There's something you should know . . . ."

****

Dear Molly, this is probably the three thousandth letter I've tried writing you in eight years.

Dorker sat in the arena stands watching The Thieving, sucking on the end of a pencil, and trying to think. His father was doing what he always did—walking through the arena handing out pastries. Dorker always carried a notebook with him to write down his ideas for stories on the theory that one day, he might actually write one. He thought he probably *could* write a story, but the problem was that he felt like he never had anything to say. That seemed like a problem. But seeing Molly in the first round of The Thieving had inspired him.

Dorker re-read the first line of his letter. While it was true that he had been trying to talk to Molly since he had been about five, he wondered if that was the right tone to strike on a letter as important as this. He crossed it out and tried again.

Dear Molly, have you ever seen someone do something so amazingly incredible you realized your whole life up until that point had meant nothing?

Again, Dorker wondered if that was really the best introduction. Surely, his life had meant *something*. He didn't know what, exactly, but it seemed like a reasonable proposition, and he shouldn't dismiss it so quickly. But what he had to say to Molly was big. Really big. The whole arena was abuzz with what she had just done, but for Dorker, it was something more. Seeing Molly had *changed* something inside him. Something fundamental. He had never seen anyone do anything like it. Granted, he was only thirteen and hadn't seen a lot, but Dorker knew what he knew. And he knew he would never be the same.

Dear Molly, you are amazing, and I will follow you to the ends of the earth.

Too much? Dorker worried it was too much. And too soon. The statement was true, of course, but something told him this was one of those occasions where the whole truth might be better served by suppressing it. He wondered briefly if he should talk to Shaun about his feelings. Shaun had written whole books on lying and the truth, and probably even love, so he would know, wouldn't he? He knew everything.

Hey Molly, your pal Dorker here. Wow! Great Thieving, huh! Wanna hear something neat? I love you!

Writing this letter was proving to be a lot harder than expected. Which was weird. He'd read about revelations, and they always seemed to bring absolute clarity to whoever had one. Dorker had absolute clarity, but how to talk about it with Molly was anything but clear.

A cheer in the crowd brought Dorker back from his thoughts to The Thieving. He had stopped paying attention after Molly found her gold, but it looked as though everyone had passed the first round, even Gregory, Celli, and Daen. That was good. At least no one was banished. Now it was Molly's turn to hide.

Dorker set his pad of paper down for a moment to focus on Molly, but the pencil stayed firmly in his teeth. As the auditors retired to the waiting room underneath the arena, he saw Mr. Links glare at Molly. Molly glared back. Dorker didn't know what was going on, but she was angry, he could tell. Clearly, Mr. Links had provoked Molly somehow. When he was gone, Dorker saw her lips mouth what looked like the words:

"Nuts to Mr. Links!"

Molly clutched her five gold pieces and dashed into the woods again. Dorker's heart thrilled. She ran, ducked, and turned around trees like she had in the first round. But it wasn't like before. Something was wrong. In the first round, Molly had looked almost like a bird flying, or a shooting star—a pure force obeying some ancient and primal energy. Not even magic could look as natural, as elemental as Molly had in the first round. If Truth looked like anything, Dorker was pretty sure it looked like Molly.

This didn't look like Truth. This looked like Desperation. Molly stopped and looked around, her hands clutching her head. Whatever had powered her in the first round seemed to have vanished, and now, time was running out. Dorker held his breath as Molly began to dig furiously right where she stood. He wanted to run down out of the stands and help her, but he couldn't, of course. He stood up and sat down several more times, hardly daring to look. After Molly tossed in the gold, she filled in the hole with impressive speed, but now she had to get back to the starting area and she didn't know the way.

"No, Molly! Turn back! Other way! Go the other way!!" Dorker yelled frantically, but she couldn't hear him. Molly got lost several times before finally making it back to the starting area with seconds to spare. Dorker sat down and exhaled.

"Okay, auditors," Morgus announced, "you have two hours. Be careful, contestants! These auditors are tricky! Let round two BEGIN!"

Dorker collected himself so he could focus. He put in the magical earpiece that had been distributed to the audience at the door so they could hear the Questioning, and tuned it to Molly.

Mr. Links emerged from the waiting room and wasted no time walking straight to her. He glared silently, breathing through his nose in short bursts.

"Did you cheat?" he demanded.

"What?!?"

"In the first round—how did you do that?"

BOOK OF LEPRECHAUNS: THE LORE GATHERERS

"I—I don't know, I—"

"Was it magic? It couldn't have been magic."

"No, I don't—"

"Did you cheat?"

"No!"

Mr. Links looked her up and down doubtfully.

"You buried it, this time, didn't you?"

"Yes. No! Wait, what?"

Dorker clutched his hands over his mouth. Mr. Links was clearly an expert questioner and Dorker was sure Molly was done for. But instead of pressing his advantage, Mr. Links stopped questioning, turned, and sat heavily in a chair.

Was this a trick? It seemed like a trick to Dorker. But if Mr. Links wasn't even going to look for the gold, Molly couldn't lose. Thank Shillelagh! Dorker didn't like competition. It made him tense. Only when an hour passed, and Mr. Links still hadn't moved did Dorker relax and go back to composing his letter. Soon, he was barely even aware of the announcer's voice reverberating around the stadium.

"The contestants have done an outstanding job this year. I've never seen auditors look so flummoxed. And to the contestant who persuaded a badger to swallow your gold pieces—I won't say who!—fantastic stuff! Definite points for creativity there."

Dear Molly, I have been watching you since you were four years old.

Dorker scratched that one out immediately. Even writing it felt creepy. Dorker stared at the white paper in front of him, his mind as blank as the page.

"And an auditor goes down!" cried Morgus, as the audience gasped. "Sorry, Mr. MacDonald, the spell placed over the arena to prevent magic applies to the auditors too. It's pretty unforgiving." The audience chuckled uncomfortably. "Don't worry folks, his face will return to normal in a day or two. All the same, can we get Jerry some ointment?"

Dear Molly, congratulations on passing The Thieving.

Dorker looked at the sentence. It was bland, but it was the best he had written so far. A start, at least. Maybe he just needed to move on.

Dorker spent the rest of the round staring at the sentence, trying to figure out what to say next. As the minutes wound down, he finally concluded that maybe he didn't need anything more than that. Maybe he should just sign it and give it to her. That might be enough. Until today, he had probably never said anything more than "Hi" to Molly. He had always been too shy and intimidated. As of today, of course, those days were over, but she didn't know that. She didn't really know anything about him. Expecting her to suddenly receive with open arms his deepest, most profound declarations of love might be expecting too much. A short note was better. It was thoughtful and left open the exciting possibility of a future conversation. Dorker signed his name.

"Fellow villagers," Morgus intoned, "what a year! For the first time in a long time, every single contestant has passed The Thieving!"

The audience jumped and cheered. Dorker saw Molly leap into the air and cry, "YES!"

Dorker smiled. Clearly, Mr. Links had realized there was no point in trying to find Molly's gold. She was too wonderful. Clearly, Molly deserved to pass The Thieving, no matter what. Dorker neatly folded his note, wrote "To Molly" on it, and left the arena early to avoid the crowd. He decided he would stop by her house and drop it off for her to find later, and then figure out when he might "accidentally" run into her again to finally say more than "Hi." It would be easier to say all the things he wanted to say to her face to face. He was sure of it. In any event, he decided there was no need to watch the very end of the ceremony.

Which was too bad because it wasn't until after Dorker left that Molly failed The Thieving.

* * * *

Shaken, and somewhat incredulous, Caesar sat staring at Dorn.

"After all this time?" Caesar said, his voice hollow.

"I'm afraid so," said Dorn mournfully.

"But . . . humanity . . . civilization . . ."

"Gone," said Dorn. "The twenty-first century is no paradise, my friend. A jungle, more like. Dangerous, too. That mechanical bird we saw? Machines like that *rule* the world now. We're just lucky it didn't see you. They *eat* people."

"What?!?"

"Yes. The one we saw? Just ate. I could tell. It was *full* of people. You think Roman streets are dangerous? In the twenty-first century, humans are slaves to machines."

"I don't understand . . ."

"Been like that for centuries. Well, I mean it's hardly surprising. After the Roman empire fell—OOPS! I shouldn't have said that . . ."

"What? What was that? Tell me."

"I shouldn't."

"You must."

"I shall. The world fell to pieces, O Caesar. Today . . . well . . . the truth is, humans barely even know how to speak anymore. They can only communicate with little hand-held machines they carry everywhere."[F]

"This is . . . I don't . . ."

It is a little known fact that when Julius Caesar was twenty-five years old, he was captured by pirates. Before long, he was running the pirates' ship. Which is to say, he was not a man who was easily flummoxed. He could just about wrap his head around a seven-inch-tall man appearing out of nowhere, but his ancient-Roman mind didn't stand a chance comprehending a twenty-first century passenger plane. Julius Caesar had short-circuited.

"Seems to me—" said Dorn, "—if I may say, O Caesar—it seems to me, you've got an *opportunity* here. Maybe you can't rule this world. But take me back and maybe you can save—"

"No." Caesar was calm and determined. "You must show me. I have to see it for myself."

"Nooooooooooooo!" said Dorn. "You can't just go walking out there among the machines! Far too dangerous! Even for the likes of me. And I have magic to protect me."

"Magic? You have magic? What kind of magic?"

"(Bingo!)" said Dorn.

"Excuse me?"

[F] A textbook example of Cruciale Lye number thirty-five: the Lie Ironic.

"Nothing. Yes, I have magic."

For all his immense gifts, Caesar was a sucker for magic and superstition. Here, he felt on firmer ground. Unfortunately for him, so did Dorn.

"Are you a demon?"

"More like a god, really," said Dorn.

"A god? A god of what?"

"A god of luck, my friend," said Dorn. "For lucky it is that you found me. Come. Let's take a walk."

"Show me your magic," said Caesar. "If you are a god."

"I'd love to," said Dorn, "but alas, my power is weak. I need your help."

"I see. You're a fraud," said Caesar. He turned to walk away. His mind was stretched, and he had had enough of Dorn. Whatever he was, Dorn was probably more trouble than he was worth. But Dorn summoned his best impersonation of divine fury.

"Oh, look who knows so much about Gods! Talking to a God expert, am I? Know all about regenerative omnipotence, do you? Know how magic works? How *DARE* you doubt me? Who summoned the mechanical bird, eh? Ever seen anything like that before? Ever seen *anything* like *ME?*"

Caesar stopped, uncertainly.

"I didn't think so," said Dorn.

Caesar looked at Dorn, standing there on a rock, chest thrust forward, looking not at all like a god of thunder. It would have been comical, but that airplane had been all too real.

"I respect the Gods," he said uncertainly.

"Then you better start respecting me, pal!" said Dorn. "'Cause I got news for you—you want to save the world? You want to go home? I'm the *only one* who can get you there."

Caesar considered doubtfully. "How?"

"What we need, my little friend, is gold."

"Gold? Why gold?"

"Gold helps my magic."

"How?"

"No more questions."

Caesar thought for a minute, then reached into his toga and produced one gold Roman coin. "I have this," he said, flipping it to him. "Do your magic."

Dorn looked at it, felt the smallest surge of magical power, and grinned. The coin displayed a perfect profile picture of Caesar (though the nose didn't do him justice). It gave him an idea.

"Not nearly enough, O Caesar," Dorn grinned toothily. "But not to worry. I know where we can get more."

"Then why do you need me?"

"Because I like you, O Caesar. And I hate to see what the world has become. Getting you home might help humanity, and I want to help humanity. I'm generous like that. Benevolent, you might say. But the thing about the gold—it's hidden."

"Mm-hmm. We're going to steal it, aren't we?"

"Borrow. More like borrowing. And a little digging. It's not far. Don't worry, the owner will never know. Trust me. Hey, I'm a just god. Once we get back to your time, we'll rebury it in the exact same place and in two thousand years, it'll be like it was never gone!"

"Whose gold is this? Is it someone important?"

"It's nobody."

Caesar didn't believe Dorn, but he had never been above breaking a rule or two to get what he wanted. And now he wanted to go home. Besides, whatever Dorn was, if he truly did have magic (and gold), he could be useful. Caesar's past was littered with the bodies of those who thought they were smarter and craftier than him. What did he have to lose?

"What do we have to do?"

Dorn smiled. "Just take my hand and repeat after me: I wish for Shaun McClanahan's gold."

* * * *

The Thieving had been wildly successful—a one hundred percent pass rate! When round two was over, the arena crowd celebrated rapturously. Whoops and shouts rang around the stadium like bells.

Only Mr. Links stayed quietly seated. Molly didn't know why he hadn't looked for her hidden gold pieces, but she didn't care. She had won, and that was all that mattered. She extended her hand and said: "Not even going to shake my hand?"

Mr. Links looked up at her and said simply: "Congratulations, Molly. And now, will you please go collect your gold pieces and bring them back?"

"Bring them . . . ? What?"

"You've got to collect your gold pieces, Molly."

"Wait, wh . . . but I . . ."

"Hiding gold isn't much use to anyone if you can't find it again, Molly," said Mr. Links solemnly.

She couldn't remember where it was. Her path had been too random. Desperately, she ran into the woods and searched for it, but it was no use.

After far too long, she sat down heavily on the ground, feeling like she had committed the world's dumbest, most obvious mistake.

And now she was banished for it!

How could she face her father?

Mr. Links, who had been following her, walked up beside her and knelt down. Gone was any hint of antagonism or judgment. To Molly's surprise, his demeanor was respectful and gentle.

"How did you know?" she asked.

Mr. Links smiled. "I've been doing this a long time, Molly. I've learned to read contestants pretty well." He looked at her kindly. "Tell me, in that first round, what were you thinking about?"

"Well, nothing really. Just finding the gold."

"And the second round?"

"I was thinking about beating you."

Mr. Links nodded. "Anger. Revenge. Yes? You were focused on beating me and not on winning the real game, which is protecting the gold—protecting the village. Little good comes from seeking revenge, Molly, in magic or in life. If you come away from today with no other lesson than that, it will have been a good day for the village, believe me. Anyway, after your reaction in the hallway . . . well, it seemed reasonable to think you'd make a mistake."

"But how could you be sure?"

Mr. Links shrugged. "Have you ever done what you did in the first round before?"

"Maybe," she said, with a touch of defiance.

"Well, *I've* never seen anything like it, and I've seen quiet a lot. I suspected you were as surprised as I was. I figured you'd try it again, but I didn't think you could pull it off twice. And frankly, if you can do that *without magic—*" a flicker of doubt crossed Mr. Links's face. "It wasn't magic, right? It couldn't have been. You'd have been disqualified instantly."

Molly shrugged. She didn't know how she had done what she had done. Right now, everything was a blur.

Mr. Links nodded. "Well, if you could replicate that at will, then not only would you pass the test, but I'd be recommending you as an auditor next year!"

"Yeah, well . . ." Molly sniffed. "I won't even be here next year," she said, wiping away a tear.

Mr. Links stood her up, took her by the shoulders, and looked directly into her yes. "I'm going to talk to the committee, Molly."

"What?"

"Mark me now—I don't know what you did in that first round, but . . . I don't even know what to say. It was *extraordinary*. Truly. I don't use that word lightly. Ask your father. No twelve-year-old has ever just . . . *read* me like that before. Ever. It's a little unnerving, to be honest. But whatever you did, you hang onto it, and you'll be fine. More than fine. We'll all be fine. I'll see what can be done. I know the rule, but this is . . ." Mr. Links looked around as the crowd was filing out. "We can't lose you. We've made a terrible mistake. This whole thing was a mistake. I see that now. I'm so sorry. The committee will just have to listen to reason." He turned back to Molly. "You just keep your head down for the next day or two and don't do anything foolish."

CHAPTER 3

Responsibility

"Check the gold tomorrow morning all by myself?" said Molly, as her father looked at her excitedly. "Me??"

We should back up a bit.

After The Thieving, Molly went down to Holly's Hedge to "keep her head down," as Mr. Links suggested, but also to distract herself and try to pretend nothing had happened. She had made mistakes before, and her father never handled them well. But this—nothing had ever been as bad as this. What a nightmare!

Dorker was right, Holly's Hedge was nice. It didn't have any hedges or even any holly, but it was secluded and had a small waterfall where she could be alone and wash herself off. She told herself she needed to be alone, but it wasn't true. She was scared and mad and embarrassed and upset and—she had forgotten you could feel so many awful things at once. And now she didn't know what was going to happen. Banishment, maybe. Shillelagh's breath! How could it be worse? So no, she didn't need to be alone. What she needed was comfort.

Unfortunately, her father could barely comfort himself, much less anyone else. Comfort only ever seemed to make him more uncomfortable. As far as Molly could tell, he didn't trust it and never would. Her hopes, therefore, were not high when she finally decided to stop putting it off and come home.

"There you are!" he said as soon as she walked in the door. "Where have our gold for the first time by myself?"

Molly shook her head. Shaun never talked about his family, much less about his gold.

"I was your age. Terrified. He was an awful man. You can't even . . . . just wretched. But I did it. I followed the same route you'll take—one I had taken a thousand times. I said the same magic words and did the spells faithfully, just as he had taught me. And do you know what I found when I dug up our chest?"

"The gold, just where it had always been," said Molly, rolling her eyes.

Shaun shook his head. "Nothing," he said.

"What?!? *Nothing?*"

"Not even a scrap of metal. The whole chest was gone."

"What?!?"

"I panicked. I couldn't believe it. I thought I had come to the wrong place. I retraced my steps five times to make sure I hadn't made a mistake. Then I dug like crazy. I must have shifted thirty tons of soil looking for that chest. When I was done, the whole area looked like it had a bad case of the humans."[*]

"Did you find it?" Molly asked.

"No! It was gone!"

"What did you do?"

"What could I do? I went home and told my grandfather. I thought I was dead for sure. And do you know what he did when I told him?"

Molly shook her head.

"He laughed."

"What?!?"

"The old liar had moved it himself the night before."

Molly was appalled. "Why would he do something like that?"

"To teach me a lesson, chick. He wanted me to know what it felt like to lose everything so that I would never want to experience it for real."

"That's terrible!" said Molly.

"Yes, it was," said Shaun. "But I learned the lesson."

Molly went quiet. Between this and The Thieving, she was starting to seriously question leprechaun teaching methods.

"Don't worry, Molly," Shaun smiled. "That's not going to happen to you.

---

[*] "A bad case of the humans" = general reckless destructiveness or characterized by willful disregard for anyone or anything.

I wouldn't do that to you. Especially now. Remember: leprechauns lie, yes. But family doesn't lie to family. Ever."

"Your grandfather did."

"Yes, but as I say, you just can't even . . . he was terrible."

The moment had come, once again, for Shaun to say something supportive as he let Molly go do something on her own. Immediately, he thought about Alice. He tried to steady himself and took a deep breath.

"Molly. I know I'm not always the best . . . your mother was always better . . . I've always thought . . . you would have been better . . . better off without . . . is what I mean . . ." he trailed off and turned his back, choking back sobs. Finally, without looking at her, he reached back and squeezed her hand, barely squeaking out the words, "You'll be fine."

Then he abruptly picked up his bag and walked out.

"Okay, Da'," Molly said softly, as the closed door behind him.

Now she was alone.

She felt too queasy to bother with the hot breakfast her father had made her, so she ate a piece of dry bread, hoping to settle her stomach. When that didn't work, she decided to just get it over with. She gathered her shovels and the accounting records and set off.

The walking calmed her. She remembered the route, and all the spells worked perfectly. Before digging, however, she put down her shovels and books, and performed a precautionary sweep of the area to make sure that she had not been followed (she knew that would make her father happy). Finding nothing unusual, she pulled out her shovels and began to dig.

Molly was a good digger, but even with her mother's shovels, doing it by herself took more than twice as long as it did when she and her Dad worked together. She focused on her breathing and concentrated on the task at hand. The physical exertion and release of adrenalin felt invigorating. For the first time since The Thieving, she allowed herself to hope:

Hope that her father's plan might actually work.

Hope that, if she could handle checking the gold, maybe her dad would trust her with other things.

Hope that they could spend more time together.

Hope that they might talk about things—*real* things, not just the tasks on his lists or whatever happened to be worrying him that day.

Hope that everything could finally be different between them.

All of which collapsed, of course, when she opened the chest and found it empty.

CHAPTER 4

The Story

The very first thing children in Finnegan's Wake learn when they start school at age four is *The Story*. Its full title is longer, but for now, just know that *The Story* was so important, it was commonly referred to by this shortened version. Molly hadn't thought about *The Story* for a long time. Mostly because it reminded her of the worst week of her life, but more on that later.

Telling *The Story* was the first big rite of passage for young villagers and each year, the school's great hall was redecorated especially for the occasion. Molly remembered it was like walking into an autumn forest, with trees sprouting to a high ceiling, vaulted with branches, where fireflies danced amid the orange, red, and yellow leaves. Torches had been lit, filling the canopy with a golden glow, and on the floor, different types of interlocking wood planks created a complex knot design.

The children all dressed in their ceremonial robes. This was important. Molly's teacher had told them: "Your parents have made you these robes, just as their parents made robes for them, and their parents before them. We are craftspeople. There is nothing a lore gatherer cannot make. As Shillelagh made the universe, we make and remake our world. You wear your robes as a reminder."

In addition to their broader cultural significance, ceremonial robes are deeply personal works of family art. What they all have in common is, in accordance with long-standing tradition, every robe is green. Beyond that, each is utterly unique. Designed by a child's parents before their first day of school,

Molly's had a lattice-work pattern sewn into it with finely spun gold and actual wildflowers here and there that never died or dried. As Molly walked, the gold flashed and vanished, shimmering in its folds. Even years later, when Molly put it on, she felt awash in sunlight. Nothing made her feel closer to her mother than wearing that robe.

Though the ceremony was held at the school, it was technically run by the village Bickersmiths.[†] The Chief Bickersmith herself came down from the Narratorium at the top of the hill to tell *The Story*. Bickersmiths were highly revered. Their job was to go out and mingle with the villagers, collect their stories, and study them for patterns and deeper meaning. Stories of all kinds were catalogued and stored, but every now and then, a story was important enough to be included in THE BOOK OF LEPRECHAUNS, which lore gatherers considered their entire species' collective memory. THE BOOK OF LEPRECHAUNS was millions of years old (possibly older) and almost incomprehensibly vast. Some of the stories were beyond ancient, but new ones were always being added. No one knew anymore how factually accurate the stories were, but no one cared. THE BOOK OF LEPRECHAUNS contained Truth, if not incontrovertible fact.

Before the ceremony, Molly and the other children were only allowed to know that *The Story* told of the greatest trick ever played. It taught lessons about leprechauns, magic, humans, and gold—especially gold—all wrapped up in a tale that struck, it was generally felt, just the right balance between entertaining the children and scaring them silly.

The text of *The Story*, roughly translated from THE BOOK OF LEPRECHAUNS, vol. 49,304, *The Book of Consequences*, is as follows:

> Once upon a time, there was a lore gatherer from the village of Finnegan's Wake. One evening, after a long day of thieving, he grew tired and fell asleep against a tree out in the open—in plain sight!
>
> A young human named Lucky Jim spotted him and knew what good fortune had brought. He reached down and picked up the lore gatherer right where he lay.

[†] So named because every Saturday, villagers gathered at The Narratorium to sit and listen to the Bickersmiths tell or sing stories from THE BOOK OF LEPRECHAUNS, and then argue about them.

The love gatherer immediately knew his danger. But if he was afraid, he did not show it because, as every leprechaun knows, humans are stupid, vain, and easily manipulated. He smiled at Lucky Jim.

"Ah, can it be?" he said. "I have heard stories of powerful humans with strong, broad foreheads, arms like carved oak, and a piercing gaze in their eyes! In all my years . . ."

"Stop your yammering, leprechaun," said Lucky Jim, "Flattery will get you nowhere. I'll not trust a word you say."

"And right you would be not to trust me!" said the love gatherer. "For a leprechaun is a lying miscreant if ever there was one! Why, I could tell by the arch of your eyebrows that your mind was sharp and keen. The very idea is insulting that I could tempt you with talk of **gold at the end of a rainbow** . . ."

The children giggled. The good ol' "gold at the end of the rainbow" routine was one of the oldest tricks in the book. As Shaun explains in his famous compendium, *Great Lies Through the Ages*, a long time ago before they understood anything about refracted light and prisms, humans made up all sorts of theories about what rainbows were and why they appeared. In their ignorance, humans were more than willing to believe that rainbows are primarily a mechanism for locating leprechaun gold. Thus, the "gold at the end of the rainbow" routine was born. That so many humans *still* believe such obvious nonsense amazes and delights leprechauns.

"No," said Lucky Jim, "it's three wishes I'll be asking for."

"Crackled acorns!" cursed the love gatherer melodramatically. "Ah, well. Tell me then, fine sir, what is your first wish? Shall it be gold? Shall it be power? Perhaps you'd like to be king? Or an emperor? No doubt you would be a wise and just ruler. Or perhaps it's love you crave? The most beautiful woman in the world to be your wife?"

Money and power. The love gatherer knew well how to tempt humans into making foolish choices—and how one poor choice so often leads to another.

"My first wish" said Lucky Jim, who had considered his

wishes carefully, "is to wish you incapable of tricking me."

"You are as clever as you are wise, young sir! Very well. Your wish is granted. I am now incapable of tricking you."

It was true. Once bound to the magical wish contract, no leprechaun—not even one as crafty as this one—could break it. But he was not worried. Every human wish carried with it the seeds of its own destruction.

"What is your second wish, O great wise one?" he said, bowing low.

Lucky Jim considered carefully.

"A promise—I wish you to promise that you will give me your personal pot of gold today."

A promise? No one had ever wished for a promise before. Even so, the lore gatherer did not worry. But he wanted to be rid of this pesky human.

"Very well," he said. "I promise to give you my personal pot of gold this day. Now what is your final wish?"

Lucky Jim smiled.

"I wish for you to keep your promise!"

The lore gatherer was beaten and ashamed. No human had EVER outwitted a lore gatherer. But he had no choice. He dug up his gold and gave it to Lucky Jim.

Fortunately, Lucky Jim was not so lucky. On his way home, lore gatherers from Finnegan's Wake dropped a tree branch "mysteriously" onto his head, knocking him out cold. When he awoke, his gold was gone, and he never saw another lore gatherer again. [*]

The children always enjoyed *The Story*, but they never got too excited about it afterwards. If anything, they were always a little disappointed. To their young ears, it sounded like the sort of story they had been hearing all their lives about stupid, easily-outwitted humans.

Frankly, they had hoped for a better trick.

---

[*] Over the millenia, humans have told so many stories about leprechauns that they think they know how wishes work. They are wrong. More than anything, what humans fail to appreciate is that even if a leprechaun does give you their gold, nothing prevents their friends from stealing it back. And it won't stop there. You may also find yourself the victim of all sorts of impractical jokes for the rest of your life. A practical joke is one that, while inconvenient, does no permanent damage. An impractical joke is the other kind.

What they didn't realize was that the trick was on them. The reason the village told and retold *The Story* every year wasn't because a human got outwitted; it was because the lore gatherer got *caught*. Molly vividly remembered the ripple of terror she felt when the Chief Bickersmith told them that for losing his gold, the lore gatherer had been banished from Finnegan's Wake, never to be heard from again.

Though Molly could not yet appreciate its significance, the story's full title was *The Story of Dorn*.

CHAPTER 5

Crisis

Molly stared at the empty chest where her father's gold should have been.

She closed the chest.

Then she opened it again.

Then she closed it and opened it a few more times.

It was two long minutes before what she saw fully penetrated her shock.

"The chest is empty," she said. "The chest. Is empty. Why is the chest empty?" She closed her eyes, and exhaled slowly, trying not to panic. Panicking was bad. Her dad always said panicking makes your brain stop working. Well, he would know! He always yelled, "Don't panic!" just as he collapsed into a cataclysmic, end-of-days, world-champion-level, meltdown panic!

She opened her eyes again.

The chest was still empty.

This was ridiculous. How could the chest be empty? She lifted it up, as if all that gold might somehow be hiding underneath the chest.

It wasn't.

Was she dreaming? She had to be dreaming.

She wasn't.

She stared at the chest. It wasn't, in fact, *completely* empty. One small, gold coin lay at the bottom of the chest—sad, alone, and slightly accusatory. Maybe one gold coin was better than nothing?

No, it wasn't. It absolutely wasn't.

The spells—maybe it was the spells; maybe the gold wouldn't appear unless you said the spells correctly? Maybe she had made a mistake somehow.

Desperately hoping against hope, she quickly closed the chest and locked it with the keys and various spells her father had taught her. Then she ran through the whole the sequence again.

Still empty.

She locked the chest, reburied it, walked home, and methodically went through the entire process from beginning to end in case there was something she had somehow left out.

Empty.

Her imagination raced.

Maybe this was the wrong chest; maybe another lore gatherer had buried their gold in the same area and had dug up Shaun's by mistake and carried it away? It didn't seem likely, but better safe than sorry. Molly dug up the entire area, unearthing acres upon acres of dirt. In the process, she found an old human shoe, five tin cans, a license plate, and a family of irate wood mice, but no chest of gold.

Hours later, exhausted and filthy, she stood alone with the empty chest on what now looked like an excavation site. A thousand catastrophic scenarios played out in her mind, culminating in the thought that this might actually kill her father. How many times had he said, when recovering from some calamity, "Well, at least the gold is safe"? He never said, "Well, we've still got our health," or "At least we're all still breathing," or anything that might express care for their personal well-being. The gold was always the important thing.

And now she understood: gold was the glue that held him together. She had lost the only thing her father truly cared about. It was gone.

She leaned against a tree to steady herself.

There was nothing for it, she finally decided. Best to put the area back together again and replace all that dirt. Things would only be worse if she didn't.

By the time she finished, the shadows were growing long, and the air was cooling. She had no sooner wondered whether her father had gotten home yet, and how she was going to tell him, when he ran up from out of nowhere frantically out of breath.

"Da'! What are you—?"

"Molly! You should have been home hours ago! I came home expecting to find you working in the garden or with the bees or having dinner or . . . and what do I find? Nothing! An empty house! You were nowhere to be found!"

"Da', I'm sorry, I—" Molly began.

"I called for you and called for you. Naturally, I thought the worst! What was I supposed to think? I figured something must have happened to you in the forest!"

"Well, actually—"

"Molly! I thought maybe you'd fallen and gotten hurt, or got caught in some human trap, or by a fox, or . . . I was so *worried*, Molly. You can't *do* that!"

"I'm sorry, Da', I didn't mean to scare you."

Shaun took a few deep breaths, trying to calm down. He was doing his best not to overreact.

"Okay. It's okay, love, it's okay. You just . . . you *scared* me, is all. But you're okay. Yes. I'm glad you're okay. Whoo! Thank goodness. Ha! Ha!"

"Da' . . ."

"So, you did it. And all by yourself, yeah? I knew you could!"

"Da'—"

"This is *great*. And everything was alright, wasn't it? The gold was still there." Shaun was speaking a mile a minute. All his panic had transmuted to manic cheerfulness, which wasn't much better.

"Da!"

"So we can *use* this now! We can show the counsel that you're reliable and—"

"The gold is gone, Da'!"

Still smiling, Shaun shook his head as if trying to clear his ears. "What did you say?"

"Well, not completely gone. There was just this gold coin." She handed it to him. "But other than that, the gold is gone. I'm sorry, Da'! I'm so sorry! I don't know what happened!"

Shaun looked at the gold coin in his hand blankly, then looked back at Molly. "The gold . . . is *gone?*"

Shaun's hand still had not closed around the coin. Molly now saw that though he still smiled, he wasn't actually breathing. Then he blinked, and his face collapsed in slow motion like a tower demolished by explosives.

"Da' . . . ?"

"The gold. *Isn't*. There."

Molly shook her head.

Shaun grabbed the shovel from Molly and, dirt spraying from the earth like a geyser, quickly dug down to the chest.

It may interest you to know, at this point, that Shaun once wrote a military history of the great leprechaun general, Rictus O'Reilly, titled *The Gift of Calm*. General Rictus was known chiefly for the number of battles he didn't win. More specifically, General Rictus was famous for the number of battles he never had to fight. A brilliant tactician, General Rictus was also uncommonly cool-headed. No soldier who had served under him could ever recall him losing his temper or appearing even mildly flustered. He exerted an almost preternatural ease that affected everyone around him, including the enemy. On the eve of his greatest battle, when his army was outnumbered five to one and seemed to face almost certain annihilation, he invited the opposing general to dinner. General Rictus served his enemy a light meal, artfully and lovingly prepared, with a fine bottle of wine made from the local berries and flowers that grew in the area. The wine was not magical (so far as anyone could tell), but it was so good, it placed the drinker in a state of almost perfect empathy. His enemy thus disarmed, General Rictus patiently explained how his victory was not only inevitable, but how the entire dispute could be resolved to each party's mutual advantage. A few days later when the peace accord was finally signed, the enemy general resigned his commission and took up dancing, his first great passion in life. According to General Rictus, his victory had been quite straightforward: "With perfect calm, comes perfect insight. And that goes for all concerned."

As Shaun's book explains, General Rictus's traveling winery was among the most feared (and desired) in the world. He had an uncanny ability to capture the life essence of the local soil in fermented form. All his enemies knew its power, yet none could resist its temptation. General Rictus was characteristically placid about his controversial use of battle wine. On the eve of a great victory in Germania, he famously said: "To taste of the soil is to know those who work upon it. When you know them, you love them, and love is the first step to victory."

All of which is a long way of saying that all the calm General Rictus possessed, Shaun did not.

"Oh no! No no! No no no no no no no no no no!! Oh! Shillelagh!! NO!!!"

He looked up at Molly, who shrank back from the lip of the hole.

"What have you done?!? What did you do? You told someone the spells, didn't you?"

"What? No! Da'..."

"You did! You must have!" Shaun looked possessed. Molly had never seen his face so contorted with tears and rage. It was like being yelled at by a stranger.

"You must have told someone! Who was it!!" Shaun was climbing out of the hole towards her.

"Da', I didn't..." she said, backing away.

"Don't give me that!" Shaun snapped. He got very quiet as he approached. "Listen to me. No one. NO ONE could have found that gold, much less have taken it. Not without knowing the spells. Now tell me—" Shaun stood right in front of her, "Who. Did. You. Tell?"

Tears streamed down Molly's face, but she was so scared she could hardly speak.

"ANSWER ME!!" Shaun yelled.

"Da'," Molly managed through silent, choking sobs, "You're scaring me."

In the confused, swirling chaos of his mind, the small part of Shaun that was still sane took control. He turned slowly and dragged himself away.

"Okay." He took a breath to steady himself. "Okay.... Maybe you didn't tell anyone. Maybe... maybe... maybe someone followed you? Did you notice anything when you came this morning? Anything unusual?"

All of Shaun's yelling had turned Molly's thoughts to confetti. "I...I...I don't think so...."

"You don't THINK so? I need you to KNOW so, Molly!"

"No, Da,' I didn't see anything unusual!"

"You're sure?"

"I checked, Da'! Before I even started digging, I checked the area to see if anyone had followed me. But even if they had, how could they have taken the gold before I opened the chest?"

"Oh, Molly! All kinds of ways! So, I'm going to ask you again. Are. You. Sure?"

"As sure as I can be, Da'. I mean, I checked. I checked I checked I checked! I don't know what else I was supposed to do."

Shaun was suddenly cold. "You were supposed to protect the gold,

Molly."

His words were worse than if he had struck her. Shaun turned and, using Molly's shovels, began filling in the hole with dirt. Cautiously, Molly came to help.

"I'll do it, Molly. Sit down and wait please."

Molly found a log and sat down, not daring to move. Her father's digging was the only sound in the forest, as if even the birds knew better than to chirp near him. When he had finished, he gathered their things wordlessly and started off for home, barely glancing at Molly as he passed. Molly hesitated, then got up and followed. For just a moment, she wasn't completely sure he even wanted her to come. All the way back, she could hear him muttering.

"No one must know. Ah, don't be ridiculous, of course they're going to find out. They always find out. Especially after The Thieving? Maybe if we keep our mouths shut? But that's not possible. Molly already gave away the secrets. The Council knows already, for sure. We don't have much time."

"Da'?" said Molly.

Shaun stopped, turned, and looked at her wide-eyed, as if he had forgotten she was there.

"I really didn't tell anyone the secrets, Da'," she said quietly. "Why won't you believe me?"

Shaun looked at her and nodded vacantly. His mind was racing, and she didn't know where it was taking him. She wasn't even sure how much of her father was actually present behind those eyes. They walked the rest of the way without speaking.

By the time they got back, it was night. Bioluminescent lanterns had been hung across the village roads bathing them in warm, soft light, and the village was still lively. Harvan O'Higham was out on his stoop weaving his brooms; Dorothy McStaron was giving a demonstration of a candle she had created that magically recycled wax as it burned; Ellen O'Brundage was having a spirited discussion with some other village engineers about revamping the power supply to harness geothermic processes, as well as wind, water, and solar energy.[*] When they passed Mr. O'Doud, the local butcher who was out sweeping in front of his shop, he gave them a wave.

---

[*] Lore gatherers have electricity, but for the most part, they don't see the point.

"Evenin' to you, Shaun, Molly! How does this glorious night find you, then?"

Shaun plastered a smile across his face and waved a little too enthusiastically.

"Just fine Thomas nothing's wrong nothing, nothing at all wrong with me. Or Molly! We're both just fine just very very fine thank you for asking yes, and, we're fine and . . . how are you?"

Mr. O'Doud looked at Shaun's frozen smile and Molly's terrified face and stopped sweeping. "I'm well, Shaun."

"Yes fine fine fine," Shaun babbled. "Why why why . . . why do you ask? We're both just fine. Thanks!" Shaun looked down at Molly, saw her face, and quickly shoved her behind him. "Oh, you're talking about Molly! Of course. Ha ha! Yes, she's just fine nothing wrong. A stomachache! Yes, she has a little stomachache that's bothering her that's all, it's just a little stomachache, isn't that right Molly? Tell him how you have a little stomachache but will be feeling just fine in no time at all, go on tell him!"

Molly peeked out from behind her father and said in a small voice, "I have a stomachache."

This was one hundred percent true.

"Shaun," said Mr. O'Doud, "is everything okay? You don't look well."

Shaun's eyes went wide. "Well, I can't stand around chatting, have a lot of things to get done today. This evening I mean! I mean tonight! Day's over. Ha ha! Have a lot of . . . things . . . tonight . . . and Molly! Yes, Molly. Of course, have to get her home before she . . . her stomach, you know . . . well, good evening!"

He grabbed Molly by the arm and walked home as fast as he could, almost dragging her behind him. On their way, they passed several more well-wishers, but Shaun pretended not to see them by covering his face with his free hand. As a way of hiding, it was a bit divorced from reality, but then, Molly was beginning to suspect, so was Shaun. When they got home, he slammed the door behind them and exhaled as though he had been holding his breath the entire way.

"Shillelagh!" he exclaimed. "That was close. I *don't think* anyone noticed anything. But we have to move quickly." He began closing all the window blinds, locking all the doors, and turning the lights down.

As Shaun frantically raced around the house, Molly stood in the middle of the room, not knowing what to do. When he finally noticed her, his face grew dark.

"Pack your bag, Molly."

Molly wasn't sure she had heard him right.

"Pack my bag?"

"Yes, Molly, pack your bag!"

"But . . ."

"But what?!" he said impatiently.

Molly swallowed. "But why?" was all she could manage.

"We may have to leave very quickly and with very little notice. We need to be ready."

"But why?"

"Just do it please!"

"Sh-sh-should I pack one for you, too?"

"Yes," he said curtly. "Light enough to carry, but enough to last a week. *Essentials only*, Molly."

Molly nodded, went to her room, and closed the door. She tried to settle herself. She had never seen her father so—she didn't know how to put it. "Intense" didn't even begin to describe it. Not unhinged, exactly, but not entirely hinged, either. With Shaun, there was often little room between "Everything is fine," and "THE WORLD IS GOING TO END!" The smallest thing could always tip the balance, even at the best of times. This, however—this was something else.

But she couldn't think about that right now. "Essentials only," he'd said. She had to decide what to pack that was "essential." The ceremonial robe her parents had made her was obviously essential; and the yellow and orange quilt her mother had made; and the book her dad had dedicated to her when she was born. Molly defined "essential" generously, and by the time she got out her travel bag to pack it, she had assembled a heaping pile of possessions that completely failed to include even a change of socks. Looking at it, she suspected her father's definition of "essential" might be drastically different from hers, and if she didn't want to see her father melt down again, she should probably narrow her list.

Quickly, if reluctantly, she put everything back in its proper place and began pulling out what she imagined her father would define as "essential." It was a depressingly less interesting pile: socks, underwear, pants, shirts, some soap, a brush, and her ceremonial robe. She didn't know where they might be going, but stubbornly, she included a small, framed picture of her mother on the principle that "essential" was not necessarily the same as "important." Then she went and packed a bag for her dad.

When she was done, Molly risked a peek at her father from down the hall through the crack in her bedroom door. Shaun sat hunched over a pile of maps in the kitchen, studying them intently, when a knock at the door shattered his concentration, and made him jump out of his chair. He froze, maps hanging precariously from his arms. Molly held her breath.

Another knock.

Shaun didn't move. A single, rolled map fell from his arms to the floor.

"Shaun?" called a voice from outside hesitantly. "I know you're in there."

Shaun swore under his breath, looked around, then began frantically clearing the maps off the kitchen table.

"Sorry, Shamus!" he called, cramming the maps into a cupboard. "Fell asleep at the kitchen table. Must not have slept well last night. I'll be right there. Fancy a cup of tea?"

"No thanks, Shaun."

"Right!" Shaun was doing his best to sound normal as pots and pans clanged to the floor around him. "I'll be right there!"

Shaun slammed the cupboard shut and locked it, then looked around wildly, trying to decide what to do next. Finally, he ran to the door and wrestled with the handle, unable to open it.

It was locked!

He had locked it.

Right. Of course.

He unlocked the numerous bolts, latches, and chains that comprised his home security system, and opened the door.

"Shamus, old friend!" Shaun exclaimed, ushering Shamus in with a smile. "How goes the night?"

"I'm fine, Shaun, just fine." Shamus wiped his feet awkwardly on the door mat. "Um, yourself?"

"Couldn't be better, couldn't be better. Come in, come in. Have a seat."

"No, Shaun, I—"

"Shamus!" Shaun interrupted. "Don't worry about your shoes! *Do* take a seat and let me give you a cup of tea."

"That's awful kind of you, Shaun, but—"

"No time for a cup of tea and a chat with an old friend?"

"Shaun, you know, I . . . I just—"

"Shamus, just one."

Shamus took off his hat and twisted it like a wet rag. "I'm sorry, Shaun, I didn't want to be the one to tell you—"

"Tell me what, Shamus? I hope nothing's wrong?"

Molly strained to hear from down the hall in her bedroom. Shamus looked miserable.

"Well, the council's called an emergency meeting, Shaun. Tonight. They want to see you now."

"About what, Shamus?"

Shamus shuffled his feet and looked pale.

"About your lost gold, Shaun."

Shaun deflated. Shamus put a beefy hand on his friend's shoulder.

"They asked me to fetch you because they thought it'd easier coming from me. You know how it is when someone loses their gold. Barty Links almost got the council to agree to let Molly stay, but with your gold stolen . . . well, that implicates both of you."

The sound of breaking glass startled them. Shaun looked at Shamus, then ran back to Molly's room. The bags she packed sat in the middle of the floor, but the window was broken, and Molly was running off into darkness.

CHAPTER 6

The Reminiscence

It hadn't been a conscious decision. Molly just ran. She wanted to be away—somewhere she didn't have to worry about gold, or her father, or banishment, or anything.

She had really done it this time. If she thought she had messed up at The Thieving, being summoned by the council made this the grand, super-spectacular, prize-winning, all-time, championship mess-up of mess-ups. The words that kept repeating over and over and over in her head were: "It's all your fault. It's all your fault."

Her dad probably thought it was all her fault too, but a bitter suspicion nagged at her that the window she had accidentally broken might have temporarily erased all other concerns. He had a thing about broken glass. Any time Molly had ever broken a glass or a windowpane, Shaun always yelled, "MOLLY, DON'T MOVE!" and the world had to stop spinning until it was all picked up. Every little problem ballooned into a crisis with him. And now, there was a *real* crisis, and it really *was* her fault, and he had already handled it *really badly*, and she knew it was only going to get worse.

Unlike the main village road, the back paths she had taken were not well lit, and the night was so dark, and her mind so frenzied, she didn't even see Dorker running towards her until they slammed into each other.

"Uhnnhnn . . ." Dorker observed, lying on the ground.

"Dorker!! What are you doing?!?"

"I was comig to see you," he groaned. His face was covered in blood. She was happy to see a friendly face, but at the same time, it wasn't as if Dorker seemed like he would be particularly capable in a crisis. Kind of the opposite, really.

"I thig you brohg by doze!" he said.

"Your what?" Molly said.

"By doze! By doze! I thig you brohg id!"

Molly silently mouthed his words, trying to understand him.

"OH! You think I broke your nose?"

"Yes, you brohg id!"

Molly examined his face. Then she remembered the note Dorker had sent, and she reflexively hit him hard on the arm.

"HEY!" Dorker cried. "Whad was THAD for?!?"

"Why did you send me that note?! Were you trying to rub it in? What's wrong with you??"

"I'b sorry, Molly, I left early! I wouldn'd have if I had . . . I spendt all day trying . . . I wanded to . . . I'm so sorry, Molly."

Molly wasn't ready for Dorker's abject capitulation. It disarmed her, leaving her angry with nothing to be angry at. "Let's have a look at that," she demanded. Dorker was bleeding quite a lot and his nose looked crooked. She grabbed his nose firmly. "We'll have to straighten that out," she said.

"Waid! Whaddareyou—AAAAUUUUGHH!!" Dorker doubled over in pain, grabbing his face.

"Whad did you do THAD for?!?" he cried.

"Hush!" she said, grabbing a handkerchief out of her pocket.

"Well . . . does it loog bedder, at least?" Dorker's eyes were watering.

Molly considered. "Actually, it does. It's a *little* bent, but it gives you a kind of dangerous, rakish look."

"Really?" said Dorker, brightening.

It didn't. Dorker wouldn't look dangerous if you put an eye patch on him and sharpened his teeth. You would still end up feeling sorry for him and worrying he'd bite his lip.

"You'll probably have a black eye," said Molly. "So . . . sorry about that. Here—" she gave him the handkerchief, "—for the bleeding."

Gingerly, Dorker stuffed the handkerchief up his nose.

"I heard whad habbened," he said. "I just . . . I had to see you. Were you runnig to by house?"

"No, I wasn't running to your house!" Molly exclaimed. She wanted to be offended at his presumptuousness, but Dorker looked like an earnest scarecrow whose stuffing was falling out. Air whistled through his nostrils past the handkerchief as he inhaled and exhaled—a different note for each nostril—like the world's strangest clarinet duet. It was hard to stay mad. When she spoke again, her voice was small.

"Oh, Dorker. I really messed up."

"No, Bolly—" Dorker began.

"Dorker! I lost the gold!"

"There bust be some bistake," he said, shaking his head.

"You weren't there, Dorker! Either time! It's gone!"

Dorker took the handkerchief out of his nose and looked at her. "Do you think they'll banish you?"

Molly nodded. Dorker frowned.

"That's not fair. You haven't done anything wrong."

"I lost the gold, Dorker."

"No, I—"

"Yes, Dorker."

"But—"

"No, Dorker."

"Well . . ." Dorker looked at Molly carefully. "What are you going to do?"

Molly shrugged. "Run, maybe. I don't know."

"You can't run!"

Molly looked at him flatly.

"Okay, well, you *can* run . . . obviously," Dorker conceded. "But if you do . . . if you do . . . I'll come with you."

"What?!" said Molly.

"I can't let you go out there by yourself, Molly!"

"Don't be stupid! Why would you do that? You don't have any reason to run."

"No, but I . . . the reason I sent the note . . . Molly . . . the reason I sent it was because I was trying to tell you—"

"Molly!"

Running up the path came her father, followed by Shamus, William

O'Toole, and five other Council members. Shaun grabbed her by the shoulders. "What are you doing?! Why did you run? Are you okay?"

"Yes, Da'. I'm fine. I'm sorry, I just . . ."

"Hi Mr. McClanahan!" said Dorker with a friendly smile, extending his hand. Shaun looked up.

"Dorker," said Dorker, re-introducing himself. "We saw each other yesterday. Just before The Thieving?"

"Ah," Shaun nodded. He whispered out of the corner of his mouth to Molly, "Why is Dorker here?"

"Oh, it's okay, Mr. McClanahan," said Dorker happily. "I'm going to help clear all this up."

"Really? How?"

Dorker thought for a moment. "I don't know," he said confidently.

Shaun didn't know whether to laugh, cry, or get angry. It was a common reaction to Dorker. Shaun turned to Molly.

"Let's go home and get those bags you packed. And we'll grab a loaf of bread before we go." Shaun lowered his voice even further. "And don't say *anything* to the Council. Let me do the talking."

"Ahem—" coughed William, the unofficial chairman of the Council. William was the type who, even though he didn't wear spectacles, generally sounded as though he were peering disapprovingly over the top of them at you. "Shaun, I hate to be a nudge, but now that we've found Molly, I really think . . ."

Shaun nodded. "Yes, of course, of course. Alright, everyone, come on. Let's get on with it."

As a group, they trooped back to Molly's house silently.

"Go in and grab everything you can carry from the larder," Shaun said when they arrived. "I've got some game that's defrosted, fresh vegetables from the garden; there's likely some fizzed chutney and spliced relish that would go well with the meat. There may also be some leftover stew and some beer I brewed last week. Bring it all." Shaun turned to William. "That's correct, right? I mean, I read rules and provisions back when I was on the Council, but that was a while ago. I assume you've been reviewing the ritual?"

"Yes, yes," William sighed. "Yes, the village hasn't had to do one of these since way back when—" William caught himself and looked at Shaun. "Yes, you are correct. Don't worry, we'll do it right, Dorker," he said turning, "time for you to be getting home. Does your father know where you are?"

"Yes, I told him," he said, following Molly into the house. "But right now, I'm going to help Molly carry her bags."

William grunted and looked at Shaun, who just shrugged. As long as Dorker's father knew where he was, Shaun wasn't going to worry. He had bigger problems than Dorker.

When Molly came back outside, she ran to her father.

"Da', they're ransacking our kitchen!! Why are you letting them take all our food?"

"It's part of the ritual, Molly," he said, smiling. "Besides, *we're* not going to need it."

"You don't know that. We're going to fight this, aren't we?"

"I'm sure we can clear it all up," said Dorker.

"Molly," whispered Shaun, "resign yourself. There's nothing to discuss. Just enjoy the ritual."

"You're just giving up?"

"Molly! Hush now! Someday you'll understand."

"I want to understand *now!* I want—"

"This'll make a grand banquet, Shaun," said Liam, emerging from the house with the rest of the Council, all of whom carried armfuls of food and drink. "I've got a new bottle of blackberry wine that would pair well with this pigeon. Let me go get it. Go on without me, everyone, I'll meet up with you there!"

* * * *

When they arrived at the meeting hall, William and the other Council members put down the food and took their seats at a long table where roughly twenty other villagers sat, politely bickering. Lore gatherer politics is a relatively laid-back affair. Lore gatherers would never consent to being governed by one villager alone, elected or not. Accordingly, all adult men and women of the village took turns as Council members, rotating one member out every month to maintain continuity. Council meetings were largely an excuse to get together, eat some good food, or drink someone's latest beer or wine experiment, and argue.

"Right!" said William. "Well . . . let this meeting come to order, I guess. Um . . . Well, we are here to discuss the matter of Shaun McClanahan and the loss of the gold entrusted to his charge."

Everyone murmured embarassed agreement, avoiding each other's eyes.

"Yes," said William, tapping his fingers uncomfortably on the table. "Well, no use dithering. Um. Let's, let's just . . . Gray?"

"Yes, Mr. Chairman?" said Gray, standing.

"Put the kettle on!"

"Second that!" said another Council member. Grateful for something to do, Gray got up, put several pots of water on the stove, and began mixing tea leaves.

"Everyone else, let us begin." With that, the Council members rose, rolled up their sleeves, and began preparing the food.

As has been mentioned, like all leprechauns, lore gatherers care about gold, but what they really love is art. Watching them prepare a meal as a group is like being thrust into a five-star kitchen staffed entirely with master chefs. Everyone brought food and drink, and everything was used. They made pheasant, brazed in a mint-pesto reduction; rusted squirrel stew; garlic-infused venison with a turtle-shell glaze; spring vegetable medley in rose-blossom herb butter; game hen in a frog sauce; frog's legs with toasted hen feathers; beer-basted new potatoes; goat's milk stoat on macerated blackberries; firefly flan (which glows in the dark); caramel-encrusted grasshopper wings on an apple pudding crumble; creamed weasel on toast; and a variety of beers, wines, and pastries.

In the joy of creation, everyone's discomfort melted like butter in a saucepan. Soon, all were chatting as if nothing was out of the ordinary.

When they were finished, William pronounced: "Marvelous work, everyone, thank you so much!"

"Hear hear! Pass some of Shaun's bread, if you would, William."

"Wait your turn, Timothy," William said, happily carving himself a sizable slice.

"I've got some fresh butter," Sheila volunteered. She was the village blacksmith [F] and best butter maker.

[F] For obvious reasons, lore gatherer blacksmiths have no need to shoe horses, though they are skilled enough with iron that they could probably manage it. Mostly, they make shovels, picks, and other digging equipment (Sheila helped Alice make her shovels), but they have substantial engineering skills and are generally involved with all major building projects in any lore gatherer village.

"Ooooooh, that'd be grand," said William.

"Mmmm! Oh my gosh—that bread, Shaun!" said Liam. "Did you make it yourself?"

"It's Molly's," said Shaun proudly, spooning some mushroom bisque with tomato cream into his mouth. "She's been making all our bread for months now."

"You don't say!" said William. "Isn't that something? You've got your mother's touch, and no mistake, Molly."

Molly perked up at the mention of her mother. Until then, she hadn't really been paying attention because she was too upset to eat. Dorker (who, in solidarity with Molly, wasn't eating anything either) surreptitiously snuck a couple of pieces of bread into his pocket when he heard that Molly had made it.

"Your Alice always did make the best bread, Shaun," said Liam, taking another scoop of wobbling goose delight.

"Ah, thanks, Liam. That's good of you to say."

"It's true!" said Liam. "Molly, leprechauns used to come from all over the world just to buy a loaf of your mother's rosemary-splint sour dough."

"Really?" said Molly.

"Oh yes," said William. "'There is no snack in the world as good as the world's best bread and the world's best butter,' she always said."

"Speaking of," said Shaun, "excellent butter, Sheila!"

Glasses tinked, plates were refilled, and the conversation was lively. All topics focused on Shaun and Molly and their time in the village, but best of all, Molly heard stories about her mother. So many stories she had never heard before. Not only that, Shaun spoke about Alice without falling to pieces—he even laughed! He also cried a lot, to be sure, but it was the first time Molly had ever seen him talk about her mother and look genuinely happy.

For example, two years before the events of this story, after much trial and error (and some unfortunate trampling), the village trained a cow in one of the nearby fields to separate itself from the herd and loiter near the far edge of its owner's property. Gray, who was better with animals than he was with people, had been the cow-whisperer. Afterwards, in the dead of night, a team of villagers could crawl under the fence and acquire a day's supply of milk for about a quarter of the village in just a few hours.

To account for the disparity in size between cows and lore gatherers, Gray, working with Shiela, had developed an ingenious method for milking using pullies, levers, and a sophisticated hydraulic system that not only milked the cow, but transported the milk back to the village with speed, efficiency, and minimal discomfort to the cow. The farmer kept the cow, despite her almost non-existent milk output, because she had become the happiest cow he had ever seen, and her calm, good-nature seemed to transmit to the entire herd via its cheerful "Moo."

"Shaun, I've always wanted to know," said William after a few too many glasses of lilac wine, "how did you and Alice ever end up together? Wasn't she supposed to marry Shamus?"

Shaun took a long swig of horseradish beer and smiled. "William, it's like this. When Shamus and I were lads, we fell in love with the same girl."

"Ahhh," said Gabrielle, who had made the celery-seared cucumber spice biscuits. "He won her heart, but you stole it away?" Rivalries in love were generally frowned upon in the village, but a good theft was a good theft to any self-respecting leprechaun.

"You could look at it like that," Shaun said thoughtfully. "He had won her heart, that's for sure. They had been seeing each other for about a year and everyone said they would be married. You all knew that. And they were happy. But . . . I don't know, the first time I laid eyes on her, I was a goner. I just knew she was the one for me."

"Did she feel the same?" said Liam, grinning.

"No," said Shaun flatly. "But I didn't care, y'see? I knew we were meant to be together. Come to think of it, it's the only thing I've ever been sure of in my whole life. I never . . ." Here, Shaun got quiet. "I felt safe with Alice. I never worried as much. About anything. You all know what she was like."

Everyone in the room nodded. They did know. Everyone knew.

"So," Shaun continued, wiping away a tear, "I started trying to get noticed, right? Mostly, I just made a fool of myself. You know, stupid things like walking into trees, pratfalls down the stairs, that sort of thing. You know, just trying to get her to laugh."

"And did she notice you?"

"Oh, yes. She thought I was an idiot!"

Everyone laughed.

"She's not the only one, Shaun!" said Timothy.

Everyone laughed harder.

"Anyway," said Shaun, smiling, "I learned that being the village fool isn't necessarily what anyone finds attractive. So, I tried a different approach. Every morning, when I went out to check the gold with my grandfather, I would cut the most interesting flower I could find. Then I took it to her doorstep and left it for her with some little verse I had written."

"A poem? *You* wrote poems?" said Annie O'Scheer, widely considered the village's best poet.

"I didn't say they were *good* poems. But they rhymed. Mostly."

"Give us a poem, then," said Annie. She had a hard time imagining what sort of poem Shaun would write. She wasn't the only one. Molly tried to picture her father taking the time to write a poem and just couldn't do it. But imagining your parents as young and in love can be hard when you're twelve.

"I don't remember any," said Shaun, shaking his head. "Always been more interested in facts than romance. Oh! I do remember the best passage I wrote. I was rather proud of it at the time, as I recall. It went something like:

> Had Amon writ upon this page you hold,
> Your eyes an epic of themselves would read
> And steal the love that there was told
> So like as Hornof did with Dadne speed. [*]

The room gave an appreciative round of applause.

"Very nice," said Annie, generously. "Did she fall for it?"

"Not at first. My poetry wasn't great. But I was persistent. I think she saw I was putting effort into it. Into her, I mean. I think that's what mattered. The point of that particular poem, as I remember it, was that you shouldn't get too excited about flowery words—pay attention to what a person does."

"Was Shamus not treating her right?"

"Treated her very well, as far as I ever knew. Shamus is a good man, and no mistake. Always has been. Better than me, in a lot of ways. But in truth, I think he may have taken her for granted. Oh, he loved her, but—and I speculate here—he had stopped investing in that love day in and day out. That's what keeps love alive."

Shaun paused.

"Something about Alice changed me. Right down to my marrow, right from the start. And she saw it—saw it was *because* of her, you see? She made me want

---

[*] Shaun's verse references the great lore gatherer poet Amon, who, thousands of years earlier, had written *Love's Destruction*, a classic epic poem about the ten-years war between two ancient leprechaun kingdoms. As the story goes, the two kings, Goreth and Nyqued, met to discuss peace. At a banquet thrown by Nyqued for his foreign visitors, Goreth's son, Hornof, was smitten by the beauty of Nyqued's daughter, Dadne, and the two of them fled back to Goreth's kingdom to marry. Feeling understandably betrayed, Nyqued invaded and lay seige to Goreth's kingdom for ten years before destroying it utterly.

to be a better man. And the more time I spent with her, the better I became. And she saw me change. That's a powerful thing, my friends, to know you have that kind of effect on another."

The room was silent, except for the occasional sound of a glass being refilled. Everyone in the village had loved Alice from the time she was little. Really loved her. Shaun on the other hand . . . well, if they thought of him at all, they thought he was nice enough, but no one saw anything very exceptional in him. When it became known that Alice—everyone's favorite—and *Shaun* were getting married, everyone was stunned and more than a little doubtful. But soon, no one could deny that opposites though they were, it worked. Alice was happy. And Shaun became more than anyone would have expected—a real value to the village.

"So, what happened?" asked William.

"Well, Shamus got wind of what was going on and he came to my house one evening and we had it out."

"Meaning . . . ?"

"He hit me."

"What?!?"

"Yes. I mean, I got a few good licks in, but basically, he flattened me. He cried the whole time, too."

"And was that it?" said William.

"More or less. Alice was mad at both of us for fighting. But she came to my house every day for a week as I healed. THAT was a great week, let me tell you. She stayed with Shamus for a while longer, but I think we all knew it was over."

"How did she know that?" said William. "I mean, forgive me Shaun, what did she see in you that the rest of us missed?"

Shaun shook his head. "I asked her that, William. Asked her that many times. All she ever said was, 'We do what must be done.'"

Everyone nodded silently. No one knew what it meant, but it was the kind of thing Alice always said. Her smile was so radiant and powerful, you tended not to ask questions.

"Well, Shaun," said William, downing the last of his drink, "This has been delightful. Truly." The whole room murmured a drunken agreement. "Um . . . Well. I guess . . . I mean, you know what's next . . . I guess we should get on with it."

"Sure, William, sure," said Shaun. "I understand."

"Shaun, you've gone and let your gold get stolen," he said helplessly.

Shaun sighed. "It looks that way, William, I won't deny it."

The Council exchanged meaningful glances and murmurs.

"Any idea who?"

"No." Shaun took a bite of bread and looked out of the corner of his eye at Molly, who looked at him sullenly.

"Well, that is . . . unfortunate," said William. "Molly, you were the one who first found the gold missing, is that right?"

"How do you know that?" Molly was calm and fixed her eyes on his.

"Molly!" snapped Shaun under his breath.

"It's alright, Shaun," said William kindly. "Molly, never mind about that, just answer my question please,"

"No, I won't be never-minding about that," said Molly in the same calm tone. "It seems awfully interesting to me that I was completely alone when this happened, yet everyone seems to know so much about it."

"Molly," said Shaun, putting his hand on the table, "of course they know! Please don't embarrass me."

"Embarrass you?!?" Molly couldn't believe her father.

"Sorry about this, William," said Shaun.

"No, no! Don't give it another thought, Shaun," said William. "She's never been to an official Reminiscence, and she's upset, I can see that. I know I would be if I had lost all my gold."

"I didn't *lose* it!" Molly fumed. "It was *stolen!* Why isn't anyone interested in finding out who did it?"

"Molly, listen to me," Shaun said quietly but firmly, "lost or stolen, it's the same thing. It's shame on our house, do you understand?"

"No!" said Molly. "I don't understand. I understand it's not fair, is all I understand. Da', why aren't we trying to get it back, instead of standing around drinking tea and eating bread and butter and—"

"I would just like to say," Dorker interjected, raising his hand, "I don't think Molly could have been in any way responsible."

The room went quiet as all heads turned to Dorker. Most hadn't even noticed him until now.

"And upon what do you base that belief?" said William in the confused silence.

Dorker seemed genuinely puzzled by the question. "I just know."

Shaun shook his head, covering his eyes.

"Drop it, Dorker," said Molly out of the corner of her mouth.

"Thank you, Dorker," said William, "but if you don't have any actual evidence to offer . . ."

"Evidence?" said Dorker. "My evidence is I know Molly."

"No, you don't!" Molly exclaimed.

"I know enough!"

"Well, Shaun . . ." William scratched the back of his head. "I'm afraid there's little choice we have. I think you know what needs to happen."

Shaun nodded. "I do."

Everyone sat in silence for several uncomfortable minutes, reluctant to take the next step.

"Look," said Shaun, "let's just do it, alright?"

"Wait, I'd just like to say—" Dorker began.

"Very well," said William, ignoring Dorker and opening a dusty book with a creak. Delicately turning the old, yellowed pages, his tone became formal as he read. "(Ahem) Shaun. Molly. Your gold has been lost in violation of your most sacred duties. The shame on your house is perpetual and cannot be undone."

"What's going on?" said Molly.

"The village must know its secrets can be kept." William read.

"Da', what is he saying?"

Shaun kept his eyes on William, trying to maintain his dignity.

"You are no longer worthy of our trust."

"Da', answer me!" cried Molly.

"By the power vested in me . . ." William continued.

"Wait, what are you doing? Are you throwing us out?" Molly demanded.

". . . as head of the High Council . . ."

"No!" Molly ran to each of the Council members who had all become suddenly quiet in deference to the solemnity of the moment.

". . . I hereby declare . . ."

"Da', do something!"

". . . that you both be banished from our village effective immediately. Do you accept this sentence?"

"I do," said Shaun.

"I DON'T!" cried Molly.

William scanned the rest of the page. "Well, I think that's really all there is to it," he said. "Any other business?"

The Council members stayed silent. No one wanted to move. Finally, Liam got up and shook Shaun's hand.

"Thank you, Shaun," he said. "That was wonderful."

"Yes," said Shaun. "I'll remember it fondly."

"Thanks for the food, Shaun," said Timothy, clapping him on the back and giving him a hug. "Great meal."

"Indeed, it was. Thank you. Thank you all. Well, no use putting it off," said Shaun. He looked at the assembled villagers, and a tear came to his eye. "Don't know what to say, really. Take care of yourselves. Give our love to your families."

Tears streamed down the Council's eyes, as they gave their good wishes.

"Cheers, Shaun."

"You take good care, now."

"Alright, Shaun," muttered William, "if we could just get you both to stand up, please."

Shaun gestured to Molly. They stood side by side as the Council members got up and joined hands around them.

"Wait, what's happening?" said Dorker.

"Stand back please, Dorker," said William. "You don't want to be in the circle when the spell is cast."

"Be well," said Timothy through a choked sob.

The Council reluctantly joined hands, raised them above their heads, brought them down forcefully, and shouted:

"BANISHED!"

There was no blinding light. No crack of thunder. Nothing at all to suggest that powerful magic had just been performed. All Molly knew was that one minute, they had been standing in a large room in the village where she had lived her entire life. The next minute, she and her father stood alone in the forest.

Alone, that is, except for Dorker.

CHAPTER 7

A New Life

"Dorker! What are you doing here?!?" said Shaun.

Molly looked around wildly. "What happened? Where's—"

"Dorker—" said Shaun.

"THAT was AMAZING!" said Dorker, patting his body to see if it was all still in one piece.

"But where's—"

"LOOK OUT!"

A rust-colored blur with fangs shot past them as Shaun tackled Molly and Dorker to the ground. Quickly and quietly, Shaun hustled them into a hollow log before the blur saw where they went.

"WHAT IS GOING O—?!?"

Shaun clapped his hand over Molly's mouth. He edged closer to the log's opening and heard soft feet padding carefully just outside the log. He sniffed the air. Then he turned, put his finger to his lips, and mouthed silently:

"Fox."

Finnegan's Wake was untroubled by forest predators due to its various magical protections. Having grown up in relative safety, Molly had not yet fully registered their danger.

"Did they magic us away?" she whispered.

"Technically, they magicked *themselves* away, isn't that right, Mr. McClanahan?" said Dorker quietly.

"*Quiet!!*" Shaun hissed.

The fox was getting closer.

* * * *

Poor Reynard (for so the fox called himself) perked up his ears. The food—he was pretty sure it was food—could not have gone far.

What the food was, exactly, he didn't know. One minute he had been making his usual rounds, hoping to find a rabbit or an unsuspecting squirrel, the next minute, three creatures appeared from out of nowhere two meters in front of him. He had pounced without thinking. "Pounce first, think later" was a motto that had served Poor Reynard well in his short life. Placed as he was in the middle of the food chain, lightning reflexes were critical. A fox who hesitated might find himself going hungry for the night, or worse, in someone else's stomach. Besides, who was he to question food deposited so helpfully at his feet?

But he was surprised at how quiet and fast the food had been—certainly faster than your average critter. So fast, in fact, that he had no idea where it had gone.

That was okay. Poor Reynard liked a challenge.

* * * *

"Magicked themselves away? What does that *mean?*" whispered Molly desperately.

"It means," said Dorker, "that we are in the same forest we've always been in, at the exact same spot, but the village is now forever hidden to us! That's really advanced magic!!"

"The village is hidden from us?"

"Shh! This way!" Shaun quietly urged them out the back end of the log, while the fox sniffed at a bush several feet away. They scrambled up the side of a willow tree with the agility of squirrels and stopped on a branch about halfway up so that Shaun could better observe the fox's movements.

"Molly," said Dorker, "ask yourself—why has no human has ever found our village?"

"Well . . . it's protected by magic?" said Molly.

"Dorker—" said Shaun.

"Right!" said Dorker. "And as long as we belong to the village, the magic does not affect us. We're part of the spell, so to speak."

"Part of the spell?" said Molly.

"Please be quiet!" said Shaun.

"This is all in your Dad's book, by the way."[F]

* * * *

Food is quick and hard to kill,
But Poor Reynard can smell you still!

. . . thought Poor Reynard, who, as all foxes do, thought in rhyming couplets.

Snout to the ground, the fox searched for the whiff of a scent he had only barely sniffed. Given the kaleidoscope of smells swirling around the woods, it was a little like trying to identify one sock in a crowded locker room. But he would know if he found it. It was unlike anything he had ever nosed before. He stopped, fluffed his tail quickly and, satisfied with its sheen, put his nose to the ground again, tail raised like a flag. Style was important to Poor Reynard. A kill performed in an ugly way was hardly worth eating.

His ears flattened. The food was close; he could feel it in his fur. Placing one paw carefully in front of another, he skulked beneath the bracken, nostrils flared. Slowly, almost imperceptibly, a hint of a remnant of a scent distinguished itself from the metaphorical cacophony of background aromas—human-ish, yet not.

The fox let the smell take shape in his mind, homing in on its source and direction. He closed his eyes, and turned once or twice on the spot, letting his nose guide him. He looked up.

There!

* * * *

"Come on," said Shaun quietly. "We've got to move."

Dancing along the interlacing tree branches like tight-rope walkers, they leapt from tree to tree. Leprechauns generally can't climb to the tops of trees like squirrels because they weigh too much, but they can scamper through a tree-filled canopy in a similar fashion. Even so, navigating tree branches is not

---

[F] *Elements of Magic*, by Shaun McClanahan.

easy in the dark of night. More than once, they hit dead ends where the distance between trees was too great, and they had to double back.

As they ran, Dorker explained to Molly how the banishment spell worked. Long, long ago when the village was founded, all the villagers were united by the same need and desire—to protect themselves from humans. When true need and powerful desire are one and the same, that makes the most powerful spells. Further, all magic contains an element of the one casting it. What makes a village's concealment spell unique is that it is cast by *everyone*, so each villager is woven into it, just a little bit. This "weave" gets passed along in the DNA (or the leprechaun equivalent) from generation to generation.

"So, what the Council just did," Dorker said, slightly out of breath from running, "was to basically unravel us from the weave!"

"So there's no way to find the village again?"

"Right! Isn't that AMAZING??"

"DORKER!!" Shaun hissed, almost losing his footing on a knotty branch. "WHAT are you doing here?"

"Oh, sorry Mr. McClanahan. I jumped into the circle at the last moment. I didn't want Molly to be alone."

"Dorker!"

"Yes, Mr. McClanahan?"

"*I'M* here! Her *father!* She wasn't going to be *alone!*"

"Yes, I see that now, Mr. McClanahan. I'm sorry, I completely forgot about you."

"I WAS STANDING RIGHT IN FRONT OF YOU!"

"It's hard to explain, but I didn't see you, Mr. McClanahan. I was kind of focused on Molly."

Shaun was not the most sensitive reader of emotions, but the love-sick look on Dorker's face was hard to miss, even in pale moonlight. This was a complication Shaun really really really didn't want. But right now, the fox was still following them, moving slowly and unmistakably in their direction.

"We've got to get to the river," he said. "Come on."

* * * *

Food can hop from branch to tree,
But Poor Reynard can patient be.

. . . thought Poor Reynard.

The fox had never seen a leprechaun before, but the glimpses he caught of them darting through the forest canopy persuaded him they would be delicious. New food was always thrilling. These creatures looked like humans (whom he hated), but were small enough to eat (which delighted him). The tallest one looked like he might be a bit stringy, but that was fine. Three distinct tastes were promised: one brittle, one bony, one fresh. A range of flavors. His mouth watered.

* * * *

Dancing over branch and twig, Shaun, Molly, and Dorker advanced towards the river. They made rapid progress, but they couldn't shake the fox.

When they arrived near the river's edge, another problem: how to get across?

"Listen to me, we don't have much time," said Shaun quickly. "Dorker, Molly—I need you to search the area and as quickly as you can, bring me every stick you can find that's at least as big as Dorker and lay them down, side by side at the water's edge."

"Yessir, Mr. McClanahan."

"Da', why?"

"Just do it please! That fox will be here soon!"

They scrambled down the tree and as Molly and Dorker scoured the area for dry sticks, Shaun waded into the water. With a small pocketknife, he began cutting and ripping off green strips from the reeds. When he thought he had enough, he used them to tie the sticks that Molly and Dorker had found.

"It doesn't have to be pretty, it just has to hold us . . ." Shaun muttered.

"Da' . . ."

"Not now, Molly!"

"DA'!"

"WHAT IS IT?!?"

"Fox."

Lurking in the high grass about fifty feet away, a pair of hungry yellow eyes stared at them.

"Grab the other end," Shaun whispered, seizing the makeshift raft he had built, "and push it into the water."

"But you haven't finished tying—"

"NOW!" Shaun yelled.

The fox charged.

Grabbing the loosely assembled branches, they struggled into the water as the fox sped towards them. Pushing so much wood through the mud wasn't easy, but eventually, the water was deep enough that they began to float.

"KICK!" yelled Shaun.

The fox leapt. Molly gripped the branches for dear life and kicked the water as hard as she could. Yellow-fanged jaws snapped so close to Molly, she could smell the fox's sour breath. But a face full of water was all Poor Reynard got for his effort. Shaun, Molly, and Dorker drifted out into the river's current.

Relieved as they were not to be inside the fox, they now faced a new problem. The river was wider and the current stronger than they had realized. If Shaun had had more time, he certainly would have built a raft that was both elegant and seaworthy. As it was . . .

"Da'!"

"I know!"

"The branches aren't—"

"I know!"

Only about halfway across the river, the binding that held their raft together loosed and fell apart, sending branches floating off in different directions. Shaun, who had managed to hold onto one of the largest branches, reached desperately for Molly and Dorker.

"Grab my hand!" Shaun yelled. Molly and Dorker grasped for Shaun, but only Molly reached him. Dorker sank completely beneath the white caps for a long moment before surfacing again, sputtering water.

"Swim Dorker!!" Molly yelled.

"Okay!" Dorker coughed.

Clinging to their branch, Molly and Shaun struggled to the opposite side. Breathlessly, they turned and scanned the river for any sign of Dorker. There, on a small rock about one hundred feet away in the middle of the current, they spotted him.

"Dorker!" yelled Shaun. "Are you okay?"

"Probably not!" yelled Dorker.

The stone was not big, and some of the larger fish in the river had begun circling it, as had a small insomniac hawk overhead. All were curious about how Dorker might taste, and it was only a matter of time before one of them found out.

"Dorker!" yelled Shaun. "Have you read the story of Kilvan O'Loggergraun?"

"Yes?" yelled Dorker nervously.

"It's all true!" yelled Shaun.

Dorker straightened and looked at Shaun with a mixture of inspiration, awe, and disbelief. Then he looked at the churning, fish-filled water surrounding him. He reached into his pocket, pulled out the bread he had stashed during the Council meeting and without a second thought, began running. Molly screamed, expecting him to disappear down the gullet of a largemouth bass, but to her incalculable surprise, Dorker ran on water! As he went, he quickly ripped pieces off the loaf of bread and threw them into the water directly in front of him, one after another.

The hawk that had been circling above—agitated to the point of madness by the sight of Dorker, the swarm of fish, and now breadcrumbs near the surface of the water—could stand it no longer and fell into a dive, talons flashing.

"DORKER!!" Molly yelled. "JUMP!!"

Dorker didn't even see the hawk screaming down from the sky behind him. Propelled by adrenaline and some primal sense of self-preservation, Dorker hurled himself towards Shaun and Molly, who splashed into the water, caught his arms, and yanked with all their strength. The hawk splashed into the school of fish, missing Dorker by inches. As it flew away, wet but happily holding a large perch in its talons, Molly, Shaun, and Dorker lay panting for breath.

"Thanks!" Dorker gasped.

* * * *

Poor Reynard was now as wet as he was hungry. He retreated from the water to shake himself off and groom while he watched the lore gatherers try to cross the river. Dorker running on water got his attention. As far as Reynard knew, only certain birds and insects could do that. He was also impressed (and, for selfish reasons, relieved) that Dorker dodged the hawk. Clearly, there was more to this food than met the eye. It would almost be a shame to eat them.

Almost.

Finally, he watched them retreat past the tree line on the other side of the river.

Satisfied that his coat was dry, beautiful, and possessed of just the right *je ne sais quoi*, he considered his options.

Food is tired and water-tossed;
Reynard knows bridge that can be crossed . . .

. . . thought Poor Reynard.

* * * *

Dripping and exhausted, Shaun, Molly, and Dorker moved away from the river gratefully. They paused to catch their breath.

"Dorker," said Molly, "how did you do that?!?"

"The story of Kilvan O'Loggergraun," panted Dorker.

"Who's that?"

"Leprechaun who could train fish," said Dorker. "They say that when he whistled, fish would jump out of the water and right into his net. Legend has it that once when he was being chased by humans, he escaped across a lake by throwing breadcrumbs into the water, and the fish lined up like a bridge in front of him. This is all in your dad's book, by the way.[†] I didn't think that story could possibly be *true*."

"Neither did I," said Shaun.

"It's one the most unbelievable—Wait, what?!?" said Dorker.

"It's interesting," said Shaun, "they didn't line up like a bridge, but at least we proved the fundamental premise is possible."

"But you said—"

"They lined up more like movable stepping-stones, really," said Shaun. "But if your timing hadn't been perfect—"

"No, wait, go back—" said Dorker.

"Dorker, I said what I had to say to get you across the river before you got eaten," said Shaun. "It was all I could think of. I'm sorry. I'm *really* glad it worked."

[†] *Leprechaun Apocrypha*, Vol. 7, by Shaun McClanahan.

"I don't feel well," said Dorker.

Shaun patted him on the shoulder and then noticed Molly was sitting on a log a little way away with her back to them. He went over to her.

"Dorker will be fine, Molly, I just—"

"What are we going to do, Da'? Where are we going to live?"

Shaun took a deep breath and took in the area. "Not here, that's for sure. But right now, I'm tired. Let's set up camp. You didn't eat much at the meeting. We'll get you some food and then we'll get a couple hours of sleep. Wherever we're going, we can go when the sun is up. Why don't you go gather some wood for a fire. I'll scrounge some kind of meal together and set up a few traps and alarms in case there are any other creatures out there looking for a late-night snack."

"I'll help Molly," said Dorker.

"NO!" said Shaun a little louder than he intended. Dorker was a fine, honest lad, but some basic, animal instinct deep in Shaun's paternal hindbrain was now yelling at him to erect a large "FORBIDDEN" sign between Dorker and Molly.

"No, no, Dorker, why don't you . . . ah . . . you know how to pitch a tent?"

"Oh yes, Mr. McClanahan. My Dad and I have gone camping lots of times."

"Good," said Shaun tossing him one of the backpacks. "There's a tent in there somewhere. Pitch it."

"Yessir, Mr. McClanahan," said Dorker, who was just happy to be included. "My pleasure!"

As Shaun set off in search of food, Molly stood and watched Dorker struggle with the various poles and ropes of the tent. He didn't seem to have any idea what he was doing, and his efforts looked like a circus act gone wrong. It just made her feel more helpless and angry.

Not knowing what else to do, she started gathering firewood. When Shaun returned, she had a sizable stack of branches and kindling.

"I found a squirrel," said Shaun, "some herbs and roots, some good honeysuckle, and a few crickets, [F] so we should be able to make a reasonable

---

[F] The cricket's song is a key element in many lore gatherer dishes. As explained in Shaun's *101 Movable World Recipes: Food for the Leprechaun on the Go*, taste varies according to the frequency of the cricket's chirp, which, in turn depends on the temperature at which the cricket is captured. For best results, capture at 15° C, or 59° F.

stew."

Dorker raised his hand.

"Um . . . Mr. McClanahan?"

"Dorker, it looks like we're going to be together for a while. You might as well call me Shaun."

"Thanks Mr. McClanahan! I mean Shaun. Ha ha! Feels funny saying that. I've been calling you Mr. McClanahan for so long, you don't *seem* like a Shaun. You know what I mean? I mean, *obviously*, you *have* a first name, but *I've* never used it, and when you grow up around an adult, it's kind of hard to see them as an actual, you know, person who blows his nose and stuff."

"Dorker," said Shaun.

"Yes, Shaun?"

"You had something to tell me?"

"AH! Yes! Right. Sorry. It's about the tent. I'm close, but I *think* I may have gone wrong somewhere . . ."

Shaun looked at what Dorker had assembled. It was monstrous. In fairness, he had managed to erect a structure of some sort. Exactly *what* sort, Shaun couldn't say. The middle had gotten twisted and bunched beyond recognition, and poles protruded at all sorts of unexpected and threatening angles. Even if he had wanted to go inside (which he didn't), Shaun couldn't tell where the entrance was supposed to be. An abomination to the joys of camping, it sat there like a grotesque and hideous spider.

"Um . . ." said Shaun, "I just . . . just leave it for now, Dorker. Do you know how to start a fire?"

"Oh yes, Shaun! I learned *that* along with my camping skills."

"Molly, start the fire, please," Shaun said quickly. "Dorker, you can . . . watch."

"Yessir, Shaun!" said Dorker.

A few uncomfortable minutes of silence passed. But Dorker could only stand silence for so long.

"I remember the first time my Da' and I made a fire," he said. "It had rained all day when we got to our camping spot, so all the kindling and everything around was still wet, so he was having trouble getting the fire lit, y'see. So he pulled out some fuel to put on the kindling. *Well*, he stepped away to get the flint, and *I* decided to see what would happen if I used the lenses of my glasses, because I had been reading about optics and lenses and stuff, and I had read that you could probably focus the rays of the sun with the lens of your glasses to start a fire. Anyway, the whole campfire blew up in my face! Took my eyebrows right off! It was pretty funny. After, you know, all the screaming."

"Dorker?" asked Shaun delicately.

"Yes, Shaun?"

"I wonder if you would mind not talking for a bit."

"Righto, Shaun. If you want me to stop talking, then stop talking, I shall. My Da' always says—"

"Starting now?" said Shaun.

"Righto!" said Dorker.

"Molly, how's the fire coming?" said Shaun.

"She's just about got it going, Shaun. She's amazing. You wouldn't—"

"Dorker!"

"Right. Sorry, Shaun."

In the awkward silence, Shaun began heating some water with herbs and roots thrown in. Bit by bit, he added the squirrel meat, some wild potatoes he had found, a number of other ingredients Molly couldn't quite identify, and finally, the cricket song. Even with these meager ingredients, the smell was inviting. It wafted around them and calmed everyone's nerves. As Shaun stirred the pot, Molly realized how late it was and how tired she had become. When the stew was ready, her dad spooned out a small bowl for each of them, and they slurped together in silence. It was all Molly could do to keep her eyes open. When they had finished, Shaun collected their bowls and spoons.

"Let's get to bed now, chick. We have a big day tomorrow."

Molly got up, and Shaun got up with her. Dorker also got up, and just like that, the question of sleeping arrangements insisted itself in a heart-thumping way.

"Shaun?" said Dorker, looking at the tent.

"Yes, Dorker?"

"I don't think we can all fit in the tent, Shaun."

Shaun looked at the sprawling nightmare of a tent Dorker had constructed. Even if reassembled correctly, it was only a two-leprechaun tent, at best. Shaun desperately considered his options. On the one hand, it seemed wrong to leave

Dorker all alone by himself outside the tent (though a guilty part of him wanted very much to do just that). On the other hand, he certainly wasn't going to leave Molly alone outside while he shared the tent with Dorker.

That was when Dorker made his first really big mistake.

"Maybe . . . Maybe Molly and I could sleep in the tent, and you could enjoy a relaxing night under the stars, Shaun."

Speaking of stars, our own star, the sun, has a core temperature of around 27 million degrees Fahrenheit (15 million degrees Celsius). Though burning in a cold void, it is nonetheless so hot it warms the earth, a celestial body so far away that even light takes six minutes to travel the distance. There are stars in our galaxy that dwarf our sun and burn with an almost incomprehensible fury. The kind of fire that makes the word "inferno" throw its hands up in the air, pack its bags, and go home.

The silence that followed Dorker's suggestion could have frozen all those stars put together.

"Dorker?" Shaun mused.

"Yes, Shaun?"

"I'm going to pretend you didn't say that."

"Thank you, Shaun."

"And Dorker?"

"Yes, Shaun?"

"Call me Mr. McClanahan."

"Yes, Mr. McClanahan."

In the end, they decided it would be best for all concerned to just sleep outside. It wasn't raining, but the night was chilly. Molly put on her ceremonial robes and immediately felt warm and comfortable. Alice had designed the robe to regulate her body to an ideal temperature, no matter the weather. An ideal camping garment, it made her feel as if she lay on a smooth, comfortable mattress, even on rocky or rough terrain. To Molly, sleeping in it was the closest she ever felt to sleeping in her mother's arms.

Shaun put some more logs on the fire, and they lay for a while, lost in their own thoughts.

"Da'?"

"Yes, Molly?"

"What's going to happen, Da'?"

"Well, if the fox returns, the alarms I set will give us plenty of time—"

"No, I mean, what's going to happen to us?"

The question hung in the air just a little too long. Shaun wished he had a better answer. "Don't worry, chick. We'll be okay."

"Mr. McClanahan?"

Shaun sighed. "Yes, Dorker?"

"Um . . . Do you remember how I said earlier that my Da' knew where I was?"

"Yes, Dorker."

"Well, um, the fact is . . . when I said he *knew* where I was, what I *meant* was . . . that is, it would probably be more accurate to say that . . . in fact . . . he *didn't* know. Where I was, I mean. He sure wouldn't know where I am now . . ."

Shaun took a deep breath. Poor old Dorlish would be frantic when the Council told him what had happened. But at this point, there was nothing to be done.

"Alice?" he whispered to himself desperately. "Are you there? I need you."

But Alice didn't answer. Shaun lay in the silence for a moment, then without thinking, sang them a song. It rose from his belly unbidden. The song was old—one that had passed down through so many generations it was almost a different language. Though Molly and Dorker didn't immediately understand the words, they felt the meaning, and a deep longing welled up inside them. In those strange, exotic words, the woods seemed to disappear and the only thing in the world that was real and solid and true was the song. And though it was almost inexpressibly sad, it soothed them and brought them peace. Was it magic? Or was it just music? As she drifted off to sleep, Molly wondered—was there a difference?

* * * *

The next morning, the early birds not only got the worm, but made so much noise doing it, they woke Molly from a sound, dreamless sleep. She blinked, rubbed the sleep from her eyes, and saw the sun was already up. It was a beautiful morning. The air was fresh and crisp, and the fog that rested gently on the forest floor was slowly folding back on itself, glowing yellow. Molly could not remember ever waking and feeling such complete . . . idleness. Whatever might have been on Shaun's many lists for today could all be crossed off. She and her father had nowhere to be, nothing to do.

Just survive.

Shaun and Dorker were still snoring peacefully, so Molly decided to make breakfast. Her father had taught her how to forage, and the immediate area yielded ripe berries, herbs, nuts, mossy tree bark, and even some grains. She cleaned out their pot in a nearby spring, got some water for a soup, and started cooking. Within minutes, the aroma roused Shaun.

"You've been busy," he said rubbing his eyes. Molly shrugged and handed him a bowl. They ate in silence as Dorker lay beside them, fast asleep.

Finally, Molly said, "You slept so late."

"Under the circumstances, I thought we should all get as much sleep as—"

"What are we going to do, Da'?" said Molly.

Shaun put his spoon down and looked at her. Molly just stared at her food. Not knowing what to say, Shaun sighed and finished the last few mouthfuls of his breakfast. Then he stood and looked around the campsite awkwardly.

"We had better clean up," he said. "Save a bowl for Dorker when he wakes up. You um . . . you clean the bowls, and I'll try to do something about that tent Dorker mangled."

"What about Dorker?" she said.

"Let him sleep."

"Da'—"

"Off you go now," said Shaun, waving his hand.

"Fine," she said coldly.

Molly roughly gathered the wooden dishes, then stamped back to the spring to clean them. She was mad. She didn't like being dismissed like that.

Why can't he comfort me? she thought bitterly. *A kind word, a hug—or just answer my question, for Shillelagh's sake! Can't you do that, Da'? Can't you answer your child's question? Like a PARENT??? I lost The Thieving, the gold, got you (and Dorker!) banished, and now a wild animal is hunting us. Maybe some COMFORT would be okay!!*

As she sat by herself scrubbing the dishes, even the birds sounded strange. Almost alien. Molly had never been to this part of the forest before. Normally, she liked exploring new areas. The forest had always been home. But not anymore. It didn't feel threatening (which would have been bad enough).

Instead, it felt . . . indifferent. It didn't care if she lived or died.

Sort of like Da', she thought bitterly. *Feels like that sometimes, like he doesn't care. Maybe he's right. Maybe I don't deserve any comfort. Certainly not any special attention. I just keep messing up. Maybe I am just a burden. Just another problem on his list. Another thing to worry about. Maybe that's all you are, Molly. Maybe you're nothing. Maybe you're worse than . . .*

No! URRRGH! Ma' always . . . I FEEL like Ma' always made me feel special. It didn't matter what I did! Even when I messed up, I felt . . . I KNEW she loved me. Him, I don't . . . He CARES for me . . . or about me . . . or . . . I don't know. I'm no different than a crack in the wall. A problem to be dealt with.

Why can't he be like other Dads? Why can't he be like Dorker's Da'? Dorker's Da' LOVES him! You can tell just walking into the bakery. The way he looks at him, even when he's spilled flour all over everything. And just look at Dorker! He's so HAPPY all the time. Must be nice. Must be nice to be happy once in a while. To have a Da' who's happy.

I want to be happy for once. The other night after The Thieving—preparing me to go check the gold—it was so good! He . . . he . . . TALKED to me. He LAUGHED. He never does that! Why doesn't he ever DO that?!?

I mean, I know why . . . I think I do . . . But . . . But we were like . . . like . . . like a real TEAM—a FAMILY, even. Maybe for the first time since . . .

. . . It was all a lie, she thought, shaking the excess water off the dishes. *He didn't mean any of it. He just wants to go on like before, treating me like nothing.*

Molly's jaw set. She was done feeling sorry for herself. Her father's way didn't work, she decided. Their world had changed. Shaun must change too.

* * * *

Poor Reynard can slip a trap,
And soon his jaws will snicker-snap!

. . . thought Poor Reynard.

We should back up a bit.

Poor Reynard had to travel half a mile or so out of his way to find a human bridge leading to the other side of the river. He disliked traveling on man-made roads and structures, but the nearest natural crossing was miles away, and time was precious.

Once across, he scrambled down to the river's edge, closed his eyes, and let his nose take over. Human scientists have long known that smell is a powerful trigger for memory, but they don't know the half of it. In the fox's nose, past and present were almost one and the same. Downstream of their last encounter, the lore gatherers' scent lingered and floated along the watery currents. If he concentrated, Poor Reynard could smell the past in the subtle aromas dancing on the water's surface, forming an olfactory vision of Dorker's narrow escape from the hawk. Most importantly, he could tell the food had not doubled back.

Taking off upstream, Poor Reynard ran along the riverbank, nose twitching, seeking the lore gatherers' unmistakable scent on every passing breeze. On another night, he might have noticed the moonlight glistening like diamonds on the river, or the crisp chill of the breeze, or the crickets' musical quintet. On another night, he might have paused to capture this fragile beauty in a perfectly-phrased haiku that would be as beautiful as it was fleeting (foxes don't publish or remember their greatest works). But not tonight—tonight, Poor Reynard was hungry, and poetry would have to wait on his stomach.

By morning, after many hours of starting and stopping, success! The smell of lore gatherer grew pungent in his nose.

As it did, his exquisitely coiffed fur bristled. Honed and refined by generations of evolution and personal experience, his keen senses detected—traps! Any fox worth his tail has an extensive knowledge of human-made traps, and any fox that doesn't, doesn't stay a fox for long. These were different, however, which excited Poor Reynard. Human traps had horrible wires, ferocious jaws, or other vicious metal pieces that bit, chewed, and mangled. He sensed none of that here. He had no word to describe it, but a concept formed in his belly that felt less like "trap" and more like "alarm."

Every new thing he learned about this food exhilarated him. He had never hunted anything quite this interesting. The traps would take some figuring out, but the trap had not been invented that Poor Reynard could not slip through.

****

When Molly returned to the camp site, the only evidence that anyone had been there was Dorker, who lay snoring like an asthmatic wildebeest. Shaun sat ripping the bark off a small branch to fashion himself a walking stick. Molly marched up to him.

"Okay. Now what?" she asked simply.

Shaun looked at her. He got up, put on his backpack, and said, "Come on, let's wake up Dorker."

"Where are we going?"

"Just wake up Dorker, please."

"No," said Molly. Shaun turned to her.

"No?"

"No." Molly stood looking at her father meaningfully.

"What do you mean, 'No'?"

"I mean, you need to tell me where we're going, Da'."

"Do I?"

"Yes. It's time you start telling me things."

Shaun looked into her eyes. "I told you how to find the gold. And how did that turn out?"

If he had said just about anything else, they might have talked calmly and rationally. That's what Molly had wanted to do. She very specifically didn't want to lose her temper. When demanding to be treated like an adult, she reasoned, you have to act like one. But all the blood rushed to her face, tears geysered forth, and with them, a shaking hot fury she could not contain.

"NOW YOU LISTEN TO ME!" she erupted. "I DID *EVERYTHING* YOU TOLD ME! I DIDN'T TELL *ANYONE* THE SPELLS! *NO ONE* FOLLOWED ME! I'D HAVE *KNOWN!* BUT IT DOESN'T MATTER WHAT I SAY, DOES IT?!? YOU DON'T CARE! I LOST THE GOLD AND THAT'S *ALL YOU CARE ABOUT!* 'MOLLY LOST THE GOLD!' NO MATTER WHAT I SAY! 'MOLLY LOST THE GOLD!' YOU DON'T CARE! YOU DON'T CARE THAT IT WAS *YOUR* IDEA! YOU DON'T CARE THAT SOMEONE ELSE TOOK IT! YOU DON'T CARE THAT WE JUST LOST OUR *HOME!* AND YOU SURE AS SHILLELAGH DON'T CARE ABOUT *M—*"

"HAWKFOX!!" Dorker yelled, waking suddenly. Disoriented, he looked around groggily and saw Molly and Shaun: "Oh. Hey, where'd the campsite go?"

Molly turned and looked at Dorker, breathless, her face soaked with tears and almost purple with rage. Dorker's smile evaporated.

"Wha'd I do?" he said.

Shaun looked from Dorker to Molly and sighed.

She's right, he thought. *She would have been better off with her mother. Everything I touch gets ruined. What is wrong with me? I'm so stupid. Why did I give her the spells? I shouldn't have told her how to find the gold. Of course she lost it. What is wrong with me? I should have seen it coming. I failed her. And it's my fault. It's all my fault. It's your fault, Shaun. You weren't vigilant. You know you weren't. You're so stupid. You know what happens. This is what happens. What is wrong with me . . . ?*

"Dorker," he said quietly.

"Yes, Shau—I mean, Mr. McClanahan?"

"Eat some food, please," he said, gesturing to the bowl they had left for him.

"Oh, that's okay, Mr. McClanahan. I'm not that hungry. I can—"

"Molly made it."

"—but if it's already made . . ." said Dorker, leaping to his feet and grabbing the bowl hungrily.

"You'll have to walk and eat," said Shaun, picking up his backpack. He turned and started walking.

"DAAAAAAAAAAA'!" Molly shrieked.

"We're going to ancient Rome, Molly," he said simply.

"Ancient . . . ? Wait, what—?"

"But we have to get to Italy first. C'mon, take my hands, both of you, and . . . I promise, I'll explain."

* * * *

From the outside, what happened next would have looked like a staged magic trick. Three lore gatherers joined hands, took a step together, and vanished.

But if you had, for example, been lurking in the bushes hoping for a breakfast of raw lore gatherer and then pounced at Molly, Shaun, and Dorker at *exactly* the right moment, the world would have blurred for an uncomfortably long minute, your head would have felt as if it were being stretched like taffy and twisted across several hundred miles, sounds would have warped and distorted, and when everything snapped back into shape, the world would have gone silent and still.

That is what happened to Poor Reynard.

CHAPTER 8

Cross Countries

Leprechauns are capable of moving at great speeds. This is only part of why it's so hard to catch one. You could call them nimble, but that wouldn't speak to the subtle and remarkable magic at work within their autonomic nervous systems.

Think of it like this: when you run, your body makes all sorts of unconscious adjustments to help your body to go faster: your lungs work harder to suck in more oxygen, your heart beats faster to circulate oxygenated blood to your muscles, and so on. You don't have to think about it; it just happens. It's so remarkable, in fact, that it could look a lot like magic, if you didn't know any better.

Something like that happens when leprechauns want to travel long distances quickly. Some chemical in their hindbrain stimulates their internal time and space glands, and they become like black holes that suck all surrounding time into themselves. This leaves very little time for anything or anyone else to use. From the traveling lore gatherer's point of view, the ultimate effect is that time around them stops almost completely, while they carry on at normal speed. Thus it was that Molly, Shaun, and Dorker walked from Ireland to present-day Italy in about five minutes, all at a leisurely pace.

They did not, however, see Poor Reynard pounce at the exact moment time slowed down around them. To this day, Shaun has not worked out the mechanics of how it happened, but somehow the fox got sucked into their time vortex and essentially drafted behind them all the way.

But we're getting ahead of ourselves.

When Poor Reynard shook off the feeling that his head had been snapped in and out of shape over and over like a rubber balloon, he almost collided with a robin that had just taken flight. Suspended only a few inches off the ground, wings mid-flap, the robin clearly had been trying to avoid Reynard as he came crashing through the bushes. But now, the robin didn't stand a chance. Reynard plucked it from the air like a candy cane on a Christmas tree.

If it helps, the robin never felt a thing.

As Poor Reynard supped on this unexpected-but-welcome pre-meal snack, he finally registered that only he and the new food were still moving. The rest of the world had stopped: wind, leaves, sound—everything. Deep in his foxy brain, a little voice hinted that since *he* certainly didn't do it, the new food might be responsible and, perhaps, he should weigh his dinner plans carefully. Traps were one thing, but food that could do something like *this* was food that might have other, more deadly, tricks up its sleeve.

* * * *

"What?!? What do you mean, *ancient Rome?*" Molly demanded, as they trooped through the unmoving and silent Irish landscape.

"You asked where we need to go, so I told you," said Shaun. "But Italy first. Then time travel."

Her father might as well have said they were going to Saturn. Had he finally lost it? Assuming they could even get there, what on earth did he think they were going to do in ancient Rome—go sight-seeing? Take in a play? Have tea with Julius Caesar?

"Da', are you feeling alright?"

"I've been better . . ." he said calmly.

"Ancient Rome, eh?" said Dorker through a mouthful of food. "That sounds fun. D'you know, I've always dreamed about going there. They have great ruins. Of course, if we're going to be in ancient Rome, they won't be ruins because it won't be ancient, will it? Some of them might not even be built! It'll be Not-Ancient Ancient Rome. Or maybe Current Ancient Rome? Ancient (But Not Really) Rome? Not-Yet Ancient Rome? Or maybe just Rome."

"Dorker!" Molly yelled.

"Shutting up!" he said, cheerfully turning back to his breakfast.

"*Why* do we need to go to ancient Rome?"

"Because I'm desperate, Molly," Shaun said matter-of-factly. "The one thing—the *only* thing—we've got to hold on to is that gold coin you found in the pot. I don't know what it means, but we're going to follow that gold coin."

"And the gold coin leads us to *ancient Rome?!?*"

"Look at it, Molly."

"I saw it."

"But did you really *look* at it?"

"Well, I didn't *memorize* it, but—"

"Look at it," said Shaun, flipping it to her. "What do you see?"

Molly turned it over in her hands skeptically.

"I see the profile of a man who looks like he has a veil over his head and who also has an *enormous* nose."

"It's Julius Caesar!" exclaimed Dorker over Molly's shoulder. Molly frowned.

"How do you—?"

"Right there," said Dorker, pointing to the coin. "It says 'CAESAR.'"

"Right," said Shaun. "Julius Caesar! So now you understand."

"Um, *no*."

"Oooh! Let me try!" said Dorker. He scrunched up his eyes in deep contemplation. "You think that Julius Caesar rose from the dead to steal your gold?"

"No, Dorker," said Shaun.

"Thaaat . . . Julius Caesar built a time machine?"

"*No,* Dorker," said Shaun.

"Thaaat . . . the coin is a message somehow?"

"Dorker, will you please—!" Molly snapped.

"Yes, actually," said Shaun with surprise. "That's exactly what I think. Well done, Dorker."

Molly looked at Dorker, who was beaming.

"A message?" said Molly. "From who?"

"I don't know," said Shaun.

"It'll probably be from whoever stole the gold," said Dorker.

"Yes. Thank you, Dorker," said Molly, pinching the bridge of her nose. "How do you know it's a message, Da'?"

"Because," said Shaun, "I didn't have any Roman coins in my pot."

Her father would know that. He probably knew the details of every single coin in his treasure chest down to the nicks and scratches. He might even be reviewing them in his head right now to pass the time. If he said he had no Roman coins, then he had no Roman coins.

And that did seem significant.

"Who do you *think* it is?"

"I don't know," said Shaun, pocketing the coin. "But that's why we're going back to ancient Rome."

They walked together in silence for some time as Molly processed this new information.

"Okay, ancient Rome," she finally said. "How are we going to get *there?*"

"Shakespeare," said Shaun.

* * * *

Poor Reynard delays the slaughter,
For Reynard can walk on water!

. . . thought Poor Reynard.

The fox followed them at a distance, trying to stay out of sight. Concealing himself had been easy enough as they moved through the Irish countryside, but now that they were out on the open English Channel, it was more challenging. Generally, his nose was good enough that he could keep a healthy distance and duck behind a small wave if they threatened to see him. As it was, they were too focused on their conversation to notice much else anyway, which was just as well. Poor Reynard was too overcome with wonder to be at maximum stealth. How, you ask, did he walk on water? Among the benefits of slowing down time is that atoms behave differently at super slow speeds. Large bodies of water, for instance, behave almost like a solid landscape. Reynard didn't sink because (a) the water molecules were moving too slowly to engulf him, and (b) he was moving so fast relative to the water that his feet could hardly be said to have touched it at all. Poor Reynard was elated. To a fox that hated—*hated*—water and had spent his life studiously avoiding it except when thirsty, the feeling was triumphant.

Every follicle of his exquisite fur told him he should turn back and steer clear of these strange and unexpectedly powerful creatures, but he was captivated. He could no more go back than a chicken can go back to its egg.

* * * *

"Shakespeare?!?" Molly sputtered. "What are you talking about? What does Shakespeare have to do with anything?!?"

"'But soft!'" said Dorker, gesturing to Molly. "'What light through yonder window breaks? It is the east, and Juliet is the sun! Arise, fair sun, and kill the envious moon, who is already sick and pale with grief that thou, her maid, art far more fair than she!'"

Molly and Shaun turned to Dorker.

"*Romeo and Juliet.* I thought we were talking about Shakespeare," said Dorker. "What?"

"You've read Shakespeare?" Shaun asked.

"Well . . . I read *Romeo and Juliet,*" said Dorker, looking at Molly meaningfully.

"*Anyway,*" coughed Shaun. "Yes, Shakespeare. Human writer. Wrote some plays about four hundred years ago, a bit of poetry. *Some* like it." Shaun glanced sideways at Dorker. "But what's really intriguing about Shakespeare—did you know that people who have never read a word he wrote quote him without even knowing they're doing it?"[⸸]

"Really?" said Molly.

"We think," said Shaun, "it's because Shakespeare's consciousness was particularly attuned to what we call fixed points in time."

"What???"

"Sorry," said Shaun. "Before we talk about Shakespeare, we need to talk about science fiction."

* * * *

O'er fields and hills and wooded green,
Reynard has ne'er such wonders seen.

. . . thought Poor Reynard.

[⸸] If you have ever "turned the tables" on someone, been "in a pickle," or "caught a cold," you've quoted Shakespeare. You've also quoted Shakespeare if you have ever said, "What, you egg!" but hey, they can't all be gems.

BOOK OF LEPRECHAUNS: THE LORE GATHERERS

In the distance, way out on the Atlantic, Reynard saw thunderstorms frozen in time. Hundred foot waves, with white frothy caps lurched in perfect stillness, as lightning bolts lit the darkening sky. Under his own feet (where the English Channel was thankfully less tumultuous), the silhouetted ghost of a mighty leviathan lurked eerily beneath the frozen currents. Poor Reynard was a stranger in a strange land.

Humility is not a natural state for a fox. But it is the first step towards wisdom. Wondering if anything he thought he knew was true, Reynard felt his head crack open and the universe stream in.

* * * *

"Humans have no idea what's going on," Shaun snorted. "In the universe, I mean. Just, y'know, to be clear. They have what they call 'science,' which, don't get me wrong, is solid stuff if you want to focus on the basics, but if you want to know how things really *work*—read science fiction. Stories. Pay attention to stories. That's where you're going to find the deeper patterns of creation. That's why we're lore gatherers!" Shaun was getting animated. Other than his worries and his lists, there was nothing he liked better than to talk about his research. He was like a different person. Almost charismatic. "For example, humans like to imagine future times, advanced technologies, alternate realities, that kind of thing—"

"You'll learn about it next year in your Human Cultures class, Molly," interrupted Dorker. "Except . . . we're banished now, so you won't even be in sch—"

"We look at science fiction," said Shaun, patting Dorker's shoulder, "because themes, patterns, or ideas repeat . . . Like portals, for example—wormholes, otherworldly doorways, that kind of thing. That idea shows up a lot. Accelerated pathways between different worlds, or different realities—"

"—or different times," said Molly.

"Exactly!" said Shaun. "O'Doul's 'Portal Thesis'—we've been studying that for a long time now.[F] Portals of one kind or another show up in enough stories that it seems like it must mean something. Turns out they're real. You just have to know how to find them."

[F] Named for the lore gatherer Flannery O'Doul (b. 1783, d. 1952), author of *Music of the Spheres: Humanity's Accidental Discoveries and Other Revelations*.

"And do you know how to find them?" asked Molly.

"Let's hope so," said Shaun.

* * * *

Pauvre Reynard a connu l'amour,
Mais la France est amour encore et encore. [†]

. . . thought Poor Reynard.

The fox was glad to be off the water, exhilarating though it had been; he was even gladder to have arrived in France. France was his kind of place. The weather was sunnier here, and the Gallic countryside was stunning. His artistic sensibilities swelled. Around him, hills teemed with wild flowers and grapes practically burst on the vines. Fields of lavender carpeted the world and on the outskirts of Lyon, they walked through a light rain shower that, under normal circumstances, would have put him in a foul mood, but which now inflamed his passion even more as each raindrop reflected the sun, flooding the world with a million points of sparkling light. If he had known what jewelry was, he might have said they hung in the air like diamonds.

They even produced a rainbow.

As he walked, he had visions of himself sitting in a café, eating a baguette with some gruyère cheese, and sipping strong coffee, all while painting vibrant still-lifes and impressionist oil-color landscapes.

He didn't know what these visions meant, but he was determined to find out.

* * * *

The waves and natural roll of the English Channel can leave a leprechaun very seasick, even moving in slow motion. Shaun once crossed the Atlantic Ocean during the height of hurricane season to a conference in North Carolina and barfed for two hours afterwards. But Molly, Shaun, and Dorker did not throw up after reaching France. They were too engrossed in conversation.

"Wait!" said Molly. "Portals. Is that why you were looking at maps last night? Are they on those maps?"

[†] [Loose translation] "Poor Reynard knew love back when;
But France is love—and love times ten!"

"Nooooooooo," said Shaun. "You can't just have magic time portals appearing on maps for everyone to see."

"Then why—?"

"Magnetic field lines!" exclaimed Dorker.

"What?" said Molly.

"Waves of energy that—"

"It's like this," said Shaun. "Think of time like a river. Individual rocks and stones in a river may get tossed around randomly and unpredictably, but the destination of the river remains the same. You can even change quite a few rocks and stones without altering the outcome of history substantially. A corollary of the idea is that because the ultimate destination of the river is unalterable, there may also be certain fixed points that cannot be changed. Those fixed points show up as poles in the Earth's electro-magnetic currents. Where you find a high concentration of magnetic field lines, there's a good chance you've found one of these fixed points in time. We think this is where time portals are located."[F]

"Why?"

"Well, think of time like a rubber mat."

"Wait," said Molly. "I thought time was like a river?"

"It is," said Shaun, "but now it's probably more helpful to think of it like a rubber mat."

"Well, which is it?"

"It's actually both, but for now, just focus on the rubber mat, okay?"

"O-kaaaaay." Molly felt herself getting lost in a maze of mixed metaphors.

"Now," said Shaun, "if you were to drop a big, heavy lead ball onto a rubber mat, what do you think would happen?"

"It would sink down?" said Molly.

"Exactly! It would sink down and stretch the rubber. These poles, these fixed, unalterable points in time are like gigantic lead balls on a rubber mat. Metaphorically, they sink down, and where they do, the rubber mat of time gets

---

[F] Mance O'Flattery, who lived in the second and third century A.D., was the celebrated lore gatherer time scholar who first posited the River of Time theory. In an early experiment, he moved to the North Pole on the hypothesis that, during the polar summer when the sun almost never sets, he would not need as much sleep and could therefore perform more experimental research. Surprisingly, the cold didn't bother him and, in fact, actually made some of his magical equipment work more efficiently. But the sleep deprivation almost drove him mad. "Whatever else we may say about time," he later wrote, "it is apparently an immutable rule of the universe that sometimes we all need a break from it."

stretched very thin and you can, kind of, as it were, sort of stick your boot in a metaphysical door and cause it to swing open." [*]

"So, time is like a door?" said Dorker.

"No," said Shaun, "the portal is like a door—is a door. Time is like a rubber mat."

"You said time was like a river," said Dorker.

"It is, but . . . Look, that was before. Forget about the river. We've moved on from the river. There is no river. Time is like a rubber mat. The portal is like a door," said Shaun.

"I thought the portal was like a lead ball," said Dorker.

"The fixed point in time is like a lead ball. The lead ball creates the portal," said Shaun.

"Then what's the door like?" said Dorker.

"The door is like . . . a door." said Shaun. Now he was getting confused.

"In the rubber river of time???" said Dorker.

"No, the door—" said Shaun.

"I think I get it," said Molly.

"Really?" said Dorker and Shaun in amazement.

"No, not really. But I get that we're looking for a time portal, and you think you know where one is." said Molly. "But how do you know which portal is which?"

"Well now, this is where it gets *really* interesting," Shaun began enthusiastically. "We don't really know."

Molly had noticed that often when her father said something was "interesting," what he really meant was he didn't have any idea what he was talking about. Molly didn't know if that's what being a researcher was all about, but she decided that "interesting" was a word she should pay more attention to when talking to her father.

"But if we don't know," she said, "we could end up anywhere, couldn't we?"

"Ah! This brings us back to Shakespeare!" said Shaun.

Dorker's eyes gleamed.

"Does it have to?" said Molly.

---

[*] "Monaghan's Rubber Mat" theory of time travel was first postulated by Maug Monaghan in his controversial book, *Mance O'Flattery Was Full Of It*.

BOOK OF LEPRECHAUNS: THE LORE GATHERERS

* * * *

"!!!"

. . . thought Poor Reynard.

The fox was having an existential crisis. They say that travel broadens the mind, but Reynard's mind had broadened so much, he feared his head might explode. His life until now had been almost entirely about survival—eating, sleeping, hunting, hiding, the occasional haiku, etc. Such mundane concerns now seemed small and insignificant. The world was more remarkable than he had ever imagined.

But what does a fox *do* with such information? He was still hungry. Other predators still wanted to kill and eat him. Fundamental realities could not be ignored. Yet as he followed these strange creatures across a continent, he could also not ignore the dawning realization that although he had become very good at surviving, somehow he had never learned to *live*.

How strange that he had never appreciated—well, *everything*—until it had all been stopped completely. All sorts of details jumped out at him that, until now, he had never even noticed: light particles filtering through trees; the subtle architecture of a leaf; the delicate acrobatics of a bumblebee balanced on the petals of a rose. The cosmic dance of life and death—the grace of all things great and small—pierced his hungry heart, and he experienced what can only be described as an all-embracing love he had never known before. Love that encompassed even this new food.

And yet, he had to eat.

Reynard once slept; but now awake,
Poor Reynard has choice to make.

. . . thought Poor Reynard.

* * * *

"Shakespeare wrote a play about Julius Caesar,"[§] said Shaun, "and one of the most famous lines in it is 'Beware the Ides of March.'"

[§] The plot briefly: a group of conspirators headed by Cassius plot to assassinate Julius Caesar. A friend of Caesar's—Brutus—has initial misgivings, but Cassius ultimately persuades him to join the conspiracy.

"But that's just theatre and poetry," said Molly.

"Just poetry? *JUST* poetry? Oh, dear, oh dear," said Shaun, shaking his head. "Molly, poetry *is* a kind of magic! And theatre is the greatest lie ever created. Humans call it 'the lie that tells the truth.' Any self-respecting leprechaun had better pay attention to a lie that good. And Shakespeare—Shakespeare combined both poetry *and* theatre. Personally, I've never cared for him. But you better believe I, and any serious lore gatherer, read him veeeeeerry carefully."

Molly and Dorker walked in and out between the legs of immobile Italian vineyard workers who were walking home single file as Shaun continued.

"Humans believe that time moves in one direction only, which," Shaun laughed, "of course, is nonsense. The rubber mat of time goes on and on in *all directions*.[†] So to know which portals are which, you have to know what the fixed points in time are. It's not easy to identify them, but for some reason, they resonate powerfully in the human psyche. They seem to get passed down through generations, often in story form.

"So," said Molly, "the Ides of March is . . . ?"

"It's the day Julius Caesar was assassinated," said Shaun, "around March 15, 44 BC."

"And why are we going there?" said Molly.

Shaun took a deep breath. "I am hypothesizing that the reason so many people know the line 'Beware the Ides of March' is because the assassination of Julius Caesar is one of those fixed, unalterable points in time. I also hypothesize that the portal to this fixed point will be near the place he was assassinated."

Molly nodded. "So, based on some *human* story, we're looking for a time portal that may or may not exist, that may or may not lead us to ancient Rome at the exact point in time Julius Caesar was assassinated??"

Shaun nodded. "I did say I was desperate, Molly."

They assassinate Caesar, which leads to civil war, and both their deaths. Despite what Shaun says, it's a good play. You should read it.

[†] As the famous lore gatherer philosopher Bogus McCool notes in his highly regarded book, *Life? Don't Get Me Started!*: "Und who sayz events are linear, jah? Maybe life goes back to front, or zide to zide, who knowz?" Bogus controversially wrote all his books in a thick German accent because he felt it gave his philosophical pronouncements intellectual heft. You can read more about Bogus McCool in the popular compendium of lore gatherer philosophers, *Great Ages of Philosophy: What, If Anything, Is Going On Here??* by Shaun McClanahan.

CHAPTER 9

Italy

In real time, Shaun, Molly, and Dorker arrived just outside of present-day Rome approximately five minutes and thirty-eight seconds after they left their campsite in Ireland. Even though the trip took so little actual time, it *felt* like walking hundreds of miles, and they were exhausted. ⸸ They collapsed

---

⸸ Interestingly, leprechauns have the strength and stamina for this sort of trip due to the energy that accompanies the extra time they absorb. As Corbin Garth O'Venturary (one of the first lore gatherer time historians) explains in his book, *Time: This Is A Thing Now?*, it turns out that time is an infinite resource. Our lives may be limited—the Earth, our solar system, and even the universe may have an end date—but time itself goes on and on. "Hang on," I hear you object, "time is only a manmade construct. It is no more than our way of measuring one complete revolution of this planet around its Sun using very small increments. If our solar system were gone, then our conception of seconds, minutes, hours, and years would be meaningless." This is true, but remember the rubber mat of time. It is infinite and goes in all directions. Just because our personal yardstick for measuring it may be lost, doesn't mean the rubber mat disappears along with it. This insight would have made Corbin's career, had he not gone mad soon afterwards, demonstrating once again that we mess with Time at our own peril.

What the world of time research lost to Corbin's insanity, however, the world of poetry gained. His subsequent incoherence of speech was matched only by his eloquence in written verse, and his *Dally Ye Not, For Time Is Short* (an epic poem/meditation on time and impermanence) is still considered an unparalleled triumph. A brief sample:

> *Dally ye not, for time is short,*
> *And lest ye go a-Maying,*
> *Know faithful hearts sworn true today,*
> *Tomorrow will be straying.*

Much of it has been lost, but it is believed to go on for another 400 quatrains. Some attribute the genius of this poetic masterpiece to his time studies, while other more cynical critics attribute it (and his madness) to the fact that his wife, Elise, had just left him for someone else. Unlike Corbin, Elise's new husband gave her and their marriage as much time as he did to his work, and though he made no comparable contributions to lore gatherer culture, he did have a happier life and marriage.

gratefully in a field just outside the city limits.

"We'll camp here tonight," said Shaun catching his breath as time resumed around them. "Rest up a bit. Tomorrow, we'll try to find the portal. Dorker?"

"Yes?"

"When you catch your breath, help Molly collect some firewood."

"Will do, Mr. Mac Leanna-uuhuhurUUPP!!" said Dorker, whose first lesson in long-distance travel was that seasickness is sometimes a delayed reaction.

As Molly turned from the spectacle of Dorker depositing the contents of his stomach on the Italian soil, she saw the fox. Their eyes locked ten feet from each other.

Unexpectedly, Molly felt calm. The fox clearly wanted food, but its eyes were not hungry like a predator's. The fox looked curious. It sniffed its way cautiously towards her, tilting its head this way and that, as if it were trying to *read* her. Without thinking, Molly decided to let it. She knelt down slowly, alert and prepared, but also—she didn't know how else to describe it—*available*. As she did, the fox's ears twitched, and its neck straightened. A pathway of some sort opened between them. Molly couldn't tell exactly what or how much she communicated, but through a hazy fog of intent, emotion, and need, she felt certain they shared at least one clear signal:

"FRIEND."

That was enough to establish a connection—a psychic link, binding Molly and the fox forever in a—

"MOLLY, LOOK OUT!"

Shaun's walking stick flew over her head and speared into the ground right next to the fox.

"NO!" Molly yelled.

The fox's ears flattened as he looked at Molly and darted away.

"Wait! Please!" Molly yelled out to the fox. It stopped about fifty yards away and turned, crouching low to the ground.

"Ratcrap!" said Shaun. "Almost got him."

"DA'!"

"You're lucky he didn't pounce," said Shaun. "He looks hungry. You and Dorker go gather some firewood. Stay together and be careful. I don't think the fox will bother us again, but you never know."

"Da', I don't think he . . . I think he was trying to talk to me!"

"Don't be silly," said Shaun. "It's just a dumb fox."

* * * *

Reynard protect! Reynard defend!
What once was food, shall now be . . . friend!?!

. . . thought Poor Reynard.

Something had changed. Something remarkable—more remarkable than all the other remarkable things that had happened since Reynard started chasing this remarkable new food. Reynard had bonded. For the first time in his life, he *cared* about another creature at least as much as he cared about himself. Possibly more. He didn't know how, he didn't know why; he only knew that, come what may, he would do everything in his power to protect the life of this new food that, he now understood, called itself "Molly."

Troublingly, to Poor Reynard's way of thinking, this was not very foxy behavior. Here he was, almost beside himself with hunger, but the idea of eating Molly—or her companions—was now unthinkable. This, more than anything else he had experienced, shook him. What was a fox to do? He crouched within sight of Molly, his mind a jumble of conflicting impulses.

It didn't help that he could now hear Molly's thoughts as clearly as he heard his own.

* * * *

The pickings in the area were sparse. Nonetheless, Shaun managed to capture a rabbit and began making a light soup with some herbs and succulent roots he had dug up.

"We should share some with the fox," said Molly.

"What? No!" said Shaun. "I don't want it getting ideas."

"But it's hungry, Da'. If we feed him, maybe he'll be less hungry. You know? Less likely to eat us?"

"And more likely to keep following us. No, I want it to go away," said Shaun.

"I agree with Molly," said Dorker.

"Big surprise," Shaun muttered, rolling his eyes.

"I feel bad for it," said Dorker.

Shaun looked at their expectant, pleading faces. He was hungry after their long walk and giving away half a rabbit meant less food for them. But sometimes, Molly really did look *a lot* like Alice.

"Keep an eye on the pot," he said. He walked to the edge of the magical protections he had put up and threw the carcass as far as he could in the fox's general direction. "Enjoy it," he said without much feeling.

The stew was flavorful, but thin—little more than a few scraps of rabbit in seasoned water. Still, it was enough to quell their rumbling stomachs long enough for them to get to sleep.

"I don't think it's going to rain," he said. "What do you say we forget about the tent and just sleep outside again?"

But Dorker had already passed out with his head on a rock. Molly was too tired and hungry to argue. She pulled out her ceremonial robe, rolled it up like a pillow, and as she drifted off almost instantly, she saw the fox in the distance slink up to the rabbit and grab it.

* * * *

The next morning at sunrise, they cleaned their campsite and started off for Rome in search of something to eat. Molly noticed the fox trotting behind them at a cautious and respectful distance. Would it follow them all the way into the city? She had a feeling it might, though she could have sworn she could feel its reluctance.

What foxes and leprechauns have in common is that they are naturally rural creatures. Cities, by and large, make them uneasy. Molly had never even been to a human town before.

"Where are we going, Da'?"

"The Roman Colosseum."

"What's the—?"

"I'll show you when we get there."

Shaun was jumpy as they made their way into the heart of the city. Navigating the Roman streets by himself would have been difficult enough, but having two children along (and a fox bringing up the rear) only heightened his anxiety, on top of which, his empty stomach was growling impatiently. The prospect of travelling back in time more than two thousand years also had him on edge. Time travel can be wildly disorienting, even if going back only a few minutes. And, as noted, more than one lore gatherer has gone mad toying with time.[†] Besides, let's face it: though fixed points in time cannot be altered, most of us are not fixed points. No one wants to go back in time, do something stupid, and come back to find they never even existed.

But despite Shaun's worries, they easily stole a loaf of bread from a local bakery and some cheese from a nearby shop and, finding an alley that looked quiet and out-of-the-way, they ate in the shadows of two large dustbins. The smell of trash did nothing for their appetites, but it did provide an extra layer of protection from unwanted human attention.

But not from all attention. As Molly sank her teeth into a thick piece of white cheddar on a slice of rosemary bread, a small face peered around one of the dustbins. It was a leprechaun. Dressed casually, he wore an unbuttoned white shirt, a patterned, tailored vest, and dark denim trousers, which taken together, communicated a clear understanding of his natural good looks. Young, clean cut, wearing a cheeky grin and a twinkle in his pale green eyes, he leaned rakishly against a trash can.

"You must be Shaun," he said with satisfaction.

＊＊＊＊

Let us pause here to emphasize, if you had not already guessed, that lying is an unfortunate, but intrinsic part of being a lore gatherer (the wider population of leprechauns is not so reticent about it). Lore gatherer anthropologists blame humans. For eons, non-human predators posed the only real threat to leprechauns, and most animals are pretty straightforward: they catch you, they kill you, they eat you—The End. But when humans shifted gears on the evolutionary bicycle and bi-pedaled down from the trees, they became a different beast altogether. Humans do not want to eat creatures like leprechauns; they want to *possess* them.

[†] Another famous example involves Bonflan Connecticut, a seventeen-year-old lore gatherer who was fascinated with dinosaurs. He spent many a day fantasizing about what it would be like to see them live. Somehow (and no one really knows how), he found a portal that took him back to the Cretaceous period, and his dreams were wildly fulfilled. Upon his return, he was initially coherent and told amazing stories about his adventure. After a few days, however, he slowly lost the ability to speak, and began tramping around the house, roaring like a velociraptor. Fortunately for his parents, he alternated between this and lumbering around slowly like a seventy-ton sauropod. His parents were refreshingly open-minded about it all. In his raptor phase, he was an exceptional hunter and brought home fresh meat regularly. In his sauropod phase, they kept his food on high shelves.

In a way, this is just as disturbing, but new threats also offer new opportunities. If you're not being eaten, you are free to flatter, cajole, plead, beg, argue, threaten—whole catalogues of tactics become available to manipulate and control the relationship, and humans, unintelligent as they are, proved exceptionally susceptible to deceit and treachery. The rest, as they say, is history.

The downside is that the introduction of fraud to the lore gatherer world, over time, corroded what used to be an otherwise perfectly harmonious subculture. The lore gatherers of today distrust almost everyone—even lore gatherers from villages they do not know.

* * * *

Molly looked at her father. "Da', how did he know—"

"Shh!" said Shaun sharply.

Shaun smiled broadly and bowed to the stranger. He wasn't much of a liar, but here was on firmer ground. Gone was the distracted, anxiety-ridden father Molly was used to and in his place was an expansively extroverted charm machine.

"Dear Sir, you must please excuse my daughter's impertinence, but this is her first trip abroad and she does not know better than to speak out of turn. As for who I am, maybe my name is Shaun and maybe it is not. Either way, I am sure you will understand if, whatever my name, I am reluctant to divulge it to a complete stranger without first knowing to whom I speak. Why, as a father, I could hardly look myself in the face were I to act so imprudently! My mother's mother would roll in her very grave! Whom, may I ask, do I have the honor of addressing?"

Molly looked at her father, open-mouthed. She had never seen such a bare and open display of ingratiating nonsense. Leprechauns only talked like that in stories, or so she had assumed. Surely, the stranger would be revolted.

But no, the stranger caught her eye, winked, and said with a deep bow of his own: "The honor, I assure you, is all mine, dear sir. How right you are to point out my foolishness in presuming to make such an outrageous request without having first introduced myself. Why, if my old mother ever heard that I had behaved in so reckless and—may I say—*inappropriate* a manner, she'd box my ears for sure."

Molly's surprise at this ostentatious display was easily explained: she had not yet studied the *Thyrty-Two Cruciale Lyes*, which, in Appendix D, details embellished forms of flattery that are highly useful "when Truth ys not thyne objecte." But even Molly's untrained eye quickly saw that her father and the stranger were playing something like a game of poker, except instead of cards and chips, they played with fawning politeness. Her dad wanted, without appearing to be insulting, to keep his own name secret, yet delicately force the stranger to reveal his own. The stranger was trying to do the same, but he had the advantage—somehow, he already knew Shaun's name.

What else the stranger might know, Shaun could only guess, so he launched an all-out suck-up offensive.

"Sure, your mother must be an *exceptional* woman to have raised so upstanding a gentleman as yourself, good sir. A man so open and forthright in his heart and mind is a jewel to the world indeed. A prince among men, I might say. A fine woman your mother must be."

Despite all the warmth and smiles, the two leprechauns circled each other like panthers.

"Ah, you are good to say so, sir," said the stranger, "but alas, my dear old mother has long since left this world."

The "dearly departed mother" gambit! Shaun had walked right into it! That gave a player leverage that was hard to overcome. In the card game of sycophantic flattery, the stranger had just played an ace. Shaun kicked himself, but like a martial arts master, he absorbed the blow and redirected it.

"Say it isn't so!" he said, radiating concern and sympathy.

"'Tis true, 'tis true," said the leprechaun. "A better woman you never will meet." A single tear rolled slowly down his cheek, which Molly thought was a nice touch.

Shaun saw the stranger's tear, and raised him a gusher, spontaneously spouting them from his eyes like a faucet. "Oh, dearest sir," said Shaun, pulling out a handkerchief and blowing his nose loudly. "When I lost my own mother, lo these many years ago, the pain was a thing I wouldn't visit on a human!"

The two men were now sobbing and embracing each other warmly. If she hadn't known better, Molly would have sworn they were long-lost brothers reuniting after a lifetime's estrangement. The only clue that something fishy was afoot was that, as they embraced, each was trying to pick the other's pockets.

This led to a complicated series of behind-the-back parries and thrusts that looked like a combination of physical affection and aikido.

Clearly, here were two masters of the obsequious arts.

They released their embrace, with no clear winner from the melee.

"Let me offer you my deepest condolences for the loss of your dear old mother, who taught you so well," said Shaun.

"Sir, you are every inch the gentleman and no mistake," said the leprechaun, smiling gratefully. "I remember the last words she ever said to me. She said: 'Son, where'er ye go, and whoe'er ye meet, let nothing come between two hearts of honesty.'"

Still no names had been exchanged, Molly noted.

"A finer sentiment has never been expressed, I do believe," said Shaun, wiping his face with his handkerchief again. "And so eloquently stated! It does my heart good to know that there shall be no secrets between us." Shaun placed his hands on the stranger's shoulders. "Shall we then, as your dear old mother would have wanted, exchange our names, and bury all fears and suspicions between us."

It was an artful move, but the stranger was ready for him.

"Nothing would give my heart more joy! You go first."

"No, you!" said Shaun.

"Honor my mother," said the stranger.

"Honor her by honoring yourself," said Shaun. "Your mother wished you to be free and open with the world. A mother's dying wish is a son's command. Now is your chance. Tell me your name, and with the gladdest of hearts, I shall tell you mine."

"Sir, you are as generous as you are wise, but 'tis what my mother would have wanted—that I should yield the honor to one so noble as yourself."

"Sir, I insist," said Shaun.

"No, sir, *I* insist," said the stranger.

The two men sized each other up.

"Tell you what," said Shaun, "let us both honor her by saying our names at the same time."

"On the count of three?" said the stranger.

"You have read my mind, good sir," said Shaun. "One."

"Two," said the stranger.

"Three!" they said together.

. . . .

Shaun and the stranger stood face to face, smiling through steely eyes.

"Well," said Shaun.

"Well," said the stranger.

They stood awkwardly for a moment.

Molly had had enough.

"YOU HAVE BOTH LOST YOUR MINDS!!" she cried. "You!" she said, pointing at the stranger. "What's your name? No funny business!"

Shaun's eyes widened; Dorker cringed. But the stranger burst out laughing. When he recovered, he bowed low to Molly.

"Well, my delightful young lady, my name is Antonio, and that's the truth of it. And what may I call you?"

"Molly," said Molly before Shaun could stop her. "He's Shaun."

"It is truly a pleasure to meet you, Molly," said Antonio, shaking Molly's hand and dropping all pretense. "Shaun, you have nothing to fear from me, I give you my word. I needed to make sure you were who I thought you were and . . . well, to watch you lie, to be honest. But now I've seen you lie, and you've seen me. And you've seen me tell the truth. Good! We all know what that looks like. Now we can trust each other. I'm a lore gatherer. I'm here to help. I think Molly here is rightly telling us that we'll all do better if we don't play games."

Shaun regarded the lore gatherer calling himself Antonio. "Never trust a leprechaun you haven't met" was Shaun's motto. On the other hand, this one *had* given his name. And his response to Molly had been genuine—Shaun detected none of the sixty-five "tells" that reveal a liar.[F] That was big. It showed real trust. Plus, something about him struck Shaun as basically honest. Not *too* honest, of course, because you can't go around being honest all the time and still call yourself a leprechaun. But honest enough that Shaun took Antonio's hand and shook it.

"Please," said Antonio, "come with me back to my home, get a decent breakfast into you, wash up if you want, and I'll explain everything."

[F] For a complete list and full descriptions of all known tells, see Shaun's book, *Oh, What A Givaway! Why You're A Terrible Liar*.

As they walked, Antonio showed them the sights. "My family came to Italy in the year 523 B.C.,"[ƒ] he said. "We've lived here in Rome ever since."

"You don't sound Italian," said Shaun.

"But I speak it, which is easy enough. But I also speak Latin, which, I dare say, might be of use where you're going?"

Shaun shot Antonio a look.

"Da', how does he know——" Molly began.

"No, no, forgive me, all in good time," said Antonio before Shaun could shush her. He turned and bent down to Molly. "I promise you, your questions will be answered, Molly. But let's have some food first, yeah?"

Molly nodded.

"Um, hi, I'm Dorker," said Dorker, who despite his size, was easy to overlook.

"Dorker!" said Antonio, slapping his head and shaking Dorker's hand vigorously. "My deepest apologies! How rude of me! *So* glad to meet you, Dorker! Truly! Welcome to Rome, all three of you!"

Sticking mainly to side streets and back alleys, they made their way through the busy city until they arrived at the Colosseum. Even in ruins, it was impressive. Molly had never seen anything like it. The size alone was overwhelming. The arena, where all sorts of grisly displays were staged in its day, was big enough that, when flooded, sea battles could be recreated with actual ships.

"You should have seen it in its prime," said Antonio, leading them away from human entrances. "My family lived here during the Empire, and some of the stories they recorded . . . you just can't imagine. The Colosseum has fallen into a bit of disrepair over the centuries," he said, feeling around the outside wall with his fingers, "but it still retains a bit of magic."

"A bit of magic?" Molly asked.

Antonio waved his hand over a crack in the wall and an opening appeared

---

[ƒ] For convenience, all dates are given in human years. As you might expect, because lore gatherers have been walking the planet for eons, they have their own calendar. In fact, they have their own method of telling time that is so accurate, they don't have to bother with leap years every four years. When he first heard about the human calendar, Gormish McSpenderton, a famous lore gatherer mathematician and astronomer, couldn't stop laughing for three solid hours. When he could finally speak again, all he could say, tears still streaming down his face, was, "What do they measure speed with, a hammer?!?"

where none had been before. Antonio gestured them in.

"The Colosseum was a place of violent ends, Molly. Many who died here were foreigners captured by the Romans only to be thrown to the lions or killed as gladiators. Many of them were actual magicians. The death of a magician leaves echoes."

"But Da'," said Molly, "I thought you said humans can't do magic."

Antonio laughed. "I didn't say they did it well, Molly!"

As they wound their way through the hidden lore gatherer passageways in the Colosseum, Antonio explained that, over the centuries, there have been humans who could actually do some pretty impressive magic. Not just tricks—the real thing. The kind of magic that makes you rethink the laws of physics and wonder what else the universe has up its metaphorical sleeve.

Merlin, who was King Arthur's magician, is of course the most famous example, though he didn't do half the things he claimed to have done. Frankly, he was better at self-promotion than he was at magic. What he did do exceptionally well was understand people. And he could legitimately summon fog. A cagey businessman can turn a talent for summoning fog into a whole catalogue of magical abilities. No one doubts a good fog. You can either summon fog, or you can't. A man who can summon fog on an otherwise sunny day might be capable of just about anything. And once people believe you can do just about anything, there's almost nothing you can't do (or at least, take credit for)—earthquakes, plagues of locusts, the sun going dark at midday, etc.

That's because most humans desperately want to believe in magic. They want to believe in it so badly they will go out of their way to ignore reasonable explanations for anything that seems remarkable. Above all, humans crave mystery. Where humans find mystery, they somehow find meaning (which is, when you think about it, a kind of magic in itself). That's the key insight ancient magicians like Merlin understood: a mystery is just a great big gap in our understanding waiting to be filled. Whoever fills it most convincingly—which often means, whoever lies the best—gets to define what the mystery means. Control the mystery, control the world.

"That's daft," said Molly.

"No, Molly, not daft," said Antonio. "Quite important, really. The world is a big, scary place. Making up a story about things you don't understand is a pretty reasonable way to control your fear."

"Or someone else's," said Molly.

"Spoken like Merlin himself!" Antonio grinned. "Anyway, the background magic of the Colosseum is still strong enough to give our village an added boost of protection from intruders."

"Wait, you *live* here?" said Molly.

"Indeed, I do!" said Antonio. They had stopped in a corridor which, long ago, would have been under the center of the Colosseum's arena.

"This is AMAZING!" said Dorker. "*I* want to live in a Roman ruin!"

"There's a lot more here than ruins, Dorker," said Antonio. "Give me your hands,"

"There's *more?!?*" said Dorker.

Shaun, Molly, and Dorker gathered around Antonio and put their hands on top of his. "I speak with the authority of the Council," said Antonio. "FÁILTE!"

He flung their hands upward, and suddenly, where there had been nothing but a vast, ancient Roman ruin, a small village now surrounded them with busy lore gatherers going about their day. It was not dissimilar to Molly's village, but it had a distinct Mediterranean flair. For example, the roofs were not thatched, but layered with terra cotta tiles that also served as solar panels to generate energy for the village. The roads were cobbled, like in Molly's village, but here they looked as if they had risen from the depths of the earth itself, artfully designed to collect and filter rainwater.

"Woah!" gasped Dorker.

"This way," said Antonio. "With any luck, my mother will have made breakfast. I told her to expect us."

"Your mother?" said Molly.

"Oh! Yes, she's not dead," said Antonio. "Sorry, I thought you knew. That was just standard leprechaun blarney. Very useful to mention a dead mother if you ever find yourself captured by a human. Hard to argue with a man crying over a dead mother, isn't that right, Shaun?"

Shaun had stopped abruptly.

Dead mother? he thought. *Alice! I forgot about Alice! Oh no! No! No! No! No! No! How could I have forgotten about Alice?!?*

Antonio turned and saw Shaun's pale face. "Have I said something wrong?"

Alice? Shaun searched in his head for a whisper of her voice. *I'm sorry. I'm sorry, I'm sorry, I'm sorry! I forgot about you. When I was . . . sparring with Antonio and he mentioned his dead mother, I just . . . I was caught up in the game I think and . . . I was having fun. It was fun. And I forgot about you. I NEVER forget about you. Shillelagh, I'm sooooooo sorry! How could I forget you! I don't ever want to forget you! I'll never forget you again! Ever! I swear!*

Molly looked at her father. Why did he have to do this in front of a stranger? She looked back at Antonio. "My mother is dead," she said bluntly.

Antonio stopped smiling. He looked from Molly to Shaun. "Is that true?"

"Yes," said Molly.

Please Alice? Let me hear your voice?

Molly approached her dad and tried to put a hand on his arm. Shaun winced at her touch, abruptly brushed her hand away, and turned from them.

You have to talk to me! he thought. *I haven't heard your voice since The Thieving and I . . . Please, I need to hear your voice. Won't you just say a word? Just one? I won't ever forget you again! Please, please, please, forgive me. Talk to me. Alice . . . ? Stupid! I'm so stupid!* Shaun began hitting his forehead with his hand. *Stupid! Stupid! Stupid! Alice, please! Don't leave me in this head alone . . .*

Antonio watched this spectacle for a moment and didn't know what to say. But he was acquainted with the face of loss well enough to recognize its features. He quickly ascertained Shaun was unlikely to speak again until whatever was moving through him had passed. He also saw Molly quietly reeling.

Antonio approached her, knelt down, put his hands on her shoulders, and said gently. "I am so sorry to hear it, Molly. It's a terrible thing to lose your mother so young, and no mistake."

"It's okay," Molly shrugged. "I didn't know her very well. She died when I was little."

Antonio looked at her carefully. Molly felt like he was reading words written on the inside of her head, and she suddenly wondered why she had said losing her mother was "okay." It was not "okay." It was far from "okay." It was awful. Held in Antonio's sympathetic and penetrating eyes, the years since her mother's death suddenly vanished, and it might as well have been yesterday. The memory slammed into her like a freight train.

She really didn't want to cry in front of Antonio. It was not the first impression she wanted to make. But grief is rarely a convenient caller.

Fortunately, Antonio read her well. He stood and smiled graciously. "Well, Molly," he said, "I would be honored if you would come inside and meet *my* mother. I think she will be very happy to meet you."

CHAPTER 10

The Message

"Antonio, is that you?"

The voice that called from the kitchen sounded like varnished oak and aged brandy. Something about it lingered in the walls and got into your bones, making it hard to think about anything else. It commanded attention. Molly instantly wanted to meet the owner of that voice.

"Sure, 'tis I, O mother o' mine!" Antonio called cheerfully once inside the house. "And I come bearing gifts!"

"Is that right? I love gifts. I'll be right in."

"My Ma' *lives* in the kitchen," Antonio said conspiratorially to Molly. "Her favorite room in the house—just making, creating, inventing, all day. And nothing makes her happier than to cook for those she cares about. Her favorite thing in the world."

"Now, Antonio," said the voice, entering the room, "what have you brought—Oh! Oh my."

First impressions are important, and the woman who walked in made a lot of them. She was almost perfectly round, with wild, wiry, grey hair sprouting in all directions from under the knit hat she had made. She had a large nose and looked like she was missing at least one front tooth. To look at her, you could imagine that a knot from some ancient oak had decided to climb off the tree and pursue a life in the culinary arts. But though her face was as gnarled as a gourd, it was also as round and open as a harvest moon. She was instantly warm and likeable, and smelled of warm bread and fresh vegetables. The word "autumnal" jumped to Molly's mind. She wouldn't have been surprised to see an owl fly out of the woman's ear.

Upon seeing Molly, the woman's face didn't so much break, as cascade into a smile. "Well, Antonio, what *have* you found?" She looked at Antonio. "Where's Shaun?"

Antonio shook his head and gestured outside. Aggie nodded then looked back at Molly. "Come here, girl; let me look at you."

There was no resisting that voice. Molly blushed and walked towards her automatically. The woman's grin stretched from ear to ear. As Molly approached, the woman bent over, took Molly's hands and gazed deeply into her eyes. Molly gazed back and what happened next surprised her. It was as if a tunnel of light opened and connected them and all they could see was each other—like what had happened with the fox, only more vivid and more intense. The room around them seemed to dissolve, and in that tunnel, Molly revealed herself to the strange woman without a word exchanged, as if her whole life was a book, and the woman was reading it.

The woman also revealed herself, but it was too much to take in. Molly could see the wide, panoramic landscape of the woman's life, but no one could digest that much information all at once. Molly was overwhelmed, but the one thing she did grasp firmly was that this woman was an ally.

Then abruptly, she dropped Molly's hands. The connection was broken, and all warmth drained from the woman as if a sieve had opened beneath her. She said curtly, "What's your name, girl?"

Molly got instantly defensive.

"Molly."

"Made a mess of things, have you?"

"WHAT?!?" Molly thrust out her chin and squared her shoulders.

"Antonio, what do you mean by bringing . . . *this* . . . into my home?" The woman now peered at Molly through narrow eyes, as if she were considering a piece of spoiled meat.

What had felt so warm and generous a moment ago now felt like all-out war. Molly stood nose to nose with the woman, glaring back at her, getting angrier by the second without even knowing why. She wasn't even thinking any more, just reacting. Molly literally saw red. Her hands balled up in fists and the room crackled with hatred.

"Oh! Am I going to have trouble from you, miss?" the woman said, raising her voice.

Molly's face got hot. "YES! YOU! ARE!" she screamed.

With that, Aggie reached down and touched the very top of Molly's head. Her touch was light, but as she flung her hand upwards, Molly felt like the top of her skull had burst open. A ball of blue fire erupted and hit the ceiling, crawled along the rafters like a thousand spiders, then dissipated.

As fast as it had gone, warmth flooded back into the room.

"HOO!" said the woman, shaking her hand and waving a dishcloth to disperse the smoke. "That was a big one! Open a window, Antonio!"

She flipped the dishcloth over her shoulder, smiled broadly and took Molly's hand.

"It's okay, Molly. It's okay. I'm sorry. You're okay."

"What was *that?*" said Dorker.

The woman winked at him. "Cheap tricks."

Molly was dizzy and disoriented. She looked around the room as if she had forgotten where she was and who she was with.

"Feel my skin, Molly," said the woman, patting and rubbing Molly's hand. "You're safe. You're okay. Say 'yes' if you can understand me."

"Blarghlgah" said Molly.

The woman chuckled and kept rubbing Molly's hand. "Takes a minute sometimes," she said to Dorker. "Molly, tell me you can understand me."

Molly blinked at the woman's wide, open face, and then everything came back to her.

"Yes," she said.

"Good," said the woman. "Good good. That's good, Molly. I'm sorry to spring that on you. Better out than in, as they say. Come. We haven't much time."

"I think I'm going to puke," said Dorker.

"How old are you, dear?" said the woman.

"Twelve," said Molly.

"And when did your mother die?"

Molly looked at Antonio in astonishment. How could she know? Antonio shrugged and grinned.

"I was four."

"Oh, my dear!" the woman exclaimed embracing her. Molly instinctively stiffened. In the space of minutes, this woman had sent deeply conflicting signals, and Molly didn't know what had just been done to her. But it slowly dawned on her that she now felt happier than she could ever remember feeling. The woman's arms were soft and pulsed with strength and kindness. What else could Molly do but sink into them gratefully?

Finally, the woman released her and said, "Come and have some breakfast. Antonio, fetch Shaun in as well, there's a lad."

"Yes, Ma'."

"Umm . . ." said Dorker, "I'm Dorker, ma'am. Dorker. I'm with Molly, Ma'am. Um."

The woman turned to look at Dorker and smiled. "Well, if you're with Molly, you'd better come here and let me look at you."

"Yes, ma'am," said Dorker hesitantly. "Are you going to . . . you know . . . do that thing you did to Molly?"

"Let's find out," she said with a wink.

She grabbed Dorker by the chin and eyed him critically. Almost immediately, she raised an eyebrow and smiled in spite of herself. She patted his cheek.

"Whatever else you are, Dorker, you've got a light and generous heart and you're welcome here. Molly's lucky to have you."

And if Dorker's heart had been a balloon, he would have floated to the sky.

"What should we call you?" asked Molly.

"Oh, yes! My name. Forget my own head next. You can call me Aunt Aggie, if you like, but if you don't like, you can just call me Aggie."

Molly felt like she *would* like to call her Aunt Aggie, but she knew she should ask her father first. He could get . . . particular about that sort of thing. Shortly after her mother had died, a few unfortunate women in the village who were close friends of Alice made the mistake of dubbing themselves "Auntie" this or "Momma" that in Shaun's presence. Molly hadn't minded. It didn't make *her* feel any better, but it seemed to help them. Shaun *really* didn't like it, and no one did it twice.

Dorker was definitely going to call her Aunt Aggie.

Aunt Aggie led them into the most magnificent and inviting kitchen Molly had ever seen. It had reddish brown tiles on the floor, and yellow-orange stucco walls. Pots and pans of all shapes and sizes hung from the walls and ceiling, and vegetables and fruits filled baskets everywhere. By a pair of large and airy widows, sat various ceramic pots in which grew mint, rosemary, cinnamon, vanilla, and so much more, audaciously hurling their scents into the air. The kitchen felt so organic, Molly wouldn't have been surprised if it could grow and cook its own food.

"Sit here," said Aggie, pulling out stools from under a counter. In front of each of them she placed a bowl of potatoes, vegetables, and meat, along with some bread fresh from the oven. "Eat that," she said, smiling, "for starters." Molly bit her lip. She was suddenly ravenously hungry. She looked around uncertainly.

"Your dad will be in directly," said Aggie. "Don't worry. Tuck in."

And tuck in they did. The smell of stew was overpowering. When Molly picked up her spoon and took a bite, she almost fell off her stool, it was so good. Dorker groaned audibly at his first taste. It had technically only been a day or so since they'd had a proper meal, but a lot of miles had been traveled in that time. Molly suspected that even under normal circumstances, this would have been the best food she'd ever tasted.

She got so lost in her meal that she almost didn't notice her father and Antonio come in. Her dad was pale and moved slowly and deliberately.

"Well now, you must be Shaun," said Aggie brightly. "Come in, come in, make yourself at home."

"Shaun . . ." said Shaun distantly.

". . . Yes," said Aggie. "Shaun it is." She briskly set a bowl of food in front of him. "Eat that. No arguments."

Aggie spoke to Shaun in crisp, clear commands. It took no magic to see the dark state he had fallen into. Aggie saw it, and though she was giving him space, she was not giving him time to think about it.

They say that with a long enough lever and a firm place to stand, you can move the world. Molly saw that Aggie got what she wanted almost invisibly, with no apparent effort. It reminded Molly of her mother, and she wondered if, to people like Alice and Aggie, everything in the world was a lever—words, food, kindness. Maybe that was true for everyone, and people like her mother and Aggie just always knew exactly where to stand. Shaun ate, and Molly saw his mood change with his first mouthful.

Aggie left the room for quite some time, while Antonio sat quietly apart at a bookstand by the window, making notes in a large tome, and letting good food do for weary travelers what words never could. Eventually, Aggie rejoined them and sat with Antonio watching the three of them intently, her eyes bright. When Shaun put down his spoon, Aggie got up and put a cup of fresh coffee in front of him. Then she gave one to Antonio, one to herself, and a glass of fresh pear juice with honeyed sunlight [*] to Molly and Dorker.

"Now Shaun," said Antonio, putting down his pen. "Where to start?"

"Is this food magic?" said Molly.

"All good food is a little bit magic, Molly," said Aggie, winking.

Shaun took a sip of the best coffee he had ever tasted and said: "Why don't you start by telling me how you knew my name?"

"Ah yes, that," said Antonio with a smile. "Well—the fact is, we've been expecting you."

"Expecting us?"

"Well, no—just you, Shaun," said Antonio. He smiled at Molly and Dorker. "Though we are very glad to have you all."

"How could you have been expecting me?" Shaun frowned.

"Maybe it would be easiest if we start with this." Antonio put down his cup and left the room. When he came back, he put a large, hardcover book on the table in front of Shaun. The book was old, its binding cracked, and its pages yellow.

"What's this?" said Shaun.

"This, my new friends, is a history of the human Roman Empire written by my family. One volume of it, anyway. My family watched it rise and watched it fall. They kept detailed records of its people, places, and events."

"Why?" asked Molly. "The Roman Empire was just humans."

"History is also a kind of magic, Molly," said Aggie. "Unlike human historians, lore gatherers study *all* the stories. Big events leave big echoes. Even the smallest event can ripple out through time like a stone dropped in a pond."

"Da', is that like the fixed points in time—" Molly began.

"Molly, don't interrupt," said Shaun. Aggie frowned at him, briefly.

---

[*] If you think about what bees do, honey is just liquified sunlight. But as Shaun explains in his book *A Leprechaun Cocktail Codex*, lore gatherers have learned how to extract the sunlight from the honey, which makes it sweeter than ordinary sunlight and useful for infusing all sorts of beverages.

"Like ripples in a pond," Antonio continued, "history also has recurring patterns. Some repeat rapidly; others take centuries. But once certain patterns are set in motion, the number of possible outcomes diminish until they become inevitable. If you know how to read those patterns, you can predict the future with a fair degree of accuracy."

"So . . ." said Shaun, "you *predicted* my arrival?"

"Oh that," said Antonio. "No, someone warned us."

"What?!?"

Antonio flipped through the pages. "As I say, most of this book concerns human history. But there was a notation made over two thousand years ago in the margins of the history of Julius Caesar that not only relates to lore gatherers, but speaks to my family directly." Antonio looked up at Shaun and pointed to the page. "Would you like to read it?"

Shaun looked at Antonio doubtfully. Then he read aloud what he saw written in the margins:

In March 2016, Shaun McClanahan (lore gatherer) will come to Rome looking for Julius Caesar. If you want to save the world, you must help him find the way.

"That," said Antonio, "was written the year Julius Caesar was assassinated. The handwriting does not belong to anyone in my family. Any idea what it might mean, Shaun?"

Shaun reread the note and shook his head. "I'm not here to save the world. I'm just following a clue. I have no idea what this is or why it's here."

Shaun's words hung in the air like the smell of old fish as he continued staring at the page. Antonio and Aggie didn't buy it, but nor did they challenge him. Finally, he looked up.

"You've had this for over two thousand years," he said. "Do *you* have any idea what it means?"

Antonio turned to Aggie, who looked at Shaun for a long, uncomfortable moment.

"No," she finally said. Then she sighed. "I don't know how or why, but all of this feels both familiar and strange. Like I'm having a memory of something that never happened. And the questions are driving me crazy!"

"What questions?" asked Molly.

"What questions?!?" Aggie threw her hands in the air. "Will this have happened before? Will we have never not met?"

"That's gibberish," said Molly.

"Of course, it's gibberish!" said Aggie. "But these are the sorts of questions that come up when people start messing around with time travel! I strongly advise against it. Scary business. Easy to end up haunted by your own ghost!"

Aggie sat staring at the assembled group, tapping her finger on the arm of her chair. She looked hard at Shaun in particular.

"But," she said, coming to a decision, "we've been the keepers of these books for thousands of years. If they tell us to help you, we help you." She looked at Shaun and said pointedly: "No questions asked. You want to go back to ancient Rome? The pathway leading to our house is also a corridor in the Colosseum. You'll find the portal you're looking for at the end of that corridor."

Shaun nodded.

"Also, I have spoken to the fox."

"WHAT?" said Shaun.

"Don't worry, he won't hurt you. Molly has seen to that. And I gave him a good meal, so he'll be well-fed, to start."

"Wait, what did Molly—?" said Shaun.

"The fox will be joining you," said Aggie. "His name is Reynard."

"How did Molly see to THAT?!?"

"Molly . . . ?" said Aggie, turning to her.

Molly looked at the others in the room staring at her in disbelief. "I . . . I don't . . . I don't know what I did."

"You'll figure it out," said Aggie with a smile. "But I will tell you the rabbit made a big impression."

Shaun was bewildered. First Dorker, now a fox. He was rapidly losing control of his entire banishment.

"Shaun," said Aggie gently, "I said no questions asked, and I meant it. But it might help if you tell us *why* you want to find Caesar."

Shaun hesitated, to Molly's growing frustration. Why wasn't he more forthcoming with people who obviously wanted to help?

"Our gold was stolen," said Molly.

"Molly!" snapped Shaun.

"Stolen?" said Antonio, putting his hand to his head. "Shillelagh's Shoes! How did that happen?"

"It was my fault," said Molly quietly before Shaun could answer. Antonio and Aggie looked at each other.

"How . . ." said Aggie carefully, "How *exactly* . . . was it *your* fault?"

Molly told them the story (with some help from Dorker), which Aggie listened to patiently. When Molly finished, Aggie's expression didn't change. She looked at Molly and spoke gently.

"Molly, if you go out into my back garden, you will find a lemon tree. I'm going to make some tea, and I'd fancy a drop of fresh lemon in it. Would you pick out the best one you can find for me?"

"Okay," said Molly.

"I can go!" Dorker volunteered.

"Yes, you should help," said Aggie. "Molly, you should let him help you. Put some thought into it now! Look carefully! Don't just grab the first one you see. Be sure to find one that is perfectly ripe. I want the best. And you both have to agree on the choice. Look at me." They did. "I take my tea very seriously, d'you understand? Can I trust you?"

"Yes," said Molly and Dorker solemnly. They had no trouble believing Aggie took everything she ate seriously.

"Good. Then off you go," said Aggie.

When they had gone, Aggie looked at Shaun. Or maybe she looked through him.

"Shaun, why does that girl believe she lost your gold?"

Shaun was taken aback. "What?"

"You heard me."

"Well . . . she told you the story . . ."

"That gold was yours."

"Yes, but—"

"*Your* responsibility."

"Yes, but—"

"It was *your* idea to have her check it."

"Yes, but—"

"And the gold was stolen, not lost."

"Yes, b—"

"So why does she believe it was *her* fault?"

"Because—"

"Yes . . . ?" Aggie leaned forward, eying him carefully.

"Because . . ."

"Because you told her it was her fault, didn't you?"

"Well, I . . . I might have—"

"Children believe their parents, Shaun, even when they're wrong."

"I wasn't . . . She failed at The Thieving!"

"Okay. And?"

"And . . . and she doesn't take anything seriously!"

"She takes you seriously."

"No, she—"

"Yes, she does."

"Look, it . . . It's my job to—"

"Do you take her seriously?"

"What? No! I mean, yes, of course! I mean . . . she's just a child."

"SHE," Aggie said, pointing outside, "is much more than that, Shaun!"

Shaun fidgeted in his seat.

"You shouldn't have told her that, Shaun."

He got up and started pacing.

"You need to tell her," said Aggie.

"She distracted me!" Shaun burst out.

"What? How did she . . . what?"

"She failed The Thieving, and then she got upset and I didn't . . . I never know how to . . . and so YES! Yes, yes, yes! I said she should check the gold all by herself. It's my fault! Stupid! I'm so stupid!"

"Shaun, you weren't—"

"I didn't check on her."

"What?"

"I didn't check on her! I should have checked on her! I'm so stupid! Why? Why, why, why? Why didn't I check on her?!? You have to be vigilant. Always. Always. Always. But she's always distracting me! But you can't let her. You can't do that. You can't ever do that. Because there are consequences. Always. Terrible, terrible consequences. *You* know what happens. But what can I do?!? You could have *checked* on her, Shaun, that's what! If you had checked on her, she wouldn't have—"

"Shaun. Shaun!" said Aggie. She had seen men breaking down before—often because she was doing the breaking. She was good at it. But now Shaun was doing it all by himself, which had her feeling a little left out. She tried a different approach.

"Shaun," she said gently, "I know how hard it must have been for you since your wife died—"

"What? What are you talking about?" he snapped. "How dare you! What does that have to do with anything? What do you know about any of it? You don't know! You don't know anything—about me, about Molly, about Alice! You talk to us for an hour and think you *know* what we've been through?"

"Shaun, I knew what you've been through the minute I saw you!" said Aggie, her face turning red. "You're not that hard to read! Your wife died, and you're still grieving! But whatever you've been through, so has *she!* Your *CHILD! She* lost her mother! How do you think she feels? Have you ever *once* thought about that? Has she ever told you? Have you ever *asked?*"

Shaun's face fell.

"I didn't think so!" Aggie stopped and took a breath. "Shaun, listen to me: You're right, I don't know all the details. You've had a hard time of it. Anyone can see that. And I am truly sorry. But right now, forget about what happened before. Now—*right now*—your daughter is angry. Boy, is she! I don't know if she's angry at you, or her mother, or at life, or death, or all of the above, but it's powerful! Look at me, Shaun!"

He did.

"Nothing else matters. Do not dismiss *this!* Your daughter . . . that anger? It's growing every day. And it's going to keep growing, and Shillelagh help you if anger is the force that drives her when she figures out what she can do!"

Shaun frowned. "What do you mean? What can she do? Other than . . . talk to foxes . . . ?"

Aggie paused. "I don't know yet. But I'd bet a pot of gold Alice knew. Didn't she."

Shaun sat down quietly, his hands between his knees. He nodded. "Why can't I see it?" he whispered.

"Look at me, Shaun," she said.

He did.

"Trust her."

"No! I can't—"

"Trust her!"

"I tried that and look where we are!"

"Trust her again."

"You don't under—"

"You have to keep on trusting her! Again and again and again! She can *help* you, Shaun. And if you don't start trusting her," Aggie said, shaking her head, "You will lose her. Forever."

Shaun looked down and buried his face in his hands. His shoulders started to shake. Aggie walked over to him and placed a hand on his shoulder.

"Shaun, you're not alone. Your young girl out there. She *needs* you. Not for food and shelter. Not to teach her about *gold*. She needs *you*. Her father. Try to imagine how *she* feels, *just for once*. It's like you're blaming her for—I don't know what—this and that and everything else! But ask yourself, Shaun—who are you really trying to punish?"

Shaun covered his mouth for a long moment and stared straight ahead.

Aggie watched him carefully. Beneath all of Shaun's anxiety and sadness, she suspected, was a perfectly competent father. One with a lot to offer Molly. He just didn't believe he was. But he also seemed like someone who knew how to pursue something he wanted. And just now, Aggie had coaxed him to the most delicate of tipping points where he stood perfectly balanced on the precipice of change.

The problem with tipping points is that the person standing on them can just as easily fall the wrong way.

"I've got your lemon, Aunt Aggie!" Molly said, running back into the kitchen.

"*Aunt* Aggie!" Shaun said, standing. "*AUNT* Aggie? When did this start?!"

"Oh! Sorry, Da', I meant to ask you—"

"The mother she never had, is that it?" he said, looking at Aggie.

"WHAT?" cried Aggie.

"You think I'm a terrible father!"

"I never said—"

"You didn't have to!"

"*Shaun!*" said Aggie.

"Da'!"

"Shaun, don't be ridiculous!" said Antonio.

"Ridiculous!? No, no! I'm the only one here who really cares about Molly! Cares enough to do the hard thing. You want to know why losing the gold is Molly's fault? Because *someone*—ME—has to teach her responsibility. It's not fun or exciting like food or pretending to talk to animals, but it's the most important thing, right? Horrible things happen to irresponsible people! Things you can *never* get back! You can plead and beg and wish as hard as you like to get them back, but you won't, no matter what! Not your home, not your village, not your ... *Someone* has to teach her! Teach her that when you are entrusted with something precious, you watch over it! You never let it go! You're *supposed* to watch over it! You're *supposed* to care for it! Every single day!" Shaun voice was rising and his face was red with tears. "You *don't* joke about it. You *don't* make mistakes. You take it *seriously!* You *don't* get distracted. THAT'S how she lost the gold! THAT'S how we got banished! THAT'S how I killed her mother! THAT'S how she ..." Shaun stopped.

"No. Wait, I mean ..."

His eyes bulged and he clapped his hands over his mouth.

"Wha—?" said Molly.

"No, not killed," he said, looking desperately at Molly. "No no no no no no, I didn't ... no, I ... !"

Shaun stared at them all, stumbling backwards into a corner, knocking things to the ground haphazardly as he fell. His head snapped back and forth violently as if he was trying to lasso the words back into his mouth. Sliding down the wall and crouching to the floor, he beat his head with his hands and when he finally looked up, his face looked hollow. No one dared breathe.

"It's all my fault," he whispered.

Aggie took a tentative step towards him.

"Shaun ..."

"Aunt Aggie, I found this lemon," said Dorker, bursting back into the house, "which isn't as good as the one Molly found, probably, but I'm trying to figure out—"

"We're leaving," Shaun said, abruptly getting up and shoving past Dorker.

"Right! Wait, what?" said Dorker, turning to follow Shaun. He turned right back around again. "Sorry, here's your lemon, Aunt Aggie! Um. Thanks for the food! It was the best I ever had. Um, what's going—"

"DORKER!" yelled Shaun from outside.

"Coming!" yelled Dorker, running out.

Molly stood in the middle of the kitchen holding a perfect lemon. Stunned, she looked at Aggie and Antonio, not knowing what to do. Aggie rushed over to her.

"You'd better go," she said, taking the lemon and giving her a quick hug. "Antonio, get her the book. Don't worry, Molly." Antonio nodded and quickly disappeared into a back room.

"What book?" said Molly, bewildered.

"It's a book of Latin," said Aggie.

"Oh," said Molly without enthusiasm.

"I know it's not much, but you may need it," said Aggie.

"Molly!" her dad called sharply from outside.

"Coming Da'!" Molly called back.

Antonio came back in and shoved the little book into Molly's backpack.

"I'm so sorry, Molly," said Aggie. "If we had had more time . . . . But never mind. It'll be alright. Don't worry! Your dad is . . ." Aggie shook her head. "Look, I've known people who've killed, and . . . that's not your dad. I don't know what that was about . . . he's just raving. Blame me. I pushed him too hard, too fast. He'll be okay, Molly. So will you. He loves you. I know it. Now go. I feel certain we'll see each other again, maybe sooner than you think." Aggie hugged her and put a hand to Molly's cheek. "Goodbye, chick."

"MOLLY!" her dad called.

Molly didn't want to leave. But her dad was calling. Not knowing what else to say, she turned and left.

When she got outside, her dad grabbed her hand and Dorker's, gave a complicated turn of his wrist, and what had been a pathway in a lore gatherer village, snapped back to being a corridor underneath the Roman Colosseum.

And there stood Poor Reynard patiently staring right at them.

"*SHILELAGH!*" yelled Shaun, jumping back. But the fox was unperturbed. He looked at Shaun quizzically, then fixed his eyes on Molly. He crouched down and slunk up to her feet, sniffing and whimpering plaintively. Molly reached out and cautiously stroked his face. That seemed to satisfy him.

He rose from his crouched position and sat down waiting for whatever was next.

"Um . . ." said Molly. "I think he's—I mean, Reynard—is ready to go."

Shaun frowned darkly. "Come on," he said, stalking ahead of them.

"Da'?" Molly whispered.

"Shhh!" said Shaun. He was concentrating, moving quickly along the stone corridor, examining every inch. He pointed at something up ahead.

"There it is," he said.

"There what is?" Molly squinted.

"Up there." said Shaun, pointing. Molly saw a stone plinth about two feet high.

"What, that?" asked Molly.

"Come on," said Shaun.

"What's so special about that?" she asked. In the low light of the corridor, she could just make out faint ripples surrounding the pedestal, as if it were a pond into which someone was throwing pebbles.

"I think that right here is where the rubber sheet of time is stretched," said Dorker quietly. "Wow, the light bends around it."

"Is this where Caesar was killed?" asked Molly.

"No! Of course not!" said Shaun irritably. "He was killed in a meeting house at the far end of Pompey's Theatre."

"Then why is the portal here?" she asked.

"Things shift over time," Dorker whispered, "rocks, mountains, continents, planets. Everything affects everything else. After more than two thousand years—"

"Okay, so, what now?" she asked.

Shaun hoisted her up onto the pedestal, then he and Dorker climbed up. There was no room for Poor Reynard, so he stood on his hind legs and put one of his paws on Molly's foot.

They all stood for a moment. Molly looked up at her dad. Shaun looked down at Molly and they all took each other's hands.

Molly could scarcely believe it.

They were actually going to do this.

Dorker smiled at her as if he didn't have a care in the world.

"Da', what did you mean back there when you said—"

"Never mind."

"DA'!" Molly jerked her hand free and looked up at him with tears welling. Shaun sighed heavily.

Alice, help me! he thought, *what do I say? I'm so sorry! How do I tell her? What do I say? She hates me. I know she does. She hates me so much, and who can blame her? I'm difficult. I'm so difficult. I was never as difficult when you were here. But you're not here anymore. You never will be again. I'm so sorry! And now I'm driving her away. I'm losing her, Alice. Just like Aggie said. I can't lose her. I can't lose you both! But I don't know how to . . . help me, Alice! Please help me! I can't tell her. If she knew what I did, if she knew how I . . . she'd never forgive me. How could she forgive me? I've never forgiven myself. Alice, please . . . ?*

Shaun shuddered. He didn't know if going back to ancient Rome was the right thing to do. Right now, he didn't know much of anything. There was only one thing he knew with any certainty.

He looked at Molly. "You know that message in the book Antonio showed us?"

Molly and Dorker nodded.

"The handwriting was mine."

They stared at him open-mouthed as Shaun gently took their unresisting hands. He whispered, "*Taistil am!*" and they were gone.

END OF PART I

Part II

CHAPTER 1

Alice's Shadow

When Molly was four, she knew as well as anyone that if caught, leprechauns must grant humans three wishes. She also knew that nine times out of ten, humans wish for a leprechaun's pot of gold. But Molly had never heard leprechaun's talk about what *they* would wish for if matters were reversed.

This did not seem fair.

So she had asked her mother, of whom she asked all her most important questions. Alice stopped lacing Molly's boots and thought about it.

"I would wish to know what *you* would wish for, chick," she said very seriously.

Molly blushed.

"I would wish I was more like you, Ma'."

"I think you're already like me, chick," said Alice, tying the final lace.

Molly beamed. Being like her mother would be the best thing ever. Molly told people that her mother was what you would get if a small sunflower came to life: looking into her face, no one could be unhappy. Her father said Alice could charm the lights off a field of fireflies. She wielded a kind of magic with people. And she wasn't afraid of anything.

Molly wasn't afraid of much, but right now, she was . . . anxious. The first day of school was a big deal. Among other things, today was the day she and all the other new school children in the village would finally hear *The Story of Dorn*. Molly *desperately* wanted to ask her mother about *The Story*, but she wasn't allowed. It was an informal rule of the village: No One Shall Spoil *The*

Story For The Children. Molly was excited to hear it, but she had other things on her mind.

"Yes, but," Molly said, "I wish I was *more* like you."

Alice looked at Molly out of the corner of her eye. "Wish to be more like yourself, Molly. I promise you, that's all you need. You're the real pot of gold, you are!"

Molly had her doubts. It seemed to her that her mother was amazing, and she was just . . . Molly.

"I would also wish Da' liked me as much as you do," she said in a small voice.

Alice looked at Molly with a bear hug of a smile and eyes like gimlets.

"Molly, I want you to listen to me carefully. Your father loves you very, very much. He's just sometimes . . ." She sighed and shook her head.

". . . awkward about how he shows it."

"I know he *loves* me, Ma'. I wish he *liked* me."

Alice peered thoughtfully at Molly.

"Do you remember what I've told you about stories?"

"There's always a story behind the story," said Molly eagerly. Alice nodded.

"Well, it's the same with people," said Alice. "With most things, really. Sometimes you have to look deeper than what you see on the surface. Trust his heart, Molly." Alice stood and touched her cheek. "I do, and it's worked out for me. And don't worry," she whispered conspiratorially. "I'll talk to him. Now, have you got your robes for the ceremony?"

"Yes Ma'."

"Excellent! Off you go!"

Molly darted towards the door, then stopped. "Ma'?" she said.

"Yes, chick?"

Molly hesitated.

"Ma' . . . what if *no one* likes me? What if I make a fool of myself?"

"Molly, what are you doing here?" cried Shaun, appearing at the top of the stairs. "You haven't left for school yet?!? Molly, Molly, Molly!! What's wrong with you? You've got to get going!! You'll be late! Alice!!"

"Shaun," said Alice lightly, holding up her hand. "I've made you some breakfast. Why don't you go and get started and I'll come join you directly?"

"But—"

"Shaun," Alice interrupted, turning to him with a smile. "We do what must be done. Go now."

Shaun clapped a hand over his mouth, nodded, and went into the kitchen without another word. Molly didn't know how her mother did it. Her father's worries always melted around Alice like snow in a blast furnace.

"Now, look at me, chick," said Alice. "You're worried. I understand. Of course you are. I was on my first day of school. Perfectly normal. But excited, too, yes?"

Molly nodded and grinned.

"I'll tell you a secret, Molly: excited and scared are the exact same feeling, just looked at from different sides. Focus on the excitement," said Alice brightly. "Ooh! And since we're talking about 'the story behind the story,' today would be a good day to practice."

"Really?" said Molly, swinging her bag over her shoulder.

"No better day than today. Give it a try and we'll talk about it after school, okay?"

"Okay, Ma!"

Alice patted her on the back, and Molly was gone.

* * * *

Molly's first day was a disaster. When the Chief Bickersmith told the children *The Story of Dorn*, Molly tried to listen to "the story behind the story" and it worked for the first time ever, which was actually pretty overwhelming (and scary). Much later, Molly would remember it as being a lot like what happened to her in the first round of The Thieving: her senses had sharpened so acutely that she felt as if she had left her body and seen the shape of all the stories surrounding her—Freddie McGill, who wet his pants every fifteen minutes; Michael O'Halloran, who drooled so much it was like talking to a portable shower unit; Thomas O'Henry, whose nose was constantly runny; all the adults, the school, the chairs, the bugs in the walls, the village—everything. *All* the stories.

Unfortunately, she also foresaw that Dorn would be banished at the end of *The Story* and blurted it out, ruining the surprise for everyone in her entire class.

BOOK OF LEPRECHAUNS: THE LORE GATHERERS

It was the first time that *The Story* had ever been spoiled for a new class of school children. Shaun was beside himself. The Bickersmiths at The Narratorium were apoplectic.

But not Alice. When she heard what Molly had done, her eyes twinkled. Then, in that way she had, she simply went to everyone who was mad and listened and talked and laughed and soon, everyone calmed down. By the end of the week, hardly anyone could remember what they had been mad about.

Alice also had promised to talk to Molly about what had happened, which excited Molly. Her mom knew everything. Unfortunately, they had gotten busy and it kept getting put off.

Then one morning a week later, Alice woke up with a cough. It didn't seem like anything serious, but in the afternoon, she decided to lie down.

"Everything okay?" Shaun had asked.

"Just a sniffle," she said blearily. "I'll be fine. I think I just need to sleep it off."

"Okay. I'll come check on you in a bit."

Alice went to bed, and Shaun got on with his research, his writing, his lists—all the lists—as well as taking care of Molly. He wasn't used to working Molly into his daily routine. It was a disruption, and Shaun wasn't good at having his routine disrupted. But little Molly kept pestering him with games, and needs, and questions, and all the attention a four-year-old demands. He spent most of the day feeling overwhelmed and slightly put out, and he forgot to check on Alice.

When he finally cracked open the door to their bedroom that night after Molly went to sleep, the air was still and Alice lay motionless.

"Alice . . . ? Alice . . . ?"

No response.

He crept in quietly and put his hand on her shoulder. What he felt—or rather what he didn't feel—he had never recovered from. Alice was gone. Just like that. As quick and quiet as a kidnapping. He sat paralyzed with shock for a minute or two, then ran to the doctor and frantically dragged her from her bed back to the house. The doctor was at a loss.

"What's wrong with you, Shaun? How could you have let this happen?!?"

. . . is what Shaun remembered the doctor saying. What she really said was this:

"Did she get up at all after she went to bed?"

"I don't know, I was . . . I don't know."

"Did you see any other symptoms?"

". . . I don't . . . I don't know."

"Did you check on her?"

"No, I . . . I was with Molly . . ."

"I'm so sorry, Shaun. It's just one of those things . . ."

Everything after that was a blur. The doctor had asked some other questions and offered what comfort she could, but she might as well have been talking to a stone.

Shaun stayed up the whole night with Alice, hardly able to think straight or even breathe, wishing he could have the last twelve hours back.

The next morning, Molly knew something bad had happened. When she got up, her father looked . . . empty, and he immediately hustled her outside for a walk without any breakfast. He never did that. Shaun always insisted she eat breakfast first thing every morning, no matter what. It was one of his Rules. Also, he was so quiet as they walked. Shaun was never what you would call chatty, but as he walked heavily up the hill that rose behind their house, a silence hung over him darker and thicker than the early morning fog.

Shaun had no destination in mind, but they found themselves climbing to the big, flat rock high on the hill where they had picnics in the summer. The forest looked so peaceful from up there in the grey light of early dawn. They sat quietly for a while just taking in the view until at last, Shaun told Molly she would never see her mother again.

Molly had questions. So many questions. Shaun answered what he could, but to the only question that mattered—why?—well, what could he say? How could he tell her she died because of his carelessness?

Finally, Molly ran out of questions and just cried and cried and cried and cried. Shaun cried too, and held her tightly, and they sat there together until the sunrise penetrated the fog and its golden light wrapped itself around them as they wrapped themselves around each other. When the fog had burned away, so had Molly's tears.

The sky was blue.

The sun was warm on her face.

It was a beautiful morning.

They spent the whole day in the woods because Shaun couldn't bear going home to an empty house. Late in the afternoon, as sunlight streamed through the trees, they passed an hour or two gathering food, and Shaun even caught a grouse that he roasted over a fire. He didn't have much of an appetite. Molly ate it hungrily.

But as the shadows lengthened and darkness closed in around their campfire, Shaun could no longer put off the inevitable. He cleaned the campsite, and they went home to say goodbye. Shaun had asked some neighbors to bury Alice in a quiet, shaded spot at the back of their garden. He had wanted to bury her himself because he felt he owed it to Alice, but he had to protect Molly. Such things were nothing a four-year-old needed to see.

That's what he told himself, anyway. The truth was, he just couldn't face putting Alice in the ground.

* * * *

That night, Molly dreamed of spending the day with her mother—just walking in the house, the garden, everywhere. They didn't talk. It was one of those dreams where it felt like they were always *trying* to talk about something important and secret, but couldn't find any place to do it privately. Still, it was pure happiness just to be near her. The dream was so real that when she woke the next morning and felt her absence, she started crying all over again.

Wiping her eyes, she went to find her father, but he wasn't in the kitchen. No breakfast had been made. That wasn't right. Her dad always made breakfast. Without breakfast, without her dad banging around in the kitchen, the house felt even emptier. She looked into her dad's room and saw him lying motionless. Terrified, she ran to the bed and shook him.

"DA'! DA'!!!"

Shaun just moaned and rolled over slowly. Molly sighed with relief.

"Da'," she said softly, "I had a bad dream. Actually, it was a good dream, but I felt bad after."

Her father didn't move or even open his eyes. Finally, Molly asked, "Da', can I please have some breakfast?"

"Uh-huh," Shaun grunted. Then he rolled over and went back to sleep.

After a few minutes of watching her father snore, Molly decided that she was on her own for breakfast, so she tip-toed out of the room, and made herself some bread and butter. She also ate a few berries because her father always insisted on having fruit with breakfast. Then she cleaned her dish, just as she had been taught, and sat back down at the table, not knowing what to do.

Fortunately, Ms. O'Leana, the neighbor who lived next door, came calling. Molly liked Ms. O'Leana. She was elderly, smart, and above all, friendly.

When Molly opened the door, she said, "Molly! Oh, I'm so glad to see you!" Ms. O'Leana gave her a hug and knelt down. "I'm so sorry, Molly. Listen to me: no matter what, we're all going to make sure you're okay. Alright? Everyone. The whole village. We all love you. Understood?"

Molly nodded.

"Now, I need your help," Ms. O'Leana said, standing briskly with a groan. "Mr. O'Finn brought me a fresh egg he stole from a farm this morning, and I would love to get your opinion. I cooked it up, but I *think* I put in too much parsley. Mr. O'Finn says it's fine as is, but I want to know what *you* think. You have such good taste in food. Would you try some? I'm always trying to refine the recipe. After forty-some years, I think I've *almost* got it. I also brought some bread and butter to go with it. Want some? I always think bread and butter makes eggs taste better, don't you?"

Molly did think bread and butter made eggs taste better, and she was happy to give Ms. O'Leana her opinions about anything and even happier to have a hot breakfast. Also, having something to do—and someone to do it with—felt better than sitting alone with her thoughts.

Ms. O'Leana stayed with her all morning and into the afternoon. When they went over to Ms. O'Leana's house to make dinner, Molly noticed that the village was . . . different. Alice's death had shocked everyone. Without discussion or any official planning, people had been quietly gathering on the streets. All was solemn at first. People shared their hugs and tears, followed by stories and songs, and then a bottle. After a few hours, you might have thought it was a festival, if not for all the crying. They lit firepits and placed makeshift grates over them so that food could be cooked for all. Beers and wines, jealously guarded for years, now poured freely. In the village square, Gwynn McWalker played her reed whistle with Kris O'Vancher on his spider's harp, Bitty McGlynn on an oversized rabbit-skin drum, and Kate and Macky McSchark on grasshopper fiddles.

Together, the village sang Alice to her rest.

BOOK OF LEPRECHAUNS: THE LORE GATHERERS

* * * *

Ms. O'Leana quietly spread the word that Shaun was in a bad way, and for a week or two, a steady stream of friends and neighbors began showing up at the house, bringing food and drink and idle gossip. No one gave Molly or Shaun any advice. They just cleaned the house, washed clothes, warmed up meals, and repaired whatever needed to be mended. Some even coaxed a few morsels of food into Shaun, who didn't get out of bed for weeks.

Mostly, they looked after Molly. They made sure she never felt alone, got her to bed on time, got her meals, read her stories, played, and listened to anything she wanted to talk about, which included just about everything, except her mother.

Then, on the first morning of the fourth week after Alice died, Shaun was startled awake by a voice in his head that was as loud and clear as a bell:

Shaun, get up this instant and take care of our daughter!

It was Alice's voice. Shaun didn't even question it. Then it came more soothingly.

Shaun, we do what must be done.

Shaun had lived most of his life based on one unbreakable rule: Always Listen to Alice. He had never gone wrong listening to Alice, and it seemed foolish to stop now just because she was dead. If Alice was still talking to him, maybe everything would be okay. Eventually.

So, Shaun pulled himself out of bed slowly, washed and dressed himself with considerable effort, and did his best to choke down something more substantial than crackers.

Things got better after that morning.

Molly often saw her father talking to himself, but she didn't care. Nor did she ask who he was talking to (well, she tried once—only once—and her father broke down crying; he was fragile these days and she didn't want to risk losing him, too). Nor did it matter that Shaun now began obsessively checking their gold every single morning. None of that mattered. All that mattered was that she had one of her parents back.

A piece of him, at least.

CHAPTER 2

Ancient Rome!

By now, you have probably figured out that, contrary to what we see in movies, lots of serious magic happens without big flashing lights, claps of thunder, or even orchestral accompaniment. Lightning bolts, wind machines, and Dolby-quality sound effects are rare. Movies and stage magicians traffic in such flourishes because they have to spend their special effects budgets on something. But leprechaun magic—the real thing—does not need to draw attention to itself.

So, when Shaun whispered his spell, there were no fireworks or dazzling displays. The only clue any onlooker would have had that some seriously impressive magic had just occurred was that Molly, Shaun, Dorker, and Reynard abruptly found themselves in the middle of an open-air market in the center of ancient Rome surrounded by people in strange clothing busily going about their day.

The first thing Molly, Shaun, and Dorker did was throw up.

What no one ever tells you about time travel is how completely different the world *smelled* even one hundred years ago. The stink that accosted their noses with the savagery of a rhinoceros was what you get when a large population of people is crammed into a relatively small area with only a rudimentary sewer. Even with the Roman sewage system, which was revolutionary at the time, people still emptied chamber pots out their windows onto the streets. Plus, horses were a primary mode of transportation, so there were a lot of them on the Roman roads. Add to that all the cattle, chickens, pigs, and other animals that paraded through the streets every day, none of whom were very particular about where they (let's just say it) pooped. In short, the vast Roman citizenry shared their streets—and their bodily waste—with a well-represented segment of the domesticated animal kingdom. The ancient Romans didn't appear to mind. They were used to the smell, just as we are used to the smells of our day, all of which illustrates just how adaptable human beings can be.

But because Molly, Dorker, and Shaun had not lived their lives inside a cow's small intestine, the olfactory assault was overpowering. Their nostrils almost involuntarily sealed shut.

The upside was that it diffused the tension they were all feeling. You can only be so angry when you can barely breathe.

"Phaw! What a stink!" said Molly when she had recovered a little. "What happened to the Colosseum?"

"If we're where—I mean *when*—I hope we are," said Shaun covering his nose with his sleeve, "it hasn't been built yet."

"How do we figure out the date?" asked Dorker.

Shaun ignored Dorker, closed his eyes and made some complicated movements with his wrists.

"What are you doing, Da'?"

"Time bubble," said Shaun. "It's a little pocket of today held in place, so that if we come back tomorrow or next week, we can still get home."

When he was done, they quickly scuttled into a nearby alley. As Molly sat down with her back against a wall, the weight of what had just happened washed over her. The world she now walked had already happened—over two thousand years ago! All the people, all the animals, talking, braying, going about their lives—every one of them—had been dust in the earth millennia before she

---

As Shaun explains in his book *History's Great Time Travelling Disasters*, it turns out that a time portal is a bit of a one-way street. Whowood McFardlesbear, an early lore gatherer time traveler, was the first to discover this unfortunate fact. As a test, shortly after the birth of his daughter, Whowood went back in time exactly one year, having stumbled upon a portal. Thinking he had time to kill, he spent a week or two enjoying himself on a nice secluded beach, away from the massive responsibility he knew awaited him as a new father. His distress was almost unspeakable when he tried to go back to his family and found that the time portal had disappeared. He spent a year desperately trying and failing to return, and when the year had passed, he finally went home on the very day he had left. When he did, he met himself (before his unfortunate trip to the past), his wife, and—to his devastating shock—their new baby *boy*.

Fortunately, the other Whowood and his wife were very open-minded about the whole thing and invited him to come live with them as the baby boy's uncle. He accepted their generous offer and stayed with them for a few years, but he was always tormented by the loss of his baby girl. One day, he simply vanished, never to be heard from again.

was even born. The more she tried to wrap her head around it, the more she felt her brain expand and contract like a bellows. She felt herself drifting away as if in a dream when her father grabbed her arms.

"Molly!" he said, giving her a shake. "Molly, look at me! I'm your Dad. You're Molly." He slapped her hands. "These are my hands. These are your hands. Look at me!"

Molly blinked and looked at her dad.

"Say it, Molly," said Shaun. "You're Molly. I'm your dad. Say it!"

"You're Molly. I'm your dad."

"No," Shaun shook his head. "Try again. Say, '*I'm* Molly. *You're* my dad.'"

"I'm Molly, you're my dad," she muttered indistinctly.

"Good! Say it again!"

He made her say it several more times until it sounded like she believed it. Then he gave her some water.

"What happened?" she said. Her head was still swimming.

"Never mind. Follow m—" Shaun began, but Dorker came up behind him and gave him a big hug.

"I'm Molly; you're my dad," said Dorker with a dazed, but blissful smile.

"Shillelagh!" cursed Shaun as he turned and grabbed Dorker.

What Molly had experienced—and Dorker was now experiencing—was a "time snap." Imagine for a moment that you are in outer space. Out there, ideas like "up," "down," "North," "West," etc., have little meaning because there is almost no gravity and no other point of reference. On Earth, these ideas are easy to grasp because we're firmly stuck to the ground. No one needs to tell you that birds are above us and worms are below because it's obvious. But if you and your friend are floating in space, are you above her? Is she above you? Who can say?

A similar thing happened to Molly and Dorker, only with time instead of space. Finding yourself suddenly two thousand years in the past can leave you with no understanding of who you are, and no way to figure it out.

When Dorker finally sounded like he knew he was Dorker again, Shaun summed it up thusly:

"Time travel can be rough."

Molly nodded. Dorker threw up again.

"So, what now?" she asked.

"We need to learn Latin. Come on."

"But Da'!" said Molly, "Aggie and Antonio gave me a Latin dictionary!" She reached into her pack and pulled out the book triumphantly. It did not produce the "Molly Saves the Day" reaction she had hoped for.

"Why would they—?" said Shaun, perplexed. "We don't need that. Come on, Molly. Dorker . . . try not to throw up again."

* * * *

Aromas fair and odors sweet
Unto my nose this world doth greet.

. . . thought Poor Reynard.

The fragrances of ancient Rome were an evolving landscape to Reynard. Smells from the dung of a thousand animals (humans included) wafted around him, flooding his brain with information.

Imagine a complex computer network with twenty times more data than the system was designed to handle surging through it. Something like that was happening in the olfactory centers of Reynard's brain. Systems long dormant reawakened, popping and fizzing to life, re-forging connections evolution had selected for extinction generations ago.

He didn't know where he was, but he knew almost instantly that this was no mere change in geography. This world was old. The stresses of Rome's livestock floated through the air directly into his nostrils, and then individual stories took shape: a cow who had been whipped one too many times and was looking for the moment to escape; a horse whose rider did not know (or care) that she had a bad tooth and the bridle hurt her mouth; a human who had not eaten in days on the verge of starvation.

The smells swirled around him, weaving a tapestry of casual brutality and neglect that warned him of danger at every turn.

* * * *

After some furtive sneaking around Rome's open-air market, Shaun finally saw a stall selling pottery where a couple of Roman legionaries were chatting. It was perfect. A colorful piece of fabric was draped over the stall's table and hung all the way to the ground, providing ample cover for all of them, even the fox. As furtively as possible, they made their way under the table and ducked out of sight. It was cramped and a bit stuffy among the collection of pots and figurines, but at least it was out of the sun.

"Molly," whispered Dorker. "Can I see it? The dictionary? I've got a terrible ear for languages."

Molly handed Dorker the dictionary as they settled in and listened.

What Molly did not know (because she was only twelve years old and had never been outside her village) was that leprechauns pick up languages very quickly. This is because they have been around longer than any other creature on Earth. Some lore gatherers subscribe to the controversial theory that leprechauns predate the Earth itself. Whether or not this claim is true, what is certainly true is that because their civilization was rich and thriving long before the first proto-humans got the brilliant idea of walking upright and shaving, leprechauns have been in a unique position to influence human evolution. In short, every language spoken on planet Earth, no matter how different from other languages, has its roots in ancient Leprechaun. Human ears have difficulty identifying the numerous common characteristics of English, Mandarin Chinese, and Swahili, for example, but to a leprechaun, these languages will all sound relatively the same, as well as familiar. As a result, almost any leprechaun can listen to a new human language and pick it up within about ten minutes. A human linguist, who was once fortunate enough to capture a lore gatherer, asked how they do it. The lore gatherer reportedly shrugged and said, "Once you figure out the vowels and consonants, the rest is just talking."

Dorker, unfortunately, was the rare exception—a leprechaun with no ear for languages. On a vacation with his father, he had once spent three fruitless months trying to learn Welsh. His father picked it up quickly, but Dorker complained: "They might as well be talking with a mouthful of raw carrots." What he lacked in natural ability, however, Dorker made up for in diligence.

Molly, on the other hand, was amazed to find that what had initially sounded like garbled nonsense was quickly resolving into comprehensible speech—like slowly tuning a radio to the correct frequency. As the speakers' words became clearer and clearer, this was what she heard:

". . . asfxcecm weepoue xxcwfffff and that is why all leave is cancelled," said the smaller of the two Roman legionaries. He looked both extremely fit and extremely cagey, fully capable of holding his own against the bigger soldier (who was really big) and possibly two or three more just like him.

"That stinks," said the bigger one.

The shorter one shrugged. They looked at the pottery in silence for a moment, but it was clear that something else was bothering the big one. After some painful and difficult thinking, he asked:

"Lucius, what's an Ide?"

"An Ide?"

"Yeah, you know. The Ides of March, like that Soothsayer said."

"Are you serious, Gracus?"

At this point, the street peddler—who was old, more than a little deaf, and tired of these two men talking instead of buying pots—intervened. "What's he talking about?"

"Ides," said Lucius.

"Why're you talking about that?"

"Because someone claiming to be a soothsayer—"

"A what-sayer?" said the peddlar. "Tooth? Is that like a speech impediment? What do teeth have to do with it? I thought you were looking at my pots!"

"SOOTH-sayer!" Lucius shouted. "It's someone who can see the future. This one really is magical, apparently. He yelled out at Caesar the other day: 'Beware the Ides of March!'"

"Why'd he do that?"

"How would I know? I wasn't there. All I know is, he shouted it. Everyone's talking about it. Caesar was pretty upset," said Lucius.

"Anyway—"

"I hear Caesar has bad teeth," said the street peddler conversationally.

Lucius blinked.

"What?" said the street peddler. "Don't look at me like that. You hear things in my line of work. Anyway, who cares? Do you want to buy a pot?"

"*Anyway,*" said Lucius meaningfully, "it's all to do with the moon."

"What is?" said Gracus.

"Ides," said Lucius.

"*Tides* is also to do with the moon," said Gracus, pleased with this intellectual contribution. "And you know what? 'Tides' rhymes with—"

"Yes," said Lucius wincing. "You're right. Well done."

Gracus scowled. "But what's the moon got to do with Ides?" he said.

"You know who has good teeth?" said the street peddler. "My granddaughter." He felt on firmer ground now that he had cunningly steered the conversation towards a familiar topic. From there, he hoped to drive it back towards his pots, re: the purchasing thereof.

"Okay look," said Lucius, "Before Caesar's new calendar, you had your standard lunar calendar.[*] In every month of a lunar calendar, you've got the Nones, the Ides, and the Kalends, yes? You know that, right?"

"Yes," lied Gracus.

"Excellent," said Lucius.

"Got a smile that would warm your heart, my granddaughter does," said the street peddler. "I've made a pot with her picture on it, look."

"*And*," said Lucius, forging onward, "in the course of a month, you've got the half-moon, the full moon, and the new moon, right?"

Gracus had never thought about the moon much beyond knowing it was there at night and sometimes had different shapes. He didn't know what the shapes meant, but this didn't seem like the right time to admit that to Lucius.

"My poor granddaughter," said the street peddler sadly. "She has a rare medical condition. Needs to make a special sacrifice at the temple of Apollo. But she has no money. Now if you were to buy this pot . . ."

"So," said Lucius, who, plowing through fields of idiocy, could now see the finish line and was determined to get there, "the Nones of a month is when the half-moon appears, Kalends is the new moon, and the Ides is the full moon." Lucius looked at Gracus triumphantly.

Gracus looked at the street peddler.

The street peddler looked at Gracus.

They both turned back to Lucius.

"And what was the part about teeth . . . ?" said Gracus.

---

[*] For those readers not up on their history, Julius Caesar introduced a new calendar to the world that went into effect on January 1, 45 BC. The prior Roman calendar had been based largely on the moon's revolution around the earth, but people who studied such things had determined that a calendar based on the revolution of the earth around sun could be more accurate.

No one knows what the lore gatherer calendar is based on, but it has been speculated that it is keyed to some fundamental rhythm driving the universe. As has been noted, its accuracy would make a Swiss watch maker lay down his tools and take up knitting.

Lucius gave up. "It's tomorrow, alright? The Ides of March is tomorrow."

"Are you two going to buy anything or not?" demanded the street peddler. These two clearly had no interest in his granddaughter, and he was tired of this conversation.

"Well, why didn't he just *say* that, then?" said Gracus. "Why go on about Ides, when he could have just said, 'Hey Caesar! At the full moon, watch yourself!'"

Lucius sighed. He was not a complicated man. Like many born in this era, he never had any formal education. Through a combination of native cunning and raw intelligence, he had risen through the ranks of the Roman military to a level of leadership few recruits could ever hope to achieve. He liked his life, and he liked the men he commanded. But he also had a certain poetry in his soul (which he kept carefully hidden), as well as a natural understanding of people. On another day, he might have attempted to explain to Gracus that sometimes a good lie has to be dressed up a little to get anyone to pay attention. But just now, the effort felt like more trouble than it was worth.

"How much for the pot with your daughter on it, then?" said Lucius.

"Ah!" said the street peddler. "Good sir, don't waste your time on that old chamber pot. I can tell you're a man of taste and sophistication. Have you, by chance, ever seen the sculptures at the Oracle of—"

Without looking at what he was doing, the street peddler reached under the table as he spoke, expecting to grab a small statuette of the Roman goddess Athena. Instead, he grabbed a very surprised Molly, pulled her out from under the table, and presented her to the Roman legionnaires. Dangling by her backpack, Molly looked into Lucius's astonished eyes and blinked.

A very crowded moment followed in which many thoughts passed through the minds of the various players in the unfolding scene, and several things happened in rapid succession. Let us therefore slow down the clock so that we don't miss anything.

Molly thought: *Gulp!*

The street peddler thought: "Hmm, that's odd. Statuettes aren't usually so wriggly. I don't recall any of the Roman goddesses carrying a bag on her back. By god, this sculptor was good. You can almost see it breathe! Wait a minute— It IS breathing! Eeeaauuuuaghghg!!! WHAT IS IT? AHH! KILL IT! KILL IT! KILL IT! OH NO! MY POTS!!"

Gracus thought: ". . . ."

Shaun thought: "Good, the portal worked! We're back just in time for—where's Molly?!? I told her to sit still and listen! Can't I trust her for anything? She can't be running around ancient Rome on her own! What can she possibly—Oh no! No! No! No! Hurrrup! OOOOOF!"

Lucius thought: "This statuette looks like a very small girl. Wait, it *is* a very small girl. A very, *VERY* small girl! What on earth—Wait! What the? OWWWWWWW!! OW! OW! OW! OW! STOP IT! STOP IT! STOP IT!"

Reynard thought: *Nor man, nor beast shall Molly fear*
 While Poor Reynard's sharp teeth are UNGH!

Dorker thought: "Wow, Latin is a fascinating language, but I bet the verb declensions are tricky. I've never been good at verb declensions. What *is* a verb declension? I've never been sure. What does 'declension' even mean? That's one of those words that loses its meaning the more you say it. Declension, declension, declension. How does a verb declenzsh? Declense? Declench? Maybe Mr. McClanahan will know. Hey, where'd the table go? Aren't we meant to be hiding? HEY, LET GO! HEEEEELLLLLLLLLLLPPPPPPPPPP!!!"

Now that everyone's thoughts are clear, let's rewind and start the clock in real time.

When the street peddler realized that he was holding a—well, he had no idea *what* it was he was holding, but whatever it was, he didn't want to be holding it anymore—he dropped Molly onto the table.

Before Molly could move, Shaun, who had figured out what had happened, upended the table, hoping to cause enough chaos that they could escape.

As various ceramic pots went flying through the air, the upended table launched Molly onto the head of Gracus, who had become suddenly paralyzed at the sight of a very tiny girl dangling from his nostril.

Poor Reynard's fur bristled as he stood ready to attack. Unfortunately, one of the pots came down squarely on his head, leaving him badly dazed. Unable to see straight, he stumbled to find somewhere safe where he could lie down and, hopefully, pass out.

Lucius, who had recovered his wits more quickly than Gracus, made a grab for Molly, but not before Shaun drove a well-aimed kick into Lucius's shin.

Lucius yelled out in pain, stumbled and, unfortunately, fell right on top of Shaun.

The street peddler, meanwhile, had grabbed a broom and started hitting Gracus repeatedly on the head in a desperate attempt to kill whatever this thing was that was destroying all his pots.

Molly dodged a few blows, but upon seeing her father fall under Lucius, she pushed off from Gracus's chest, leapt to Lucius's shoulders, and began hammering his head with her bare fists.

Dorker had barely registered the chaos, when from out of nowhere, a chicken whose cage had been unlocked by a falling pottery shard (and who had some attachment issues caused by the loss of so many eggs), picked him up in her beak by the shirt collar and ran off down the street beating her wings furiously.

As Molly pounded on Lucius, let us note that leprechauns are small, but harder and tougher than you think they're going to be. Humans have never been able to determine their true origins, and even lore gatherers themselves disagree. As has been noted, some think they have been around since at least the earliest dinosaurs, and some think long before that. The point is, humans don't really know what sort of . . . *stuff* leprechauns are made of. Their muscles are tough and sinewy, and their bones are hard and dense. A 15-pound leprechaun has the approximate strength of a 75-pound human.

Lucius may have been among the first humans to experience this fact, because Molly's blows, while hardly incapacitating, hurt a lot more than he expected. It was as if someone had attached two walnuts to a string and was repeatedly whacking him on the forehead with them. But you don't get to be the kind of seasoned soldier Lucius was without knowing how to take some painful hits and keep your wits about you. Through the pain of Molly's whirlwind fists, he realized that one of these creatures was trapped underneath him, and the other one was, rather excruciatingly, right in front of his nose. With the practiced skill of a man used to fighting more than one assailant, Lucius rolled, grabbed Molly in one hand, and reached under himself to grab Shaun with the other. Shaun was unconscious.

Lucius looked at Molly.

"Hello," he said, trying to focus his eyes.

Molly spluttered with rage, hammering her fists on Lucius's hands. "LET

US GO!! LET US GO!! YOU BIG . . . YOU BETTER NOT HURT HIM!!"
But Lucius held on.

"Settle yourself!" said Lucius. "We can do this easy, or we can do it hard," he said, giving Molly a little squeeze.

Molly shrieked a little and began hitting him even harder and more ferociously.

Lucius was impressed.

"Or perhaps I should squeeze him," he said, holding up Shaun to her face.

"DON'T YOU DARE!! DON'T YOU DARE!!"

A veil of rage fell before Molly's eyes and the world went red. Yes, her father was infuriating, but she loved him. The thought of this soldier torturing him to manipulate her was more than she could take. She began vibrating like a small earthquake, as power surged through her. She didn't know where it came from, but it felt like all the anger, frustration, and injustice of the world now compressed into her muscles as concentrated hate. She hated this soldier. She hated feeling so powerless. She hated that her father had been knocked out and that their gold had been stolen and that they were in a strange place and her mother was *dead* and nothing was fair and she wished she could HIT the whole world!

So that's what she did.

In the space of a breath, she saw the world in her mind's eye as if she were floating in space—saw all its cruelty and intolerance and wanted to smash it all. Her hatred gathered in her forearm like an electrical storm. At the very last moment, a small part of sanity behind her eyes saw what she was about to do—saw that she might smash way more than she wanted to—and *PUUUULLLLLLLLED* back.

She was able to restrain the worst of it, but she could no more have stopped her fist than a cloud can stop a lightning strike.

* * * *

"I don't know what you did," said Lucius carefully as Molly slowly regained consciousness, "but you probably shouldn't do it again."

Molly groaned and opened her eyes to see the huge, slightly charred face of Lucius looking at her. "What happ—Oh." Molly blinked and looked around. Human bodies lay on the ground around them, though some were slowly coming to their senses. Even Lucius looked a little shaky, like he was still getting his bearings, but he was a man who had been knocked down so many times he knew how to get up quickly. Everything else around her—carts, tables, chairs—was in pieces, as though a bomb had detonated. The pot seller's collection was little more than dust.

"No," she said, horrified. "I didn't mean to—"

"You almost killed that man," said Lucius gesturing to the pot seller. Gracus, who still couldn't quite stand up, had managed to wake him, but he was lying very still. Molly put her hands to her head.

"No, no, no, no, no!" she said. Then she remembered. "Where's—?"

"I've got him," said Lucius, gesturing. Shaun was cradled in his arms. "He's still unconscious, but I don't think he's any worse than before."

"You give him to me!" Molly said, getting up and squaring off with Lucius.

"No!" he said, raising his voice for the first time and standing. Then, more gently, he said: "I mean you no harm, but we have to get you out of here. People are coming. And I know someone who very much wants to meet you."

Molly paused to look at Lucius more closely. On the one hand, his face seemed open and honest; on the other hand, he was holding her father. How far could she really trust him?

"This is your father?" Lucius asked.

Molly said nothing.

"Look, I'm sorry about what happened. From when I fell, I mean. It was an accident. I didn't mean to hurt him. But we need to go. Now."

Molly frowned and quickly considered her options. She could start hitting him again, but that didn't seem to do much good. And she clearly needed to control her temper. Having almost accidentally killed someone *really* upset her. She could run, but where on earth would she go? She looked around and didn't see Dorker anywhere, which was annoying. She ought to go and find him, but she couldn't leave her father in his present state. Certainly not with Lucius. The fox had disappeared as well.

She decided her first priority was to make sure her dad was okay. And, truth be told, Molly was scared. She felt safer staying with her father, even if he was unconscious.

"Put him down too!" she demanded.

"I can't do that. I'm sorry. I have to take him to see my friend, or it'll be my head on the chopping block. And since your father—it is your father, isn't it?" Lucius asked, attempting a friendly smile.

Molly didn't return the smile, but nodded reluctantly.

"Good. I thought so," said Lucius. "As he is, I think I better carry him. C'mon. I promise not to hurt him."

"You better not!" Molly warned.

"Gracus!" Lucius barked. "Stay here and make sure everyone is okay."

"Where are you going?" said Gracus.

"Hey!" said the street peddler, who was now conscious enough to realize his entire inventory had been reduced to powder. "Look at what you've done! Who's going to pay for all my pots?"

Lucius smiled.

"Pay the man, Gracus," he said, and marched off.

"What?" said Gracus helplessly. "Wait, how much is it? I don't have that much!"

The street peddler smiled. He had been a salesman on the hard-scrabble streets of Rome during a politically tumultuous and unstable time for over forty years. You don't survive in that kind of environment without an almost feral sense for opportunity. The street peddler could smell a sucker the way a shark smells blood, and open-mouthed Gracus was a wounded carp thrashing in the water. Large and intimidating as he was, Gracus shuddered involuntarily when the street peddler laid his head back on the sand, closed his eyes and said:

"Not to worry. I'm sure we can come to an . . . *arrangement*."[*]

---

[*] Lest the historical significance of this scene get lost, it is worth remarking that, due to Gracus's empty coin purse, the street peddler invented the world's first installment plan right then and there.

CHAPTER 3

Captive

Things were moving quickly. Too quickly for Molly. No sooner had they traveled back in time than her temper had *literally* exploded (she hadn't really digested what *that* meant just yet), Dorker and Reynard had gone missing, and her father was unconscious in the hands of a human. All in all, it seemed like a bad start.

Also, ancient Rome was waaaaaaay hotter than Ireland. Dustier, too. The roads in the marketplace were a combination of cobblestones and dirt, and because millions of feet and hooves traveled across them daily, the dust never really settled. It hung in the air like a haze and stuck to sweaty skin. When the light was right, Lucius looked as if he had been sculpted from sand.

Molly regarded the man carrying her father. He had a jaw like a shovel, his muscles were thick and ropey, and his hands looked like they were made of knuckles. His was a body hewn by years of hard labor, combat training, and actual combat. Scars on his arms, legs, and face declared him the survivor of more than one violent military battle. He radiated granite hardness but moved with disarming fluidity. And true to his word, he handled Molly's father firmly, but with care.

He was trying to get Molly chatting, but it wasn't easy. Not because Molly wouldn't talk, mind you. Far from it. No, the problem was that leprechauns are very good at not being seen when they put their minds to it, and Molly had put her mind to it like a hammer to a nail. They can't actually disappear (at least, not without some seriously advanced magic), but they can take advantage of humanity's natural blindness. Humans go through most of their lives so focused on other things—work; who won which sports event; am I too fat; am I too thin; will other people like me; do my clothes look okay; etc.—that they often never see what is right in front of them. Which is too bad, really. The world is full of some pretty amazing things. Leprechauns are only one of them.

In particular, humans do not see what they don't expect to see—and let's face it, *no one* expects to see a leprechaun. Even Lucius, who held all the evidence you could ask for right there in his hands, still couldn't quite believe what he saw. That disbelief was all Molly needed. She didn't disappear; she just . . . arranged matters so that Lucius couldn't see what he didn't believe in. She hoped this would keep him off-balance and perhaps create an opportunity for escape.

"Can I ask you a ques—hey!" said Lucius spinning around. "Where'd you go?!"

"What are you talking about? I'm right here," said Molly, reappearing as if she had never left.

"Oh," said Lucius. "For a minute, I thought you had—HEY! Stay where I can see you!"

"I am where you can see me," said Molly in a reasonable tone, appearing at his side again.

"You keep disappearing!"

"Disappearing?!" said Molly. "Everyone knows that's impossible, don't be ridiculous. I'm right here. It's not my fault you can't see what's right in front of you. Shouldn't go blaming me for that. Fancy blaming me for you not being able to see what's right in front of your face. You just worry about not dropping my Da'."

"I'm not going to drop him. Look, I'm—HEY! COME ON!" At this point, Lucius was practically turning in circles. He had faced challenging opponents in his military career, but nothing quite like a recalcitrant pre-teen lore gatherer.

"I. Am. Right. Here. Are we walking or what?" said Molly.

"Stop doing that!"

"Doing what? I'm just trying to walk," said Molly matter-of-factly. "You're the one who can't seem to walk. What's the matter—heat getting to you? My Da' getting too heavy? Want me to take him?"

A crowd had started to gather. The sound of Molly's explosion had drawn a crowd to the general area, and so far, the emergency had allowed the three of them to pass largely unnoticed. But a soldier wildly spinning in circles and talking to himself while carrying a very, very small man—that tends to draw attention. Noticing this, Lucius put his head down and quickly continued on his way. Molly gave a few curious Romans a swift kick in the ankle to drive them away.

After walking for a few minutes and feeling confident they had escaped any meaningful notice, Lucius said under his breath:

"Are you still here?"

"'Course I'm still here," said Molly. "I never left."

"Look why don't we start with names. What's your name? I'm Lucius. What should I call you?"

There was a troubled silence, but finally Molly spoke.

"My name is Molly."

"Molly. Hello, Molly. Er . . . It's nice to meet you."

"Whatever," Molly sniffed.

"And what's your father's name?"

"My name is enough," said Molly.

"Now Molly, don't make me do something to your father I'll regret."

This threat was met with a sudden sharp blow to Lucius's right temple that briefly left him seeing stars. He shook it off quickly, but Molly was now standing on his shoulder, leaning over, and grabbing him painfully by the ear.

"You understand now, yes?" she whispered fiercely. "You're not the only one who can hurt someone, right? I'm following you by *choice*, not by your say so. Anything happens to my Da' . . . you'll feel it *double*."

Molly jumped back down to the ground.

Lucius recognized bravado and desperation when he heard it. He rightly guessed that if Molly could overpower him, she already would have done so. But she was scared and angry, which made her unpredictable. Rather than escalate an already volatile situation with further threats (and to avoid more hits to the head or another possible explosion), he decided to try a different approach.

"Where are you from, Molly?"

Molly didn't know how to answer that in a way that wouldn't sound insane.

"A long way away," she finally said.

"Are there more like you and your father?"

This was met with silence.

"Let's just back up," said Lucius. "What *are* you and your father?"

Still silence.

"I mean, you're not just very small humans, are you?"

"Pfft! Humans! Ha!"

"I'll take that as a 'no,'" said Lucius. "Are you demons?"

"You really don't know anything, do you?" said Molly.

"You're right, Molly, I don't know much," said Lucius. "But I do know one thing. You're a very brave young girl."

A current of unnurtured pride surged through the silence. Lucius decided to nurture it.

"And strong. Take it from me, Molly, I've fought a lot of men, and that knock you just gave me—WHOO!"

"You think if you compliment me, I'll start liking you," said Molly, who was too smart to fall for anything like that.

"No, Molly," said Lucius solemnly. "I can already tell you're much too smart to fall for anything like that. I wouldn't insult your intelligence."

Molly knew what he was up to. She wasn't starting to like him. Definitely not. It took more than a compliment or two. Humans really weren't as clever as they thought they were. That said, this *was* the very first human she had ever spoken to, and she *was* in an unfamiliar time and place. Maybe this was an opportunity. It was risky, but she didn't know how badly her father had been hurt, and it would be nice to know *someone* in ancient Rome, someone who actually knew their way around and how things worked—a friend maybe . . . ?

No. Not a friend *really* because . . . well, how would *that* work? Besides, she didn't even like him—*at all*, she was very definite about that—much less trust him. But where else was she likely to find help? No, she would just talk, she would learn what she could, and if they became friends—if she started to like him—well that wasn't her fault because, as Lucius observed, she was too smart for that.

Molly was glad to get that straightened out.

"Soooooooooo, Lucius," she said casually. "Who wants to see us so badly?"

"I'll tell you what, Molly," said Lucius, "why don't we play a game?"

"What sort of a game?"

"A game of questions. You ask me one; I ask you one."

"What's the catch?"

"The catch is we have to tell the truth."

Molly paused.

"No tricks?" she said.

"No tricks," said Lucius.

"Okay."

"Can I go first?" said Lucius.

"Yes. My turn!"

"I thought we said no tricks," said Lucius smiling. But Molly was so proud of herself, he gave in.

"Okay, fair enough," he said. "But no more of that, agreed?"

"Who are you taking us to see?" said Molly, ignoring him.

"I'm taking you to see Julius Caesar," said Lucius.

Molly couldn't believe her luck. Just who her dad wanted to see. She didn't know why her dad wanted to see him, but she felt certain he would be pleased.

"Why?" said Molly.

"Ah-ah! My turn," said Lucius.

Molly didn't want to wait her turn, but she bit her lip.

"What *are* you and your father, if you're not demons?"

"We're leprechauns," said Molly.

"What's a leprechaun?"

"Ah-ah! My turn," said Molly with satisfaction. "Why does Julius Caesar want to see us?"

"I don't know," said Lucius.

"You said you'd answer me truthfully!"

"It's true, I don't know!" said Lucius.

"You're a cheater!" said Molly.

"No, I . . . Look, Molly, all I know is that Julius Caesar issued a standing order to all legionnaires to report anything unusual. Something his soothsayer warned about. And I'm sorry, Molly, but you and your father definitely qualify as unusual. I have a hunch you're exactly what Caesar was talking about."

"What's he going to do to us?" said Molly.

"Again, I don't know, Molly. I wish I did."

"He could kill us?"

"He could try," said Lucius with a gleam in his eye. "Something tells me you and your father are not so easy to kill."

"So, you could be taking us to our deaths!" said Molly.

"I told you I would tell you the truth, Molly, and I have. Now, if you want to know what I *believe* . . . I don't believe he wants to kill you."

"But how do you know? You don't know anything!"

"You're right, Molly, I don't. But I've served under him for a long time. He's a smart man. Ruthless, yes, but smart. I don't think he'd try to kill something like you without trying to learn what use he might make of you."

Molly shuddered. She knew this was a brutal time in human history. For most ancient Romans, slavery and other atrocities were a given—just the way of the world. She wondered—did humans consciously ignore the evil in their own souls, or just explain it away? She had to be very careful.

"I think I've earned another question, don't you," said Lucius.

"Go on then."

"What's a leprechaun?"

"What's a leprechaun? That's a stupid question. We're leprechauns! Leprechauns is what we are. Look at us! What more d'you need to know?" Molly snorted. "Right here in front of him, and he asks 'what's a leprechaun?'"

"How am I supposed to know? You're the only two I've ever seen! Just tell me something about yourself."

"Too late, my turn!" Molly enjoyed seeing Lucius getting frustrated. She almost felt sorry for him. He was trying so hard to be fair and nice. Molly decided to go for broke.

"Where does Caesar keep his gold?"

"Why do you want to know that?" said Lucius, suddenly suspicious.

Molly hesitated.

"I think he may have stolen ours," she said.

"You have gold?" he said. The conversation had just taken an unexpectedly interesting turn. Lucius might be willing to withstand any number of blows to the head from Molly if a pile of gold lay at the end of them.

"No, he—" Molly caught herself. "I mean um . . . yyyyyyes? Yes! We do. Pots of it. We're leprechauns, you know. You wanted to know interesting facts about leprechauns? We are known for having pots and pots of gold."

"Really," said Lucius flatly.

"Yes, really!" Molly protested. She was now beginning to appreciate how difficult lying can be. A bungled lie makes the truth hard to swallow.

"No, that's actually absolutely true!" she said. "If there is one thing anyone knows who knows anything about leprechauns, it's that they always have a pot of gold. Humans usually think we keep it at the end of a rainbow, but that would just draw attention. Much better to use concealment spells."

"Spells? You mean like magic? You can do magic?"

Molly gulped.

"Did I say spells? I didn't say spells. Who said spells? I don't know what I said. What do you mean? Anyway, yes, leprechauns have gold. But I expect you probably wouldn't have any use for gold, being a soldier and all. Probably get all the gold you can handle, conquering new countries and killing people and everything. Just forget I said anything about gold. Except the part about wanting to know where Caesar's is. His gold, that is. Where is it?"

In the midst of Molly's confusing, but transparent, efforts to manipulate him, Lucius was actually unable to tell what was true and what was false. Even Shaun might have been impressed.

"Molly, we made a deal," said Lucius. "Truth, okay? I'll tell you what I know about Caesar's gold; you tell me about yours."

Molly hesitated. "Okay, but you have to promise to keep it to yourself. You can't tell anyone. Especially not Caesar."

"Molly, Caesar will question me. He's a good lie detector. I like you, but I'm not *quite* ready to risk my life for you yet. What I will do is promise that if there is any way that I *can* keep it to myself, I will. I can't do any better than that. I'm sorry."

The fact that Lucius said he liked her had not gone unnoticed.

"Not even with the promise of a pot of gold to call your very own . . . ?" Molly said with what she hoped was a beguiling smile.

"Even if I believed you had a pot of gold to give me right here and now, Molly, I can't do any better."

Desperation sometimes requires a calculated risk. Lucius might know something about Caesar's gold that could help them, and right now, he was the best lead Molly had.

"Alright, it's true," Molly said. "Where I come from, humans believe leprechauns have pots of gold. And most of the time, that's true enough. But our pot—my father's, I mean—was lost. Or stolen. I *think* my father thinks that Julius Caesar had something to do with it. That's why we're here. That's why we need to see him. That's the truth. And if you promise to help us, I promise to do my best to see that you share in some of it, if we ever get it back. That's the best *I* can do."

Lucius looked at Molly. "How do I know you're not just here to steal Caesar's gold?"

Molly shrugged. "I guess you don't."

Lucius looked back at the road. If asked to describe himself (and no one ever had), Lucius probably would have used the word, "Professional." He was not a greedy man. He liked what he did and tried to do it well. He had no illusions that history would ever remember someone like him as a "Great Man," if it remembered him at all. Mostly, he was pragmatic. He knew the Roman Gods existed but didn't see much point in believing in them. They did what they did, whether you believed in them or not. Might as well believe in a table. But he had enough imagination to entertain the notion that Molly and her father were . . . what? Not Gods, that seemed certain. Out of the ordinary, yes. Supernatural? He had never seen anything like them before. Clearly, an opportunity of some kind had fallen into his hands. It might be an opportunity to get into enormous trouble, but it might also be something more. The point is, greed is not what drove him to say what he said next, nor the promise of riches and wealth. Call it curiosity. Or maybe even faith. Faith enough, at least, to risk something—but maybe not everything.

"Okay, Molly. I'll tell you what I can about Caesar's gold. But then I have to do something else before I take you to Caesar. And you're going to have to trust me."

"What do you mean?"

"I mean that I have to put you in jail."

CHAPTER 4

Prison

"Where am I?" said Shaun, slowly regaining consciousness. From what he could see through his pounding headache, he was lying on a dirty flagstone floor in a poorly lit room. His last memory was of a human crashing down on top of him, so he considered this an improvement. Turning his head painfully, his blurry eyes discerned Molly's shape sitting over him.

"Are you and Dorker alright?" he said groggily.

"I have good news, and I have bad news," said Molly, weighing her words.

"What happened to Dorker?" said Shaun. Whatever the bad news was, he just assumed it would involve Dorker.

"That's only part of the bad news."

"What's wrong? Where is he?"

"I don't know," said Molly.

"What do you mean you don't—"

"He disappeared in all the commotion when the solider fell on you. I think I saw him being carried off by a chicken."

"A chicken?"

"Yes."

"Seriously?"

"Yes."

"Well . . ." said Shaun. ". . . okay. What's the good news?"

"We're going to see Julius Caesar."

Shaun was impressed.

"That is good news," he said, struggling up onto his elbow. As soon as he got even a little bit upright, however, the room spun three or four times around his head, and he lay back down.

"Just stay still," said Molly. "You took Lucius's full weight."

Shaun closed his eyes and groaned. Then he opened them again.

"*Lucius?*" he said, frowning. "Who's Lucius?"

"The Roman solider that fell on you."

"But you called him Lucius."

"We might be . . . sort of becoming friends."

"Is that more bad news?"

"I don't know yet," said Molly. In their further discussions, Lucius had confirmed that a substantial portion of Caesar's gold was located in Rome, but he hadn't said where. "It may be both. But we'll see."

Shaun didn't have the energy to be outraged. "Okay," he said.

"No, the other bad news is we're in jail."

Shaun sighed heavily, reached over, and put a shaky hand on Molly's leg. "Molly," he said, "I've been unconscious for—how long?"

"Close to six hours," said Molly.

"Six hours, right. So being careful not to overly upset your old Da', who might not withstand the shock, I want you to choose your words carefully and tell me if there is any more bad news."

"Shaun? Shaun McClanahan?" said a voice.

Shaun and Molly turned. Chained to the wall behind them was a thin, grey leprechaun, who was so old and gnarled he practically blended into the rocks of their prison cell. Molly hadn't seen him until now and didn't know how she could have missed him.

"YOU!" said Shaun, his eyes growing wide. "It can't be! Ohhhh, why YOU?!? Oh, no, no, no, no, NO!"

"Oh, yes, yes, yes, yes, yes, YES!" said the leprechaun, gleefully rattling his chains. Molly wished he wouldn't grin. The few teeth protruding from his mouth looked as if they hadn't been cleaned in a generation.

"Do you know him, Da'?" Molly asked incredulously.

"Unfortunately, yes," said Shaun. "Molly, meet your great grandfather, Dorn O'Hanrahan."

The silence rang like a bell with a pickle for a clapper.

"Great grandfather?!?" Molly said. "*Dorn*—as in Dorn-from-*The Story Of Dorn*—is my great grandfather?!?"

"I'm afraid so," said Shaun wearily.

Dorn cackled to himself through his long white beard.

"Why're you laughing like that?" Molly snapped, rounding on him.

Dorn didn't miss a beat. "Can't a man be overjoyed to finally meet his great granddaughter? Why in all my years—"

"Why didn't you ever tell me?!" Molly exclaimed, turning back to her father.

"Yes, Shaun," said Dorn, with feeling, "Why did you never tell your daughter about her great grand—?"

"Quiet you!" Molly snapped. "I didn't see you when we came in. Why didn't I see you when we came in?"

"Well, of course you didn't, lass!" said Dorn with deep sympathy. "You were too busy tending to your dear ol' Da'. And right you were to do it! He was in an *awful* state when he came in." Dorn turned to Shaun, radiating concern. "How are you feelin' now, Shaun my love, any better? How's the head?"

Shaun said nothing.

"And, of course," said Dorn, turning back to Molly, "let's not forget . . . you were chattin' up that handsome Roman legionary fella. Shaun, you need to watch your daughter. I think she's got a soft spot for that human." Dorn's grin was so suggestive, Molly blushed.

"EW!" she said. "What do *you* know about it? He's nice enough. Anyway, why'd you wait so long to speak up?"

Dorn smiled and wiggled his eyebrows at Shaun. "She likes to ask inconvenient questions, doesn't she, Shaun?"

"You have no idea," said Shaun.

"Well, Shaun," said Dorn, ignoring Molly, "I expect I'm the last person you expected to meet in ancient Rome, aren't I?"

Shaun looked at Dorn warily but didn't respond.

"And I expect you'd be wondering what I'm doing here, am I right?"

"I don't care," said Shaun.

"Why didn't you say anything when we came in?" Molly insisted.

"Ah, see? Now *that's* a smart lore gatherer! You spotted that I ignored your question, but you're not going to let me off the hook, are you? Get the real story!

Good girl, Molly! Bravo! That's right! You press on, girl! Oh, she's a fine one, Shaun!"

"Still haven't answered me," said Molly, tapping her foot. Dorn smiled, but now there was an edge to it. It vanished almost as fast as it had appeared. Molly was amazed that a man chained to a wall could so completely dominate a room. He seemed to fill up every corner.

"Molly, I'll come clean with you. I can see there's no getting anything past you. Too smart, you are! Shaun, you raised her right! Molly, don't you think I *wanted* to shout for joy, run up and take you both in my arms when I saw you? My chains prevented me. But when you first walked in—I, I, I was so surprised to see two leprechauns, I couldn't believe my eyes. And not just leprechauns—lore gatherers! Lore gatherers I knew and loved! Well, I was speechless. Shocked beyond belief, I was! Giddy, even! I wanted to hold you and sing your names to the skies! But I didn't dare. No! Not until that Roman soldier had left. Didn't want to give anything away, did I? Can't trust 'em! And to tell the truth . . ." Dorn paused, as if struggling with a painful admission. "The truth is, I wanted to eavesdrop on what you and your dad said. I *spied* on you, Molly, that's the cold, honest truth of it. I *spied* on you! There, I said it! I'm a bad, bad man, just ask your father. No! I'll not deny my past, Shaun! I can only imagine what you've heard about me Molly, and now this? It's a bad way to start a *relationship*, Molly, I know that. I know it. I only hope that you can find it in your heart to forgive your old, wayward great grandfather, who has always loved you, even though he's never laid eyes on you until this very moment."

Dorn's most ingratiating smile spread across his face like a disease, tears running down his cheeks.

Throughout his speech, he had ricocheted from one emotion to another—from giddy happiness, to dark paranoia, to bitter regret, to weepy sentimentality—each shift accomplished in the space of a breath and each emotion totally infectious. It was like watching a masterclass in acting. He was captivating. Molly was conflicted. She didn't believe a word Dorn said, but she *wanted* to believe him. His charm was so weaponized, he made her want to give him every benefit of every doubt, even though she knew—with absolute certainty—that he would betray her without hesitation. It was almost like magic. She watched herself in horror as the words "I forgive you" started to form on her lips.

Shaun broke the spell.

"Spare us, Dorn."

Dorn frowned. "You wound me, Shaun, you really do. How can you doubt my love for my only great grandchild? What did I ever do to you to make you so unfeeling, so uncharitable?"

"What did you do?" said Shaun, his face turning red. "What did you *do?* Where do I start?!? What didn't you do?!? You betrayed your family, you lied constantly, you cheated, you stole—"

"I'm a leprechaun!" Dorn protested.

"You cheated *us!* You lied to *us!* Your *family!* And after all *that*, you lost your gold, Dorn. You were careless with your most sacred charge."

"Which scared charge would that be, Shaun," Dorn said with a wicked glint in his eye, "my gold or my family?"

"You're g—" Shaun stopped.

"Ahhhh . . ." said Dorn. "I thought so," he said, looking meaningfully at Molly.

"You're a disgrace!" Shaun put his head back down, closed his eyes, and muttered: "And you broke Grandma's heart."

Dorn was quiet, but never took his eyes off Shaun. It was like watching a cat regarding a wounded mouse.

"I think we have a few things in common, Shaun. Wouldn't you agree, Molly?"

"Not anymore," said Shaun. "And leave her out of it!"

"One thing, at least," said Dorn, grinning.

Shaun opened his eyes. He had to be careful. Dorn was as skilled a liar as there ever was. And every lie would have three or four different agendas behind it. His subtext would have subtext.

"What do you mean?" he said cautiously.

"Well, correct me if I'm wrong, Shaun, but you're here in ancient Rome because *you* lost *your* gold, isn't that right? Like grandfather, like grandson?"

"What do you know about it?" said Shaun, struggling to prop himself up on his elbows.

"He always was a bit thick, Molly." Dorn whispered. "But you've figured it out, haven't you?"

Realization dawned.

"*You* took it," she said in disbelief.

Dorn's delight was palpable. Even chained and immobile, he looked as if he was dancing.

Shaun's eyes narrowed as he turned back to Dorn. "He what?"

"Oh, *now* you're interested in what I have to say," said Dorn, his voice like silk. "Well, it's like this—"

What happened next was predictable, really. No one who knew him would have ever called Shaun relaxed or laid back. And in the past few days, when all his worst fears had become reality, Molly had seen him more tightly wound than ever. But as far as she could recall, she had never seen him try to deliberately harm anyone. He was not a violent man, despite his temper. She was therefore not prepared to see her father—in one fluid movement—spring from the floor, leap across the room, and wrap his hands tightly around Dorn's throat.

"WHAT HAVE YOU DONE?!? YOU BASTARD!! YOU SELFISH, SELFISH BASTARD!! YOU'VE RUINED MY LIFE!!"

"DA'!" cried Molly, trying to stop the throttling.

As quickly as he had attacked, Shaun fell to his knees, gasping and dizzy from his head injury.

"How could you do that to me?" Shaun said with his head in his hands. "How could you?"

"I had no choice, Shaun," said Dorn, coughing for breath. "You've got to believe me. I had no choice!"

"No choice!" Shaun spat. "No choice?!? Of course, you had a choice!" Shaun sputtered. "YOU . . . of all people, *always* have a choice!" Shaun dragged himself back to where he had been lying on the flagstone floor. "And you always choose yourself," he said collapsing again.

"No, Shaun, listen to me," said Dorn. "Do you want to know what really happened to me all those years ago?"

"NO!" said Shaun. "I don't give a rat's tail what happened! Everyone knows what happened to you. You were away from home—like you *always were*—got outwitted by a human, and then you disappeared again—like you *always did*. Only this time, it was for good. I don't know why Grandma still cared, but she did. But don't expect me to."

Dorn went quiet.

"She was a good woman who loved me. I didn't deserve her, Shaun, I know that." Dorn shook his head. "Shaun. A human captured me. Yes. And I lost my gold. But more important is what happened *after*."

"Who cares what happened *after?*" said Shaun.

"Shaun, that's why I'm here! That's why *you're* here!"

Shaun rolled over, turning his back to Dorn.

"Shaun," Dorn pleaded, "will you not give me a chance to explain?"

Shaun sighed and closed his eyes. "Molly, I want you to take off my left sock. And I want you to shove it in Dorn's mouth. As far in as you can get it, okay? Would you do that for me, please?"

"Shaun, Shaun, Shaun," said Dorn. "Listen to me, Shaun. Yes, I was banished. Might as well have ripped my heart right out of my chest. You probably won't believe it, but my heart *was* broken, it truly was. For the first time, I realized . . . *everything*. I had lost *everything*. Your grandmother, you. All I ever had in life, I had squandered on . . . well, nothing as it turns out. Shaun, I cried myself to sleep those first few months. I did. I can still feel a pit in my stomach when I think about it. I wandered for years—lost count how many. But I always came back to the forest, hoping I could find the village, knowing I never could. Well, it's my home, isn't it? I couldn't bear not to be near my own family, even if I could never see them again. I wandered those woods imagining what my children, my grandchildren—what *you* were doing. Ah, my heart aches just remembering it. I *missed* you, Shaun. You probably don't believe that, but I did. I loved you, Shaun. We had fun telling stories, didn't we? Telling you stories when you were little was one of my favorite things to do! He was the best audience, Molly! Such a great laugh he had! I wanted to tell you the stories of where I'd been, what I'd been doing. I wanted to hear you laugh again. Not a day went by that I didn't hope to catch a peek, just a glimpse of you."

Shaun lay silent, unmoving.

"Shaun," Dorn went on, "I know I was never much of a grandfather—or a father, for that matter. Or husband. Or friend. Shaun, let's face it, I'm not much, period. I wish it were otherwise, but there's the truth of it."

"How did you survive on your own?" Molly asked.

"As best I could, Molly. Then one day . . ." Dorn looked for the right words. "It sounds stupid to say—even I still hardly believe it. I was captured by an ancient Roman soldier."

Molly blinked.

Shaun just laughed.

"Oh! Of *course* you were! How foolish of me! Why didn't you say so sooner, Dorn? I'm so sorry I doubted you. All is forgiven."

"It's the truth, Shaun! I was walking through the forest a long way from the village, poking around for nuts and berries because I was ever so hungry." He winked at Molly. "I came around a tree, and he was just standing there. Didn't know where he was or how he'd gotten here. Can you imagine that?"

"Who was it?" said Molly.

"Doesn't matter. No one special."[†]

Shaun grunted.

"Well, he was startled and no mistake," said Dorn.

"Wait," said Molly, "How did he get there?"

"That's what I'm saying, Molly, he didn't know! Utterly clueless. But there I was. Caught again! The bond that attaches when a human catches a leprechaun is unbreakable until three wishes are granted. Once I explained to him how things are with leprechauns and wishes,[††] what d'you suppose his first wish was, Shaun?"

"To be free of you?" said Shaun.

"To go home," said Molly.

"Right you are, Molly! That's exactly what he wished for! To go home. *Home*, Shaun! Well, I don't mind admitting it, it had been so long since I had seen my own home, my heart almost cracked in two, it truly did. And so I . . . well, I came up with a plan that would force you to come to me. To rescue me. To help *me* get back home! And because I *missed* you, Shaun! So I might have . . . sort of . . . *suggested* to the Roman that I knew where some gold was . . . and that he could have all of it . . . if he would wish specifically for your pot."

[†] An example of *Cruciale Lye* Number 1: The Baldfaced Lie.

[††] As you may have heard from other sources, wishing comes with rules. The most famous is that you can't wish for more wishes. However, as Shaun chronicles in his book, *The Evolution of Wishing: Deals With Devils*, in 1423, a human named Rob McLean captured a leprechaun in Edinburgh at the top of Arthur's Seat, and thought he had found a loophole in the rules. His exact words were: "No wishing for more wishes, eh? Then I wish for more leprechauns!" Instantly, Arthur's Seat was swarmed with literally every leprechaun in the world, all of whom were infuriated at having been so inconveniently summoned. The idea that they all owed him three wishes was clearly out of the question, and so, in one of the few recorded instances of worldwide leprechaun cooperation, everyone combined their magic to alter the rules subtly to prevent another such occurrence. They also erased the Rob's memory. Previously, he had been a rough man with a violent temper, but he returned to his family as a peaceful, if vacant sort of fellow.

"You stole our gold," said Molly.

Dorn's eyes twinkled.

"But it worked, Molly! Worked better than I could have imagined. You found the Roman coin! You guessed the riddle! You're here! We're all together again! You can free me! Listen to me, Shaun. Once I had your gold and felt that magical power again, I had *another* idea. Oh, you're going to love it. If we can find enough gold, accumulate enough of it, we could go home! With enough gold, we'd have enough magic power to break the village protections. We could get in and erase our debt! Wipe the slate clean! They'd *have* to take us back! Don't you *see* that? Don't you *want* that?"

"What happened to the Roman?" said Molly.

"*Used* me, he did!" cried Dorn. "Got him back to Rome, gave him the gold, and what d'you think he did? How d'you think he thanked me?"

"Baked you a cake?" said Shaun.

"His third wish, Shaun! His third wish was that I let myself be captured by Julius Caesar!"

Shaun frowned. "Why would he do that?"

"Thought he could earn special favor from Caesar by offering my services to him, didn't he? What could I do, Shaun? I didn't want to, but I had no choice!"

"You've already seen Caesar?"

"Well, of course I've seen him!" Dorn laughed incredulously. "Why d'you think I'm in these chains? Gave him his wishes and he locked me up! But I told him nothing! Mad with power, he is! And terrified about the Soothsayer's prediction. He's a lunatic. Shaun, you know what humans are like. And now that he feels trapped, he's more dangerous than ever. I know you're going to see him. You've got to be careful. He's going to try to capture you to get more wishes! You mustn't let him!"

"How do you know?" said Molly.

"I offered him gold. He said he needed none! Can you imagine that? A human turning down a leprechaun's pot of gold! But that's when I realized something, Shaun."

"What's that?" said Shaun.

Dorn rattled his chains. "Shaaaaaaauuuuun! Don't you get it? This is Julius Caesar! The man who rules all of Rome. He must be sitting on *piles* of gold already! It's the opportunity of a lifetime! The greatest caper, the greatest theft a leprechaun ever pulled!"

"So, if he didn't want gold, what did he want?" said Molly.

"Information!"

"Information?"

"I know! What kind of man wants information? He said information was worth more than gold to him. That's why he wants more wishes!"

"What kind of information?" said Shaun.

"Oh, just what people are thinking, you know, the Senate, his rivals, the people, blah blah blah. But Shaun, the gold—"

"Did he say why he wanted information?"

"Shaun," said Dorn with an exasperated smile, "he's still not an emperor, is he? He's gambling everything to become one. His life stands on a razor's edge and he knows it. It hasn't happened yet, but you know how all this ends."

"The Ides of March," said Molly.

Dorn smiled. "At least *you're* thinking, Molly, even if your father isn't." Dorn winked at her again.

Molly wanted Dorn to stop winking at her. She didn't like him taunting her father, either.

"So, what are you waiting for?" asked Shaun. "Why haven't you found his gold yet?"

"Um, I'm a little tied up at the moment, Shaun. Now that he's used me, Caesar doesn't want anyone else to capture me. He's left me here to rot!"

"Why should that stop you?"

"I'm trapped, Shaun. He has a magician!"

"A what?" said Shaun incredulously.

"I know! You could have knocked me over with a feather! It's that wretched Soothsayer! He works for Caesar now. It turns out he's a real magician. Powerful, too! He enchanted these chains so I can't break free."

"Impossible," said Shaun. No human has that kind of magic."

"See for yourself, Shaun." Dorn struggled briefly against the chains to demonstrate.

Shaun got up unsteadily and, with some caution, approached Dorn. He reached out to touch the chains and instantly snatched his hands away in agony.

"Da'!" cried Molly.

"Hurts, doesn't it?" said Dorn.

"Shillelagh!" groaned Shaun. "What is it?"

"I told you, an enchantment! Some sort of charm that burns anyone magical if you try to fiddle with them."

"How on earth did he do *that?*" Shaun said, sucking his fingers. He couldn't believe how much it had hurt. If the Soothsayer did this, he was formidable.

"Never mind Shaun, it's done. We don't have much time. We need to focus on getting Caesar's gold before he's assassinated. Otherwise, Rome will be plunged into chaos, and who knows how long it will be before we can lay our hands on that kind of stash!"

Shaun was just about to tell Dorn to stick Caesar's gold somewhere *incredibly* inappropriate when they heard Lucius coming down the hall outside.

"Listen to me, Shaun," Dorn whispered. "I know you don't trust me. You have every reason not to trust me. But trust me or not, the only thing that will get us back into our village is gold and a good story. That's true, and you know it. And stealing Caesar's gold can give us *both*. You can't let him do to you what he's done to me. You've got to find out where his gold is! It's my—It's *our* only way out!"

They heard the rattle of keys in the jail cell door. Shaun frowned at Dorn.

"Help me or don't, Shaun," said Dorn simply. "It's up to you,"

The door swung open, and Lucius stepped in.

"It's time, Molly," he said.

CHAPTER 5

Gladys

Dangling from your collar in the beak of a runaway chicken is no way to travel. Dorker felt badly jostled. The chicken who carried him emitted a steady stream of muffled squawks—the sort of sound you might expect an over-excited chicken to make with a mouthful of gangly leprechaun.

It was a magnificent creature. Larger than your average egg-layer, its plumage was extravagant and imposing. It carried itself with a kind of regal majesty—or as much majesty as a chicken can muster, which, admittedly, isn't much for most chickens. But this was a Brahma chicken. Between its enormous size and blossoming feathers, you could almost believe it descended from a line of chicken Gods who once strutted the earth. [*]

The chicken seemed powered either by righteous fury or unfiltered insanity—possibly both. On the one hand, every turn, every change of direction felt purposeful, and if he could have seen its eyes, Dorker would have seen laser-like focus—a fevered single-mindedness found only in the most highly-trained assassin. On the other hand, the route the chicken actually travelled was chaotic—a random path determined as much by whim and chance as by any pre-determined plan. It dashed through the Roman marketplace turning this way and that, down one street, up another, in and out of alleys, upending

---

[*] This particular chicken believed fervently in such Gods. In its religion, these Gods scratched and pecked into existence the mountains and valleys of the earth. The sun is the magnificent comb of Great A'Tilla, the giant space chicken. The moon is Great A'Tilla's eye, always watchful, ready to strike down and eat bad chickens. The stars are the feathers of bad chickens Great A'Tilla has eaten and pooped out into space.

baskets and tables all the way. It even made an unfortunate diversion through a sewage ditch. Every now and then, it flapped its wings violently, to Dorker's great distress. He sincerely hoped the chicken couldn't fly.

When it finally paused to rest and deposited him in an open field on the outskirts of town, Dorker had no idea where he was. He was game for new adventures and was by nature optimistic. No one could find a silver lining like Dorker, but even he was distressed. When you are far from home, two thousand years in the past getting carried around by a chicken, and separated from the only two people you know, the word "lost" doesn't even begin to describe your feelings.

As the chicken pecked the ground looking for food, Dorker decided to weigh his assets.

Asset 1: He knew that he would see Molly again. He didn't know how he knew it or how that helped him right now, but it still felt good.

Asset 2: He was a smart, young lore gatherer in good health. That had to count for something, though he wasn't sure what.

Asset 3: . . .

Maybe Dorker didn't have as many assets as he thought. And now that he thought of it, his deficits loomed large. He couldn't make a fire. He didn't know how to cook. He never learned much magic and had no idea how to get back to the twenty-first century, much less home. A small, detached part of his brain noted with irony that for someone who always paid attention and did well in school, he didn't really know much of anything. Nothing useful, anyway. A larger, more realistic, part of his brain also noted this and panicked.

What he wanted more than anything was to sob or possibly scream, but he shuttered those impulses and tried to pull himself together to start finding Shaun and Molly. He stood up and looked back at the chicken.

"I don't suppose you know your way around Rome, do you?" he said as calmly as he could.

"Cluck," said the chicken.

"No, I didn't think so," said Dorker, turning away.

"Cluck cluck," said the chicken meaningfully.

Dorker looked back. The chicken was looking right at him. It was eerie. What goes through a chicken's brain at any given moment is almost impossible to know. Brains are an afterthought for most chickens; what purpose they serve is anyone's guess. Once, a Colorado farmer's plans to eat chicken marsala for dinner were completely derailed when he cut his chicken's head clean off and the chicken went on to live without it quite happily for another eighteen months.[F] So, when dealing with an animal whose brain seems vestigial at best, trying to discern ordinary thought processes might be missing the point.

Looking into the eyes of this particular chicken, however, Dorker perceived the mind of an exceptional bird.

"Did you . . . *say* . . . something to me?" said Dorker.

"Cluck," said the chicken, bobbing its head. Chickens bob their heads a lot. Dorker couldn't tell whether this was just one of those reflexive bobs, or whether it was something more.

"Was that a nod or a bob?" he asked.

"Cluck," said the chicken, bobbing its head again.

"Okay, so I still can't tell—"

"CLUCK!" the chicken clarified.

Dorker paused.

"Okaaaaay. I'll take that as a nod."

"Cluck," said the chicken.

"So . . . you understand what I'm saying to you?"

"Cluck cluck," said the chicken. It scratched the ground and ate a beetle that was scuttling away.

Dorker got very still, as his perception reoriented. The world held its breath. The chicken's clucks and movements seemed somehow connected—as if all those bobs and scratches expressed something more than a random search for food. You wouldn't call it sign language exactly, and certainly not mime[FF] or dance, but Dorker sensed the chicken intended something deeper. Uncertain where it could possibly lead, he decided to test his theory.

"So," he said casually, "tell me what you think about . . . foxes?"

The chicken erupted in a fusillade of clucks and bawks and frantic scratching as it ran around in angry circles. Dorker was momentarily overwhelmed by the sudden flood of communication, but then something clicked.

"Wait!" Dorker interrupted. "Say that last part again!"

[F] This is true. Look it up. The chicken's name was Mike.
[FF] There are, sadly, no chicken mimes. But there should be.

"Cluck cluck," said the chicken, scratching the ground.

Dorker couldn't believe what was happening.

"I . . . I think I understand you," he said excitedly. "Keep talking! Uh, um . . . Tell me again, do, do, do you . . . can you tell me where those Roman soldiers took my friends?"

The chicken clucked and scratched. The sound and movement rearranged itself in Dorker's head and refined into something comprehensible. Dorker was learning his very first foreign language—no dictionary required! He was exhilarated.

The chicken, as it turned out, had a lot to say. Faced with a captive audience, it let loose its opinions on everything. Thoughts and feelings it had bottled up for years came pouring forth in a torrent of chicken-speak. Admittedly, lots of it was complaining, but her vocal and gestural display was wonderous to behold. The chicken engaged like a machine gun nest, rattling from one topic to another, all with equal intensity. Even the most esoteric corners of the avant guard never produced such an angry, squawking, pecking, flapping modern dance. Dorker felt his head spin.

"Okay, okay," said Dorker interrupting the chicken. "Let's just go back and take this one step at a time. I think you said you know where they took my friends?"

"Cluck."

"I'm sorry, you're right, that was rude of me. My name is Dorker. Do—do you have a name?"

The chicken paused. It wasn't sure if it had a name. It had never needed a name. But a name now seemed like something it wanted.

"Can I call you Gladys? Only, I've been sort of calling you that in my head anyway."

"BAWK!" said the chicken, indicating that yes, Gladys was her name, and her name was Gladys.

"Okay, great! Gladys. I think you said you know where my friends might be?"

"Cluck," said Gladys.

"In prison?"

"Cluck cluck," Gladys confirmed.

"Why would they take them to a prison?"

"Cluck cluck cluck."

"Standard procedure??" said Dorker, doubtfully.

"BAAAAWK!"

"Fine, I believe you, but how does a chicken know the Roman military's standard operating procedures?"

"Cluck cluck."

"Their pet? How long?"

"BAWK!"

"Mascot, sorry, I'm still learning the dialect. How long?"

"Cluck cluck [peck the dirt, scratch scratch] BAWK! [eat a grub]."

"That long?"

"Cluck [bob the head]."

"So where are you from?"

Gladys let out a slow, mournful, "Baaaaaaaaaaaaaaaawwwwwwwk."

"Wow. That's far. How did you escape?"

"BAWK! Cluck cluck cluck. BAWK!"

"That's hard to believe."

"Cluck [peck the dirt]," Gladys emphasized.

Dorker paused and wondered what kind of life this chicken must have had roaming the streets of Rome alone.

"Do you have any friends?"

"Cluck."

"Me neither."

"Cluck cluck."

"No, you're right, I do have one friend. At least, I *think* we're friends. I mean I'd like to be more than friends, but she doesn't seem interested. In fact, she generally seems irritated by me. Honestly, I'm not one hundred percent sure she's even my friend."

"Cluck cluck?"

"Because she's terrific, that's why! She's smart, she's brave, she's . . . I dunno. . . . But it's more than that. When I see her, I want to be . . . more than me. You know? I mean . . . not that there's anything wrong with me, but . . . it's hard to put into words."

"Cluck?"

"Yes, she's beautiful!"

"Cluck!" Gladys protested.

Dorker rolled his eyes. "No, not as beautiful as you."

"Bawk [scratch scratch]."

"I've *tried* to tell her. I *want* to tell her."

"Cluck cluck cluck."

"You're right, you *do* only live once." Dorker got quiet. He wasn't sure what was weirder: the fact that he was talking to a chicken, or that the chicken was giving him dating advice.

"Do you miss it? Home, I mean?"

"Cluck," said Gladys.

"Me too," said Dorker.

The two of them sat for a moment not saying anything. Dorker looked at Gladys. Gladys looked at Dorker.

"So, they're in prison, huh?"

"Cluck."

"Any ideas on how we can get in?"

"BAWK!"

"To rescue them, that's why!"

"Cluck cluck cluck."

"I bet I *can!* And that's not a very nice thing to say!"

"BAWK!" said Gladys pointedly.

"I don't care, I have to try."

Even to one not versed in chicken-speak, it was clear Gladys was uneasy. Or rather, more uneasy than usual. Uneasy is a chicken's default state. Gladys regarded Dorker and spoke cautiously.

"Baaaaaaaaaaaaaaaaaaawwwwwwwwwwwwwk bawk bawk bawk bawk bawk bawk . . . ."

"Yes, yes," Dorker interrupted, "but you do know a way in?"

"Cluck."

"Will you take me?"

"Cluck cluck cluck."

"What's in it for you? I don't know. What do you want?"

Such a simple question. But it now struck Gladys that as far back as she could remember (and she wasn't certain exactly how far back that was), no one had ever asked what *she* wanted. It's not the sort of thing people ask chickens.

In fact, Gladys couldn't remember anyone saying much of anything to her other than "Hey, get out of that!" Few care what a chicken wants any more than they care what a tuna fish sandwich wants. And frankly, even if they were asked, most of the chickens Gladys knew didn't have any interesting answers. But Gladys had answers. More than that, Gladys had questions. Oh my, did she! And Dorker's question hissed and popped in her brain like the fuse of a dormant firework ready to explode into an idea that would light up her chicken-mind.

She launched into a complicated series of clucks, bawks, pecks, and scratches (with more than a few of the pecks aimed directly at Dorker's head) that may have been the most complicated thought Gladys (or any chicken) had ever tried to communicate. She wanted to get it right. When she was finished, she stood looking meaningfully at Dorker, who was lying on the ground, rubbing his head where Gladys had hit him.

"I think we need to work out some less concussive ways of communicating."

"BAWK!" Gladys insisted.

"But yes," said Dorker. "You've got a deal."

CHAPTER 6

Hail Caesar!

Shaun was woozy and his head still throbbed. He leaned on Molly to steady himself as Lucius led them through the back corridors to Caesar's quarters.

Dorn! he thought. *Farking barkwards!*[†] *That's the last thing we need! The charm of twelve leprechauns and the reliability of none. Isn't life hard enough without Alice? I need Dorn coming back to make it harder? And what's he really up to, anyway? Who knows with him. It won't end with stealing Caesar's gold, I know that much. He's slippery as an eel dipped in grease, marinated in oil, and glazed with pig fat. More slippery—even eels tell the truth sometimes. And now we're mixed up with Julius Caesar. This is bad business. Coming here was a mistake. Ratcrap! Ratcrap! Ratcrap!*

Shaun had been raised by his grandmother and Dorn. When Shaun was very young, he never understood why his grandfather would disappear, often for weeks at a time, but his return always excited him. Whatever else Dorn was, he was a great storyteller and Shaun was a rapt audience. Dorn would take him on his knee and spin fantastical tales of his grand adventures, while Shaun's grandmother quietly did the dishes, biting back her rage. When Shaun was old enough to understand that Dorn's stories were all lies; that everything about him was a lie; that every lie cut a piece of his grandmother's heart away; that his

---

[†] An exceptionally coarse expletive whose origins are unknown. Some lore gatherer linguists speculate it could relate to a very rare, very unpleasant gastrointestinal condition that can afflict elderly leprechauns, commonly referred to as "farting backwards," the details of which, the editorial staff will spare you.

grandmother deserved so much more than Dorn could ever give her in a thousand lifetimes, Shaun grew to hate him. And when Dorn's banishment brought shame on the entire family, Shaun vowed he would never make the same mistake. Now Dorn had ruined that too.

Okay, okay, okay, he thought. *Deal with the problem in front of you. Isn't that what Grandma always said? Well, she had lots of practice, married to Dorn! We're banished and in ancient Rome.*

We should just escape, get home as fast as possible, accept our banishment, and start rebuilding our lives. Right? Wouldn't that be the smart move? That would be the smart move. The second we get mixed up with Dorn, he holds all the cards and I'll never beat him. He's better at this than me.

But he is right. If anything would impress the village it would be lots of gold and a good story about stealing lots of gold. A gold thief with flair has good standing in any village.[F] *If we can outwit Julius Caesar and steal his gold, well—that's the sort of thing that makes an impression. It could end our banishment.*

* * * *

Ow . . .

. . . thought Poor Reynard.

We should back up.

When the pot-seller grabbed Molly and chaos ensued, a falling pot struck Poor Reynard on the head, rendering him useless just when Molly could have really used some foxy heroics. He felt like a failure.

Now, his head hurt, he had lost sight of Molly completely, and he had no

---

[F] Take, for example, Borumund O'Reilly. As detailed in Volume 4 of Shaun's *Rogues, Rascals, and Ne'erdowells: A Compendium of Leprechauns Who Went Too Far*, in 1743, Borumund stole his entire village's hoard of gold while *at the same time* having a cup of tea with his neighbor, old Ms. McKulick. Many theories have been floated as to how exactly he did it, and few agree. What is undisputed, however, is that the magical power he acquired from the sudden accumulation of gold all in his possession was so substantial that he transformed into a ten foot tall golden phoenix right in front of Ms. McKulick, blew through the roof of her house, and flew away in a blaze of fire that lit the sky for three days and nights. As the embers of her roof burned and collapsed around her, Ms. McKulick was bemoaning the spilled tea on her new carpet, when the residual magic from Borumund's flight transformed her into a young woman of twenty. The village was distraught, of course, but the caper had been executed with such panache they decided to let him go with the full understanding that if he ever returned, there *might* be consequences. In all likelihood the concentration of so much gold in one leprechaun destroyed him, but for her part, Ms. McKulick spent the better part of five years trying to track Borumund down so she could thank him.

idea where he was.

Stupid pot. Stupid humans.

After getting hit, he had managed to slink shakily out of sight behind some abandoned crates to close his eyes. Then, an explosion of some kind knocked him further back, obliterating the crates and filling him full of splinters. Bruised and concussed, he dragged himself into an out-of-the-way side street. It was some time before he could remove all the splinters and his head stopped throbbing.

When he felt more like himself again, his nose took over and the world of smells revealed the events he had missed. Molly (who smelled like burning leaves and angry sunflowers), had gone *that* way, following a human who smelled like old hard leather, flint, and garlic. The human was carrying Molly's father (who usually smelled like a mixture of paper, ink, and worrying), but something was amiss. Shaun smelled like worrying even when he slept, but that particular aromatic thread was nowhere to be found. Reynard surmised that Shaun had been knocked unconscious somehow. Meanwhile, the tall, skinny one who, no matter how dirty he got, always smelled like sunshine and soap—the one Molly called Dorker—had run off with a . . . could it be? Yes, a chicken! A big one, by the smell of it!

Poor Reynard's mouth watered. The promise of chicken was beguiling, and it was all he could do not to follow it in the hopes of a hearty meal.

But no, he had to find Molly.

Watching the ancient Roman streets carefully, Reynard began following the trail of Molly's scent. As he did, his mind reached out to her like an antenna, trying to find that psychic connection again . . .

Probing . . . probing . . . probing . . .

There!

✶ ✶ ✶ ✶

Julius Caesar! When Molly and Shaun entered his chambers, he was flipping through parchments, upright and alert like a cat. Even Shaun felt an icy excitement thrill down his spine. Here was a man he had only read about in history books. His movements were poised and relaxed, but his body bristled with energy. You could almost see the wheels of his mind turning. As they walked in, Caesar glanced up briefly—it was no more than a moment, but it gave the impression he had read them like a papyrus codex.[※] Shaun had almost felt him turn the pages. The man's charisma was palpable and, of course, there was that nose. Caesar's nose perched upon his face like a maestro tuning the music of the spheres. When he left the room, it left a gap in nature. It was truly one of history's great noses.

Shaun took in the room as Lucius gently made them kneel. The only real decorations, besides a marble bust or two, were a few long, deep-maroon curtains draped elegantly around the room. Otherwise, the room was spare, but comfortable and tastefully done. Certainly, no one would think a monk lived here, but it wasn't as extravagant or lavish as one might have expected. The first word that came to Shaun's mind was "control." It was as if every fold in every curtain that hung had been put there intentionally, creased to the exact millimeter. The overall effect projected cold precision. If the room maketh the man, the man who stood before them was a razor blade.

Standing just behind and to the left of Caesar was the most physically handsome man Shaun or Molly had ever seen: Marc Antony—a greyhound made human. His muscles moved beneath his skin even standing still. He carried himself with a self-assured arrogance and grace that filled the room up, competing with Caesar for every available corner. As he looked at Molly and Shaun, an amused and disdainful smirk curled on his lips. It somehow made him even more attractive. He leaned over and whispered something to Caesar.

"Handle it, Antony," said Caesar. "You're always so good with words." Antony nodded and swept out of the room with a leisurely sneer at Shaun and Molly, leaving them alone with Caesar.

Caesar jotted a few notes on his parchment, then put down his quill and looked at them impassively.

After a very long, uncomfortable minute, he finally asked: "Will you give me three wishes?"

Shaun and Molly looked at each other.

"What?" said Shaun.

Caesar raised his eyes to the ceiling, containing his impatience.

"Give. Me. Three. Wishes." he said, over-enunciating his words.

"Ummm . . . No . . . ?" said Shaun.

[※] A type of early Roman book.

Caesar sighed and snapped his fingers. Enchanted shackles flew from his table and clamped around Shaun's wrists, burning him like Dorn's had and making him cry out in agony. Lucius, his jaw wide open in astonishment, opened the door as the shackles dragged Shaun from the room, as if pulled by an invisible jailer.

"Molly!" he cried. But before she could say anything, he was gone.

"I was told you might resist," said Caesar. "So now we try it this way: Molly, give me three wishes, or I will imprison your father forever. In a cell worse than the one you came from. Are we clear now?"

"How did you do that?" Molly demanded.

"It's useful to have a magical soothsayer. Are. We. Clear?"

"Where did you take him!"

"Molly," said Caesar, rising, "you will find that I am not unreasonable. I'm trying to be polite, but I will hurt your father." He crossed to a table and poured himself a goblet of wine. "Believe me when I tell you: What I want, I get."

"Where did you take him!"

Caesar turned to Molly. "Away," he said coldly.

Caesar stared at her with eyes like a vice. Molly's jaw and fingers clenched, but she said nothing.

"Good, now you will listen," he said. "I will be brief. Rome is in chaos. The Senate—our government—is toothless and corrupt. Without strong leadership, Rome will fall. Within the year, I fear. I can save it, but there are many who, for various reasons, would see me fail."

"So what?" said Molly. "You drag my father away in chains and I'm supposed believe you have *good intentions?*"

Caesar smiled. "You are right to doubt me, Molly. I would not believe you, if our positions were reversed. You should always distrust the words of powerful men who want something. Under the circumstances, nothing I can say will persuade you. So I'm not going to try."

Molly frowned. "Then what do you want?"

"Excellent," said Caesar. "To the point then. Molly, I have learned from a source—my soothsayer—about a plot on my life. I need information."

"Information?" said Molly.

"About the plot," said Caesar. "It must be stopped. The Gods themselves have chosen *me* to bring peace to Rome, Molly. I *know* it. This is not my choice.

In all things, I serve only the Gods."

Molly looked into his eyes and for the first time felt terrified. Not because she saw ruthlessness or cruelty or even desperation (though she saw all that, too). No, what she saw was belief. Powerful belief. In the right person, belief can move mountains and change the world. But that is exactly what Molly was afraid of. History's pages contain those whose belief made the world a better place, but also millions more who were trampled under foot in the name of some "greater good" that was too often no good at all. Caesar didn't breathe fire and brimstone or rave like a lunatic. He didn't even preach. He was simply convinced he was a god—or the next best thing. He believed—no, he *knew*—the Gods commanded his actions. And if Caesar was the Gods' chosen one, Molly wondered, where did that leave everyone else?

"You have to promise not to hurt my father," she said carefully.

"Yes, of course," said Caesar, smiling thinly. "Just as you will promise not to play games with my leprechaun wishes." Caesar leaned over and put one finger under her chin. He spoke quietly. "I know all about leprechauns, Molly. Do not test me. You will find I know more about you and your father than you know about me."

Caesar straightened. "*If* you grant my wishes, and *when* I am satisfied that you have not played any tricks, we shall discuss the terms of your release—which will *not*, I assure you, involve surrendering my gold. But you shall find I am not unreasonable. Or ungrateful."

Never trust the words of powerful people who want something, Molly recalled. Caesar had clearly learned a great deal about leprechauns and about she and her father, despite what Dorn had said. How much had Dorn told him?

"Take the night to think about it," Caesar said, nodding to Lucius and going back to his papers.

Lucius put a hand on Molly's shoulder and led her out of the room.

*****

"Molly, I swear I didn't say anything about you stealing his gold," said Lucius softly once they were safely down the hall from Caesar's chamber.

Molly didn't say anything, and Lucius didn't know what else to say. In his experience, Caesar was a hard man. Vain? Yes. Cruel? Sometimes, but so what? The world was cruel. Caesar was as cruel as circumstances required. He was also sharp, clear-eyed, and a strategic leader. Cool under pressure and fair to his men (or at least, as fair as can be expected), he was practically legendary for his steely nerves. Death and danger were no strangers to this man. And he never lost his capacity to surprise.

But beneath his controlled exterior, Lucius realized, Caesar was terrified. Lucius had never seen Caesar afraid of anything. The Soothsayer had really gotten under his skin. And where had all that talk about being an instrument of the Gods come from? Lucius had never heard *that* line before. Questioning his superior went against all his training, but everything about this felt very, very wrong. When great men shudder, Lucius realized, the whole world quakes.

They walked in silence the rest of the way to the prison. When they arrived, Molly's cell was empty.

"Where's my father?!" Molly demanded.

"I'm sorry, Molly, Caesar wants to keep you separate."

"What?! Why? Is he okay? Just tell me that at least!" she pleaded.

Lucius looked up and down the hall of the prison to make sure no one was coming.

"He's okay, Molly," he whispered. "He's not in any pain. I promise I'll keep him as safe as I can."

"And how safe is that, exactly?" Molly asked pointedly.

Lucius looked away. He had no answer. All he could do was close the cell door and lock it.

Molly slumped to the ground. The air was dank, and the stone walls were lonely and cold. When she closed her eyes, she kept seeing her father's face as he was dragged away from her in chains. She desperately wanted to believe that he was okay, but not knowing was torture. What she did know for sure was that Caesar *wanted* it to be torture. He wanted her to feel isolated and alone, which would make her more pliable to his demands.

Well, nuts to that, Molly thought. If Caesar wanted her to fret and cry while sitting alone in a prison cell, then that's exactly what she wouldn't do. She got up, wiped her eyes, and began exploring the stone walls, the door, the floor—every inch of the cell, hoping to find some sort of weakness she could exploit. She had no idea whether escape was even possible, but trying was better than sitting and feeling sorry for herself.

Unfortunately, after two hours of close scrutiny, she had found nothing.

She was ready to scream.

Then, a crazy idea: it couldn't possibly work, but she what did she have to lose? She sat down and tried to settle herself. As she did, she concentrated on Reynard. The connection she and the fox had shared on the outskirts of Rome had been brief, but intense. Ever since, Reynard had seemed strangely attached to her. Aggie said Molly had done something to ensure he wouldn't hurt them, but Molly couldn't imagine what that could possibly be. *She* hadn't tossed him the food after all, she had just thought of it. Currently, however, she was sitting in a prison cell two thousand years in the past. She had just *talked* to Julius Caesar. Maybe it was time to stop thinking sensibly.

She had sat completely still for several long minutes when she felt a tickle behind her eyes. The fox was out there. She didn't know how she knew it, but she could feel him looking for her. Not knowing what she was doing, she reached out to him with her thoughts:

Find me.

As soon as she did, a large stone block in the wall she was leaning against moved. It was only an inch, but it definitely moved—and it was moving into the room! Bewildered and more than a little excited, she got up as, inch by inch, the stone slowly pushed itself from the wall. When it came loose, the face that came poking through the hole made her jaw hit the floor.

"Dorker?!?"

"Oh, hi!" he said, getting up and dusting himself off. "I was hoping you'd be here."

Molly was conflicted. On the one hand, she was a little disappointed not to see the fox. She really had thought she had made some sort of telepathic connection with him. But the fact that Dorker of all people now stood before her was even more miraculous.

"What . . . how . . . why . . . ?" Her jaw moved up and down noiselessly for a moment. Then she flung herself at him, beating on his chest repeatedly. "Where! Have! You! BEEN!?!"

"OW! Hey!" Dorker protested.

Molly stopped hitting him. She stepped back for a moment frowning, then lurched forward and hugged him tightly.

Momentarily confused, Dorker tried putting a tentative arm around her. She didn't push him away. Then he put his other arm around her . . .

This exciting state of affairs lasted a good ten seconds before they both suddenly felt very self-conscious and separated. They stood awkwardly for a moment, uncertain what to do or say. Molly pulled at a lock of her hair and looked down at her shoes. Dorker's big silly grin made him look like a puppy waiting for another treat.

Finally, Molly said: "So, uh . . . where *have* you been?"

"What?" said Dorker, whose thoughts had not yet moved on from the hug. "Oh, right. I've just been, you know . . . well, let me back up—"

Before Dorker could go on, Gladys burst into the room with a giant squawk.

"Sssshhhhhhh!" Dorker shushed. "Gladys! You've got to be quiet or you'll give us away!"

Gladys quieted, but made it clear she didn't like being shushed. Dorker would definitely hear about *that* later.

Molly's eyes grew wide at the size and plumage of the gargantuan bird before her.

"?!??!?" she said helplessly, gesturing at the chicken.

"Oh! Yes!" said Dorker, "So, when you and Shau—I mean, your dad—got mixed up with those Roman soldiers, I didn't really understand what was going on because I haven't *quite* got the hang of Latin yet. I'm getting there, you know, but I'm still missing the nuance of a native speaker. I get the general gist, but I miss *a lot* of—"

"Dorker! The chicken?!"

"Right, sorry. Yeah! So, she's the one who carried me off, as you may recall. Her name's Gladys, and she's—"

"Wait," Molly interrupted, "*whose* name is Gladys?"

"The chicken."

"The chicken's name is Gladys," said Molly flatly.

"Uh-huh," Dorker smiled. "She's really smart. You'll like her. She's the one who showed me how to break into the prison."

Molly looked blankly at Dorker, then at the chicken, then back at Dorker.

"The chicken. Showed you? How to break into a prison???"

"Uh-huh," said Dorker matter-of-factly.

Molly still couldn't quite believe her ears. "So, you just . . . broke in here . . . with the help of a chicken?"

"Well, it wasn't easy! Gladys knows all the hiding places and ins and outs and stuff. We did have to try several cells before we finally found yours. Though, in fairness, there are a *lot* of cells, and the guards recently changed who gets placed where, so Gladys was making her best guesses. Oh, and here's something I never knew about—all these cells have secret exits! Or most of them, at least. Gladys wasn't *perfectly* clear on that point, but it seems like over the years, the criminal element in Rome have gotten good at tunneling and maintain a fairly up-to-date map of escape routes, which, if you're clued in to that world, can be really helpful. Anyway, Gladys is very good at pecking away old mortar, so . . ."

"So, wait, Gladys—is a criminal?"

"BAWK!" said Gladys.

"No!" said Dorker. "But I mean, be fair, a chicken on her own in a big city does what she has to."

What could Molly say? The story was oddly plausible. It would have been hard to imagine Dorker showing this much resourcefulness on his own, but hearing that he did it all with the help of a criminal chicken mastermind gave his story a strange credibility.

"Um . . ." said Dorker. "So, anyway, how are you?"

Molly caught Dorker up on what he had missed. When she finished, Dorker's eyes were wide.

"Dorn?!? THE Dorn stole your gold? Wow! That's . . . actually kind of cool," said Dorker. Then he saw Molly's expression and backtracked. "From a . . . y'know, thieving . . . historically . . . kind of point of view."

"No, it's not cool, Dorker. He's not to be trusted. For anything. Are we clear about that?"

"Okay, Molly." They stood silently for a moment. Finally, Dorker said hesitantly, "Um, should we go? I *have* come to rescue you."

Dorker hadn't meant the question to sound so much like he was pleading. In fact, this whole scenario was not playing out as he had imagined it. In his fantasy, he burst through the stone walls, grabbed Molly by the hand, swept her into his arms, and said in a deep, husky baritone: "It's alright Molly. I'm here to rescue you." At which point, he assumed, swooning would be involved. He'd read about swooning in romance novels and was keen to experience it firsthand. He wasn't entirely certain who was supposed to swoon, but he hoped the dramatic rescue might clarify things. Unfortunately, he didn't have a husky baritone voice, and Molly was too lost in thought to swoon.

The hero business is a lot harder than stories make it look.

Uncertain if Molly had even heard him, he decided to try again.

"So, um . . . come on, Molly! Let's get out of here and we can figure out how to rescue your dad!"

"Dorker, I can't leave," she said.

Gladys squawked. Dorker squeaked. He wished he could pick Molly up, toss her over his shoulder, and say, "Sorry, Molly! No time to argue!" while riding out dramatically on Gladys. Unfortunately, he didn't have much shoulder to speak of over which anyone (or anything) could be tossed, and besides, he suspected that would only make Molly mad. He defaulted to plaintive bewilderment.

"Are you crazy, Molly?!"

"Dorker, he's got my Da'!"

"Well . . . we can rescue him. Can't we?"

"They've got him locked in magic chains, Dorker. You didn't see them. Not even my Da' knows what kind of magic it is!"

"Well . . . but we can figure that out, can't we? We're both young and . . . and smart . . . and . . . and we've got a chicken!"

If this were a story, thought Dorker, surely two plucky young protagonists who believed in themselves and worked together as a team could come up with a cunning plan to rescue Molly's father, steal Caesar's gold, and find their way back home. He was sure of it. That said, he was also pretty sure that no inspirational speech in history had ever concluded with the phrase: "and we've got a chicken!"

"So, what do we do, Molly?"

She weighed the options.

"You need to go find Caesar's gold. As much of it as you can. Ask Lucius. He owes me."

"Lucius?"

"The smaller soldier from the pot seller's stall. Ask Gladys to help find him."

"What are you going to do?" said Dorker.

"I need to find out more about Caesar's Soothsayer so we can figure out how to break the magic on those chains."

"How are you going to do that?"

"By staying close to Caesar."

"What do you mean?"

Molly sighed. "I mean, I have to grant him three wishes."

CHAPTER 7

Caesar's Wishes

Marcus Junius Brutus, senator of Rome, Praetor of Gaul (i.e. France), and close friend of Julius Caesar, sat alone in his bedchamber eating dinner. Physically powerful, his every move bespoke discipline. He was the sort of man who, if board games had existed, would have memorized the rule book before playing and quoted it at you throughout the game. Even alone, he sat at attention.

His friend and brother-in-law, Gaius Cassius Longinus (Cassius, to his friends) had been to see him earlier, and Brutus was chewing over their discussion as fitfully as he chewed his light salad.

Brutus didn't like him. Cassius was a hothead, always ranting and raving about injustice and trying to stir up trouble. Usually, in a day or two, he would forget all about whatever he had been yelling about the day before and move on to the next perceived outrage. Most of the time, you could ignore him, but today, he had gotten under Brutus's skin.

I should have told Cassius to go jump in a well, that's what I should have done.

Brutus stabbed a recalcitrant cherry tomato with his knife.

But no. I listened to him. Respectfully. As always. I argued calmly and rationally. As always. Didn't let him see how angry he was making me. What a jerk! Once—just once—I'd like to punch Cassius right on his nose.

Julius Caesar and Molly hovered nearby like ghosts, unseen and unheard (or perhaps merely occupying some theoretical, non-dimensional, magical space between the neurons of Brutus's conscious thought).[†]

Caesar was fascinated. "This is remarkable," he whispered. "How can we hear his thoughts?"

"Um . . . magic?" said Molly. "Obviously. Also, you don't have to whisper. He can't see us or hear us."

Caesar nodded, but he hadn't gotten where he was without a well-developed sense of paranoia. "How do I know this is real? How do I know this isn't a vision you've conjured to trick me?"

Molly shrugged. "I guess you don't. But magic has rules. You wished to know what Brutus was thinking. One of the rules is that you get what you wish for."

"Mmmm . . ." said Caesar skeptically.

"So be careful what you wish for."[††]

"Noted," said Caesar.

What a nerve! Brutus thought. *Didn't even thank me for that nice amphora of wine I brought him from Greece. See if I ever haul twenty pounds of Greek ceramics hundreds of miles for him again. Coming here, uninvited, trying to get me to join some sort of conspiracy to assassinate Caesar!*

"You see?" said Caesar. "Plots . . ."

Brutus sniffed contemptuously, wiping salad dressing from his chin. Then he paused, his knife hovering over a ripe cucumber. Something didn't feel right. He got up and looked outside the casement of his window.

Darkness. Wind. A dog barking in the distance.

He searched the room. As he overturned cushions and looked behind drapes, his thoughts were too frantic to follow with any clarity.

"Does he know we're here?" Caesar asked, as Brutus cautiously waved a hand right through the space where Caesar stood. "Because it looks like he might know we're here."

"I seriously doubt it," said Molly dismissively.

Brutus returned to his seat and sat down. He frowned for a moment,

---

[†] Lore gatherers who study theoretical magic have been unable to determine how, precisely, the magic works in situations like these. Part of the problem is that field research is so tricky. "Wish magic" is a special type of magic that only activates when leprechauns enter the magical contract with a human counterpart. But no one wants to be caught by humans to do the necessary experiments. There's just no telling what humans will wish for.

[††] Caesar didn't know how lucky he was that he had wished "to know what Brutus was thinking," and not, more poetically, "to look into the heart of Brutus."

shrugged, then speared a carrot drenched in sweet vinegar that had previously escaped his notice.

Caesar has some sort of magical soothsayer working for him now. THAT'S a problem. How could we even kill him if Caesar has magic?

But Cassius says Caesar is ambitious. Well, obviously! Who isn't? And that Caesar wants to be king of all Rome. Well, maybe he does, but would he really try to make it happen?

Brutus stopped chewing.

Well, of course he would. The real question is: could he?

Brutus swallowed.

Yes, he could. And that's also a problem. And, gigantic pain in the neck though he is, Cassius IS an honorable man, whatever my wife and mother may say about him. As are they all—Casca, Cinna—all of them are honorable men. Well—for a given value of "honorable," I suppose. Still, honor ought to count for something.

"Casca and Cinna?" said Caesar. "Interesting. Who else is involved? How far does it go . . . ?"

* * * *

Dorker and Gladys roamed the streets searching for Caesar's gold. Molly had decided that, whatever else happened, they ought to know where the gold was. They were leprechauns, after all. Gold and leprechauns went together like . . . well, leprechauns and gold. She also didn't trust Dorn farther than she could throw him, even if he was magically chained to a wall. If Caesar had any gold to steal, better they know about it before Dorn. Dorker needed information.

The problem was that Dorker's Latin was still basic at best. Aunt Aggie's dictionary was useful, but didn't help with, for example, conjugating verbs, or everyday conversation. Plus, no one—leprechaun or human—could just walk up to an ordinary Roman citizen and say, "Hey you! Show me where Caesar's gold is, okay?" People would look at you as if you're crazy, dangerous, or both. Even Gladys, with all her knowledge of the Roman streets, alleys, and secret passages didn't know where the city's gold was stashed.

Finding Lucius was also proving difficult. Dorker had tried to explain to Gladys who Lucius was but had hit a snag—as far as Gladys was concerned, all Roman legionnaires looked alike. Frankly, most humans looked alike to Gladys.

They had almost no distinguishing plumage to speak of. And as intelligent as she was, you couldn't really brainstorm ideas with Gladys.

So they wandered Rome looking for inspiration. Dorker vaguely hoped an ancient tourist map that showed city landmarks—"CAESAR'S GOLD KEPT HERE!"—might blow accidentally to his feet. Or maybe some rich Romans might casually glide by, discussing their finances. Perhaps one might say to the others—in English (somehow): "Oh, *WE* keep all of *OUR* gold in the same place Caesar keeps *HIS*, doncha know—the New Bank of Rome, located at Third and Herculaneum, business hours six to midnight, maintaining a minimal guard presence between two and three a.m."

Both these things failed to happen.

What did happen was that while he and Gladys were wandering cautiously through a market square, someone threw a burlap bag over Dorker's head and silently dragged him away.

* * * *

Where she is, Reynard can't tell;
Molly's gone from sight or smell.

. . . thought Poor Reynard.

He was frustrated. Molly's scent had led him to Caesar's prison but breaking in posed obvious problems. On top of which, he was no longer confident she was even in there. Shortly after picking up the clearest psychic signal from her he had ever received—one that practically lit the way to her on the map in Reynard's mind—she had disappeared completely. Reynard would have assumed she was dead, except that he could still hear her thoughts quite clearly. It was confusing. His ordinary five senses were not equipped to find Molly in the strange, pseudo-neural space she currently occupied with Caesar listening to Brutus's thoughts.

But Reynard was nothing if not resourceful. He closed his eyes and focused on Molly. As he turned his mind's eye inward, a sixth sense engaged—one he had not known about until this moment—and a different sort of path opened before him. A path to a realm the likes of which Reynard had never experienced. But Molly was at the end of it, he was certain. And she was drawing him towards her. His teeth tingled.

Cautiously, he stuck out a paw, placed it down carefully, gave it a twist, and vanished from sight.

* * * *

Lucius sat in his barracks playing dice with Gracus and a group of six or seven other soldiers who participated in their semi-regular game. The game had no set time, but they all had an unspoken agreement that, if and when the opportunity presented itself, they would play. It was a good way to pass the time, and they enjoyed each other's company in an aggressively competitive sort of way. None possessed what Lucius would call real genius, but one or two did have a kind of feral street cunning that made them formidable gamblers. Lucius was better than all of them, by far. He was also a better cheat. Another man might have used those advantages to rob the other players blind—over and over again. But Lucius rarely played to win, at least not with the soldiers he commanded.[*]

"Is that all you're going to bet, Gaius?" said Gracus. "C'mon, you can do better than that. I'm on a hot streak today!"

"Shut up and roll," said Gaius through gritted teeth.

Lucius smiled inwardly. For him, the real game wasn't the game, but comradery, loyalty, and unit cohesion. He saw to it that he won enough that no one doubted he was the best player, but not so much that they felt totally outmatched. It was a delicate balance to maintain, but getting it right reinforced his dominance as their superior officer in a friendly way that encouraged creative competition. As long as he won slightly more overall, and everyone else won roughly the same amount, everyone felt good about the order of command, everyone maintained a keen competitive edge, and everyone was more or less happy.

"By Jupiter!" said Gaius, throwing up his hands. "Again?!"

"Read it and weep boys!" said Gracus, scooping a stack of coins into his growing pile.

Today, it was Gracus's turn to be the big winner. The pot salesman had taken all of Gracus's money, and Lucius felt a little bad about that. Not so bad

---

[*] When he played with soliders of his own rank, however, he was ruthless. He liked playing men who hated losing. Their repeated efforts to avenge themselves in subsequent games provided enough ready cash to handsomely supplement the otherwise meagre earnings he made as a soldier.

that he felt inclined to pay Gracus back, mind you. Suffering abuse at the hands of your superior officer was what being a Roman solider was all about. But invisibly manipulating the game so that Gracus won big today helped diffuse any lingering resentment. Besides, he would see to it that Gracus lost most of it the next time they played. But the *feeling*—that glorious, incomparable *feeling* of winning really big—had nothing to do with money and would stay with Gracus long after the game was over.

"Tell you what," said Gracus, "I'll yield my turn. How 'bout that? That's how good I'm feeling. Gaius? You roll. No?"

Keeping the game flowing in Gracus's favor required concentration and quite a lot of math as Lucius kept track in his head of how much money everyone had and who got to roll when. Also, Gracus was a terrible gambler. But curiously, concentrating on the game freed another part of Lucius's mind to think about other things that seriously needed his attention.

"By the Gods!" yelled Marcus, hurling his cup across the room as Gracus won again.

Take Molly, for example. Lucius considered himself a man of the world, but in all his travels, he had never seen anything like her. What on earth was she? Not human, that much was clear. Lucius was not a complicated man, and generally did not believe in anything he couldn't see or touch. He counted on people to be stupid, cruel, and occasionally—in very limited circumstances—breathtakingly kind: that was the extent of his belief system. He did not, therefore, believe the Gods had thrown Molly in his path as part of any grand design. Gods, in his experience, didn't work like that. But whatever she was, Molly was real. Not human, but real.

It might not *mean* anything in the grand scheme of things, but the mere fact of her existence suggested that a lot of what Lucius thought he knew about the world was drastically wrong.

* * * *

Dorker's abduction had been so fast and unexpected, he wasn't sure what had happened to him. He also had no idea what had happened to Gladys. He hoped she was okay.

Dorker suspected he was now being led through a Roman sewer. He couldn't imagine anything else smelling quite like this. The smell had weight.

Even the Roman streets didn't prepare him for it. It mauled his senses the way a mother bear might maul an animal threatening her babies—indiscriminately, relentlessly, and from all sides. He was almost grateful he had a bag over his head.

Eventually, he was thrust onto a hard, wooden chair and told not to move. He didn't really know what they were saying to him, given his still-rudimentary Latin, but he figured it wasn't anything good and that his best move was probably to just stay still.

Faced with danger, Dorker's gut impulse had always been to smile a lot and adopt an air of good-natured stupidity. He had discovered in his relatively short life that he was quite good at it. It was like a natural talent. He *wasn't* stupid, but when people believed he was, they were much more forgiving of his other shortcomings. Somehow, it made them feel safe. They let their guards down and revealed more to him than they might to their closest friends.

But stressful circumstances sometimes bring clarity: the night before a battle, a soldier realizes she should marry the person she loves; a man with a year to live decides to write that novel he's been planning; and sitting in an ancient Roman sewer with a bag over his head, Dorker suddenly knew why he liked Molly so much. When Molly looked at him, she seemed to expect something more from him than good-natured stupidity. In fairness, she also looked disappointed quite a lot. But she did seem to assume that a brain of some sort was operating between those sizable ears of his, and it dawned on him (somewhat unpleasantly) that not many people looked at him that way. And maybe that was his fault. He considered—maybe he didn't have to act stupid all the time. Maybe it was time to find out if there was (as Molly seemed to think) anything more to Dorker.

* * * *

Brutus fought with himself.

Okay, yes, Caesar is ambitious. Why wouldn't he be? We're all a little bit ambitious, aren't we? Who doesn't fantasize about being king? I know I do. But would he act on that ambition? That's the question. If I were in his position, would I? No, of course, I wouldn't. No honorable man would do such a thing!

"Aaaand there it is," said Caesar with a satisfied smile. "We all lie to ourselves, Molly. No one wants to believe that he—" Caesar glanced down at

Molly, "or she—is a bad person. But watch now. In a few minutes, he will have convinced himself that not only am I ambitious, but a danger to Rome."

Molly frowned. "How will he do that?"

Caesar shrugged. "I've known Brutus for a long time. He believes himself morally superior to other men. He believes that he would never act inconsistently with his honor or values, but that everyone else does so regularly. He is not wrong about that second part."

"But *are* you a danger to Rome?"

Caesar looked at her. "Of course I am. Any ambitious man with an army at his command is dangerous. No, what Brutus is wrong about is believing that he would be any different."

* * * *

Lucius also thought about gold. Whatever Molly was, she and her kind apparently had quite a lot of it. That was . . . intriguing.

"Thank you, my friends," said Gracus, raking in another pile of coins. He was having the game of his life. "It's a pleasure doing business."

"I'm out," said Lepidus. "That was my whole month's pay!"

Lucius liked being a soldier, but he'd quit in a heartbeat for a pile of gold. Money may not buy happiness, but it does buy options. He didn't know what options might be available to someone like him, but some immediate ideas sprang to mind involving (1) better housing, (2) better food, and (3) not having crazed barbarians swinging giant axes at his head all the time.

"Let me roll, Gracus!"

Gracus slapped Marcus's hand away. "Ah-ah! Wait your turn."

One thing bothered Lucius. He had tried to shake it off, but he couldn't. In his not-so-humble opinion,[F] Caesar had been unfair to Molly. Or maybe what really bothered Lucius was the possibility that he, Lucius, had been unfair? But he had promised her he would tell her what he knew about Caesar's gold, and that's what he had done. He hadn't promised to tell her *everything* he knew—like where it was exactly. So, he hadn't lied. Not exactly.

Right?

Right. He had helped, just as he said he would. Besides, he couldn't control what a man like Caesar might do. No one could. Interfere with a man like Caesar

---

[F] There is no such thing as a "humble" opinion.

and you probably deserve what you get. Men like Caesar don't trouble themselves with *feelings*, or *justice*, or *fairness*. They take what they want and let others worry about how everyone *feels* about it. In lesser men, that's called "narcissism." In men like Caesar, it's called "leadership."

"Unbelievable!" yelled Marcus. "Are you sure these dice aren't loaded, Lucius?"

They were loaded, as it happens, extremely so, but it was bad form to suggest it, even in jest. Lucius glared at Marcus.

"Okay, okay," said Marcus, sheepishly. "I just . . . urrrgh!"

So no, Lucius hadn't been unfair. But he wondered if maybe Molly had understood "helping" to mean "protecting"—making sure nothing bad would happen to her. He would never make such a promise, of course. He prided himself on a sort of basic honesty, which included not making promises he couldn't keep. That worked fine with fellow soldiers. Soldiers respected brutal honesty.

"FINALLY!" cheered Gaius. "Maybe your luck's running out Gracus!"

"Hey, you can't win 'em all," Gracus said.

"*You* can," muttered Gaius, throwing a brief, suspicious look at Lucius, "apparently. But all that's about to change, my friend. Hand the dice over."

Why then, Lucius wondered, did it feel different with Molly? Not because she was a child, certainly. Lucius was not so sentimental. Could it be that he just sort of . . . liked her? *Cared* about what happened to her? Just a little bit?

"ARE YOU KIDDING ME?!!!?" Gaius yelled.

That thought *really* bothered Lucius. He didn't *like* anyone. He *got along* with just about everyone and was prepared to die for his men without hesitation. But he didn't really have what you would call "friends." He didn't trust anyone *that* much.

Or maybe he was just . . . intrigued. It's not every day that your entire understanding of the universe is upended. Yesterday, there was no such thing as magic (other than the nonsense practiced by street grifters and temple priests). Yesterday, the world did not contain winged horses, three-headed dogs, or creatures like Molly.

Today, it did.

To Lucius, that changed everything. He wanted—no, *needed*—to know more.

"Okay fellas," said Lucius, taking the dice. "My turn."

* * * *

Whate'er shall be, shall be;
Thou Universe—ope' thine arms to me.

. . . thought Poor Reynard.

In darkness, he travelled, but Reynard didn't know on what, if anything, he walked. He had no sense of himself in space. Nor did he know where he was—or if there even was a "where" for him to be. Wherever he was, the concept of "where" very likely meant something else altogether. But it did not matter that no light, or sound, or smell, or much of anything else seemed to exist. He knew he was getting closer. Molly's thoughts were like a lighthouse on an ocean.

Poor Reynard was not alarmed by these strange and unusual circumstances. Following Molly had led to so many jaw-dropping experiences that wandering through a space of near non-being was no more surprising than a sudden rainstorm. As he walked, he thought about the legendary fox Shenan'igans, who, the stories told, once broke into a henhouse intending to have a late-night snack, received total enlightenment from the chicken guru, Igrit, then spent the rest of his life travelling the earth, receptive to anything and everything the universe offered. Shenan'igans was an unusual figure in fox mythology in that his chief lessons focused on humility and wisdom, rather than raw cunning, trickery, and intelligence. He was the fox equivalent of a wandering monk.

It comforted Reynard to think that his journey had mythic proportions. There's only so much humility one fox can take.

* * * *

Dorker sat on a small, uncomfortable stool in an ancient Roman sewer. He might have felt better about his situation if he had known his captors, who sat across from him, were also leprechauns. But probably not.

His captors had seen some interrogations and knew how this was supposed to go. Their job was to menace; their captive's job was to talk. A lot.

They weren't doing badly. They had good glowers, good sneers, and were comfortable with uncomfortable silences. All in all, their natural talent combined with a seriousness of purpose that might have resulted in some first-rate menacing if they hadn't forgotten to take off Dorker's hood.

It's this sort of attention to detail that distinguishes the truly great interrogator from the weekend hobbyist.

When it became clear that silent menace was not producing the desired results, their efforts were further confounded by the fact that they were the only two leprechauns in ancient Rome whose ability to learn foreign languages was worse than Dorker's.

"Who are you and what are you doing here?" one of the captors finally demanded.

"Who are you and what do you want?" Dorker yelled back.

In the perplexed silence that followed, Dorker's captors frowned at each other.

"Look," yelled Dorker, "Maybe we could clear up this little misunderstanding if you take my hood off so I can see you?"

The first captor murmured out of the corner of his mouth, "Did you understand any of that?"

"Not a word," mumbled the second. "Maybe we should take his hood off."

"Good idea," said the first. He turned to Dorker. "We're going to take your hood off! No sudden moves, now!" He reached forward and pulled off the hood.

"Ah! Excellent!" said Dorker, blinking in the dim light. "Maybe I'm getting the hang of this language thing after all."

Now that he had a chance to look at them, Dorker saw that one of his captors was short, round, and balding. The other (as is often the case in partnerships like these) was the opposite—tall and skinny, with a mop of thick black hair on his head that completely covered his eyes.

"Tell us your name!" demanded the short one, whom Dorker, for no particular reason, had already begun to think of as "Terry." Dorker stared at them, hoping that intense concentration might somehow make the mish-mash of sounds he heard comprehensible.

It didn't.

Not knowing what else to do, to help make himself understood, he resorted to tactics known by tourists worldwide:

"WHAAAAAT? AAAAARE? YOOOOOOUR? NAAAAAAMES?"

Terry leaned over to the tall one (whom Dorker had started to think of as

"Neil") and whispered: "He's shouting at us and talking slowly. Why is he doing that?"

"Not sure," whispered Neil. "Must be a tourist. I think we should shout back."

"Agreed," whispered Terry.

"WHAAAAT IIIIIIS YOOOOOUR NAAAAAME?"

Dorker had no idea what Neil had said, but the fact that everyone was shouting now made it *feel* as if they spoke the same language. He decided to introduce himself.

"MYYYY NAAAAME," he yelled with a big smile, "IIIIIS DOORRRRRRKERRRR. DOR-KER. DORKER."

"What the—?" said Neil scratching his head.

"No idea," said Terry. "And why is he smiling?"

"I have no idea. D'you reckon he's . . ." Neil tapped his temple,

". . . all there, so to speak?"

"Hard to say," said Terry.

"I'll tell you this," said Neil, "he's lucky we found him. What kind of idiot goes wandering around Roman streets in broad daylight?"

"With a giant chicken, no less!" said Terry.

"Tell you what," said Dorker, who was feeling a little left out, "forget my name. We'll come back to it. I'm new to Rome. You probably figured that out. So listen, I'm just going to trust you. I don't have much choice at this point. I need to find Caesar's gold."

Terry and Neil stared at him blankly.

"SEEEEE-SAR'S! GOLD!" Dorker yelled. "Can? You? Help? Me?"

"Did he just say 'Caesar?'" whispered Neil.

"I think he did," said Terry. He looked at Dorker and nodded the way you might to a toddler who had just used the potty for the first time. "YES! THAT'S RIGHT! CAESAR LIVES IN ROME! BUT WHY *YOU* HERE?"

Terry's sing-song tone made Dorker smile, but otherwise he was lost. He replayed what Terry had said in his head and slowly, a candle of comprehension lit itself.

"Wait a minute! 'Here.' You said 'here.' I understood that! And 'why' . . . 'why, here' . . . Why am I here? Why I am here! Is that what you said? I think that's what you said!"

BOOK OF LEPRECHAUNS: THE LORE GATHERERS

Terry and Neil smiled and nodded encouragingly. Dorker felt a surge of confidence. He decided to go for broke and try some Latin.

"I am here to steal Caesar's gold!"

. . . is what he tried to say. What he actually said was, "Self-harmony am Caesar slinking!"

Terry and Neil gaped open-mouthed at Dorker.

Dorker tried again: "Caesar's gold. Steal!"

. . . which came out sounding a lot like: "Gold Caesar. Fly!"

It wasn't much, but all three shared a cautiously optimistic sense that they were getting somewhere, even if they weren't certain where.

* * * *

In his jail cell, Shaun dreamed. In his dream, he was back home sitting with Alice at their kitchen table. He could smell bread baking and hear birds outside the window. It was spring.

"I haven't heard your voice in so long," he said.

Alice smiled but said nothing.

"Oh, I miss you so, Alice," he said reaching across the table. Alice took his hand. "I wish you were really here to talk to."

"Then talk, Shaun," said Alice.

"I've messed it all up, my love."

"What have you messed up?"

"Everything."

Alice tilted her head. "How so?"

"I let Molly look after the gold, and now I'm sitting in a Roman prison two thousand years in the past, and I have no idea where Molly is or whether she's safe. Stupid! I'm so stupid! She's just not ready, and . . . Stupid, I'm . . . anyway . . . ."

Alice sighed and looked out the window.

"How did you get here, Shaun?"

"Well, Caesar put me in prison when Molly didn't—"

"No," Alice interrupted, "how did you get here?"

Shaun looked at her. "Um . . . Molly got grabbed by this Roman pot salesman—"

"Shaun, you're not hearing me," said Alice. "Listen to yourself. How did you get here?"

Shaun frowned. "Molly lost all our gold, so we were—"

"Shaun!" Alice slammed the table with both hands.

"WHAT?!? I don't understand!"

"Everything is not Molly's fault!!"

"Who said everything's her fault?" Shaun sputtered. "I never said that!"

"It's what you believe!" said Alice. "Even after Dorn *admitted* that he stole the gold, you still blame Molly!"

"Well, I . . ." Shaun trailed off, muttering indistinctly about responsibilities and lessons. Then he said more forcefully, "She had a job to do! She was supposed to—"

"No! Forget 'supposed to,' Shaun. You know as well as I do that Dorn would have stolen that gold no matter who was looking after it. It's Molly's bad luck it was her, *that's all! You* couldn't have stopped it. *You* couldn't have seen it coming."

"If I had—"

"No! Shaun! You couldn't. Whatever you're telling yourself you could have done, you couldn't. And neither could Molly. So just stop it, Shaun. Stop it!!"

In all their years together, Shaun had never gone wrong admitting when Alice was right, and he figured he'd be a fool to start now, even if this was only a dream. Admitting it was never *easy*, but Alice was the only true thing he knew. He took a deep breath, closed his eyes, and exhaled.

Alice smiled.

"You're not the best father in the world, Shaun. You control her when you shouldn't, and too often you leave her alone when she needs you. But I've got even harder news for you: you're not the worst father in the world, either. Molly is a smart, resourceful young woman. You had *something* to do with that."

"Did I?" asked Shaun doubtfully.

Alice got a funny look on her face. Shaun knew it well. It usually meant she was about to talk about something he wouldn't understand.

"Molly is a lot like you, Shaun. And a lot like me. But don't kid yourself. Most of all, she's a lot like herself. That is a *very good thing*, Shaun! Don't try to make her into you, or me, or anyone else."

Shaun nodded.

"And Shaun?"

"Yes?"

"It's not her fault I died."

Shaun sighed deeply. "I know that."

"It's not your fault, either."

Shaun closed his eyes tightly and was quiet for a long time. At last he said in a small voice: "I just miss you so much, Alice. All these years, I keep trying to think what I could have done differently. How I could have stopped it. If I could figure it out, I think . . . I somehow keep thinking you'll come back. That I'll get you back. That I'll wake up one morning, and you'll be there, lying in bed next to me as if nothing had ever happened. The bed will be the same as it was, and the world will make sense again."

Alice smiled.

"But you're not coming back, are you Alice?"

"No, Shaun, I'm not."

Shaun nodded gently and was quiet for a moment.

"She doesn't talk to me, Alice. Molly doesn't. Do you know she has never talked to me about you? Not once. And now, she talks to me less and less about anything."

"And do you talk to her?"

Shaun frowned. "Certainly. I mean . . . yes, I . . . Well, yes, I think—"

Alice sighed. "No, you don't, Shaun. Not really. Not about what matters. You talk about your research, your lists. You lecture her, you worry her. You panic, you fret. You YELL. You don't talk about *her* feelings, *her* life, what *she's* interested in. When I died, she watched it nearly kill you, and you never talked to her about *that*, either. Why would you think she would ever talk to you about me?"

Shaun was silent.

"You are going to lose her, Shaun."

"What?!? NO!! I don't want to lose her, too," said Shaun desperately, shaking in his seat.

"Not like that, Shaun," said Alice, smiling. "Children grow up. We all lose our children. We only get so much time before they go off and make their own life. That's the deal. And it's a *good* bargain, Shaun. *If* you take the time. Losing her may not be the worst thing in the world. If you let her go, she might just find herself. She might even find you again. If you let her."

Shaun clung to Alice's words. When she died all those years ago, he had put himself back together piece by piece, only by sheer will. All his lists and routines, all his efforts to protect or control Molly had only amounted to the thinnest thread holding all his pieces together. He could have been preparing Molly, teaching her, learning about her. Sharing his life with her. Learning from her. So much more he could have done. But that would have meant letting her make mistakes, letting her get hurt. Even thinking about it felt like another death. How could he possibly let her go?

As if reading his mind, Alice said, "Because you love her, Shaun. And because we do what must be done."

Alice's words sounded like thunder, and the kitchen, and all their surroundings began to rattle and dissolve. Desperately, Shaun grabbed for Alice's hand.

"How do I do it, Alice? What should I do?"

"Trust her, Shaun. Just trust her. What's the worst that could happen?"

"The world could end?" said Shaun.

"Shaun," she smiled, shaking her head, "you're impossible."

Shaun awoke gasping for air, as Alice receded once more into darkness.

* * * *

There's a game called "Telephone" where you sit in a circle and one person whispers a sentence to his or her neighbor and it gets repeated around the circle from one person to the next. The fun of it is that by the time it makes its way around the circle, what the last person in the circle hears typically bears little resemblance to the original sentence. Something like that was happening with Dorker and his captors.

"So, the best I can figure out so far," said Terry, "is that this guy, whose name may or may not be 'Dorker,' believes that: (1) gold is either flying all around Caesar, or Caesar is made of gold, I'm not sure which; (2) gold, or possibly a fish salad, was stolen from someone in a faraway land; and (3) he hopes at some point to carry Caesar back there and either bury him, or eat him. Anyway, there was a lot about gold."

Neil frowned.

"So, he's an idiot."

"Possibly," said Terry, nodding. "What I can't figure out is why we can't understand what he's saying? I'm generally pretty good with languages."

"Don't be ridiculous," said a voice from behind Dorker. "You and your brother couldn't pick up a new language if it fell in your laps."

The voice was familiar to Dorker, but he couldn't quite place it. It belonged to a woman, he could tell that much, but she was standing behind him in the dark so he couldn't get a good look at her. His captors, however, knew exactly who it was, and were not happy about it. When Terry spoke, he sounded like a little boy caught with his hand in a cookie jar.

"Oh! Mum!" said Terry. "We didn't know you were coming. We . . . we found this one wandering around Rome, plain as day, is what we did. So we been questioning him."

"Questioning him? You didn't bring him to me? Why?" said the woman suspiciously.

"Well . . . you know, to . . . find out . . . stuff."

The woman sighed and shook her head. "You've been interrogating him, haven't you?"

"Yes, Mum," said Terry guiltily.

"Well, have you learned anything?"

"Well, there are these flying salads—"

"I didn't think so," said the woman. "Untie him, please."

"Yes, Mum."

"Fortunately," said the woman, "I have spoken to the chicken."

* * * *

Say this for him, Caesar understood people. It had only taken Brutus another fifteen minutes of arguing with himself before he was convinced that (a) Caesar wanted to be king, (b) Caesar would be a dangerous king, and (c) he must join Cassius's plot to assassinate Caesar. For the good of Rome, of course. And if Caesar's assassination left Rome needing a new ruler (temporarily, you understand, just until order was reestablished and control of the government could be safely entrusted once more to the Roman Senate), well that was a burden Brutus would have to bear.

Molly was impressed. She had seen her father convince himself of some far-fetched ideas before, especially when he really wanted them to be true, but it usually took him a few days at least (along with a few sleepless nights) before he reached any truly radical conclusions. By comparison, the mental gymnastics of Brutus had been Olympian.

Now, however, Caesar had moved on to his second wish: Cassius's thoughts. Molly didn't understand Caesar's wishes. She figured that once he knew about the conspiracy, he would have moved on to other things. What more was there to learn from Cassius?

Cassius was nothing like Brutus. Where Brutus's room was spare and spotless, Cassius's room was filled with stuff. He clearly relished his wealth and position and wanted everyone else to relish it as well. The room was filled with artwork and elegant furniture. Objects collected from foreign lands were displayed strategically on the walls and mantles, bespeaking a man who had not only seen the world, but plundered it with exquisite taste. What Molly noticed most, however, was the disarray. The room wasn't cluttered exactly, but small details suggested a cluttered mind, and more than that, an unpredictable temper. Parchments were strewn on a desk in the corner cascading onto the floor. Cushions that should have been on a chair lay halfway across the room. And on the floor by a mantle, a telltale mirror lay shattered in pieces.

The man himself bristled with barely contained energy. His thinning, curly red hair looked as hot and tangled as his temper. His searching, saucer-like eyes darted this way and that, as if trying to capture the gnat-like thoughts swarming his head. Even sitting still, he vibrated.

He sat at a long table and shoved into his mouth a piece of steak so bloody and rare, it practically mooed.

I should have told Brutus to go stick his head in a barrel of wine, that's what I should have done. Thinks he's so much better than I am! But no! I listened to him. Respectfully. Argued calmly and rationally. Didn't let him see how angry he was making me. Once—just once, I'd like to haul off and slug Brutus right on the nose.

"Remarkable," said Caesar.

It's always such a dance with Brutus, getting him to do anything.

He wiped red steak juice from his chin.

I know just what he's going to do, too. He's going to think about it, and pace, and wring his hands, and agonize, and rationalize, and then finally—FINALLY—he'll come back to me and not only agree to be part of the conspiracy, but insist on leading it. Has to do it his way. Everything always has to be HIS way!

"Cassius understands Brutus, I'll give him that," said Caesar. "But watch what happens next, Molly."

"You know what's going to happen?" Molly asked.

Caesar smiled thinly. "I know people. They are like actors in a play. Brutus is complex. Cassius is simple. But they're both . . . inevitable in their own way."

A servant slid into the room cautiously.

"Forgive me, lord," said the servant.

Cassius looked up from a dripping, red slice of beef and went over to the servant, who cowered as he handed Cassius a parchment.

"From Brutus, my lord."

The servant slunk away as Cassius read the letter. His face got even redder than it already was. Finally, he crumpled the scroll, threw it to the floor violently, and paced back and forth slowly for a moment or two. Then, just when it seemed as if his temper might have cooled, he grabbed a nearby chair and flung it across the room, breaking a beautifully carved chair leg and taking a small side table from Germany down with it. His thoughts became the mental equivalent of pots and pans being hurled around a kitchen. Molly couldn't understand a thing.

Eventually, with supreme effort, Cassius calmed himself, went to where the crumpled parchment lay, and picked it up. He walked back to his table, sat down, and took a deep breath. Then he picked up a piece of meat with his knife and contemplated it. Finally, he ate the meat and held the parchment up to a candle, gently setting it aflame as he chewed.

As I thought. He wants to lead the conspiracy? Fine! No problem. He can lead the conspiracy. Then he can take the responsibility! And HE can deal with the magical soothsayer. And when the people riot—and they surely will—HE can try to calm them down. And when he fails, I take over!

Molly's jaw was agape. "So, they're all just plotting against each other while they plot against you?"

"Does that surprise you?"

"That's crazy," said Molly.

"That's Rome," said Caesar.

* * * *

Reynard now roams in open light,
But veiled, as 'twere, in shadowed night.

. . . thought Poor Reynard.

Brutus and his wife Portia were arguing. Molly's trail had led Reynard to their chambers and now, Reynard stood directly between them, slightly bewildered. They couldn't see him. Nor could Reynard smell them. He reached out to gently nibble Portia's ankle, but his teeth passed right through. Curious. As for what he could hear—he could hear *everything*—even their thoughts. He didn't mind hearing Molly's thoughts. Molly had earned it. These two, however—why did they deserve access to Reynard's beautiful mind? In protest, Reynard widdled on Brutus's leg.[†]

Then it came to him—he was in a pseudo-psychological, slightly notional space, possibly existing somewhere between Brutus's and Portia's neurons.

Now it all made sense.

What could Molly have been doing in such a place, Reynard wondered. She had been here not long ago. Molly and . . . someone else. Someone dangerous. Reynard's tail bristled.

****

"Gladys, try not to make any noise," said Dorker.

"Cluck," said Gladys quietly.

Dorker, Gladys, and a leprechaun named Fergus stood outside Lucius's barracks and peered in. Lucius was still in the middle of his game.

A lot had happened in a short space of time and Dorker's head was spinning. He had met with the leprechaun woman who could talk to Gladys, and his mind had been boggled, beggared, and blown. She had quickly dismissed his interrogators, who were not doing anyone any good, so that she and Dorker could talk alone. As far as Dorker could tell, the woman had an indeterminate number of children that she called upon to serve as her eyes and ears throughout Rome. As a result, very little happened in the city that she didn't know about. But that wasn't the most remarkable thing about her. No, the most remarkable thing about her had, quite simply, challenged everything

---

[†] Or where his leg would have been if Reynard had been there in any non-magical sense. It's probably best not to wonder where exactly he widdled.

Dorker thought he knew about leprechauns.

But there was no time to think about that. They had finally found Lucius.

Fergus was one of the woman's sons. The woman had insisted he accompany Dorker, and Dorker was not happy about it. As far as Dorker was concerned, he and Molly had made a plan (actually Molly had made the plan and Dorker had agreed to it), and this part was his responsibility. That is called "Being an Adult." When, however, the woman had pointed out that Dorker still couldn't really speak Latin, he grudgingly allowed Fergus to come along, but only as a translator.

The problem was, as good as Fergus was with languages, he had terrible manners. He was also shorter than the average leprechaun and made up for it with a metaphorical chip on his shoulder that far exceeded his size.

"Let me do the talking, okay?" said Dorker.

Fergus shrugged. "Talk all you want, friend. This'll never work."

Gladys shoved Fergus against a wall and glared at him meaningfully.

"What?!? I'm just saying!"

"It's okay, Gladys," said Dorker.

"Baaaaaaaaaaaaaaaawk," warned Gladys, backing away from Fergus slowly. Fergus couldn't speak chicken, but he got the point.

"S'not right, you talking to chickens," Fergus muttered. "S'not natural."

Fergus didn't like Gladys. He especially didn't like that she always seemed to be looking down on him. She *was*, in fact, always looking down on him because she was about eight or nine inches taller than Fergus. But Gladys also carried herself as if she wasn't just taller, but also . . . well, *superior* to Fergus. Worse, Fergus couldn't shake the feeling that she might be right.

"Anyway, you don't know these humans like I do," said Fergus. He tapped his head. "They're not smart like us, see? Small brains."

Dorker wasn't so sure. Time traveling had given him two thousand years' worth of perspective that Fergus lacked. Like most lore gatherers, Dorker had generally believed humans didn't have much to brag about in the brain department. And from what he had seen so far, humans hadn't fundamentally changed in two thousand years. They were just as selfish, abusive, and needlessly cruel in ancient Rome as they were in the twenty-first century.

On the other hand, the ancient Romans had sewers and aqueducts. They made art and built complex bridges. Dorker couldn't help but wonder if an animal that had done all of this might be smarter—or at least more complex—than lore gatherers assumed.

He clung to this hope as he considered how best to approach Lucius. Just walking up and saying "Hi" was probably not the best strategy, but unfortunately, he didn't know what else to do. The problem often faced by genuinely good, decent, and trusting people is that they just do not see the point in anything other than straightforward honesty. "Guile," "cunning," and "subterfuge" were not in Dorker's vocabulary.

Lacking other alternatives, he picked up a rock and threw it at Lucius. It was about as subtle as Dorker could get. It might have even worked if the rock hadn't sailed wide and hit Gracus instead.

"OW! What in the name of Jove—?!?" Gracus looked around. Dorker ducked behind the entry way.

"Nice one!" said Fergus, giving him the thumbs up. Fergus always enjoyed pointless cruelty to humans.

"What's with you?" said one of Gracus's companions.

"Someone just threw this rock at my head!"

"Why would someone throw a rock at *your* head?" said another. "Rocks can't hurt rocks!" He rapped Gracus on the head a couple of times with his knuckles, as the other soldiers laughed appreciatively. It wasn't a great joke. It wasn't even a good joke. But a joke at the expense of someone else was always worth encouraging. It meant the next one was less likely to be aimed at you.

"Ha, ha," said Gracus, swatting him away and rubbing his ear. "Just play, would you?"

Fergus, who was suddenly very glad to be on this trip, grinned at Dorker hugely. "That was great! My turn!" He picked up a rock and reared back, but Dorker caught his arm in time.

"No!" said Dorker. "I didn't mean to . . . I need to figure out how to get a message to Lucius." He had another idea. It wasn't *that* different from the rock, really, and it was a little more risky. It shouldn't have worked. But even Dorker got lucky sometimes.

"OW!" cried Lucius.

"You get hit by a rock too, Lucius?" said Gracus.

"YES!" Lucius yelled, looking around for a non-existent rock.

"Where'd it hit you? I didn't see it."

As Lucius rubbed his temple, the stinging on the side of his head stimulated other nerves in his brain. Synapse lighted synapse, one after another in a neurological waterfall of free association. Thoughts triggered feelings; feelings activated sensory recall. Lucius paused, letting the cloud of memory carefully take shape. Finally, clarity: it had not been a rock that hit him. He knew what rocks felt like. He had been hit in the head by plenty of rocks. This had felt more like a small, but very hard fist—a fist that felt suspiciously like the one that had hit him in the head not long ago. He surveyed the area more carefully.

Could Molly have escaped?

Finally, he caught sight of an optimistic little head not unlike Molly's peering around the doorway at the end of the room, smiling and waving in a way that managed to be both enthusiastic and furtive. Whatever his other shortcomings, Dorker's wide-open face was instantly disarming. Even Lucius had to suppress a smile.

"Now what?" whispered Fergus.

Dorker scratched his head uncertainly and tried to catch his breath. He had never dashed into a group of humans like that before. But they had been focused on their game, and as has been noted, humans generally don't notice leprechauns where they don't expect to see them. "We need a diversion," Dorker panted. "We have to get the rest of those soldiers out of there somehow. Maybe you could go in there and kind of—?"

"Sorry friend. I came here to translate. I'm not going to risk my—"

"BAAAAAAAAAAAWK!"

"GLADYS NO!" Dorker whispered.

Taking matters into her own beak, Gladys charged, screaming into the soldiers' barracks and flapping her wings like a deranged Valkyrie. Plumage puffed and neck stretched to its full height, this imposing bird looked even bigger and more terrifying than usual. She upended the table on which Lucius and the others played, sending dice and money flying.

"WHAT THE—?!?" yelled Gracus.

"Grab it!" yelled one of the faster-thinking soldiers. "Dinner's on me, boys!"

Turning over more furniture, the soldiers scrambled clumsily to their feet and ran around the room, trying to catch the berserking chicken. In the midst of the chaos, Lucius stayed calmly seated, looking fixedly at Dorker. Finally, when Gladys was satisfied that she had whipped the soldiers into a sufficient frenzy, she led them out of the room and down the corridor, stumbling over each other.

As Gladys's squawks (and their swearing) faded into the distance, the dust settled, and Dorker entered, smiling sheepishly. Fergus followed with his hands in his pockets, regarding Lucius as he might regard something rancid stuck to his shoe.

Lucius didn't look threatening, but he didn't look very inviting either. More than anything, he looked alert.

"I'm sorry I hit you on the head," said Dorker. "I didn't know how else to get your attention. Oh, and uh, sorry about all . . . this," he said, gesturing to the mess Gladys had made.

"I can't understand you," said Lucius steadily.

Dorker elbowed Fergus in the ribs. "Translate what I just said."

Fergus nodded. "Don't worry, I'll use small words."

Fergus cleared his throat and spoke loudly and slowly: "He hit you on head! So sorry! If he don't hit you, you don't see him because you too stooooopiiid!"

Lucius turned and glared at Dorker.

Dorker cringed. "What did you say?!?" he whispered urgently.

"Just what you said," said Fergus. "I just used words he can understand."

Dorker groaned. He turned back to Lucius.

"So, look, I'm a friend of Molly . . ."

"HE MOLLY FRIEND!" Fergus translated.

"It turns out that we may need some gold to get home. Can you tell us where Caesar keeps his?"

"YOU TELL US WHERE CAESAR KEEP GOLD, WE NOT KILL YOU!"

Lucius stood up slowly and put his hand to his sword. Dorker's eyes bulged.

"Are you translating what I'm saying?!?" Dorker asked desperately.

"Word for word!" said Fergus. "Pretty much. I told you, humans are too stupid to understand anything. Oooh! He's a live one though, isn't he!" Fergus began dancing and shadow boxing on the spot, taunting Lucius. "C'mon big boy, show me what you got!"

Dorker turned back to Lucius. "Why are you so angry?"

"WHY YOU MAD, STOOPID HUMAN?" asked Fergus.

"I don't care for threats," said Lucius coolly. "Or insults."

"Thr . . . eats!" said Dorker sounding it out. "Threats! I understood threats! YES! I understood—Wait, what threats?!? Fergus, did you threaten him?!?"

"No! Not at all! Well, maybe. I may have. Just a bit. I mean, you've got to threaten humans. Force is all they understand, really. Gotta let them know who's boss."

"Nooooooooo!!" Dorker shook his head furiously. "You're going to ruin everything! I don't *want* to let him know who's boss. I don't *want* to threaten him. Do you understand? I *want* him to *HELP US!*"

"Look pal," said Fergus, "if you want to do this by yourself, be my guest. I have better things to do."

Lucius could not understand their conversation, but he had seen enough arguments in foreign languages to get a pretty clear idea of what was going on.

"You." He pointed at Fergus.

"Oi! Oi! Oi!" said Fergus. "Don't you point that fat ugly finger at me, monkey-boy! I'll rip it right off your hand for you!"

"Ah! Excellent!" said Lucius. He leaned down, put his face level with Fergus, and said pointedly: "I understood that *perfectly*."

Fergus's eyes grew wide.

"I want *you* to translate *his* words *perfectly*," said Lucius. "Do you understand?"

"'Course I do!" said Fergus. "What do you take me for, some kind of idiot?"

"Don't treat me like an idiot, and I'll do the same for you. Fair enough?"

"But you *are* an idiot," Fergus explained, genuinely struggling with the idea. "You are a hu-man."

"I'll put it this way," said Lucius. "You're tough, I believe that. But I have this big sharp sword here, see? And do you know the best thing about a big sharp sword?"

Doubt flickered across Fergus's face. "No, what?"

"I only have to get lucky once."

Fergus considered. "Okay human. I am, for the purposes of this conversation, willing to consider the possibility that you may be smarter than a sheep. Fair enough? Come on! Can't ask fairer than that!"

"Just translate."

"Oh, alright," said Fergus, dropping his fists reluctantly.

"Good," said Lucius. "Now we're getting somewhere."

* * * *

Molly's head reeled. They had finished with Cassius and were now back in Caesar's chambers. Caesar reclined on a cushioned chair with a glass of wine.

"There you have it," said Caesar. "What do you think?"

"What do *I* think?" said Molly. "Who cares what I think. They're not my wishes."

"Humor me," said Caesar.

"I think you're all crazy."

"You are probably right about that, Molly," said Caesar, smiling. "We're all a bit crazy. Someone once said that anyone who seeks power is inherently unfit to have it."

"Is that what you think?" Molly asked.

Caesar looked at her seriously. "No," he said. "I do not. I will tell you what I think, Molly. I think some are born to lead, some are chosen to lead, and some have leadership thrust upon them. I am all three. I think Rome can be a light of civilization in a dark, unforgiving world. I think we will cultivate learning, gather it from every corner of the globe and make it our own. And through us, the light will spread. By force, if necessary."

"By force?"

"Yes, force. The world outside Rome is barbaric, Molly. I have seen it. Rome must conquer others or others will conquer us. That is the way of things. The way of the world. Wars will always be fought. People will always die in them. That will happen. As it has always happened, as far back as man can remember, no matter what you or I do. Powerful men will always seek greater power. But to what end? Isn't that the better question? If wars must be fought, if men must die, what they die *for* matters! Barbarians bring chaos, disorder, and death. But I will bring civilization, law, and life. A better life for all. That is what I think."

Molly looked skeptical. Then Caesar grew quiet.

"I'll tell you what else I think."

"Okaaaaay," said Molly.

"I think these conspirators who want to kill me—Brutus, Cassius, and the others—I think they will succeed."

Molly said nothing.

"I think you think so too," said Caesar.

Molly tried to remain calm. "You don't know what I think."

Caesar smiled. "I'm not a fool, Molly," he said simply. "Do you know why I showed you Brutus and Cassius's thoughts?"

Molly frowned. "Showed me? What do you mean? I showed you."

"No, Molly. I knew about the conspiracy. I know what they're thinking better than they know themselves. I wanted *you* to see what these men are. These so-called leaders. These men who would thwart me. If you are what I believe you are, you may already know what will happen if they succeed. War. Civil war. These conspirators will work together long enough to suit their own ends, and then they will turn on each other. Rome will be thrust into chaos. More will die needlessly. I would avoid that fate."

Molly didn't like how much Caesar seemed to know about her.

"You think I already know what will happen?" said Molly. "How could I know?"

Caesar put down his drink, dropped to his hands and knees, and crawled over to Molly, fear and desperation in his eyes.

"You know the future, Molly. And you have the power to change it. My Soothsayer has foreseen it. Molly, I have mighty works in hand. I don't want to die! My third wish, Molly! My third wish! *I wish to live to be one hundred years old!*

* * * *

The human soul Reynard's been haunting,
And ultimately, found it wanting.

. . . thought Poor Reynard.

Cassius lay sprawled on a chair of some kind, passed out from too much wine. Reynard regarded him with disdain. He wished Molly would get back to the real world. He was bored with human minds. Frankly, they weren't very interesting. This one had been a mish-mash of rage and bitterness before passing out, and even in sleep, his thoughts were a quagmire of petty resentments. Top of the food chain? Phah! These creatures wouldn't last two days as a fox. Reynard widdled his contempt on Cassius's leg and moved on.

****

Now that Fergus was translating accurately, Lucius and Dorker were talking easily and freely. ⸸ Fergus was amazed to hear a human express complex thoughts. His opinion of humans had always been pretty low. It was still pretty low to be honest, but his opinion of Lucius had improved. It was the sort of astonishment you might feel if you saw a chimpanzee playing Mozart on the piano.

"You want me to show you where Caesar keeps his gold?" said Lucius.

"Yes," said Dorker. He couldn't think of how else to say it. Then he added: "Please?"

"I see," said Lucius. "Molly asked the same thing, and I didn't tell her. Why should I tell you?"

"Several reasons, actually," said Dorker.

"Such as?" said Lucius.

"I can't tell you," said Dorker.

"I see," said Lucius. He considered for a minute. "Will your chicken be alright? There were a lot of soldiers chasing it."

"Gladys?" said Dorker. "Oh, she's not mine. We're just friends. Anyway, don't worry about her. She can take care of herself."

Lucius and Dorker shared an uncomfortable silence, which Dorker could only tolerate for so long.

"So, *mostly*," said Dorker, "what it comes down to is that Molly's great-grandfather wants to know where the gold is. And if he wants to know where it is, we think we should find it first."

"You don't trust her great-grandfather?"

"Oh gosh, no!" said Dorker.

"Why not?"

"Well, if you met him, you'd know, apparently. Among other things, he stole Molly's gold and then had this big elaborate scheme to bring us back here to ancient Rome and help him steal Caesar's gold, and then—"

⸸ Fergus's translation has been edited out for the reader to allow the conversation to flow more naturally.

"Did you say *ancient* Rome?" Lucius had interrogated many prisoners in his career and had learned to pick up on little conversational giveaways like this.

Dorker clapped his hand over his mouth.

"What exactly do you mean *ancient* Rome?"

"I probably shouldn't have said that," said Dorker. "Can we pretend I never said that?"

"I don't think we can, Dorker," said Lucius meaningfully.

Dorker sighed. Leprechauns are supposed to be such great liars, he thought. Just once, he wanted to be good at something leprechauns are supposed to be good at.

"Alright," said Dorker, bracing himself. "I'll tell you the truth. Now just try to keep an open mind, okay? This might be hard to believe . . . but we're from the *future*."

"Okay," said Lucius.

Dorker blinked.

"Okay? *Okay??* I just told you we come from the future, and your response is just, '*okay*'?!?"

"Dorker," said Lucius, "do you know what it's like to have everything you believe about . . . well, just about *everything* turned upside down?"

Dorker straightened and said earnestly, "Yes. Yes, I do, actually."

"If *anyone else* had said that to me—any human anyway—I'd probably knock their teeth out for trying to pull a fast one on me. But *you* . . . well, I will take your word for it," said Lucius. "For now."

Everything changed for Dorker in that moment. Lore gatherers do not, as a rule, reveal their secrets. They have learned that the best way to keep a secret is to simply not tell anyone. Humans have never really understood this simple fact. When humans learn secrets, they invariably tell someone else, and then that person tells someone, and they tell someone, and at some point, the secret becomes what's called an "open secret," which is not a secret at all. Eventually, the open secret transforms into "common knowledge." Lore gatherers think the fact that all this occurs, and everyone involved continues to believe they have kept the secret, tells you a lot of what you need to know about human intelligence.

But because lore gatherers so rarely trust strangers with their secrets, they do not often experience the fast bonds that can form when you do. The thought flickered across Dorker's mind that strong relationships might have more to do with trust than—well, maybe anything else. Our closest friends are the ones we trust the most. Even when we want to throttle them. They may drive us crazy, but we trust them without question.

Predictably, that thought led Dorker to Molly. She seemed to be softening to him a little. But if he could earn and be worthy of her *trust*, maybe she might even like him. He didn't know how to go about doing that, or what it might entail, but it felt like a different, more positive goal than his current strategy of showering her with fawning, desperate hope.

Flush with inspiration, Dorker went for broke. He told Lucius the whole story of how he and Molly got to ancient Rome. Lucius listened politely and carefully, not saying a word. When Dorker was through, Lucius was quiet for a long moment. He got up and paced the room a few times, occasionally stopping to put his head in his hands. It was a lot to take in. Finally, he came back and sat down.

"Okay," said Lucius. He took a deep breath. "Thank you, first of all, for telling me all that. So, as I understand it . . . most pressingly, the real threat is Molly's great-grandfather, right?"

"*Mostly*," said Dorker. "Full disclosure—I can't make any promises that we won't steal the gold. That's not our intention *right now*, but that might change. We *are* leprechauns. I *can* promise you, though, that if Dorn gets his hands on the gold, it won't be good for anyone."

"What could he do?"

"Well . . . just about anything."

"So could you, presumably."

"Yes," said Dorker brightly, "but that would be okay, because it's us."

Dorker's smile really was disarming.

Lucius frowned and looked thoughtful. "Dorn, you say. That's funny. I think Caesar's soothsayer calls himself Dorn."

It was a delayed reaction. But when realization struck, it was like getting kicked in the head by a horse. Dorker grabbed Lucius by the shirt and screamed in his face, "WHAAAAAT DID YOU JUST SAY?!?!?"

CHAPTER 8

Prison. Again.

"Whaaaaat did you just say?!?!?" cried Shaun.

"I told him, 'no,'" said Molly.

Back in the prison cell, news of Caesar's third wish was not going over well. Shaun was hyperventilating because no answer Molly could have given would have been even remotely good. Granting or refusing Caesar's wish had consequences that made his head ring. It was the very worst wish Caesar could have made.

Dorn was apoplectic. "But that's . . . you can't . . . with wishes . . . you're a *leprechaun!!*" he spluttered.

"I was going to say yes, but I wanted to talk about it with you, Da,'" said Molly.

"You did?" said Shaun. He was genuinely surprised.

"Well, I started thinking about all that stuff about Caesar's assassination being a fixed point in time. What would happen if Caesar lived to one hundred?"

"Nothing good!!" said Shaun. "This is a disaster!! What are we going to do?!?"

"Shaun . . ." Dorn began reasonably.

"Shut up!" said Shaun, closing his eyes as if trying to shut him out. "Shut up, shut up, shut up! You don't know anything!!"

"Da,'" said Molly cautiously, "listen, don't get mad, but I need to ask . . ." Molly considered how to ask her question tactfully, without hurting her dad's feelings. Normally, she would never broach a topic like this, but she had no choice. The stakes were too high. "You know how you . . . You know how sometimes . . . I mean, *sometimes*, you know how you sort of . . . *overreact* to things?"

Shaun looked at her suspiciously. "Yeeeees," he said. Molly took a deep breath and forged on.

"So, I have to ask—when you say nothing good will happen if Caesar lives to one hundred, do you *know* that for certain, or do you think maybe you're sort of . . . overreacting again?" She winced. "I'm just asking!" she added quickly.

"NO!" he said. "NO! Absolutely NOT! NO!" He took a deep breath to steady himself. "Molly, I know I don't always . . ." he trailed off. "I know I'm not always the best . . . in a crisis. I know I panic. I know. I know. I know." He took another breath. "But I *REALLY* don't think I'm overreacting this time!"

"Why?" asked Molly patiently.

"Look, I'm no expert . . ." said Shaun.

"Da'!" said Molly, rolling her eyes. If her dad wasn't an expert, who was?

". . . but remember how we talked about the rubber mat of time?"

"Yes," said Molly.

"And that fixed points in time are like places where a giant lead ball sits and stretches it thin?"

"Uh-huh," said Molly.

"Well, no one knows for sure, because no one has ever tested it, but the *general* theory is that the rubber mat of time is a little like the rubber of a balloon. Poke a hole in it, what happens to the balloon?"

"Oh."

"Yes."

"That's bad," said Molly.

"Yes," said Shaun.

"Molly, listen to me," Dorn butted in. "Listen to your ol' great-great . . . whatever I am, grandfather. You agreed to grant Caesar three wishes, right? That created a magical bond between you and him! You *have* to grant him his wishes!"

"Or what?" said Molly.

"Well, you'll never get out of here, that's for sure!" said Dorn.

"We can figure a way out of this prison," said Molly.

"No, Molly," said Dorn, "ancient Rome! You'll never leave. You'll never go home to your own time. A magical bond is unbreakable, d'you understand? If Caesar dies, and you haven't granted his wishes, the magical bond doesn't die with him. It waits to be fulfilled."

"But how can it be fulfilled if he's dead?" asked Molly.

"Exactly!" said Dorn. "You're stuck."

Molly turned to her father. "Is that true?"

Shaun nodded grimly. "The O'Reilly paradox."[＊]

"So, let me get this straight," said Molly, turning red. "My choices are, kill Caesar and *maybe* go home, or let Caesar live and maybe destroy the *universe?!?*"

"Well, let's think it through," said Shaun, trying to calm himself. "You wouldn't be killing him, Molly, you wouldn't be holding the knife. You're not responsible for his death. It's already happened. It happened more than two thousand years before you were born."

"Yes, but I'm here *now!* Caesar is alive *now!*" said Molly. "He even said it would be my fault. Looked right at me and said, 'if I die Molly, it's because *you* let me.' Pointed his finger at my face and everything!"

"That's cruel," said Shaun, frowning.

"That's goooooood," said Dorn appreciatively. "First-rate manipulation there. You could learn a thing or two from Caesar, Molly."

"Don't you talk to Molly!" yelled Shaun.

"Don't you want to go home, Shaun?!"

"We don't need your help, Dorn! Stay out of it!"

"I'll talk to my great-great-granddaughter if I please!" said Dorn. He almost

---

[＊] Named for Finton O'Reilly, an early twentieth-century lore gatherer who travelled back to the early fifteenth century and was, unfortunately, immediately captured by Joan of Arc before she was herself captured and burned alive for witchcraft and heresy at age 19. After all her military successes, Joan concluded she had been using Satan's magic and that her capture was God's punishment. Though she could have easily wished herself free, she chose instead to accept her fate and renounce her last wish, hoping to regain God's grace in the afterlife.

Finton was hurt that Joan thought him the devil, but more so that he could not return to his own time. Sensible to the dangers of time travel, and hoping to prevent becoming his own great-great-great-great grandfather, he lived out his life as a hermit in a cave in the south of France. His diary remained undiscovered for centuries until Shaun found it in a long-forgotten catacomb of the Bodleian library in Oxford, amidst a shoebox of discarded papers. He published it under the title, *The O'Reilly Paradox and Other Historical Landmines*.

managed to sound genuinely indignant.

"She's your *great*-granddaughter, and you don't—"

"QUIET!" Molly shouted.

The two men quieted, glaring at each other as Molly paced the room. It was all too much—the pressure, the choice, her father and Dorn arguing. Shaun watched her miserably. Dorn's eyes flicked back and forth between the two of them, like a hungry cat.

Finally, Molly sat down next to her father.

"Da,' I don't know what to do," she said quietly.

Shaun hesitated. Every atom in his body screamed to tell her that Caesar had to die. That one man's life was not worth the death of every other living thing. That it wouldn't be her fault.

But that's where things got iffy. The wish had been made. Molly could save Caesar's life. Shaun knew the dangers of altering the past, but how do you choose between a billion lives you'll never know, and the life that's right in front of you, begging to spared? It is no small thing to take someone's life. Was refusing to save one that much different? Especially when it would be so easy? Shaun knew the choice he would make; but the choice wasn't his.

He knew what Alice would have wanted, and he had never gone wrong trusting Alice.

"The choice is yours, Molly," said Shaun. "But whatever you do, I'll support it and be here to help you through it. No matter what."

Molly looked at her father and scowled in disbelief.

"Really?!?" she cried. "*NOW?!?* You choose NOW to let me make a decision on my own?!? When the fate of the universe rests in my hands, you decide, 'Oh, now would be a *great* time to teach my TWELVE-YEAR-OLD DAUGHTER a lesson in *self-reliance?!!?*"

"Wha—" Shaun blinked. This wasn't how it was supposed to go. "Molly, I . . . I thought you wanted me to trust you more."

"Within *REASON!!*" she yelled.

How could I be so stupid. Shaun thought. *Molly is impossible. She wants trust, but not responsibility. She wants to be told what to do, except when she doesn't. She doesn't want me running her life, except when she does. And somehow, I'm expected to just know when she wants what! I'm not a mind reader! This whole parenting thing is beyond me.*

And then he heard Alice's voice whisper in his ear gently.

Shaun, just tell her.

And with that, like magic, his anger and frustration drained away, and it all seemed so simple. He looked at Molly and possibly for the very first time didn't see a problem to be solved or a burden to be borne. He saw his twelve-year-old daughter suffering, feeling overwhelmed, and asking for his help. He didn't know how this was going to end. He didn't know whether it would be happy or sad or if the world would be destroyed or if they would ever see their home again. Maybe all was lost. Maybe Dorn was playing them both for fools. He didn't know. All he knew in that moment, looking at his daughter—seeing her now as if he had never really seen her before—was that he loved her with an incandescent fire that filled him with light.

"I wonder if now, I might be allowed to—" Dorn began.

"No!" Shaun snapped at him. He turned to Molly, who was pacing the room furiously, and said quietly, "Molly, look at me." Molly looked at her father, her eyes wet, her face red. "Molly, I'm so sorry," he said simply.

She stopped. To Shaun's surprise, she didn't lash out. She stood there, waiting for more.

"Molly, I'm not your mother."

"No, Da', I know you're not my Ma'—"

"Let me finish," Shaun interrupted. He sighed. "You probably don't remember, but your mother was . . ."

Talking about Alice, Shaun usually struggled not to fall into a million pieces. But now, he didn't care, so he didn't try. His body shook with grief. Tears flowed down his face, and he let them come. "She was really great with you, you know? Read you like a book, she did. Knew you better than anyone. Before you could even talk, she could just somehow *look* at you and know exactly what you needed. Most of the time, she knew what you needed even before *you* knew. It was a gift. Like real magic. Everyone said so. There are great mothers and fathers, lots of them. But the real gift . . . it just doesn't come around that often. I don't have it. You don't know how many times I've wished I did."

"Da . . ."

"If I could wave a magic wand and bring her back, Molly, I would. God, how I would! I'm sorry you've gotten so much of me and so little of her. If I could bargain with Death and trade me for her, I would do it. You would have loved her so much. And she would have . . . " Shaun wiped his eyes. "And I know how much she loved you, and how good she would have been for you, and how proud of you she would be."

"How do you know that?" said Molly soggily. Molly didn't feel very proud of herself; why would her mother have felt differently?

"Oh, I talk to her Molly," said Shaun.

"What?" Molly couldn't keep the hope out of her voice. "You mean, like, with magic?"

"No, no," said Shaun sadly, shaking his head. "Just up here. In my head. When I need her. And she talks to me. At least, it feels like her. She'd probably tell me it's just me talking to myself, imagining what she'd say. But it sounds like her." Then Shaun laughed. "And the voice I hear is a lot smarter than I am, so *you* decide."

Molly smiled a little. Then she said hesitantly:

"Da'? Back at Aggie's house, you said—"

"No, Molly, I didn't kill your mother. It was . . ." Shaun sighed, trembling with the memory. "Even the doctor didn't know . . . But I sure felt like I did. It was one of those days . . . I was taking care of you and I got overwhelmed and . . ."

"Da'? Can I tell you something?"

"Yes, chick. Anything."

"I'm not sorry I get so much of you. The truth is, I'm sorry I get so little."

Shaun's brow furrowed. "What d'you mean?"

"I mean . . ." She didn't know how to say it best, so she just said it. "Mostly, I don't get *you*. I get fear and worry. It's like a voice is constantly whispering in your head, and you listen to it more than you do to me. It's so much bigger and louder than you or me and it makes me feel *so far away* from you. So alone. And I don't have a mother or anyone else I can go to, and I . . . sometimes, I just want to shake you! I want to yell at that voice, 'GIVE ME MY FATHER BACK!!' But I don't, I just try to make everything okay so that you stop, and then we go back to pretending that we're not just sitting around waiting for the next disaster to arrive."

They sat in silence for several moments.

"This," said Dorn quietly, "has been *beautiful*, and I think we've all learned a lot—"

"SHUT UP!" they yelled at him in unison.

Finally, Shaun looked at Molly and said simply, "It's really that bad?"

Molly looked at her father's pleading eyes. She shrugged her shoulders.

"I guess . . ." Shaun began, "You know, sometimes a parent's job—"

"No, Da'," Molly cut him off. "You've told me all about a parent's job. That's not at all what I'm talking about, do you understand that? Please tell me you understand that!"

Now Molly was pleading.

"No, no, I know, I know," said Shaun. "I know. You're talking about . . . my temper, my worries . . ."

"Da', I'm talking about not ever—*ever*—seeing my father. Not *knowing* him. We never talk, Da'. Not like this."

Shaun was quiet for a long minute, then he sighed heavily.

"That must be really hard," he said simply.

Molly nodded.

"I'm sorry, Molly. I am who I am . . . ."

The disappointment on Molly's face could have extinguished a bonfire.

"But maybe . . ." he continued, "Maybe I can try to . . . *talk* to you more. Like this. Maybe I can do better."

Molly looked at him. Then she smiled. It was a start. It wasn't as much as she had hoped for, but it was way more than she had expected. Love can surprise you like that. Shaun had changed once for Alice; it wasn't unreasonable to think he could change for her. But maybe she shouldn't expect him to change all at once. Maybe he was, in the end—to borrow a wildly inappropriate phrase—only human. Maybe it was enough to build on.

"I know you don't want me to butt in," said Dorn delicately, "But we really do need to be deciding what we're going to do with Caesar's wish."

Molly and Shaun looked at each other. "Da', what would you do?"

"Molly, it's your decision—"

"I know, Da'. And I'll make it. But I would just like to know."

Shaun took a deep breath. "I wouldn't grant it, Molly. The risk is too great. Caesar has to die."

Molly nodded her head.

"Would you be at all interested in what *I* would do?" asked Dorn.

"No," said Molly. "But I expect you're going to tell me anyway."

"Well, (*ahem*). The truth is, Molly," he began slowly, "the *truth* is that no one really knows *what* will happen if Caesar *isn't* assassinated. It *could* just be that the fixed point in time shifts a bit and everything goes along pretty much as before. That is possible, in theory. And—noble as your dear father's sentiments are (and I'm sure he does mean them truly and sincerely)—can you really *bear* the prospect of living in ancient Rome for the rest of your life?" Dorn shook his head ruefully. "If it were me, I'd want to see my home again. My friends again. If I may say, Molly, it seems like a high price to pay for not taking what seems like—forgive me, Shaun, for contradicting you in front of your own daughter—such a *small* risk."

Molly's face remained passive as she regarded Dorn.

"Molly," said Shaun, "the only other thing I'll say is that you know what sort of man Dorn is—"

"Oh really?" said Dorn, suddenly aggressive. "And how would she know that, may I ask? What sort of lies have you been telling her?"

"Everyone in our village knows what kind of man you are, Dorn." said Shaun, his voice rising again.

"And what sort of man is that, Shaun? No, no! *Please* tell me!"

Shaun knew Dorn was trying to pick a fight. He created chaos for chaos's sake just to confuse everyone and everything. Chaos was his realm and gave him the upper hand. But Shaun couldn't resist taking the bait.

"D'you know your legacy, Dorn? Shall I tell you? You're a story we tell to frighten the children."

For the first time, Dorn looked genuinely stung. He dropped all his bluster and spoke with unnerving calmness.

"Is that right? A story, am I? Well, there are worse things to be. I lost my gold, Shaun, but *so did you!* So did *Molly!* So have lots of leprechauns!" Dorn turned to Molly. "Molly, it doesn't matter what you think of me. It doesn't matter what your father thinks of me, even if I am a liar and a thief. And in fact, you know what? Why am I apologizing? I *am* a liar and a thief! *I'm a LEPRECHAUN!!* What are *you*, Shaun? Eh? A negligent husband. Nothing more. A failed father who won't let his own daughter think for herself!"

As they fought, Molly closed her eyes and tried to listen deeply. To what, she wasn't sure, but she took a deep breath and tried to relax. As soon as she did, the yelling voices retreated into the background, and she felt the stagnant air in the room move. Particles vibrated at the microscopic level, dancing on the surface of her skin. Time slowed, and she could almost begin to see the shape of something. What it was, she wasn't sure. Like seeing the river from above, but not its destination. It was enough.

"Stop it!" said Molly. "I'm going to grant his wish."

"YES!!!" cried Dorn triumphantly, then checked his enthusiasm. "I mean . . . that's good. Oh, Molly. This is a *good* decision. You won't regret it. Soon, you'll be back ho—"

"Quiet!" Molly snapped. "I'm not doing it because of what you said."

"Molly?" said Shaun as gingerly as he could, trying desperately not to let Molly sense his raging terror. His face twisted with the effort.

"Da'," said Molly, taking his hand, "I understand. I really do." She closed her eyes. "But I don't care about Brutus, or Cassius, or Dorn, or magical theories, or whether it all happened two thousand years ago, or whether or not we ever go home. I don't even care about Caesar. All I care about is—I'm here now. It's in *my* hands, it's *my* responsibility . . . and I can't kill him. I just can't." Her voice got small. "I'm only twelve. Do you understand, Da'?"

Shaun's faith in Alice was the only faith he had ever known. Alice said he should trust Molly, and he had never gone wrong trusting Alice. Against all his better instincts screaming loudly in his head that they were **ALL GOING TO DIE HORRIBLY**, Shaun took the biggest leap of faith he had ever made.

"HUhhuuuuuuuhhhhhookay," he nodded. He smiled, but his smile was a rictus—the most tense, uncomfortable . . . *thing* Molly had ever seen on a face before. But she knew how much it cost him to let her make what he believed was likely the last mistake anyone would ever make.

"Okay. So then, um . . . I guess I need to figure out how to let him know."

"Well, *technically*," interjected Dorn softly, "since the wish is already out there, so to speak—and correct me if I'm wrong, Shaun, you're the expert—as an unresolved magical potentiality, as it were, all you have to do is think about Caesar and say, 'your wish is granted.'"

Dorn tried to keep the excitement out of his voice, but he was surprisingly no better at hiding his emotions than Shaun. He looked like a little boy about to open his first big Christmas present.

Shaun did his best to smile back at her. She closed her eyes, took a deep breath and said, "Your wish is granted."

"YES!" cried Dorn. Then he vanished in a puff of smoke.

CHAPTER 9

Lucius's Wishes

Shaun and Molly had no time to register Dorn's disappearance because at that exact moment, the world started to end. Molly had never experienced an earthquake, but she imagined it must be like this. As the whole room shook, decades of dust from the prison ceiling shook free, falling on them like snow. The ground felt as if it had turned to rubber. Even through the walls, they heard the skies tremble.

"What's happening?" shouted Molly over the din.

Shaun wisely concluded that "I told you so" was probably not the most constructive observation he could offer.

"I'm no expert . . ." he shouted.

"DA'!"

". . . but my best guess is that we are approaching the exact moment in time when Caesar is meant to die. But because that's not going to happen now, a time paradox has been created which will cause all wave form potentials—"

"DA'!! What are you saying?!?" Molly shouted.

"We're all going to die!" shouted Shaun.

One of the larger stones near the floor of the cell began wriggling loose and pushed itself into the room. Weak light streamed in through the hole in the wall, and Dorker's head appeared, radiating concern.

"The sun is going dark!" he shouted, as he crawled into the room. "Is that bad?"

"We think the world is ending!" Molly shouted back.

"So yes, then?" said Dorker. He just wanted to check.

"A less than optimal development, yes, you could say that!" shouted Shaun.

Lucius crawled into the room behind Dorker.

"*WHAT* IS HE DOING HERE?!?" cried Shaun.

"It's okay, Mr. McClanahan," said Dorker, "he's with me."

"*WHY* is he with you?!?" cried Shaun.

"Speak my language please!" shouted Lucius. "What's going on? It's like the world is ending!!"

"Yes!" shouted Molly. "That's right!" Molly quickly told him about Caesar's wishes.

"*WHY* did you grant his wish?!?" yelled Lucius.

"*WHY* is this human here with us?!?" yelled Shaun, stamping his feet.

"I told Dorker to find him, Da'. We need his help!"

"What can *he* do?!" shouted Shaun. "Can *he* stop the end of the world? Does he suddenly have some magic we don't know about?!?"

"I don't know!" shouted Molly. She turned to Lucius. "Do you have any magic we don't know about?"

"Not that I know of!" shouted Lucius. "But at least I can do this." He pulled out the keys to Shaun's chains and set him free.

"Gosh, super! Thanks for helping!" shouted Shaun. "Buh-bye now!"

"Wait!" shouted Lucius. "How do we stop the world from ending?"

"Caesar has to die!" shouted Shaun. "But that can't happen because the wish protects him."

"Could another wish . . . un-protect him?" Lucius asked. Shaun looked at him suspiciously.

"Theoretically," said Shaun, uncertainly. "McDermott's second law of magic states that last in time controls."[†]

"Then, quick, let me catch one of you and I'll unwish his wish or

---

[†] As Shaun writes in *A History of Theoretical Magic: A Look Back*, Delroi McDermott was a research lore gatherer famous for positing three laws of magic that, in three thousand years, have never been refuted. They are: (1) the law of proportionality, which states that if too much magic is concentrated in any one place, something will happen to restore magical equilibrium—usually something bad; (2) last in time controls, which means that if, on Monday I wish to get a ham sandwich delivered on Friday, and then on Tuesday, you wish to eat all conceivable ham sandwiches, then I won't get my ham sandwich; and (3) you never can tell. Number three is not considered one of McDermott's greatest insights, yet most scholars privately agree, it's probably the most reliable.

something!"

"First, you can't un-wish someone else's wish," shouted Shaun. "Second, in your dreams, pal! No self-respecting leprechaun lets himself get caught!"

"Not even to save the world?!? Are you mad?!?"

"You wouldn't understand, human!"

Lucius shook his head in disbelief. "Look, I promise. I'll waste two wishes on something silly, I'll wish for . . ." his mind raced desperately. "I don't know. But then I'll wish for the ability to kill Caesar!"

"WHAT?!?" cried Molly.

"Not on your life, human!" shouted Shaun.

"No, Lucius! It would be too dangerous!" said Molly.

"Molly, if you don't want his death on your conscious, I get that. But I'm a soldier. I've killed lots of people for reasons I never understood. It would be nice, for once, to know that it meant something!"

"Don't let him catch you, Molly!!" warned Shaun. "We have no reason to trust him! There are worse things than death!"

"Wait a minute, wait a minute!" said Lucius. "If I catch a leprechaun, I get three wishes, right? That's how it works?"

"Yes, but—" said Shaun.

"Well, I already caught Molly back in the market."

"Nice try, Roman. She got away!" shouted Shaun.

"But YOU didn't!" shouted Lucius.

"Oh," said Shaun. "Ratcrap."

"*I* fell on you, knocking you out! *I* took you to Caesar!"

"Da'! Please . . ." shouted Molly.

"I'm sorry, Molly, he's right. He picked me up. I owe the son of a—I owe him three wishes."

"But don't kill Caesar! Da', you're not a killer!"

"Molly!" shouted Lucius. "Don't worry! It's going to be alright! You, Shaun—quick now, I wish for . . . a a a . . . a cup of wine!"

"What?!" shouted Shaun.

"But not just any wine!" Lucius took a deep breath. He didn't know where the memory came from, but there it was, suddenly fresh as yesterday. "I was in Gaul. Before a hard battle. Lots of us died that day. But we came across the barrels of a great wine maker. It was the best I've ever tasted. I want that."

"Granted!" shouted Shaun with a flick of his wrist. A cup appeared in Lucius's hand. He drained it in one swallow and regarded the cup. It was the same one he had used all those years ago.

"It's good," he said, his hand trembling slightly. "It tastes like . . . I don't know what. Comradery? Survival? The memory of fallen friends? Maybe it's . . . But I guess I'll never know. But it's good." Even Shaun was surprised to see Lucius's eyes had gone misty. Lucius shook it off. "Right. Molly's father, my second wish: I wish for the ability to kill Caesar."

"You said you would waste *two* wishes, human!" yelled Shaun.

"Trust me, leprechaun!!" yelled Lucius. "You have no other choice."

"Da'!" cried Molly.

"Molly," said Lucius, "he's only giving me the power; it's up to me whether I act on it."

"But he *knows* what you're going to do!"

"Do you grant my wish or not, Molly's father?"

"Granted!" shouted Shaun.

"For my third wish . . . for my third wish . . ." Lucius's voice trailed off.

"We *literally* don't have all day!" shouted Shaun.

Lucius closed his eyes and said quietly: "I wish to be remembered. Forever. Somehow."

"Is that it?" shouted Shaun.

"That's it!" shouted Lucius.

"Granted!"

"We're done then." Lucius looked Molly in the face. "I'm sorry, Molly. Truly. Don't hold it against your father. You made your choice, and it was a good one. Trust me when I tell you that others have done far worse."

"Lucius, you'll be killed," Molly said simply.

Lucius smiled. "Maybe. But I'll make a difference. I'll save the world. How many men can say that?" Lucius turned. "I hope you find your chicken, Dorker."

Dorker gave him a small wave. Lucius turned back to Molly.

"Farewell, little one." He knelt down to the hole in the wall, stopped, and turned. "And thanks for the magic."

Lucius crawled out and was gone. The three of them stood in the cell awkwardly. Finally, Shaun turned to Dorker.

"'I hope you find your chicken??'" he said. "Is that some sort of Roman goodbye?"

"I'll tell you later," said Dorker, as a stone from the ceiling crashed down beside them. "Shouldn't we go outside?"

Shaun nodded. "Let's go!"

One by one, they crawled through the hole in the wall and stepped into daylight. Or what passed for daylight. The sky was red, and the sun looked cracked, charred, and black, like a piece of coal burning from the inside out. The air was already turning colder, and panic gripped the streets: people ran screaming as the ground shook; mothers clutched babies to their chests; animals that had slipped their tethers or had simply been abandoned charged dangerously this way and that.

"Did you ever think you would die in ancient Rome?" said Dorker, doing his best to smile cheerfully. "I sure never did."

"No," said Shaun.

"That's *kind* of cool, isn't it?"

"Not really," said Shaun.

Dorker's smile waned. "No. No, I guess not."

They stood in silence a few moments, watching the chaos, watching the sun fade, and with it, all light and life on earth. Molly turned to her father.

"Da'—"

"Molly, I'm sorry," said Shaun interrupting her. "You did what you thought was best. I did what I thought was best. In the end, that's all we can ever do."

"I know, Da'." She took her father's hand. "I just wish . . . I wish things had turned out different."

Shaun smiled. "Me too, chick. But I'm glad we're together." Molly put her head on her father's shoulders.

"I don't suppose either of you want to know what I wish," said Dorker.

Molly and Shaun turned to Dorker. Dorker, so tall, so optimistic, suddenly looked very small.

"I wish I could see my dad one more time."

The words hit Molly like a hammer. In the midst of everything, she had completely forgotten that Dorker had left his father—all because he stood up for her. Through it all, Dorker had done his best to be helpful and positive, even though there was no guarantee he would ever see his father again, and even when Molly and Shaun were not that nice to him. Yes, he could be irritating. Yes, he was clumsy and didn't seem to be very good at much of anything. But he was always in there trying, doing his best with a smile on his face. No matter what. It was like her dad said: that's all anyone can do. And seeing him stand there by himself with no parent to comfort him, Dorker's best suddenly seemed very good indeed.

No one should face the end of the universe alone. Molly gently took his hand in hers and gave it a squeeze.

"Thank you for being here, Dorker." Dorker smiled.

"Molly?" said Dorker, sneaking a glance at Shaun out of the corner of his eye.

"Yes, Dorker?"

"I was going to find a time to say this to you privately, but since the universe is ending . . ."

"Yes?"

"Well, the thing is . . . well . . . I love you."

The earth stopped shaking. The sun flared back into fiery life and the world flooded with light once more. When the Roman crowd realized that whatever had been happening had stopped happening, a cheer erupted on the streets louder than any crowd has ever cheered. And it just kept going—wave after wave of pure euphoria for minutes on end. People hugged each other and wept with gratitude. On distant planets in far-flung reaches of the universe, silicon-based life forms released plumes of sulfurous yellow smoke that mingled with the sounds of grinding minerals, indicating joy and exultation. For the first time since the universe began, in fact, almost every living thing in creation experienced at the exact same moment an overwhelming feeling of gratitude, forgiveness, and a profound connection to everything that is, was, or ever will be.

Dorker had inadvertently made the most perfectly timed declaration of love in the history of romance. How many can claim that the first time they said, "I love you," the universe rejoiced? None, that's how many. Poets say that kind of thing all the time, but that's just metaphors. This was the romantic moment of all romantic moments. And if this were any kind of decent love story, Dorker and Molly would have embraced in a kiss so beautiful, so perfect, so pure, a heavenly host of angels would have fallen to their knees and wept with joy.

The problem was—Molly's father was standing *right there*. The resulting awkwardness meant that Shaun, Molly, and Dorker were the only three life forms in the whole universe whose joy was muted by varying levels of horrified embarrassment. Really, if Dorker had said it to anyone other than Molly, Shaun might also have rejoiced. As it was, in that moment of near universal, all-encompassing rapturous harmony, Shaun just shook his head in resignation, sighed heavily, and said:

"Oh well . . ."

Molly was mortified. Her eyes went wide, and she could actually feel the blush start at her toes and work its way all the way up to her scalp, pausing to do some sightseeing along the way. Her ears went so red and so hot, she worried briefly they might actually burn right off her head. She didn't dare look at Dorker. Yet horrified as she was that he had made such an unexpected and open declaration right in front of her father, she didn't let go of his hand.

Dorker hadn't really expected to live more than a few minutes after he said those three little words. He had been kind of counting on any embarrassment he might have felt being quickly extinguished along with creation. But now, the cat was out of the bag, so to speak, and he couldn't really put it back in. He became acutely aware that Molly hadn't let go of his hand and that Shaun was pretending not to notice. What had seemed so crystal clear just a moment ago, now seemed *unbelievably* complicated and confusing.

The three of them stood, taking in the jubilant Roman street scene in front of them, not daring to look each other in the eye. Finally, unable to take it any longer, Dorker said:

"Soooooooooo . . . that's it then?"

"Think so," said Shaun.

They stood there awkwardly for a few more minutes.

"What do we do now?" Dorker asked.

"Well, for a start," said Shaun slowly, still not looking at them, "you can let go of Molly's hand."

"Yes, Mr. McClanahan." Dorker dropped Molly's hand quickly and, it has to be said, with some relief. Not that he hadn't liked it. He had been wanting to hold her hand for a long time now. But what had seemed romantic in his imagination was almost *too* heart-thumpingly exciting in reality, and he didn't want to start sweating all over everything.

"I guess this means, Caesar—?" said Molly.

"—is dead," said Shaun.

"And Lucius . . . ?"

"Got his wish," said Shaun.

"Is there any chance he . . ."

"No."

Lucius's sacrifice sank in. Molly hadn't known him well. He was the first human she had ever talked to. She had long been taught that humans were stupid, dangerous animals, and Lucius certainly fit that description. But he had also been kind, in a gruff sort of way, and he had mostly kept his promises. He was, in fact, the most fearless being—leprechaun or human—that she had ever met. When someone lays down their life to save yours, it's hard not to respect them. It's even harder when they also save the universe.

"Da'?" she said.

"Yes, chick?"

"Just make sure he gets his *last* wish." Molly's voice could have bent iron.

Shaun nodded. "I promise."

"Oh my gosh!!" cried Dorker, slapping his forehead.

"What is it?" said Shaun.

"Caesar's gold!"

Dorker took off running down the street. "C'mon!" he yelled. Shaun and Molly looked at each other, then quickly took off after Dorker.

"Dorker!" Shaun panted as they caught up to him. "What are you doing? We don't know where Caesar's gold is!"

"Yes, we do!" cried Dorker. "Lucius told me! That's why Molly sent me to find him! But he told me something else that I think is kind of important!"

"What's that?" Shaun asked, speaking through the cramp that was rapidly stitching up his side.

"Molly said Dorn talked about a magician who put the magical chains on him in prison?"

"Yes?" said Shaun.

"And you know Caesar's soothsayer?"

"Yes," said Shaun. "We already know the soothsayer is a magician!"

"No!" said Dorker. "I mean, yes! I mean, that's not what I was getting at."

They neared a large building near the center of Rome. It was heavily guarded, but it had sustained some damage in the violent shaking of the earth. A door at the entryway had broken loose from its hinges, and the chaos on the streets ensured they had no trouble slipping through it unnoticed. Once inside, Dorker stopped for a minute and looked around until he located a stairwell leading down. The coast was clear.

"This way!" he shouted in a whisper.

"Dorker, where are we?" Molly asked.

"It's kind of like a warehouse where rich people and politicians keep their gold."

"You mean a bank?" said Molly.

"*Like* a bank, but much more secret. Apparently, most people think the building is a storehouse for army supplies. Lucius guarded it a few years ago."

"Dorker, wait!" Shaun tried to insist, but Dorker turned left, then right, then right again, and down another flight of stairs, until finally he arrived at the door he was looking for. He tried to open it but couldn't.

"It's locked," he said.

"Dorker!" Shaun grabbed Dorker by the shoulders. "What is going on? What is important about the soothsayer?"

"It's Dorn," said Dorker. Shaun's face fell.

"Dorn is the soothsayer? Are you serious?" he said quietly.

Dorker nodded. "He engineered all of this right from the beginning."

"And this is where Caesar's gold is?"

Dorker nodded again.

"Stand back!" said Shaun, shoving Dorker roughly to the side. "Let's hope I have enough magic."

Shaun made a few complicated motions with his wrist and muttered a few words under his breath. It wasn't impressive, but slowly, the door unlocked and creaked open. The three of them ran into the room and found

. . . not a scrap of gold.

But the room wasn't empty. Chains sprang from the fingers of a lore gatherer sitting in the middle of the room and twisted themselves around the three of them like boa constrictors until they were chained to the wall, unable to move.

"Hello grandson!" said Dorn. "I was hoping you'd show up."

CHAPTER 10

Caesar's Soothsayer

"Oh, look!" said Dorn. "There's a new player in the game! What's your name, lad?"

"Dorker," said Dorker.

"Dorker? Delighted. What an unfortunate name you have."

"Thanks."

Dorn sat down again, as chatty as if he were hosting a tea party. Molly half expected him to pull out a tray of scones and crumpets.

"You're Caesar's soothsayer?" said Shaun.

Dorn snapped his fingers and transformed before their eyes into a tall, thin human man, grey and grizzled and wearing various animal skins crudely laced together, with a wolf's head atop his own. "BEWARE THE IDES OF MARCH!" he said dramatically. He smiled, snapped his fingers, and in a puff of smoke, the diminutive form of Dorn stood before them once more.

"The soothsayer was a useful device, nothing more. I had hoped if word got around that Caesar had a real magician working for him, it might delay the assassination. Ah well." Dorn smiled, sat down again, and crossed his legs. "Isn't this nice! I can see you've all got questions, but time is short. You took a little longer to get here than I expected (tsk tsk tsk), so let's just cut to the chase. You want to know where the gold is."

Shaun looked back humorlessly at Dorn's smiling face.

"Well, I've already taken it, d'y'see?" Dorn said briskly as he stood. "And as for your *next* question: sorry, I won't be sharing. Heartless, I know, but in my defense, I do feel a *little* bit bad about it."

"How did you—"

"Oh Shaun. Give your ol' grandfather a little credit. Once I had Caesar wrapped around my finger, finding his gold was easy. With the gold he gave me, I am *very powerful indeed*. I knew exactly when you got to Rome, exactly who you saw, when those Roman soldiers caught you, what cell you would be in, how to hide myself from you, and on and on and on."

"This was never about going back home, was it?" said Shaun.

"No, Shaun, you great dunce! It was about *gold!!* Huge hordes of gold!! A *world* full of gold!! We're in *ancient Rome!* We had one of the world's greatest military minds poised to start an empire that lasts hundreds of years, that spreads across Europe! With Julius Caesar working for me, there's no telling how much gold I could have got my hands on."

"Stupid," said Shaun. "Greedy."

"Greedy, yes; stupid, no!" said Dorn. "Have you forgotten what it means to be a leprechaun, Shaun? We lie! We manipulate! *We steal gold!* That is who we are!! I lost a lot when I was banished, but do you know what I gained?"

"What did you gain, Dorn?"

"*Perspective.*"

"Oh, good," said Shaun.

"Lore gatherers have lost their way, Shaun. Nowadays, it's all learning, working together, making things, craftsmanship. But leprechauns are nature's thieves! We *take* what we want!"

"That is *not* what the historical texts—"

"Forget the books, Shaun, for once in your life! Shaun! We are a thousand times more powerful than humans! We're smarter, craftier—and yet we *hide* from them, ashamed of who we are! We gather gold, but we don't *use* it!"

"Use it? What, like humans?" Shaun almost spat the words.

"*Power*, Shaun! Say what you like about ol' Julius, but that boy understood power. *He* wasn't afraid of it. And he wasn't afraid to take what he wanted. Tell me, Shaun, why do leprechauns share their gold?"

"Dorn—"

"Indulge me, Shaun."

"Dorn! I—"

Dorn slapped him. "Fear."

"Wha . . . ?"

"Fear, Shaun. We're afraid of our own *natural power*. Gold is an *amplifier*, yeah? A magnifier. It plugs us in to our *true* power source. Lights us up. We all *feel* that on some level, but instead of *reveling* in it, we *share* it—spread it out, dampening its effect. It's so diffuse, most barely notice it. We think our magic is stronger when we're part of a village. But I've done more than *study* magic, Shaun. I've *mastered* it. And Shaun. Oh *Shaun!* When was the last time you could lay claim to a truly vast amount of gold that belonged to you and no one else?"

"Never, Dorn! Are you mad? That's too dangerous! Everyone knows that!"

Dorn turned and walked slowly from them. "You disappoint me, Shaun."

"Dorn—"

"You're small. Narrow-minded. Like all the rest. *Afraid! Afraid* of anything you don't know or understand. *Pathetic!*"

Dorn got quiet and still.

"All those years ago, Shaun. The village . . . They took everything from me. *Everything*, do you understand? Look at you! You have Molly! You have whatshisname!"

"Dorker," said Dorker.

"I've been alone, Shaun. By myself. My wife, my children, *you*—you all stayed behind. None of you would come with me. No one would join me in my banishment. Was that so much to ask?"

"Yes," Shaun said simply. "Yes, Dorn, it was."

Shaun had been raised by his grandmother and Dorn (mostly by his grandmother). He remembered the day Dorn was banished. Shaun was six. He hadn't understood most of what was going on, but he was already old enough to distrust his grandfather. And he remembered how anguished his grandmother had been. Despite Dorn's many faults, she had loved him; but she chose Shaun over Dorn. It broke her heart, but it was the right choice. Only a fool would willingly take a child into banishment if there was another way. Besides, Dorn would have gotten bored and left them eventually.

"Dorn," said Shaun, "we're your family, but even family—"

"*Family!*" Dorn sneered contemptuously.

You could never tell whether Dorn's emotions were genuine or fake. It seemed to Molly that he wore a mask of his own face. She doubted anyone really knew him. He was always hiding, always withholding—a part of him was always detached, watching you watch him, and looking for leverage or a pressure point to exploit.

But this felt different. Now he looked raw, like an exposed and frayed nerve. All those years alone had not been good for him. Molly knew Dorn had always been more than a little bent. But only now did she see—really see—that deep down, Dorn was broken.

"Dorn—"

"Save it, Shaun." Dorn's voice was cold. "You're no different. *You* think I deserve everything I got."

"*I* don't think you deserve everything you got," Molly said simply. Dorn turned and looked at her.

"Oh really?" he said.

"Molly, don't—" said Shaun.

"No, no, Shaun," Dorn interrupted. "Let's hear what young Molly has to say. Go ahead, great-granddaughter. Do tell us why you're so different than your father."

"I'm not different from him. I just don't think it's fair. I didn't think it was fair when we got banished. I don't think it's fair that you got banished. I think it's a stupid rule."

"Ahhhhh . . . from the mouths of babes!" said Dorn, touching her cheeks.

"But I don't think what you've done is fair either," she said sharply. Dorn stepped back. "Used us. Tricked us. Love your family so much, do you? Ha! You sold your family for *gold*. And now, chaining us up! Who are you to talk about family? You didn't deserve to get banished, but for what you've done to us, what you're doing to us, you deserve far worse!"

"Molly," said Dorn, "there are things you don't under—"

"No. You know what? I don't care. I'm sick of being told what I don't understand. I understand just fine: bad things happened to you. You think that's an excuse? Well, guess what, bad things happen. To everyone. But wrong is wrong, and people do stupid things sometimes, and my Da' is a *good* man, whatever you say—better than *you*, anyway. YOU . . . I don't even know *what* you are."

Dorn regarded Molly for a moment. Then he knelt down and said gently: "I, dear Molly, am a *visionary*. And I will lead lore gatherers back to the light."

"Two of a kind, you and Caesar are," said Molly.

Dorn stood and began gathering his things.

"You're right, Molly, that boy showed promise. I *was* going to work with Caesar for a while—use his army, plunder Europe a bit, have some laughs. This world, this time—it's a good era for an ambitious lad like me. With my magic and all the gold of Europe to power it, I could have ruled the world. Could have reshaped it in my image. Shillelagh created the universe from lies and genius alone! That is what leprechauns are, Shaun! Gods! What Shillelagh wants us to be!"

Dorn stood still in the center of the room.

"But Caesar's gone now, so I've revised my plans. Scaled them back a bit. It's not as much as I hoped for, but Caesar's gold was plenty." Dorn held up his hand and green lightning sparked. As it danced and rolled around his fingers, Dorn's eye twinkled. "I'm thinking it's time I make my long-awaited return home, what d'you think? I think the village will be happy to see me, don't you? I'll be sure to let them know they have you to thank for my homecoming."

"Dorn, what are you going to do?" Shaun asked.

"Do? No more than they did to me, dear Shaun. In fact, I'm going to give them something."

"What are you going to give them?"

"Purpose," said Dorn, clenching his fist and extinguishing the lightning.

"What do you mean?"

"I'd love to explain, but it's time to be toddling along. *So* nice to see you again grandson. Or great-great grandson—whatever you are. Nice to meet you, Molly. And uh . . . thingy."

"Dorker," said Dorker.

"Whatever."

"You're just going to leave us here?" said Shaun. "Sealed in this . . . chamber? Dorn, we'll die!"

"Yes, I am sorry about that. Can't be helped, I'm afraid. Can't have you coming back to spoil all the fun, can I? Don't be mad at *me*. You had your chance to be a part of something amazing, but you blew it, didn't you? Caesar's dead. You couldn't leave well enough alone."

"*Dorn, the world was ending!*" Shaun was red in the face.

"Hardly matters now, does it?"

"Hardly matters?!? Dorn, listen to me," Shaun pleaded. "This is crazy. Please. You're not a killer."

"Sure of that, are you, Shaun?" Dorn said with eyes like knives. "Care to test it?"

Shaun swallowed.

"Dorn. I'm begging you. At least take Molly and Dorker with you. Leave me here, if it makes you happy, but you can't kill two innocent children."

"I'd *love* to take them with me, Shaun, but the problem is—I'm not going to. Besides, *I'm* not killing you. Right, Molly?" Dorn winked at her. "Just not intervening. You might survive, you never know. Frankly, I hope you do. Get out. See the world. Send me a postcard. Enjoy yourself for a change, Shaun. You're waaaaaaaaay too high strung. Can hardly believe you're my kin. If it weren't for Molly here, I would truly despair of my bloodline."

"Gosh, thanks," said Molly.

"D'y'see?" said Dorn. "Ha! Ha! That's what I'm talking about. Even in the face of death, she's got a spark, and no mistake." Dorn pinched her cheek entirely too hard, then gave her a nasty slap. "But you should never disrespect your elders and betters."

Molly was so mad she didn't even wince.

"Well," Dorn said, tipping his non-existent hat. "I'm history! No, sorry—*you're* history. Or you will be. I look forward to reading about you in the ancient scrolls, Shaun. Enjoy Rome!"

And with that, he closed the door to the room and locked it, leaving Shaun, Molly, and Dorker chained to the wall.

"Well, that went badly," said Shaun.

"Could have been worse," said Dorker.

"How, exactly?" said Shaun with genuine interest.

"Well . . . he didn't kill us."

"He might as well have," said Shaun grimly.

"Nooooooo!" said Dorker. "Molly wouldn't have allowed that," he said.

Shaun blinked. "I honestly don't think any of us could have prevented it, Dorker."

"Now she just has to figure out how to get us out of here," said Dorker.

"And how will she do that, exactly?" Shaun asked, mesmerized by Dorker's confidence.

"I dunno," said Dorker. "But she will. You'll see."

Shaun had been so fascinated by Dorker's shining optimism that he only now realized that Molly herself had been very quiet.

"Molly . . . ?" he said. *"Do you have any ideas?"*

"How could he do that?" said Molly softly.

Shaun just shook his head. "Chick, a long time ago, I learned the hard way that there is no expectation Dorn can't diappoint."

"He *has* been alone for a long time," said Dorker.

"I don't care!" Molly snapped. "Could *you* do what he did? I don't think so. You're a good person, Dorker. You never would."

"I *hope* I wouldn't," said Dorker. "But honestly, I've never been as angry as Dorn is. People don't always make good choices when they're angry."

Molly thought about her father. When he was angry, his decisions were questionable at best. Not psychopathic like Dorn, of course, but not great. As excitable as he was, though, her dad seemed more often powered by fear than anger or rage. With Dorn, it wasn't anger or fear—Dorn was powered by hate. The pain of his banishment had buried itself deep in his stomach, covered itself with layers and layers of resentment, and compressed itself into a ball of bitter hatred—hard as a diamond and just as easy to digest.

Then she remembered what had happened in the marketplace: the hatred she had felt, and the anger—the unbridled power that had come with it and what she had unleashed as a result. Fear, hate, anger—were any of these feelings a reliable place to plant your feet when pushing the levers that turn the world?

And what about now? What was she feeling now? She wasn't afraid, she knew that. The anger she felt about her own banishment, she realized, had now mixed with pity—pity for a village so filled with fear it would cast out anyone unfortunate enough to be caught by a human or to lose their gold. No one likes to be pitied, but pity at least is tinged with mercy, which is stronger than fear or hate. But neither pain, nor pity, nor fear drove her right now. Anger didn't quite describe it either, nor hate.

What she felt could only be described as clarity. Dorn was out there. He was planning something bad. She didn't have to know what it was. She understood him now. Whatever good might have been in him was there no longer. He had become something malignant. Diseased. Destructive. Willing to sacrifice the world and everyone in it to his own selfish needs. Worst of all, armed with Caesar's gold, he had power—power no leprechaun could hope to match alone. She didn't know how she was going to do it, but he had to be stopped.

At any cost.

"How do we get out of these chains?" she said.

"Oh," said Dorker, taken aback. "I'm sorry, I thought you would have an idea."

"Nope," she said.

Dorker wriggled. "Are these chains—AAAHHHHGGH!"

"Magical? Yes," said Shaun.

"What kind of magic *is* that?!?" exclaimed Dorker.

"I don't know, but it's magic like I've never encountered."

"That's because it's old magic," said a cheeky voice from the doorway. They turned, and there stood Fergus, smiling.

"Old to you, that is," he said.

"Fergus!!" cried Dorker.

"You know him?" said Shaun in astonishment. "How do you know him?"

"Okay, long story short, I got captured by some lore gatherers, one thing led to another, and Fergus here sort of helped me talk to Lucius."

"You got captured?"

"Well, you see what happened was—"

"Long story *shorter*," interrupted Fergus, who, in their brief time together, had learned all he needed to know about Dorker's ability to get to the point, "we captured him, but didn't hurt him. We helped because . . . well, any lore gatherer with a giant chicken for a friend is a lore gatherer to keep your eye on." Fergus smiled at Dorker. "No telling what mischief they might get into."

"A giant chicken is your *friend?*" said Shaun, looking at Dorker.

"Later, Da'. Can you get these chains off of us, Fergus?" Molly said.

"Can I, yes. Will I, no."

"What?!?" said Dorker.

"Just kidding," said Fergus grinning. "'Course I will." Fergus snapped his fingers and the chains fell to the ground. "We used the ol' Burning Chains trick on each other all the time when we were kids. Ma' hated it. Always sent me to my room when I did it to my younger brothers. Never understood the fuss. Scars heal, don't they?"

"Um, no," said Dorker. "That's why they're called 'scars.'"

"Oh, right," nodded Fergus seriously. "That explains a lot, actually. Anyway, Burning Chains is a good prank. I'm surprised this one didn't last until your time."

"Forgotten magic . . ." Molly muttered as she looked at the chains.

Spells go in and out of fashion. New magic came, old magic went. Only research lore gatherers like Shaun or the Bickersmiths kept catalogues of magic. Sometimes books recorded information on how they were performed; sometimes particularly talented lore gatherers could recreate spells out of whole cloth once they grasped the general shape of them. Sometimes, the knowledge was just lost. How much magic had leprechauns abandoned over the years, Molly wondered. Could Dorn be right? Maybe too much had been lost.

"Da', can you make the time portal work?"

Shaun nodded. "Should be able to."

"Time portal?" said Fergus.

"We need to get home," said Molly. "Now."

* * * *

Purple light receded slowly in the western sky when they got back outside, but the street was buzzing with exhilaration and activity. Repairing the damage caused by the end of the world was going to take decades, but the Romans were so grateful to be alive, they saw no reason to wait. Torches had been lit, casting a lively orange glow against the darkening sky, and amidst the hustle and bustle, Molly and company made their way through the streets unnoticed and quickly found the spot where they had first arrived in ancient Rome.

"Alright," said Shaun, "take my hands you two." Molly and Dorker did so as Fergus smiled broadly a few feet away.

"Bye, Fergus," said Dorker. "Thanks for all your help."

Fergus put a finger to his forelock and grinned. "C'mon," he clapped, "get on with it! I've never seen anyone time travel before. This should be good!"

"Quiet!" snapped Shaun. His eyes were shut in deep concentration as he muttered "Taistil am!" over and over under his breath.

"WAIT!" said Dorker.

"What?!" said Molly.

"I can't leave without Gladys!"

"RATCRAP!" Shaun yelled dropping their hands.

"I'm sorry, Mr. McClanahan, I know it sounds stupid, but I made a promise to her and I can't—"

"No, that's not it!" said Shaun.

"What's wrong, Da'?"

Shaun stood with his back turned, hands on his hips, and so upset he could hardly speak. "I think it's ruptured."

"What is?"

"The time bubble I left! I think the end of the world ruptured it. Or moved it. Or maybe granting Caesar's wish did it, I don't know, but this portal is *gone!*"

"But it has to work," said Dorker. "How else will we get home?"

"We won't, Dorker!" said Shaun curtly. "We won't get home. Do you understand? Without the portal, there's no way to do it! We're stuck here!"

"What, forever?"

"Yes, Dorker!! Forever!"

"Da'," said Molly. "Let's just think about it for a minute. Isn't there anything we can do? Can't we find it?"

"No, Molly! I . . . the only thing I can think . . . But I would need tools! I would need to make all sorts of measurements with tools and maps . . . *that I don't have!* Or the bubble could have just disappeared, and I'll have to find another portal somewhere! But again, no tools or maps!"

Or maybe I just did it wrong, a wretched voice in his head insinuated.

"Could you *make* the tools, maybe?" Molly asked.

"Give me about ten or twenty years, sure!"

"We could go ask Aunt Aggie what she thinks," said Dorker thoughtfully.

Molly and Shaun looked at Dorker.

"Say again?" said Molly.

"Oh, I saw her again when I got captured," said Dorker cheerfully. "She's Fergus's mom. The one who can talk to Gladys?"

Molly and Shaun tried to keep their jaws from hitting the ground as Dorker continued. "When Aggie saw her name written in that dictionary she gave us, she *really* wanted to see me. Isn't that funny? She's a lot younger now than when we first met her, of course."

Molly and Shaun were still in shock. Dorker looked at them.

"What?" he said. "Didn't I mention that I ran into Aunt Aggie?"

"No, Dorker," said Shaun. "No, you didn't."

CHAPTER 11

Deep Magic

It is not the norm, but leprechauns can be extremely long-lived creatures. Many live to be well over one hundred. Dorn, in case you were wondering, was approaching almost two hundred years. Even Shaun was almost seventy-five, though to a human, he would have looked about forty-two.

Humans who have attempted to study such things have recorded meeting leprechauns who claimed to be over five hundred years old, though anything a leprechaun tells a human should be viewed with skepticism. For that matter, you shouldn't trust any human who claims to have interviewed a leprechaun because, though the events of this story might suggest otherwise, capturing a leprechaun is unbelievably rare.

Among themselves, lore gatherers rumor that there are those who have lived to be over ten thousand years old, and some on the radical fringes of research maintain there are those among us—early rancher leprechauns—who herded the mighty sauropods.[*] Records are sparse. Besides, any leprechaun who has lived that long typically won't talk about it. They would never be left alone.

The point is, when Shaun and Molly learned that Aunt Aggie had been a mature woman long before Caesar was born, even they were overwhelmed.

---

[*] Human paleontologists have long speculated that sauropods travelled in herds. They did, but not because of natural selection. Sauropods were not only a valuable source of meat that could easily feed a community, but also provided protection against other predators. In return, leprechauns kept the gentle giants clean and healthy.

"Clean living!" said Aunt Aggie when they saw her. "That's how you do it! Stay away from alcohol and tobacco, and anyone can live to be over two thousand."

"Really?" said Molly.

"No, of course not!" Aunt Aggie laughed. She sat down, lit a big, bulbous, hand-carved pipe, and took a swig of beer.[*] "I have no idea why I just keep living. And who knows how much longer I'll go. Our very meeting may have changed everything. Who can say? Personally, I think some of us are just lucky."

"Then, would you mind not smoking?" Molly asked. "It bothers me and I don't like watching you kill yourself."

Aggie's expression hardened as she looked at Molly coldly.

"Besides, maybe me telling you not to smoke is why you live so

long . . . ." Molly could barely repress her smile. It felt good to get under Aggie's skin just a little bit, and to see Aggie squirm knowing Molly knew she had done so.

"Bah!" said Aggie crossing her arms in frustration.

This Aggie was a lot more animated and fiery than the older Aggie they had met (or was it "will meet"?) more than two thousand years in the future. She also had all her teeth, her hair wasn't as grey, and she moved with a little more spring in her step. She didn't look youthful, but the same unmistakeable warmth radiated from her like a small sun.

Finally, Aggie smiled and pointed the tip of her pipe at Molly. "I'll tell you what. Let's talk. Just you and me. You are right about one thing, at least."

"What's that?" said Molly.

"Our meeting was not an accident."

"Really?" said Molly.

---

[*] This scene provides yet another example of how human myths sometimes have their roots in reality. Many humans believe that four-leaf clovers are lucky. Leprechauns do too, but their belief is based on more observable phenomena. As Shaun explains in his book, *Fabulous Fermentations: A History of Lore Gatherer Liquor*, lore gatherer beer is magically fermented using four-leaf clovers harvested in the early spring (in the first week of April, to be exact, preferably in the hours just before sunrise). For whatever reason, such a four-leaf clover yields a beer that is rich, full-bodied, and full of nutrients. It is actually surprisingly good for you and the alcohol content is highly diluted. Beer made from the three-leaf clover, by contrast, is invariably sour and undrinkable. For whatever reason (no one really knows), the magic doesn't quite work. Lore gatherer breweries therefore maintain greenhouses and farms that have, over generations, created a genetic strand of clover that reliably produces plants with four, rather than three leafs. "Where's the magic in that?!?" you say. If you ever tasted lore gatherer beer, you'd know.

"I have no idea why I gave (or will give) Dorker that dictionary, but I must have had in mind that you'd come find me. Maybe I just wanted to be helpful or maybe . . ." Aggie trailed off, looking at the three of them. "Anyway, this sort of thing doesn't happen every day. So I'm going to listen to you. *And* I'm going to smoke my pipe *and* drink my beer! And when you and I have finished, my girl, *I'll* decide whether I ever pick up my pipe again, got it?"

"Okay."

"Fergus!"

"Yes, Ma?"

"Shaun and Dorker are hungry. Warm up something good and hearty for them, there's a lad."

"Right, Ma!" said Fergus.

Aggie turned to Molly and whispered conspiratorially, "I made a rabbit stew last night that'll stick to your ribs and never get unstuck. Your dad'll like it. Come on. Let's go outside."

The sun had set, but Aggie's garden looked green and lush. It put Molly in mind of what the world must have looked like before humans got their hands on it. Wild and overgrown, yet following a set of very clear instructions (because this was, after all, Aggie's garden). Like a bonzai Garden of Eden. It was like walking into a herbologist's dream of the first night of creation.

"This is amazing," said Molly.

Aggie took a swig of beer. "Thanks! It's a type of gardening that's going out of style. Everyone wants plants contained now—put 'em in a pot and set 'em somewhere. This . . . this is more natural. Anyway, I like it. It feels less like *my* garden, and more like . . . like I *share* the space with plants. Plants will keep you humble, and no mistake. Sorry to hear I don't live here in the future. I'm going to miss this place."

"Can you teach me?" Molly asked. "About the plants, I mean?"

"Nope. If you had more time, maybe. But I sense you're not going to be here long."

"I don't know," said Molly. "It's starting to sound like we may never leave."

Aggie brushed some leaves off a stone bench that Molly hadn't even seen.

"How long has that been there?!" Molly exclaimed.

Aggie smiled. "Possibly a very long time, indeed." She sat, looking at Molly calmly. Molly couldn't read her expression at all. It was not a comfortable silence.

Finally, Molly sat down heavily.

"I've messed it all up, Aunt Aggie."

"What did you mess up?"

"Everything."

Aggie tilted her head. "How so?"

Molly told her the whole story. It came out in fits and starts, but the general shape of events was there. Aggie listened quietly, nodding occassionally. When Molly finished, Aggie remained silent for quite some time, tapping the end of her pipe with her finger.

"Aren't you going to say anything?" Molly said.

"What do you want me to say?" said Aggie, raising her eyebrows.

"I dunno, *something*. Advice, opinions, life-altering revelations—anything!"

Aggie smiled. "I didn't know about the message your father wrote to himself in my book. That's funny."

"That's it?!?" said Molly.

"Yup. That's it. What? You want me to tell you what to do?"

"I . . . Yes. No. I don't know!" Molly was flustered. "Every choice *I* make seems to go wrong!"

"Molly," Aggie said, looking at her squarely, "choices are what life is all about. One choice closes some doors and opens others. And don't kid yourself—sometimes, the only choices you get are bad ones. You do your best. You make mistakes. You learn from them or you don't. And if you don't," she laughed, "you get to make them again and again and again! Life has a way of hammering you on the head with the same lesson over and over if you refuse to learn it. You can just trust me on that one." Aggie took a long swig of her drink.

"What would you have done? Would you have let Caesar die?"

Aggie got serious, closed her eyes tightly, and took a deep breath.

"Yes, I would," she finally decided. "Would have seemed like too big a risk not to."

"Oh."

"But I wasn't there, Molly. You were. And you considered the advice you were given, and made a choice that was yours and only yours to make. You did your best. That's all any of us can do. The only real question now is, can you live with your choice?"

"I guess I have to."

"You don't *have* to do anything." Aggie's voice was suddenly hard. "Remember that, Molly, if you remember nothing else. Your actions are *yours*. No one else's."

"Yes," Molly nodded. She looked into the branches of the old oak tree that spread above them. Its leaves had an almost silver tinge in the moonlight. When she spoke, her voice was soft, but certain. "Yes, I can live with it."

"And what about your father's choice?"

Molly thought for just a fraction of a moment. "Yes."

"Good lass!" Aggie got up. "Well, that's you sorted out. Shall we get something to eat?"

"Wait, what do you mean? What about Dorn?"

"What about him?"

"I have to do something!"

"*Have* to? Goodness. What did we just talk about?! You don't *have* to do anything, child."

"No, but—"

"But what?"

"But . . . but I want to."

"Do you? Why?"

"Because . . . because . . . urrgh, do I have to have reason?!?"

"It helps," said Aggie, smiling.

"Because . . . because he stole our gold."

"This about revenge then, is it?" said Aggie.

"No! It's . . . because it's still my village. He's going to hurt my village."

"*Your* village? It's not yours anymore, girl. They *banished* you!"

"That doesn't matter!"

"Doesn't it?"

"No!"

"Think the village will feel that way? Think they'll be *happy* to see you?"

"I don't care!"

"You don't *care?!?*"

"Why are you talking to me like this?" Molly demanded.

"Why aren't you telling me the truth?" demanded Aggie.

"I *am* telling you the truth!" Molly yelled.

"No, Molly. The *truth*. *Why* do you want to do something about Dorn?"

"Because . . . Because *someone* has to!! And I think I can!"

"You?!? Ha! You're not up to the challenge, girl!" shouted Aggie.

"Well, who cares what you think, you daft old BROOMSTICK!"

Molly's eyes went wide, and she stared at Aggie in horror. But she did not apologize. The air between them crackled for a moment, then Aggie burst out laughing.

"OOOOH! Oh my!" laughed Aggie. "I see why I wanted me to meet you!"

"Is it going to be like this every time we meet?" Molly asked, rubbing her forehead.

"Possibly," said Aggie, wiping tears from her eyes. "It could very well be. I can be difficult. But YES!" she said, sticking her finger in Molly's chest. "Who cares, indeed! *You* believe you can do it. And you'd better believe it, miss, or you'll never see home again."

"What do you mean?" said Molly.

"You're *right!* Someone *does* have to do something about Dorn. And that someone *is* you. There's not much point in life if we don't do the things we can to help the ones we love. Even if the ones we love have been thoughtless fools. Good! Big lesson, that. Takes some people their whole lives to figure that one out. Some never do. Anyway. The other point, Molly. The really important part—*belief!* Even if you *want* to do the things you can, you'll only ever get half way there if you don't *believe* you can."

Molly raising an eyebrow. "Seriously," she said flatly. "You're telling me to *believe* in myself?"

"I'm telling you to believe in *something*, Molly. But sure, why not? Believe in yourself. There are worse places to start. No magic without belief! Key lesson, there. See that? Two big lessons, right in a row. I ought to start charging!"

Molly looked skeptical.

Aggie shrugged and took a swig of beer. "Don't worry, Molly, it's hard to come to grips with. Few lore gatherers ever really do fully understand. Didn't used to be that way, though."

Aggie sighed and got quiet.

"I will tell you something. You want to hear something funny? A long time ago, before even I was born, leprechauns talked about the 'pot of gold' as a metaphor for magic. Deep magic—real vision, access to invisible power. 'That leprechaun is the true pot o' gold' they'd say. Humans heard it somehow, misunderstood it (of course), and thought we literally had pots of gold lying around. Well, that was fine with us! Misunderstandings give us the upper hand. Leverage is leverage. And can you imagine if humans had access to deep magic? No telling what harm they'd do. Leprechauns started keeping actual pots of gold not because we love gold so much, but just to keep humans from learning what we really meant! Like distracting a squirrel with something shiny. That gold amplifies our magic was sheer coincidence. But over time . . . well, with gold to help, fewer and fewer have the discipline or even the desire to get at the heart of deep magic, though some of us do have a genuine gift. Mine is cooking."

"Cooking?" said Molly doubtfully.

"Don't underestimate the power of food, Molly. Deep magic flows from core needs. Food is a core need, so it has power. It resonates on an almost unconscious level. Combine talent with belief and watch out!"

"Just belief?" said Molly.

"Molly," said Aggie, "I *accept* that there's a big, burning ball in the sky that is unimaginably far away and unbelievably hot; but I *believe* I can cook you a dish that will make you happy to be alive. See the difference? So, food, that's me. Sounds like your Ma' knew about people. Makes sense. Another core need. No one survives long on their own. We need others to survive. If I had to guess, I'd bet she believed in the basic goodness of others. Believed it so hard, others believed in it too. When she was around, at least. Few have that kind of power."

Aggie sighed and took a drink. "But more and more of us have started to think like humans—think that gold *is* our power, our core need. Your great grandfather Dorn sounds like a lot of the young ones I hear nowadays. All they talk about is gold this, and gold that. Obsessed with finding gold, stealing gold, thinking it will give them stronger magic. Phaw! Trinkets! *Toys!*" Aggie literally spat the words. "They're dead wrong! Couldn't *be* more wrong! Gold is not the important thing!"

"But belief is?" said Molly uncertainly.

Aggie looked at her a moment, and then said brightly, "You're hungry."

"I am?" said Molly.

"Yes, you are," Aggie smiled. "So am I. C'mon. Food'll do you good. And who knows, with your mouth occupied, maybe your brain will start working."

"That's not nice."

"Ha!" laughed Aggie warmly. She put her arm around Molly. "Nice has nothing to do with anything."

They went inside to find Shaun and Dorker lying on two plush couches surrounded by pillows, fast asleep. On the table were two empty bowls.

"What happened to them?" said Molly.

"Decided to sleep it off," said Fergus, smiling.

"Sleep what off?" said Molly.

Fergus gestured expansively. "All of it. Here, have some." He handed her a bowl of stew heaped with vegetables and meat that perfumed the room with the best aroma Molly had smelled since . . . since the last time Aggie cooked for her. It wafted into her nostrils and right into her brain. It was like eating without even picking up her spoon.

"This isn't going to put me to sleep, is it?"

Fergus's eyes were bright, but he shrugged. "Who knows what it'll do? Apart from fill your empty stomach."

"Don't think, Molly," said Aggie, sitting down with Fergus by a small fireplace. "Relax. Eat."

Molly's nose and stomach overruled her misgivings, and she ate hungrily. It had been several days since she had had a proper meal. The food practically liquefied in her mouth and went straight to her blood stream. Energy flowed into her tired bones, which made her realize just how tired she had really been, mentally and physically. Almost immediately, her mind cleared, and the tension fell off her body in sheets.

"Did you put . . . deep magic in this . . . ?" she asked.

"All good cooking is magic," said Aggie.

"You didn't answer my question," said Molly, smiling.

Aggie smiled. "No, I didn't, did I? Be quiet now and eat your food."

Molly ate. And ate and ate. As she ate, she became aware of the air in the room—as if she could feel the oxygen. The sounds in the background sharpened: a dog barked in the distance; a locust buzzed its sexual frustration on a tree far away; she fancied she could almost hear moonlight. Then she noticed the wood of the chair she sat on. You wouldn't see it right away, but it was all the same piece of wood. Someone had carved an entire chair out of a block of hickory. All the chairs around the table were the same. In the chairs' grain, she heard the histories of the trees they came from, saw the forests of their pasts. This chair was suddenly the most comfortable piece of furniture she had ever sat upon. It seemed to yield to her touch and conform to the shape of her body, almost as if she were wearing it.

And still the smell of the stew swirled around her, mixing with the scent of fresh herbs in the garden, whose fragrance floated in through an open window. For the first time in longer than she could remember, Molly wasn't thinking about the past or the future. She was just a young girl, having a good meal. And it was enough. It was more than enough. The word that came to her was "gratitude." Here and now, she was grateful—for the food, the house, the moon, the trees, and sky; grateful for Aggie and Fergus; grateful for banishment, and lost gold; grateful for a father that loved her; grateful for a mother she had hardly known.

And, yes, even grateful for Dorker.

Gratitude cracked her mind open, and big expansive thoughts poured in from who knows where—thoughts as ripe and round as apples swollen on the bough. She saw the shape of her life over more than two thousand years between now and the day of her birth. And as absurd as it sounded, it all made perfect sense. There was no past, present, or future. All moments were this moment. She cast her mind's eye across the globe and across centuries, feeling connected to every living thing that had been or ever would be—human, leprechaun, animal, insect, plant. The Earth inhaled, and she exhaled with it, in and out, in and out—until she couldn't be sure if she was breathing with the Earth, or for it.

And then, without really knowing what she was doing, she realized that her body was not large enough for her mind, so she decided to leave it. Her consciousness shot out through the top of her head like a fountain, and she looked down on her body, sitting in front of the bowl of stew, motionless. She saw Aggie watching her rise to the ceiling, mouth agape. Aggie nodded and said nothing, but gestured Molly on. Freed from her physical being, Molly floated up and out until she looked down on all of Italy; and then farther and farther still until she saw the Earth—the great globe itself. Molly looked down upon this blue disc floating in darkness, this little slice of creation, and saw infinite, majestic, fragile beauty, as well as infinite pain and suffering.

And with the same clarity that she saw these things, she knew she could fix them, change it all. It was like seeing a loose thread on a giant sweater. All she had to do was pull . . .

That's about enough, Molly, said a voice in her ear. *Time to come back.*

Molly didn't want to go, but she was drawn down back to Earth, back to Italy, back to Aggie's fragrant kitchen, and back to her body. She opened her eyes and blinked. She looked around and saw Aggie's eyes wide as saucers, hardly breathing.

"What was that?" said Molly, both scared and exhilarated.

Aggie finally exhaled. She picked up her pipe, considered it, then threw it into the fireplace.

"That . . ." said Aggie, "is what I think your Mother might have called the 'story behind the story.'"

Molly started at hearing her mother's phrase—a phrase she hadn't heard in years. How could Aggie have known? And suddenly, Aggie was right before her, her hands on Molly's shoulders.

"Molly, listen to me . . . You are at the beginning of a looooong journey."

"I was hoping I was near the end of one," said Molly, smiling.

"This is not a joke!" Aggie's face was stern. "I suspected there might be something, but . . . I had no idea." She closed her eyes for a moment. She was shaking, partly with tears, partly with joy. "My goodness, Molly. I was *wrong*. I've been so wrong about everything for *so long*. I've never been so wrong! You have no idea. But it all makes sense now! Oh ho ho! I told you . . . your Mother and me . . . we have a gift for the deep magic, right? The real thing, yeah? But what you have! You have something else entirely! Molly! Dorn was right!"

"What?!?"

"Lore gatherers *have* lost their way."

"What do you mean? We . . . we shouldn't share our gold?"

"No, Molly, no no no, that's not . . . Look, what's the first story you remember?"

"The story about Dorn losing his gold—?"

"No! The very *first* lore gatherer story?"

"You mean . . . Shillelagh making the universe?"

"YES!" cried Aggie. "What did Shillelagh do?"

"She lied the universe into existence."

"No, Molly! She *believed!*"

"What do you mean?"

"I know, it's hard to . . ." Aggie grabbed Molly by the shoulders. "Molly, we *are* magic. Do you see? We *are* stories. Lore gatherers, leprechauns—we are a part of the original story. The creation of everything—we are intertwined with it. Inseparable from it."

Molly's head throbbed. "I don't . . . I don't understand!"

"Don't you? Everything in the universe is a story, a narrative—everything has a beginning, middle, and end." Aggie pulled the shawl off from around her shoulders and held it up, pointing out individual threads of yarn. She was practically dancing. "Each of us is part of each other's stories—countless stories intersecting, diverging, vining around each other, a million billion streaks of light etched across an endless sky, all weaving a golden tapestry into the biggest story ever told. Humans don't see it. They're too caught up in their own stories, their own threads. They rarely take the time to experience someone else's story. *Empathy! Love! That's* what's missing! That's why there are so few humans who can even touch real magic. But lore gatherers! We are a part of the first magic, you see? The original creation. The patterns, the repetitions, variations, themes," Aggie said, pointing to the different designs woven into her shawl, "they're all *inside* us. Your Ma' and I—those of us with the gift—we can *connect* to them. But! But Molly. Few lore gatherers can do what you just did. Maybe one every several thousand years. Or more. I've been around a long time, and I've never seen it! Don't you understand?"

"No!"

"Molly. You can pull the strings! Rearrange the weave!"

"I don't—"

"Molly you're what the ancient lore gatherers were talking about. *You—ARE the true pot of gold!*"

"Me?"

Aggie laughed. "Yes, you! Why not you? Nothing wrong with you."

"But—"

"Molly, promise me. This is very important. About Caesar—it *matters* that you chose to save him!"

"What? Why?"

"I don't know, I don't know, I don't know. But it does. It *does!* I know it! Something inside you is speaking to you. Seeing what the rest of us can't. You must *listen* to it. I don't know if . . . You wanted my advice? I can't give you any. You can go where few lore gatherers have ever gone. But here it is, anyway. Do whatever it is you have to do. But do it with generosity. Whatever you do, do it with love and humility, and you won't go too far wrong, understand? Do it with anything else in your heart—anger, fear, *anything else*—and I don't even want to think about what will happen. To you, your father, or any of us."

"I still don't . . . ?" said Molly.

"Molly, the real choice you have to make? It's not what you think it is. You *must* tether yourself to love, starting now! And forever. Or you will lose everything."

Molly looked shell-shocked.

"I know, it's a lot to throw at you all at once," said Aggie, patting her on the shoulder. "But I need to know you understand me!"

There was a twinkle in Aggie's eyes, but they were also hard and cold as cut sapphires.

"I promise," she said. "But . . ."

"But what?"

"I'm not completely sure I understand."

Aggie patted her on the shoulder. "Okay. Well. Just think about it. We'll have to hope that when the time comes, you will. But listen, Molly. *I trust you.*"

Molly nodded. Then she had an idea. She went back into the house, reached into her backpack and pulled out the ceremonial robe her parents had made for her on her first day of school. It was not magic, but it was the closest physical connection to her mother—and father—that she had.

"What's that?" Aggie asked.

Molly put on the robe and looked Aggie in the eye. "A tether," she said.

Aggie held Molly's gaze for another long moment, then smiled. "Let's wake these boys up and get you home."

CHAPTER 12

Home

Shaun, Molly, and Dorker said their farewells, and thanked Aggie and Fergus. They said little, but little needed to be said. After Aggie's meal, Shaun felt better than he had in a long time; so much better he even seemed to enjoy having Dorker around. He couldn't remember feeling so at peace. But Shaun being Shaun, peace brought with it uncomfortable memories.

"You've been very kind to us," he said, pulling Aggie aside. "To Molly especially. And I just . . . that *means* something to me. She's . . ."

"I know, Shaun," said Aggie patting his arm. "You're welcome."

"No, that's not it. I know you know . . . what she means to me. That's . . . No. What I want to say is . . . What I really want to say is, I'm sorry."

"For what?"

Shaun sighed. "In two thousand years or so, I'm going to be far less gracious to you than you have been to us."

Aggie frowned. "What will you do?"

"It doesn't matter. I mean, you'll see. It's not . . . *awful*. But it wasn't right. Won't be right. And it's a bit strange, because I haven't technically done anything yet, but I also can't prevent it, which makes it even worse."

"That's time travel for you," said Aggie, smiling. "Don't worry about it, Shaun. Just take good care of Molly."

Shaun nodded. "I will do my best."

Aggie nodded and looked him in the eye. "That'll do!"

They shook hands awkwardly, and feeling unusually emotional, Shaun started to leave.

"Before we go," he said, turning back to her quickly, "can I take a quick look in your library?"

Aggie raised an eyebrow.

"Yes, I expect you better, hadn't you? Right through there," she said, pointing down a hall. "Don't worry," she winked. "I won't look."

And so, before they left, Shaun found a particular book on Aggie's shelf. It wasn't nearly as old as the last time he had seen it. It was much thinner, the binding wasn't cracked, and the pages weren't yellow. But it was unmistakable. He found the page he had seen before (or, depending on how you look at it, the one he would see two thousand years from now). After everything that had happened, he wondered if it wouldn't be more sensible to write: "Shaun—stay away. Not worth the trip." But Dorn was too dangerous to leave in ancient Rome by himself. So, hands shaking a little, he wrote a little note to himself about saving the world.

* * * *

By the time Shaun, Molly, and Dorker hit the streets of Rome once again, the sun had started to rise, casting long crimson clouds over the city. A general workmanlike air had settled on this particular neighborhood, and the daily hurly-burly of Roman commerce had begun to reassert itself. Among other things, a short-order food business had sprouted up on the streets overnight to feed those who were helping with the city clean-up. A variety of barbecued meats-on-a-stick were available from different sellers. Where the meat came from, Molly and company didn't dare guess, but the Roman citizenry was not complaining.

The food carts competed for attention with several self-proclaimed prophets who had stationed themselves on street corners, each insisting on different interpretations of recent events: one warned that the darkening of the sun had been a sign that Rome owed the Gods a greater sacrifice; another claimed that the end of the world was *still* nigh, that what had happened was just a warmup, and everyone was wasting their time rebuilding; one particularly creative thinker theorized that the world actually *had* ended, that this was a glorious afterlife, and that the Gods would be along shortly, bearing instructions.

Amidst all the selling and sermonizing, a voice called out to them: "Hey! You tried to steal my pots!! Guards!! Guards!!"

Molly turned. A group of Roman soldiers were staring at them. With them was the old Roman pot-seller who had grabbed her by the backpack and tried to sell her to Lucius. He had managed to get his hands on (i.e., stolen) a new inventory of pottery, all of reduced size, onto which he was painting quaint sayings, like, "I Survived the End of the World!" and "I came, I saw, and all I got was this lousy pottery."[§]

The soldiers would have probably ignored the pot seller if they hadn't seen three very tiny people who, as far as they were concerned, couldn't possibly exist.

"Hey! You three!" yelled the soldiers. "Stay there!"

Which is exactly what the three leprechauns didn't do.

"This way!" Molly cried. She ran down the street, with Dorker and her father close behind. They turned a corner at the first available alleyway and stopped, silently pressing their backs against the wall, hoping the soldiers would pass them by. Fortunately, most of them did. One by one, in a cacophony of rattling armor, they charged past the alley and down the road.

Unfortunately, just as the coast looked clear, a lone soldier, lagging behind for having eaten one too many bites of a street vendor's mystery meat, stopped at the entrance of the alleyway pinched with horrible stomach cramps. He looked up with a pale, slightly green face and saw the three leprechauns pressed against the wall in front of him. In one brief, paralyzing moment, he opened his mouth to call the other soldiers, but instead threw up violently into the alley.

"EEUGGHEW!!!" yelled Dorker, who had, unfortunately, been in the splash zone.

"Run!" yelled Molly.

Molly grabbed Dorker and her father, and led them around corner after corner, navigating the maze-like streets and back alleys of the Roman Forum powered more by fear than any clear sense of where she was going.

"Where are we going?" Dorker yelled breathlessly.

"I'm pretty sure we have to get to the Theatre of Pompey!" yelled Molly.

[§] The pot seller found he had a knack for coining snappy slogans (as well as for petty theft). He called the little pots "Nicked Knacks." All of which goes to show that anyone's actions can reverberate through time, even if their names are lost in history's notebooks.

"Why? I thought the portal was broken," said Dorker.

"It is, but . . . I don't know . . . I just have a feeling that's where we need to be. We've got to get to where Lucius killed Caesar."[†]

They reached the end of a narrow alley that opened out onto a main thoroughfare. Molly peered around the corner and saw a gaggle of soldiers headed their way.

"We have to split up," said Molly.

"What?!? No!" said Shaun.

"Da', it's our only chance. It'll be easier for one of us to lose them than for all three of us together. One of us needs to run across the street to draw their attention. Then the other two can make for those alleys in the opposite direction, and we'll all try to meet up at the Theatre."

Shaun looked at Molly with panic in his eyes. Everything in him screamed that splitting up was a bad idea. But Alice had been very clear with him.

"I'll go," said Dorker.

"No!" said Shaun. And before Molly could say anything, he kissed her on the forehead and darted across the street, waving his arms madly.

"Hey! Woo hoo! Over here! Come and get me!!"

"DA'!" Molly cried.

"There's one!" yelled one of the soldiers. "After him!"

Molly couldn't believe what her dad had just done. No argument. No hand wringing. He just ran. Shaun never did what Molly—or anyone—suggested so readily.

She was so shocked that, as the soldiers started after her father, she almost didn't see Dorker, who had misunderstood the plan, charge out in a different direction, yelling, "No! Follow me! Whoopee!! Come on!"

"NO, DORKER!! THAT'S NOT–!" whispered Molly, clutching her head in her hands.

"There's another one!" a soldier yelled.

Molly saw her father and Dorker disappear down two different alleys, each

---

[†] Molly correctly intuited that though the manner of Caesar's death had been historically altered, most of the surrounding circumstances had not. This is entirely consistent with Mance O'Flattery's River of Time theory, discussed earlier, which allows for isolated change without disruptions to the river. The conspirators to Caesar's assassination, therefore, were surprised when Lucius charged in and struck Caesar down before they could even draw their daggers, but they still took credit for his death, and the history books remained unaltered.

pursued by three soldiers hot on their heels.

"They ran off! They both ran off!" Molly gasped. Her mind raced, but there wasn't much she could do about it now. Now, she just had to get to the Theatre and hope they could do the same.

Then she heard a voice from behind.

"Gotcha!"

She turned. The soldier who puked at them had caught up, with ten more soldiers behind him.

"Well . . . ratcrap!" Molly said.

* * * *

Like swooping death from up on high
Comes Poor Reynard to do or die! [F]

. . . thought Poor Reynard.

We should back up.

The end of the world caught Reynard by surprise. Fortunately, it caught everyone by surprise, which gave him the advantage. The path from the notional space between the neurons of Cassius's mind back to reality had landed him smack in the middle of Caesar's chambers, which, under normal circumstances, would have been a disastrous complication. But the violent shaking of the earth and the general chaos it created gave him ample cover to navigate his way outside to the streets unmolested.

Once outside, every hair on his glorious rust-colored coat stood on end. A general existential dread electrified the air and crackled on his whiskers—something he'd never felt before. It was the sort of feeling you get when billions of souls feel the cold emptiness of space closing in around them and collectively realize that they, along with the earth and everything they had ever known, would soon be nothing more than a chunk of ice randomly hurtling through a dark, uncaring void. Reynard ducked under an abandoned linen basket to quiver.

There, shrouded in darkness, he concentrated on Molly. He sensed guilt

---

[F] Where Reynard learned the phrase, "to do or die" is anyone's guess, though it is doubtful he actually read Alfred Lord Tennyson's poem, *The Charge of the Light Brigade*. If we knew the answer to this question, we might know a lot more about foxes.

and sadness—almost as if she somehow felt . . . *responsible* for the end of everything. That's when the truth hit him like a falling oak:

Molly was a god. Most likely, she was the fox god Reynaert (for whom he had named himself), [F]—the great trickster god come back to earth in disguise as a . . . whatever Molly was. Which meant the connection he shared with her was no accident: he had been *chosen*. Molly had revealed herself to Reynard for some hidden, but holy purpose.

The darkening of the sun was therefore as a sign unto him, and lo, the glory of divine inspiration throbbing within him, verily did he disentangle himself from the linen basket of shame to receive his blessed enlightenment. The second he did (and in another moment of magnificent timing), the sun roared back to life, as if to confirm Molly's divinity.

Spiritually fortified, he homed in on Molly's mental signal as if it were a burning bush and ran off to find her. He lost her only once when, without warning, her thoughts became so expansive, so incomprehensibly huge, it was as if she filled every corner of his head, as well as every corner of the universe. The sheer magnitude and scope of mental awareness that flooded his consciousness through her was almost too much to bear.

Molly was in a place even Poor Reynard dared not follow. He found an out-of-the-way alley to hide in while he tried to fit his mind back into his skull.

When Molly's thoughts returned to normal (that is, when she finally returned to her body in Aggie's kitchen), Reynard shook it off and groomed himself. As he did, he considered: those who consort with Gods do so at their own risk.

But danger did not daunt him. The problem was that his brain now felt so elastic, he was having a hard time tuning it back to Molly. He conscientiously finished his toilette and poked his nose back onto the streets for a sniff. Almost immediately, the Roman soldiers chasing Molly, Dorker, and Shaun rushed past him and turned down an alley a block or two away. His connection to Molly locked in once more.

Between this and his extraordinary nose, a mental picture of the Roman streets seen from above drew itself in his head, and he calculated the point at which the Romans would catch her. Moving to intercept, Reynard ran laterally

---

[F]   In fox mythology, the god Reynaert "created" the universe by stealing it from the wolf god Ysengrin who, having regurgitated it into existence, wanted to eat it up again.

down a nearby side street and got to Molly first. As Shaun and Dorker ran into the streets creating their distraction, Reynard quietly climbed up onto a ledge about ten feet above Molly and waited.

Just as Molly said, "Well . . . ratcrap," Reynard leapt onto the head of the lead soldier, sinking his yellow teeth firmly into his ear.

"AAAAAAAAGHH!!!" observed the soldier.

As he struggled with Reynard, and his stunned compatriots looked on in wonder, Molly felt Reynard—yes, it had to be Reynard—*say* something to her in her head that felt an awful lot like:

O gracious Lord, exalted one,
Accept my sacrifice—and RUN!!

Shocked and more than a little alarmed that Reynard could now . . . *talk* to her somehow—???—Molly bolted, barely managing a quick, mental "Thank you!"

It was just as well that she ran because the soldiers were doing a better job of finding her, and fierce though he was, Reynard probably couldn't hold them off for long. Sure enough, in another unexpected and slightly painful jolt, she felt one of them hurl Reynard against a wall, knocking him out once more.

Molly had no time to grapple with her new and unsettling fox-centric awareness because now she was trapped. A dead end confronted her, and the soldiers wouldn't be far behind. Her best option was to run where the soldiers wouldn't look. Using the rough texture of the stucco Roman walls, she scrambled up the side of a building as nimbly as mountain goat.

Atop the roof, she peered over the edge quietly. Directly beneath, the soldiers came crashing to a halt, baffled as to where she could have gone. She watched them yell orders back and forth at each other for several minutes as they looked for her everywhere but up. Finally, they separated and ran off in different directions.

Molly sighed with relief and slumped gratefully against the ledge. She took in her new surroundings. The building she had climbed was wide and high enough that it gave her a good view of the neighborhood. She jogged its perimeter, quickly trying to get her bearings, and saw the Theatre of Pompey roughly two blocks away. The buildings between it and her were built close together and if she planned her route just right, she reckoned she could get pretty close to it, without having to come down to street level more than two or three times.

Molly calculated her path and sprinted off across the roof tops. A sudden feeling of freedom washed over her, stronger than she ever had felt. Up here, she had no one chasing her, no one criticizing her, no one questioning her choices, only her feet beneath her, the sky above, and her wits (in which she felt more confident with every step she took). Rats, pigeons, and the occasional squirrel were the only onlookers, and they were too busy with their own concerns to bother with Molly. When she did come down once or twice to cross a wide road, her rooftop view gave her the leisure to first survey the scene below to make sure it was safe. Otherwise, Molly leapt from building to building exhilarated by the sun, the wind in her hair, and the hope of going home. She arrived at the Theatre feeling strong and invigorated.

But now, another challenge: how to get into the Theatre, across the gardens in the back, and into the Senate meeting house where Caesar had been killed. It wouldn't be easy. News of Caesar's assassination had popped the lid on a pressure cooker of civil unrest. Riots were boiling up all over the city, and the crowd around Pompey's Theatre was thick with simmering anger. They were held in check by a group of soldiers lined up in the square before the Theatre, preventing anyone from entering. Their show of force was intended to keep the peace, but as so often happens, only provoked greater agitation.

Marc Antony wasn't helping. Molly recognized his unmistakably impressive physique. He stood behind the soldiers glowing like a sun. Light and even the stones seemed to bend towards him as he spoke. Over the heads of the soldiers, he openly mourned Caesar and suggested in no unsubtle terms that the crowd was right to be outraged, that a conspiracy had, in fact, killed the noblest man who ever lived in the tide of times, and what, he wondered, should any red-blooded, patriotic Roman do about it? Even Molly was moved. His voice was like rattling thunder.

The soldiers holding back the crowd exchanged worried glances. One whispered cynically to another out of the corner of his mouth: "'Join the army,' they said. 'Meet interesting people,' they said . . . ."

Fortunately, Marc Antony was so captivating, no one paid much attention to their own ankles. Molly took a calculated risk. From behind, she ran straight at the mob and into the forest of legs—a jostling, frenetic entity that moved according to no predictable pattern. But in a crowd like this, she didn't have to worry if she touched anyone. In fact, she did so deliberately. Grabbing a kneecap here, a hairy calf there, she maneuvered to the front of the crowd like Tarzan on his vines. Those in the mob who did dimly register a disconcertingly small hand groping around their naked lower legs were too squeezed by the throng to investigate. And since Molly touched no one for more than a few seconds, they quickly dismissed it, and got back to the important task of shouting.

Then came the dangerous bit. Even if she could get past the row of armed soldiers to the empty square beyond, she still had to make sure no one saw her as she traversed it. She put her odds at about fifty-fifty. But she was feeling confident and daring and besides, she had no choice. She saw an opening through a pair of soldier's legs and took her chance.

Unfortunately, just as she ran, the soldier shifted his weight, tripping Molly with his heel and sending her tumbling clumsily and, above all, conspicuously, across the flagstones. Her face smacked down hard on the ground, bloodying her nose, and leaving her dazed and disoriented. She lay on the ground for a moment, not really sure what had happened.

She got up slowly and reached into her pocket to get a handkerchief to staunch the bleeding, and as she did, she noticed that things had gone strangely silent. Then she remembered. She looked up into the astonished face of Marc Antony, then turned slowly, and saw the huge mass of Romans—citizens and soldiers—staring at her, opened-mouthed. The sight of a very small, very young girl rolling across the empty square was the last thing anyone had expected to see, even on a day filled with earth-shaking events. A small smile crept across Molly's face. She gave them all a friendly but sheepish wave as she backed away slowly. She got a lot further than she expected to before Antony came to his senses and yelled, "The very stones of Rome rise up in mutiny!"

Someone in the crowd put it more concisely: "What *is* that?!? Get it!!!"

Then Rome went insane.

The wave of sound that rose up behind Molly as she turned and ran felt like a tsunami engulfing the world as hundreds of people swarmed the Theatre. Molly's tumble through the line of guards had flipped a switch in people's heads: if Molly could be on the other side of the soldiers, why couldn't they?

Left and right, people ripped down banners, toppled statues, and generally gave a kick to anything that got in their way. The word "chaos" exists in the English language just to describe scenes like this. Most of the people were not even running towards Molly. They just ran. Defying the soldiers had been so empowering, the crowd quickly forgot about her, convinced that they couldn't possibly have seen what they thought they saw.

Molly, along with a lot of others, ran for the entrance to the Theatre. Hiding under a piece of fabric trailing from someone's ripped and low-hanging toga, she managed to escape the riot and sneak in unnoticed.

But now she had to be more careful. Being inside somehow made her feel even more exposed. Down the aisles of the semi-circular auditorium, people raced onto the stage, and disappeared out the back. At one point, a particularly blood-thirsty group chased a man across the stage, who was desperately pleading, "I'm not Cinna the *conspirator!* I'm Cinna the *poet!*"

Molly inched her way carefully around the back of the seating area, trying to keep out of sight. She hoped there was a way backstage other than directly through the house and downstage center.

As she darted between two columns scanning for an alternate route, a hand grabbed her arm and pulled her into a little alcove.

"Molly!"

"Da'!" She was so startled, she just stared at him for a moment before she flung her arms around him. "You made it!"

"Where's Dorker?"

"He ran off right after you did."

"He wha—?!"

"It's alright, Da'. Dorker will figure it out."

Molly really hoped that was true.

"Okay, well, what do we do now, Molly?" Shaun asked.

"You need to tell me the spell you used to get us through the time portal."

"But the portal's gone, Molly."

"I know, Da'! Just trust me, okay? It'll all make sense eventually, I know it."

Molly really hoped that was true, too.

Shaun took a deep breath and told her the spell. "You need to concentrate on where and when you want to be when you say it. And we must all be holding hands."

"Got it. Now," Molly took a deep breath, "we have to get to the back of the stage, through the gardens in the back, to the place where Caesar was killed. Any ideas?"

They looked around at the debris scattered all over the floor. Amid the wreckage, Shaun spied a discarded toga and several unlit torches that had fallen to the floor.

"I've got an idea," he said.

* * * *

Leprechauns, true to what you may have heard, make and mend shoes. Lore gatherers, however, are no common cobblers. As Shaun details in his book *Lore Gatherer Footwear: A Historical Study in Fabulousness*, lore gatherers create the most beautiful, stylish, and artistically accomplished shoes, sandals, pumps, boots, etc. in the known universe. A lore gatherer shoe is the perfect balance of form and function. If Leonardo da Vinci had devoted all his artistic and structural talents solely to the study of the foot, he could not ever have designed a shoe quite like a lore gatherer's. To be clear, they do not make shoes for humans, though leprechauns have been responsible for every major fashion innovation in the history of human footwear. The way it works is that when lore gatherers are dissatisfied with a design they've been working on (and it's usually women's high heels, which even lore gatherers haven't figured out how to make comfortable), they deliberately throw them in the garbage cans of the world's top human designers. These designers find them and, appreciating the superior works of bonsai-like craftsmanship they have stumbled upon, steal the design, and sell these fantastically beautiful, but grotesquely uncomfortable creations to the rest of humanity for prices that would bankrupt a small country. Lore gatherers find this hilarious.

Researchers have long speculated about the influence of magic on their phenomenal skills as cobblers. Truly, if you had looked closely at even the most functional pair of shoes lore gatherers wear (which is largely what Shaun and Molly wore), you could not fail to be overwhelmed at the craftsmanship. Leather seemed to turn to clay in a lore gatherer's hands. As liquids conform to the shape of their containers, lore gatherer shoes conform to the shape of the wearer's feet. Dress shoes are splashy and extravagant without ever lapsing into garishness. Work shoes retain a simple elegance that complements and reveals the complex architecture of the foot. Confoundingly, no magical researcher has ever been able to detect the slightest trace of magic. Leprechauns are just born knowing how to make shoes the way a spider is born knowing how to weave a web.

It was therefore easy business for Shaun to quickly repurpose his own shoes to incorporate the unlit torches, thereby fashioning makeshift stilts that not only lifted Shaun roughly three feet off the ground, but also looked sensational.

"If you stand on my shoulders, we'll be close to four feet tall," said Shaun. "Throw that toga over our heads and we may look almost human, as long as no one's looking too closely." Molly climbed onto her father's shoulders and draped the discarded toga over them both.

The results were mixed. Looking at the shuffling toga, the casual observer would certainly not have guessed that two leprechauns on stilts were skulking beneath it. But they might have suspected a pile of laundry had come to life and decided to take in a play. In short, fading into the background was out of the question. They would just have to act as human as possible and hope for the best.

Sometimes, all the world really is a stage.

"Should we wait for Dorker?" Shaun asked.

"I think we should just try to get where we're going and worry about Dorker when we get there."

". . . Okay . . ."

Checking to see that the coast was relatively clear, Shaun started down the steps leading to the stage. Though most people running around the room were preoccupied with the general mayhem, a few concerned citizens did notice—and had started following curiously—the shambling pile of clothes that had taken on a life of its own. In rapt fascination, they watched as the walking rags progressed shakily towards the stage and climbed up onto it. Had Caesar's ghost come back to deliver some dire prophesy, they wondered? Was it about to perform a bit of Terence?[F] As it wove its way through a series of columns to a door at the back, the onlookers didn't know whether to be horrified by the inhuman creature or astonished by its impeccable footwear.

"What's it look like out there?" whispered Shaun as Molly opened the door

---

[F] An ancient Roman comedic playwright. Coincidentally, Shaun references Terence's plays in his controversial book, *Laughing Matter: Why Humans Aren't Funny.*

and peered into the gardens outside.

"It looks pretty safe. We should be able to—OOF!"

A running soldier tripped over Molly and Shaun, sending them all careening to the floor. As it happened, the soldier turned out to be Lucius's friend, Gracus. His mouth opened and closed once or twice as he stared at them in confusion.

"Hey!" he said thickly. "You're those . . . Hey!"

"Hey, look!" shouted one of the more astute citizens. "It's that girl from outside!"

"Uh-oh," said Shaun. He hoisted Molly onto his shoulders, slipped through the door, and ran. Gracus was quickly joined by more soldiers as well as the concerned citizens who were already following Molly and Shaun with interest. "When in doubt, follow the mob" is the general rule of mobs. Besides, seeing a pile of laundry transform into two very small human-like creatures was unexpected and exciting, and they wanted to see what happened next.

Moving as fast as his stilts would carry him, Shaun led the increasingly fevered crowd down a straight, gravel path through a long, elegant outdoor garden lined with statues and fountains. At the other end, lay another crowd milling around the entrance to the Senate. One by one, the people in that crowd heard the commotion in the garden, turned, and saw a different crowd chasing a very small man on stilts carrying an even smaller young girl on his shoulders.

Shaun stopped in the center of the garden, caught between two dangerously agitated crowds.

"Nuts!" said Molly.

"What now, Molly?!" said Shaun desperately.

"I don't know!" said Molly. There was nowhere to run, no way out. "I think we're out of luck, Da'."

"I think you may be right."

At that exact moment, a loud voice, calling like a trumpet from the mountain tops, pierced the din of the converging mobs.

"MOOOOOOOOOOLLLLLLLLLLYYYYYYYYYY!!!!!"

Behind them, at the top of the Theatre steps, Dorker rode Gladys like a wingéd fury. He gripped a few strategic feathers of Gladys's neck with one hand, and with the other waved expansively at Shaun and Molly, as if from across the Rio Grande. Gladys, who had an innate sense for the dramatic, somehow reared like a stallion, flapped her wings uselessly, and cried:

"SQUUUAAAAAWWWWKKKK!"

Like a hero from an old American western (imagine Gary Cooper riding a chicken), Dorker rode Gladys down the Theatre steps, through the garden, and towards Shaun and Molly in a gallop that was, frankly, less than awe inspiring. If you have ever seen a chicken run, you know they are not slow, but they are hardly lightning fast either. A chicken simply does not possess the muscular explosiveness of a thoroughbred at full gallop. Perhaps the best word to describe Gladys at full sprint was "brisk." But that didn't stop Dorker, proudly astride her back, from howling like a warrior poet.

For the human onlookers, it was one thing to see creatures the size of Molly, Shaun, and Dorker; it was another thing altogether to see one ride a chicken like a demon horse spat from the jaws of hell, yodeling like Tarzan. The sheer drama of the moment conveyed a kind of inspiring heroism (and some in the crowd, on subsequent retellings, claimed to have seen it happen in slow motion). At the same time, it was a chicken. The appropriate reaction was therefore unclear: Outrage? Cheering? Laughter? Caught in the crossfire of conflicting emotions, the crowd settled for wonder and polite applause as they parted like the Red Sea.

As Dorker and Gladys approached, Shaun quickly undid the complex lacing he had devised to keep his shoes attached to the stilts. Just in time, the stilts fell to the ground as Dorker sped by crying:

"GET ON!!"

In one smooth and beautifully choreographed motion, Shaun wrapped one arm around Molly's waist, and with the other, linked elbows with Dorker as he rode past. Using Dorker's momentum, Shaun swung up behind him onto Gladys, with Molly in between. The crowd took in this maneuver and applauded again, having finally concluded that this whole scene must be a particularly daring and unusual piece of street theatre, and that the actors and the chicken were undoubtedly puppets. Some even looked skywards trying to see the strings or figure out how they were operated.

Capitalizing on the crowd's momentary goodwill, the three leprechauns rode unhindered across the rest of the gardens and into the Senate meeting house, which, miraculously, was empty. Whether the crowd had been avoiding it out of reverence or fear, Molly couldn't say, but now that their little troop had crossed the threshold, others would soon follow. Shaun dismounted Gladys and slammed the door behind them.

"Help me barricade this door!" he shouted. "That crowd won't stay quiet for long!"

Fortunately, the room where Caesar had been assassinated was still in disarray, and plenty of debris was available to pile in front of the door.

"I reckon we've got about two minutes before that crowd comes crashing through," said Shaun. "Whatever you have in mind, Molly, do it now."

"Okay," said Molly. "Come this way."

They moved to the center of the room and took each other's hands. Gladys placed a toe on Dorker's shoulder.

"Wait," said Shaun, "the chicken can't come!"

"The chicken is coming," said Dorker firmly. Shaun blinked. He wasn't used to being defied by Dorker.

"Dorker, we don't have time—" Shaun began.

"No, we don't," said Dorker. "She's coming. I made a promise."

"To a chicken?!?"

"SQUAWK!" said Gladys pointedly.

"Her name is Gladys," said Dorker. "And I'll explain later."

Shaun wanted to argue, but there was no time. Besides, Gladys had a very persuasive glare.

"Go ahead, Molly," Shaun sighed.

"We don't have Reynard," said Molly.

"The fox?!?" said Shaun. "We really don't have time, Molly. I'm sorry."

Molly knew he was right. It broke her heart, but they might not get another chance. Reynard was still alive—somehow—she could feel it. She knew so little about this strange creature that had attached itself to her, but she knew he was resourceful and would somehow be okay in ancient Rome without her. She also knew that as soon as she returned to her own time, the connection between them would cease. He would be long dead. Her eyes filled with tears as she sent out the thought: *I accept your sacrifice.* Then she whispered the spell.

Nothing happened.

"Is everything okay?" Shaun asked. "Are we missing something?"

"I don't know! I said the spell!" said Molly, trying to keep the rising panic out of her voice.

"Did Aggie tell you anything helpful? Something we need?" Shaun said it as calmly as he could, but the crowd outside had begun pounding on the door.

"She said a lot of things! I just . . . just . . ."

"Just what, Molly?" Shaun asked patiently.

The yells outside were getting louder. The door slowly began to crack open.

"She said I have to believe in myself . . ." said Molly.

Several hands clawed their way into the room.

"Belief?" said Dorker.

"Yes, Dorker, belief!" Molly shouted. "But I . . . I believe in myself! I . . . I don't know what—"

"If belief is all it is," said Dorker simply, "I believe in you Molly. I always have." Molly looked at Dorker.

"Here," said Dorker, calmly taking her hand again. "Let me show you. Say the spell again."

Two Romans squeezed halfway into the room. "There they are!" one of them yelled. "C'mon!"

Molly closed her eyes and recited the spell. Dorker's belief flooded into her like a tidal wave, her eyes went wide, and for a moment, she could hardly breathe.

What is love? Let's first clear up what it is not. Love is not passion or lust or desire. Humans often get those things confused. In fact, humans make a lot of mistakes about love. It's easy to do because love is so big and comes in so many different shapes. You may love pizza, for example, and you probably also love your mother, but probably not in the same way. But whatever love is, lore gatherer researchers have determined that in its purest, most concentrated state, love is so powerful that exposure to even the smallest quantity can have life-altering consequences.[†] That is why, as Dorker's belief flowed into Molly, so too did his love, and it felt like emerging from a cave into sunlight. She saw herself as he saw her. To him, she was not the girl who failed at The Thieving, but the girl who, doing something no other lore gatherer had ever done, secured an exhilarating, record-breaking victory in the first round. She was not the girl

---

[†] Somewhat paradoxically, as noted in Shaun's book *What Is This Love Thing, Anyway?*, researchers have been unable to determine exactly how much pure love the leprechaun heart can hold. Even under the most restrictive laboratory conditions, no matter how full it gets, there is always room for more.

who, in an act of foolishness, nearly caused the end of the world, but the courageous young woman who, in the face of an impossible choice, chose life where others counseled death. She was not the poor girl whose mother died; she was the one being on earth he *knew* could get them all home. She was, in short, his hero—fierce, strong, compassionate, caring, intelligent, creative, and resourceful. Someone anyone would look up to and admire. Through Dorker, Molly saw the lore gatherer she wished she could be.

Or maybe—whispered a voice in the back of her brain she had never heard before—*you saw the lore gatherer you already are.*

Molly saw the vague human shapes behind Dorker grow larger but more indistinct as they reached out to grab him. Then they dissolved into darkness.

CHAPTER 13

A Reckoning

First, they saw light. Bright light.

The light morphed into an indistinct mass of greens and browns.

When the trees surrounding them came into sharper focus, Molly, Shaun, Dorker, and Gladys found themselves lying in a small clearing in the middle of a forest, near a fallen pine tree. Shaun lifted his head blearily.

"Where are we, Molly?"

"I don't know," she said.

"*When* are we?" asked Dorker.

Dazed and a little dizzy, they got up and looked around.

"I assumed, if it worked, we'd end up back where we started," said Shaun, rubbing his eyes. "In the ruins of the Colosseum, I mean. Modern Rome."

He turned and looked at Molly. "What happened back there?"

"I'm not sure. Dorker—?"

"Don't look at me," said Dorker. "I mean, I believe in you and all, but I couldn't have done magic like *that*. I wouldn't even know how to start."

"BAWK!" complained Gladys, who didn't like it when Dorker downplayed his abilities. She pecked him sharply on the head.

"OW! Hey! Okay, maybe I could figure out how to *start*, but I didn't do any of that magic."

Gladys clucked with satisfaction.

"Wait!! Wait wait wait!" Shaun had gotten up and was walking around, laying his hands on the trees. "I know this place, Molly! This is where our gold was buried!"

"What?!" said Molly. "But that's not even in Rome."

"Molly, I've come here every day of my life since I was a boy. I'd know it with my eyes closed!"

"But that means . . ." said Dorker.

"That *means*," said Shaun, "you not only brought us back to the present, you brought us all the way back home!!"

"Oh," said Molly, nonplussed. "Well, so . . . okay . . . That was the plan, right . . . ?"

"Molly, from a magical perspective, that's unheard of!" Shaun spluttered. He was practically shaking. "Traveling through time is one thing. But traveling through time *and* space? *Without* a portal?!? The magical mechanics alone are mind-boggling! They've never been studied because no one has ever *done* it before!! No one knows how! Molly!" He knelt down and said softly. "You may have just done the most powerful piece of magic anyone has seen in an age."

Molly blinked. That sounded impressive. And her father was happy about something she'd done for a change—that was nice. Why then did she feel nothing but a sinking dread?

She looked around.

Then she looked again and saw it. None of the leaves on the trees were moving. Not even a little bit. The only sound she could discern was her father's voice. Even the air stood still. It was like standing in a photograph of a forest. Goose bumps rose on her skin.

"Dorn is nearby," she said quietly.

Shaun froze.

"Are you sure?" he whispered.

Molly nodded. The three leprechauns and Gladys huddled together quickly and quietly.

"What are we going to do, Molly?" Shaun asked. "I mean, I trust you, but do you have a plan?"

"No," said Molly. "Not yet."

"Molly?" Shaun spoke with quiet urgency. "You do whatever you think is best. But do not doubt for a minute that Dorn will kill us—*all of us*—if he thinks he has to. Whatever you do, you have to end it. For good. You cannot give him a second chance. Do you understand? He's too powerful."

An echoing voice boomed around them, as if the trees themselves were loudspeakers.

"No second chances, eh?"

The ground rumbled as green vines exploded from the soil and rocketed towards the sky, hairy tendrils growing at an impossible rate. Horrible, giant creepers seemed to fill the forest. They wound around Molly's arms and legs and torso, and all three of them were immobilized before they could even react. Gladys, dancing and flapping around chaotically, had a little more luck dodging the slithering green coils, but soon, she too was captured and held fast.

Then, as if an invisible veil had lifted, Dorn and hundreds of other lore gatherers from their village materialized from nowhere. Dorn was carried aloft on an extravagant throne sitting on a golden platform, which was supported by two poles and hoisted on the shoulders of four villagers. Dorn looked down triumphantly.

"Set me down, boys."

The four lore gatherers carrying Dorn looked miserable, as did all the villagers, but they obeyed, lowering his platform to the ground. Dorn arose with a sweeping gesture as the villagers bowed in cringing subservience. He walked slowly and smugly towards his captives.

Before Dorn could speak, however, a small voice called from the crowd.

"Dorker?"

"Dad?" said Dorker.

"Dorker!"

"It's okay, Dad, I'm fine!" said Dorker, contrary to all evidence.

"I didn't know what happened to you, son!" said Dorlish, unable to keep his voice from quavering.

"What's this?" Dorn cried in mock astonishment. Dorlish cowered. "Shaun *kidnapped* your son? Shaun! I shame to call myself your grandfather. Lore gatherers who lose their gold really can't be trusted!"

"That's not what happened!" yelled Dorker.

"Tsk, tsk, tsk," clucked Dorn. "Dorker, Dorker, Dorker. You don't have to protect Shaun anymore," he said lovingly. "You're safe from his clutches now, son. You're home safe at last."

"Then let me go," said Dorker.

"I wish I could, Dorker," said Dorn mournfully. "How I wish I could. But clearly your time with Shaun has corrupted you. Brainwashed you, he has!" Dorn turned to the crowd sadly. "Prisoners often sympathize with their captors, but it's just that much more tragic. No, for the safety of the village, Dorker, you must remain bound."

Dorn winked at Dorker, then turned to Shaun.

"Well, Shaun, I must say, I'm impressed. I told them you'd be back, but I didn't really think you'd manage it."

"Dorn—" said Shaun.

"I warned you they would come back, didn't I?" Dorn crowed to the assembled villagers. "Back seeking revenge!"

"What?!? That's not true!" Molly cried.

"You're too late, Molly!" said Dorn. "I've already told them about your father's plan to steal Caesar's gold. About how *unfair* you thought your banishment was. About your scheme to come home and make all these good people *pay* for what they did to you! Didn't I tell you, good people?"

The crowd shuffled their feet and mumbled that, yes, he might have—several times even—mentioned something along those lines.

"That was *your* plan, you filthy liar!"

"Your lies will not work here, Molly!" said Dorn. "How fortunate we are that I followed you to Rome and uncovered your sinister plot. How right I was—how right we *all* were to set this trap for you. Did I not say that they would return to the scene of the crime?"

The crowd looked at their shoes, scratched the backs of their necks, and muttered vaguely that, yes, he had also said that—repeatedly.

"To feed your rancor, no doubt!" Dorn enthused. "Somehow, in your twisted minds, you have convinced yourself that these good, fine people are the cause of all your life's woes: your banishment; the loss of your gold; even—dare I say it, Shaun—the loss of your own dear wife?"

The villagers gasped at Dorn's audacity.

"Don't—" Shaun began.

Dorn flashed Shaun a knowing grin and addressed the crowd. "Good people, how wise you were to entrust all the village gold to me. I shudder to think what mischief these three might have visited upon you, if you had not!"

Shaun could hardly believe what he was hearing. Stealing human gold was a foundational principle of leprechaun culture. Stealing another leprechaun's gold, while frowned upon, was not unheard of. But the very idea of stealing an entire village's gold was so depraved, so corrupt, so wantonly dangerous and immoral, it beggared the imagination.

"Their homecoming," Dorn continued, "is all the *proof* we need of their plot to harm every lore gatherer in this village! First, the gold of ancient Rome; now they've come for *yours!* Who knows what damage to history they have already done!"

Dorn climbed onto his platform and sat once more on his throne. The villagers shuffled their feet and looked at each other. They didn't like the direction this was going but didn't dare stop it.

"You're a monster," Molly said.

"Oh Molly," said Dorn solemnly. "You break my heart. Truly. There is nothing more painful than to see a child—a *child*—lost to bile and bitterness. How much greater my pain when I consider she is my own flesh and blood, and that, had I been here to guide her, I might have saved her from Shaun's pernicious influence. This is the unkindest cut of all. Truly, no one suffers more than I. But so that all may see I am a just ruler, I shall not let my personal pain— or the fact that we are family—sway my judgment!"

"Dorn—" Shaun began.

"I'm sorry Shaun. For your many crimes, and your clear intent to harm us all, there can be only one punishment—"

* * * *

Poor Reynard is on the way
To save Reynaert and save the day!

. . . thought Poor Reynard.

Let's face it, there is a lot about foxes that we just don't know. In many mythological or spiritual traditions, foxes represent intelligence and wisdom in one form or another, commonly appearing as tricksters. This is their nature. The ancient Greeks believed there once was a fox that could never be caught who was chased by a hound that always caught its prey. Seeing that the chase would go on forever, Zeus intervened, changing both to stone and hurling them into the skies where the fox looks down on us today as the constellation Canis Minor. Humans like the story; foxes know it's true. Tricksters always have a secret, something hidden up their metaphorical sleeves. Try to outwit a fox, and the fox will always run away with the rabbit you tried to pull out of your hat while you're still saying, "Abracadabra."

The point is, Shaun never figured out how Reynard followed them through time and space from ancient Rome back to present day Ireland. Truth be told, Reynard himself might not have been able to explain it. As far as he was concerned, he had just followed Molly.

When Reynard arrived at the scene, he did not understand everything that was happening, but he didn't have to. Molly was in danger; that's all that mattered. He had taken nothing but hard knocks since meeting Molly. He knew intervening might mean his death. But she was the Great God Reynaert. That's what martyrdom was all about. Otherwise, how could he live with himself?

At peace with himself and the universe, Reynard pounced.

****

"It's alright, everyone, you're safe," said Dorn. "I have saved you."

Reynard's attack had been swift and ferocious, and he'd had the advantage of surprise. He was aiming for Dorn, and Dorn alone. Dorn radiated danger like heat. But it was no use.

The crowd's screams still fresh in his ears, Dorn had turned and seen Reynard's yellow teeth inches from his face. Reflexively, he threw his arm up in defense, and miraculously, Reynard's jaws snapped closed on nothing more than Dorn's shirt sleeve. Reynard shook his head violently, and if he had had a good grip, Dorn would have been finished. Instead, Dorn's sleeve ripped from his shirt, and he was thrown free of Reynard a good ten feet away. Dorn recovered quickly, and as Reynard snarled and pounced again, Dorn snapped his fingers and Reynard collapsed in a heap like a house of cards.

"What have you done to him?!?" yelled Molly, who now recognized Reynard.

"So concerned, are you? Such concern for a creature who attacked your village!"

"He attacked *you!*"

"And for that, I have killed him," said Dorn.

Reynard wasn't dead, but Molly could see he didn't have long.

"But," said Dorn, turning to the villagers, "how does she know the fox attacked me, specifically? Oh, Molly. You wicked, wicked child. You *summoned* this vile creature! Think how many lives would have been lost had I not stopped it in time! Who would set a wild animal on another leprechaun? Your reckless, dangerous actions make it that much easier to proclaim your punishment."

"Dorn!" said Shaun.

"Death!" said Dorn.

"No!" sobbed Dorlish, collapsing to the ground.

"Alas, poor Dorlish," said Dorn. "It is cruel that you should suffer for the crimes of your child. Let this be a lesson to all wayward children. Sweet, innocent Dorlish, take comfort from the fact that your sacrifice makes all of us safer. We thank you, and we shall never forget it." Dorn turned to the rest of the village. "Does anyone here doubt the wisdom of this judgment?"

The villagers looked as if they very much doubted the wisdom of the judgment, as well as a great many other things, but no one dared speak.

"What have you done to them, Dorn?" said Shaun, looking at the cowed villagers.

"I have rescued them," Dorn said, smiling. "I have rescued them from themselves. And from you." Dorn then gestured lightly to Gladys. "Another silver lining, we'll eat well tonight!"

"No!" Dorker cried.

"It's not love, you know," said Molly quietly.

Dorn stopped and turned to her.

"They don't love you," Molly said, looking around at the villagers. "They're just scared. And it won't last."

Dorn's eyes looked hunted for a moment, shifting back and forth as if expecting another attack. Molly had hit a tender spot. He walked over to Molly, knelt down, and put a hand on her shoulder. "No, Molly," he said softly. "They're scared of *you*. You're a crazed lunatic bent on revenge, remember?"

"A lie," said Molly.

"A *story*," said Dorn smiling. "You say the truth is one thing. I say it's another. But the truth is whatever *they* believe it is. And mine is the story they will tell. I'll see to it. We will tell it and tell it and tell it, and we'll keep telling it over and over. And soon, everyone in the village will come to believe it. And in a hundred years' time, no one will know there ever was another story."

"A story," said Molly quietly.

Dorn winked at her. "Stories make the world, great-granddaughter. And winners write the stories."

"Yes," said Molly. "Yes, they do."

Dorn smiled, stood up, and started back towards his throne.

"Shall I tell you a story?" said Molly.

Dorn turned and looked at Molly, his eyes filled with malice. Not even Dorn's practiced smile could mask his agitation. He walked right up to her.

"How d'you feel, Molly?" he said under his breath, "Do you feel lucky? Think you've got enough gold tucked away somewhere to take *me* on? *Did* you steal more gold? You must have done to get back here, yes?"

"I don't have any gold at all," said Molly.

Dorn examined her face critically. "Ooooooh, Molly! I'm *proud* of you, you're getting *good!* I didn't detect even a whiff of a lie in that great whopper you just told."

"She's not lying, Dorn," said Shaun simply. "We have no gold."

Dorn raised an eyebrow.

"Right," said Dorn. "And *you* trust *her* to take *me* on without any gold at all?"

"I couldn't stop her if I wanted to," said Shaun, shaking his head.

"Ha!" laughed Dorn. "Well, that's true enough. You have always been a bit of a weakling, Shaun. Bit of a coward?"

"Careful," Molly warned. She had had enough of Dorn insulting her father.

"You. Whatsyername," said Dorn.

"Dorker," said Dorker.

"I'll know if *you're* lying. Where'd you hide the gold?"

"We don't have any," said Dorker. "It's true."

Dorn peered at Dorker, genuinely uncertain for the first time. Dorker's honesty was as impenetrable as a diamond. It glowed like a halo. Then he looked up at Gladys.

"I'm not going to ask *your* opinion," said Dorn.

"BAWK!" said Gladys, who gave it anyway.

The entire forest was silent. Dorn looked at the four of them. Self-doubt—a sensation he had never experienced before—fluttered through his stomach, and for a brief moment, he found it hard to think. A bead of sweat trickled down his forehead. The idea that Molly would dare take him on without any gold to amplify her magic was laughably insulting—so much so, he couldn't simply dismiss it and save face. And he was smart enough to know that when things seem too good to be true, they probably are.

But Dorn believed he could read a bluff as well as any leprechaun. And as of now, he possessed a truly spectacular and unprecedented amount of gold, and through it, had experienced a power no leprechaun had experienced in millennia. It was intoxicating. He felt he could handle anything a young, inexperienced schoolgirl might throw at him. He smiled broadly and turned to the crowd of villagers.

"Ladies and gentlemen. Young Molly here would like to tell us a story before we carry out the sentence. Shall we listen to her tale?"

Everyone looked at each other and nodded enthusiastically, relieved and grateful for such a welcome delay.

"Alright, Molly," said Dorn sitting on his throne. "Make it a good one."

"One you'll never forget," said Molly.

Breathe—the voice in her head whispered. Her thoughts coalesced like dust in a supernova. She was done with death. Death did not impress her, and she had seen far too much of it in her short life. It gave nothing and took away everything. Molly refused to traffic in Death, no matter what Dorn had done.

But Dorn was dangerous. Even if he had been decent once—and there was every reason to doubt it—very little of that leprechaun remained. Even so, Molly would not yield. Her father and Dorker would probably not have agreed, but that was okay. They didn't know what Molly knew. Even Molly didn't know what she knew until this moment.

Molly saw Dorn—saw him clearly. She saw his scheming and lies, and his burning resentment. She saw the vindictive, manipulative leprechaun who was a threat to everything and everyone she loved.

That was one story.

But she also saw another story—the story behind the story. She saw his need and his pain and the cavernous hole where his heart should have been. She felt his isolation and his fear. She pitied him. She empathized with all that he was and all that he wasn't. And then, to her astonishment, forgiveness flooded her and with it, a great swelling of love. Not just love for Dorn and all his failings, but love for everyone in the village that he sought to harm. Love for all who suffer unfairly, needlessly, senselessly, as well as for those who bring it on themselves.

She closed her eyes. Need and desire make the most powerful spells, Dorker had said. As it had in Aggie's kitchen more than two thousand years ago, Molly's mind cracked open, and the universe poured in. The vast tapestry of time stretched before her, and she saw the threads of everyone who has ever lived intertwined together—the shape and the patterns they made. She saw how easily those threads could be rearranged.

Reaching out and grasping a single thread, Molly began to weave.

* * * *

Later, when the Bickersmiths tried to reconstruct the story Molly had told, it quickly became clear that no one remembered exactly what it was. Its contours seemed to center around a great wound at the center of a broken world, but more powerful than any wrong suffered or need for revenge was the part about change—the need for it, and how it comes about through compassion, hard work, and trust. Overall, the consensus seemed to be that the story had been about forgiveness, and how it may be one of the most powerful forces in the world (even if it's not technically magic).[*]

Molly told the truth. Or a truth. It *sounded* true, at least, although afterwards, in truth, no one was quite sure what exactly had happened, or what was true and what was not. Certainly, no one could deny anything Molly had said.

And yet—

The Bickersmiths were also pretty sure Molly had said things that couldn't possibly be true—things that were simply not possible. For instance, in Molly's story, Dorn was stripped of all magic. No, not stripped—in her telling, Dorn simply had no magic. Of any kind. It was not a request or an order or a judgment; no one remembered any great magical spell being uttered. Molly had just made a simple statement of fact. And then somehow, though it had never happened before, though no book or historical record had ever even dared to imagine such a thing, it was now without question that Dorn was a non-magical leprechaun.

---

[*] The jury is still out on this one. Lore gatherer researchers have found testing forgiveness for magic incredibly difficult. All agree, however, that whatever it is, true forgiveness is anything but easy.

It was all a bit hazy, really, and even if they concentrated, no one could recall the details; but they had a vague recollection that at some point in Molly's story, Dorn had panicked and flown into a rage, trying desperately to stop Molly's words. But Molly's story had blown over them with the force of a tornado. It flooded their ears and filled every available space in their minds. It filtered into the ground and rose up through the sap in the trees, scenting the air they breathed. Dorn could no more have stopped Molly's story than he could have stopped the earth from turning. The assembled crowd listened to Molly and knew that what she said was truth. It had unfolded so inevitably, that they couldn't even say whether Molly had actually done anything at all.

When Molly stopped and everyone came out of whatever trance-like state they had been in, Molly, Shaun, Dorker, and Gladys were no longer bound with vines. No one could remember how they had been freed, exactly, but freed they were.

What everyone did remember with cold certainty was what happened next.

Dorn rose from his chair and with a boiling fury in his voice, pointed at Molly, and shrieked:

"DIE!!"

But nothing happened.

He yelled it again.

Again, nothing happened.

"What have you done?" said Dorn quietly, dropping to his knees.

Molly walked up to him and said, not unkindly, "We do what must be done."

"You should have killed me," he whispered. "It would have been kinder. What chance do you think I'll have out there in the world without any magic to protect me?"

"None," said Molly. "No chance at all." Then she turned to the crowd. "Which is why Dorn will remain in our village," she announced. "His banishment is lifted. He will have our protection. He will be a productive member of the village and we will help him find his way." Then she turned to Dorn and said quietly, "But you will never hurt anyone again, Great Grandfather. Or you *will* be left out on your own."

"Ahem. Point of order, Molly," said William O'Toole. Dorn's dominion over the village had been hard on the head of the village Council, and now that it was over, William could stand not being the center of attention for only so long. "But this is really a question for the Council members to decide. While we appreciate your assistance, Molly, we really cannot—"

"No, Mr. O'Toole," Molly interrupted. "There is not going to be a debate. There is not going to be a committee. There will be no vote. This is how it will be."

Molly didn't say it aggressively or as a request. It was just another irrefutable statement of fact.

"Ahem, well, yes . . . ." mumbled William. He shuffled his feet awkwardly. He was used to disagreement. Council members and villagers disagreed with him all the time. Disagreement, he could handle. This didn't feel like disagreement. It didn't even feel like a discussion. It certainly wasn't defiance (he couldn't have tolerated that). But contradicting Molly would have been like contradicting gravity.

Temporarily derailed, William O'Toole rallied magnificently.

"Well, yes, I mean, obviously. Right, you lot!" he yelled to the crowd. "You heard the girl. We're going to accept this . . . Dorn back into the village. And I'm sure we all agree."

The crowd, with what could only be described as enthusiastic uncertainty, indicated that yes, they all agreed.

"Um, Molly?" said Dorker.

Molly turned. Gladys and Reynard stood face to face, feathers and fur bristling. Two natural enemies, the only reason they were not already at each other's throats was that Dorker stood between them, terrified to his toenails.

Also, Reynard had a vague memory of nearly dying a moment ago. He didn't know why he was still alive, but he suspected it might have to do with Molly (which made sense of course), but it also hinted strongly that his God might not look favorably upon him using his unexpected reprieve to instantly kill another. Besides, Gladys was a fearsome specimen. Though Reynard believed with ancestral certainty that no chicken was his equal, any predator would think twice before taking on Gladys, who gave every indication of liking her odds.

In the stand-off, their eyes met.

Was it love that sparked between them?

No. Definitely not. But it was kinship—a thing no fox had ever felt for a chicken, and vice versa (except perhaps between the legendary Shenan'igans and Igrit). Two creatures, destined by fate and nature to hate one another, now stood opposite the only other creature on earth who knew what it meant to have a deep and profound connection with a leprechaun.

Still, kinship was hard to appreciate with millennia of evolutionary animosity lighting up their hind brains like a bonfire.

"Dorker," said Molly, "talk to Gladys. Tell her everything is going to be okay."

"But—"

"Dorker, she'll believe *you*."

Molly placed herself in front of Reynard, whose ears instantly flattened. Eyes wide, he crouched down, put his chin on his paws and, almost involuntarily, began wagging his tail. Their communication was wordless, but Molly saw Reynard's story clearly and thanked him for his help. She decided, however, not to explain about the whole god thing just yet. That might take some untangling and besides, with a fox near so many leprechauns, it was probably in everyone's interest that he be on his best behavior. When Molly finally stood and turned again to Dorker, Reynard was calmly cleaning his tail, and Gladys was happily scratching the ground for grubs.

The villagers collectively exhaled.

"Now," announced William as if nothing had happened, "um, as for your living arrangements Molly, there's a little snag . . . the thing is—"

"My Da' and I will be moving back into our cottage." Molly said simply. Once again, the fact that Molly wasn't demanding or even asking for anything threw William off his usually sharp game.

"Um . . . yes. Yes, yes. That . . . yes, that makes sense. Of course you will. I've been . . . that is to say, the *Council* has been holding your cottage in a trust, as it were, in the event that you . . . well I mean obviously no one could have predicted you'd come . . . but, yes, I will—*we* will . . . happily . . . turn the property back over to your control. We may need a day or two—"

"No," said Molly. "Starting now would be fine. Thank you for your help, Mr. O'Toole."

"Yes, well . . . yes. Of course. Effective immediately!" he said with a flourish, and the crowd cheered. William was starting to get the hang of negotiating with Molly. "Is there . . . um . . . is there anything else?"

"No," Molly sighed. She turned back to Shaun and Dorker. "I just want to go home."

EPILOGUE

Three days later, life was back to normal.

Dorker went home with his father, who was overjoyed to have his son back. Dorlish had not coped well with losing his son and had given up hope of ever seeing him again. But now, he felt rejuvenated and quickly returned to his old, booming self. Some even said his pastries tasted like joy. And when Dorker announced that Gladys was going to live with them from now on, he didn't even blink. Quick as anything, Dorlish enlisted some friends and erected a very comfortable hutch for Gladys to sleep in because there was no way she could fit in their house.

Gladys became a village favorite. That is to say, she became a favorite once Dorker trained her not to—how should we say it—*poop* whenever the mood struck her. But even that quirk spawned a new village industry. One enterprising lore gatherer had the brilliant idea that, treated correctly, Gladys's leavings might be an excellent—and best of all, free—source of fertilizer. He was right—so right, in fact, that the village farmers enjoyed a bumper crop that year and came to view Gladys with an almost mystical reverence. After that, Gladys received the best of everything.

As for Reynard, one sunny afternoon, Molly and Shaun accompanied him on his voyage back to France. The general feeling was that, though there was no bad blood between Gladys and Reynard, the village just wasn't big enough for both of them. Besides, as his God, Molly helped Reynard understand what his heart had been telling him so clearly. France was where he *belonged*. It spoke to him. The moment they stepped off the English Channel and onto the shores of Normandy, he felt it. They toured the countryside for a little while before finally settling on the outskirts of Montignac. There, Molly identified a local human butcher she intuited would be receptive to a friendly fox. The butcher, a sensitive soul himself, was just as curious as Reynard. He kept Reynard well-fed on scraps, offal, and coffee, which freed Reynard to take up impressionist painting on a limited scale. Sadly, the human world never discovered his works, but he was happy.[※]

Dorn was given a modest little cottage in the center of everything (so everyone could keep an eye on him). He went to work with one of the local cobblers, Morgan O'Flim, who was short-handed, and needed the help. Before his exile, Dorn had been an accomplished shoemaker, even by a lore gatherer's exacting standards, and had actually forgotten more about shoemaking than most leprechauns in the village had ever known. Morgan saw her sales spike.

The relationship was somewhat strained at first, partly because it took some time for everyone to accept the fact that, despite all Dorn's misdeeds, he was going to live with them once again. For Morgan, the relationship was even more difficult because Dorn never shut up. Ever the canny businessperson, however, she solved the problem by recognizing that, even without magic, Dorn was a charming and charismatic storyteller. She set up a workstation outside the shop so that Dorn could maintain his running dialogue with customers and passers-by. Not only did this ingenious piece of street theatre bring thirty percent more leprechauns into her shop on a weekly basis, but the village youth received an entertaining and first-rate education in the subtle arts of bullsh*t—a skill of unquestionable value.

Molly and Shaun went back to their old cottage. For several weeks, members of the village Council would stop by their house to check in on how they were adjusting—was there anything they needed, any problems, and by the way, the Council was thinking of doing X, Y, or Z, and did Molly have any objections? These visits finally stopped when it became clear that Molly had no interest in running things, but just wanted to get on with being a kid. This suited everyone, though Molly could not help but notice that everyone in the village now treated her and her father with new respect.

Molly asked her dad about this.

"Well, chick," said Shaun laughing, "it only makes sense. You did magic

---

[※] The leprechaun world, however, was another matter. Centuries after Molly and Shaun were gone, a group of lore gatherer spelunkers discovered his paintings in a cave not far from Lascaux.

no one has seen in an age. Is it any wonder things have changed?"

It didn't make Molly feel any better. She wished others would think more about what she had done with Dorn and why, rather than how she had done it. The idea that raw power alone yielded respect didn't sit right with her. But, she decided, change takes time. All in all, life was good, and things were much as they had been.

Except not quite.

A few days later, Dorker appeared at Molly's door. Shaun answered.

"Ah, Dorker. I've been wondering when you'd show up."

"You did? Wow!" Dorker was nervous. Shaun could almost see the beads of sweat developing on his high, honest brow.

"What can I do for you, Dorker?"

"Well, I was wondering if Molly was around?" Shaun looked at Dorker impassively.

"Really? Why?" said Shaun innocently.

Dorker gulped.

"Well, the fact is . . . I'm glad you answered the door, Mr. McClanahan . . . because, I think maybe *you*, that is *I* . . . or, *we* should probably have a talk."

Shaun's face got serious. "Should we? Well then, by all means, Dorker, do come in." Shaun ushered Dorker into the kitchen and sat him down at the table.

"So, Mr. McClanahan—"

"Tea, Dorker?"

"Oh. Um, sure!" said Dorker. "So, as I was saying Mr. McClanahan, did you—"

"Biscuit, Dorker?"

"What?"

"Would you like a biscuit?"

"A biscuit?"

"To go with your tea?" Shaun's smile radiated nothing but warmth.

"Oh. Um, sure. Thank you."

Shaun moved about the kitchen with a joyful grace Dorker had never seen before. It was unnerving. Finally, Shaun brought the tea and biscuits to the table and sat down. He poured Dorker some tea.

"Thank you very much, Mr. McClanahan. Anyway—"

"Milk?"

"What?"

"For your tea?"

"Oh. Yes please."

Shaun poured some milk into Dorker's cup.

"There you go." Shaun poured himself a cup of tea, no milk, with lemon. He took a sip. "Ahhhhhh. Nothing like a cup o' tea in the afternoon, I always say."

"Do you?"

"I do. Now Dorker, what did you want to talk to me about?" Shaun's smile was broad and bright.

"Well, it's about Molly," Dorker began.

"Yeeeesss?" said Shaun, sipping his tea.

"Well, I don't know if you remember back when the world was ending? I . . . sort of . . . *said* something? And I just thought we should talk about it."

Shaun looked at Dorker quizzically. "You said something when the world was ending? I'm sorry, Dorker, remind me—what was it you said? The excitement of the moment . . . you know how it is at my age. Some of the details are fuzzy."

"Ummm . . . I said something about Molly . . . ?" Dorker tried.

Shaun looked blank.

". . . and about how I felt about her?"

Shaun chuckled, "I'm *so* sorry, Dorker, you'll have to be more specific. My memory . . . you know."

Dorker was starting to wonder if Shaun was being completely honest with him. Shaun was making this awkward, but he had overlooked how comfortable Dorker was with awkward. Awkward was the water Dorker swam in.

"I said I loved her."

All the warmth and smiles drained from Shaun's face as he stared silently back at Dorker. Very quickly, the level of awkward reached critical levels.

"Um . . . Yes," Dorker went on, "so I said that. And I thought we should talk about it. What I said, I mean."

"Why?" Shaun's voice was flat.

"Um, well, because . . . because I plan on marrying her, Mr. McClanahan."

"She's twelve," said Shaun.

"Yes, well, I mean obviously not right this minute. The thing is, I really meant what I said, and—"

"She's twelve," Shaun repeated in the same humorless tone.

"Yes, and I'm thirteen. But someday we won't be, and the thing is, I really do, um, you know, *love* her, and when we are old enough, we'll . . . get married. That's my plan, anyway, and I thought that as her father you had a right to know, because you know, in the traditional way of things, when a leprechaun— when someone wants to marry someone . . . you know, they usually asks for a parent's permission. So that's kind of what I'm doing."

"You don't sound like you're *asking* for anything," said Shaun, raising a critical eyebrow.

"No, I guess not." Dorker scratched the back of his head. "It's more like letting you know what's going to happen. That's what it feels like inside of me, anyway."

"A warning?"

"Fair notice, let's say. I know she means a lot to you."

Shaun, took a sip of tea humorlessly. "That's good of you," he said.

"And I want you to know we will always look after you in your old age."

Even Dorker's powerful resistance to awkwardness felt the temperature in the room drop below freezing. Shaun took a deep breath.

"You're sure she'll want to marry you?" he said.

"Oh, I don't think she'll have a choice," said Dorker.

"WHAT?!?"

"What I mean is," Dorker said hastily before Shaun erupted, "I'm going to woo her."

"Woo her."

"Yes. And, as you point out, she's only twelve, and I'm only thirteen, and so I reckon I've got a lot of time on my side."

Shaun looked into Dorker's earnest and determined face and recognized that here before him was a kind of magic. Dorker was about as threatening as a duckling, but his will was deceptively strong. Truthfully, Shaun had no doubt that Dorker was a good and trustworthy boy. Dorker would never mistreat Molly in any way. More importantly, he knew Molly would never put up with any nonsense. He pitied the boy who tried to hurt or control Molly. All things considered, it could be a lot worse.

They were young. People change. Who knew what would really happen?

Besides, you had to respect a thirteen-year-old boy so willing to boldly step into the lion's den that is a father's ill-conceived idea of what protecting his daughter should look like. More importantly, Shaun heard Alice whisper in his ear that maybe Molly wasn't the one Shaun was really trying to protect. And so, though every piece of him wanted to throttle Dorker on general principle, instead, Shaun smiled and nodded.

"You do indeed have time, Dorker. Though after what we've been through, who knows what that really means, eh?"

Dorker laughed tentatively. "Sooooooooo, can I go ask her to take a walk with me?"

Shaun gripped the table so tightly he almost snapped a piece off. "Of course you can, Dorker," he said. Dorker beamed as he got up to go find Molly. Then he turned back and put his hand on Shaun's shoulder.

"It's okay, Mr. McClanahan. We'll always be here for you."

"And now you should go away."

"Yes, Mr. McClanahan." Dorker removed his hand and started for the door.

"And Dorker?"

"Yes, Mr. McClanahan?"

"Call me Shaun."

* * * *

And so, Dorker finally got his walk with Molly at Holly's Hedge. The air was warm and sunlight sifted through the trees, lighting their way, casting golden beams all around them. Dorker could hardly have imagined a more perfect setting.

After all they had been through, there was so much to talk about, they had a hard time knowing where to start. Their conversation was a little halting and embarassed at first, but generally, it all went fine until Dorker told Molly about his conversation with Shaun.

"You told my father what??" said Molly, horrified.

"I thought it was only fair," said Dorker. "It also seemed the respectful thing to do, seeing as how he, you know, basically looked out for me while we were in Rome. Or sort of looked out for me. Actually, it feels like I was on my own for a lot of that. But you know. In a general sort of sense, I'm sure he felt a certain . . . responsibility for me."

"Really?"

"Well, no, I don't know, really. But I figure I ought to show him respect. After all, he is my future father-in-law!"

Molly buried her head in her hands.

"Dorker, I'm twelve!! You're thirteen!!"

"Yes, that's exactly what Shaun said."

"SHAUN?!?"

"Yes, he said I can call him Shaun now. That seems like a good sign."

"Dorker . . ." Molly shook her head trying to find a handhold on Dorker's towering optimism. "I'm *not* going to marry you, Dorker!"

"Oh, I'm not asking you to," said Dorker cheerfully. "Yet."

"I just don't want to lead you on."

"It's okay. You don't have to believe it. I can believe it for you." He smiled.

Molly marveled at Dorker's belief. It really was a force of nature. She wasn't going to marry him. Ever. She was quite certain of that. On the other hand, Dorker had been a good friend through some very challenging times. And having a friend who cares about you and believes in you isn't a thing to be casually tossed aside.

Nonetheless . . .

"Dorker, listen to me. And I really need you to hear this. Maybe I'll change my mind some day, maybe I won't. But for now, I need you to respect the fact that *right now*, I'm saying, *No*."

Dorker's face fell like the fall of man.

"I'm not saying we can't be friends, Dorker," she added hastily. "I'd very much like to be friends, actually. I really would. I care about you. I might even feel . . ." Molly hesitated, "*someday*, I mean . . . I might even care about you . . . you know, quite a lot." Molly looked down and got quiet. Then she looked Dorker right in the eyes. "But right now, I am twelve. And I've been through a lot recently and everything is still feeling a little unstable in my head, and to get through it, I *need* to trust that my best friend hears me when I say '*No*.' Do you understand?"

The word "TRUST" echoed in Dorker's ears as if it had been shouted from a mountain, reverberating around his head from across a wide gap of time and space. This was the moment he had been waiting for—the moment to earn

Molly's trust! He hadn't expected it to mean relinquishing all his hopes and dreams, but, he reflected, Molly was showing him the way and so far, he had never gone wrong listening Molly.

"Yes, Molly. I understand," he said sincerely. "I'm really sorry."

And there and then, Dorker and Molly experienced, if not the seeds of first love, then at least the sprouts of lasting and meaningful friendship.

They walked together in silence. Then Dorker said, "Just one last point of clarification—you did say 'best' friend, right? I didn't imagine that?"

Molly punched Dorker on the arm and smiled.

They walked a little further. Finally, Dorker just came out with the question he'd been dying to ask.

"Molly," said Dorker carefully, "what exactly *did* happen between you and Dorn? I mean, I know you did some powerful magic, but what *happened?*"

Molly shrugged. "I just did what you told me to do. I believed in myself."

Dorker looked at her blankly. "Oh," he said. "Well, that's good, I guess."

"Honestly, Dorker, I'm still putting it all together. But it's all a little uncomfortable. Whatever I did, now everyone wants to know what else I can do."

"Wow!" said Dorker. "That's kind of cool!"

"No, it's not! I just want to be left alone! I mean, I guess it was . . . kind of amazing, I get that. It didn't feel amazing. Powerful, yes, but mostly just . . . necessary. I don't regret it—at all—but I didn't like doing it. It's hard to explain." Molly got quiet again, and Dorker didn't push it. Finally, she stopped and looked at him. "The thing is. The thing about having that kind of power? The thing is . . ."

"What, Molly?" said Dorker.

"The thing is, when you have that kind of power, you also realize that you probably shouldn't use it. Ever."

Dorker nodded.

"That's a strange position to be in, you know?" said Molly.

"Not really," said Dorker. "But I can imagine."

They walked on quietly.

"What do you remember about your mother, Dorker?" she asked.

"Nothing, really. She died giving birth to me."

Molly looked at him. "I don't think I ever knew that. I'm really sorry."

Dorker nodded.

And still they walked on.

Finally, Molly said, "Okay, one more question?"

"Anything," said Dorker.

"What is the deal with you and Gladys?"

"Oh, that," said Dorker. "It's nothing, really. I just agreed that if she helped me, I would help her learn stuff."

"What kind of stuff?"

Dorker shrugged. "Everything, I think. She's really quite smart."

"For a chicken," Molly guffawed.

Dorker didn't laugh. "Maybe. I think maybe she's just smart. No one's ever taken an interest in her beyond eggs, you know? And, of course, her potential as a meal. But, she's actually very keen." Dorker got thoughtful. "It's funny what you learn about people when you take an interest."

"Yes," said Molly. "I suppose so."

Dorker was one of those people who seemed so simple and easy to predict, but who always surprised you. "She's lucky to have you, Dorker."

Dorker beamed.

"Aaaaaaand now the conversation got weird," she said.

They spent most of the rest of their walk in silence. It wasn't uncomfortable. In fact, it was the exact opposite. It was a comfortable silence. It was the most comfortable silence Molly had ever experienced. But although nothing was said, a lot passed between the two of them that was more meaningful than words.

When they got back to the entrance of Holly's Hedge, Dorker asked, "Can we do this again tomorrow? I mean, you know, as friends?"

Molly smiled. "Maybe the day after. There's something I have to do tomorrow."

****

When she got home, it was almost dark. She found her father sitting over a large, thick book, sipping a cup of tea, taking notes. He didn't even look up when she came in, but said, "Did you have a nice . . . walk?"

"Yes, I did. We got some things straightened out. He's a good friend."

"Yes. Yes, he is. I fully agree." Shaun was still looking at his book and blowing on his tea to cool it down. "It was a long walk . . ."

"Yes. It was. I expect we'll take some more."

"Yes," said Shaun. "I expect so."

"But not tomorrow."

Shaun looked up. "Oh? Why not tomorrow?"

Molly took a deep breath. "Tomorrow, I want you to take me to where Ma's buried and tell me everything."

* * * *

Over a thousand miles away, something caught the eye of Aunt Aggie as she walked through the streets of Rome. Having lived in Rome longer than there even was a Rome, the sight of something new always piqued her curiosity. It was a statue, but what drew her to it was that it looked old. Really old. Ancient, in fact. And when she looked closer, it struck Aggie that though she had never seen it before, she felt certain it had been there for millenia. It wasn't of anyone she recognized, but when she saw the words carved into the statue's base, her face broke into a broad grin: "LVCIVS SALVATOR ROMANVS."

Which, roughly translated, means: "Lucius, Savior of Rome."

THE END

ABOUT THE AUTHOR

Jonathan Uffelman is a former actor turned intellectual property attorney. Other than spending time with his wife and children, he likes gardening, Grand Slam tennis, Pixar movies (and wouldn't reject their phone call if, you know, they were interested in animating *this* story), Terry Pratchett novels, sudoku puzzles, great acting, long walks, and dropping not-so-subtle hints in his author biographies.

Made in the USA
Monee, IL
09 December 2022